ONE OF US

Melissa Benn is a writer, journalist and campaigner. She has written one previous novel, *Public Lives* (1995), which reviewers praised for its 'acute intelligence' and 'incredible subtlety'. Benn writes regularly for the *Guardian* and other national publications, and her non-fiction includes *Madonna and Child: Towards a New Politics of Motherhood* (1998). She lives in north-west London with her husband and two daughters.

ALSO BY MELISSA BENN

Public Lives
Madonna and Child: Politics of Modern Motherhood

MELISSA BENN

One of Us

VINTAGE BOOKS
London

Published by Vintage 2009

2 4 6 8 10 9 7 5 3 1

First published in Great Britain in 2008 by
Chatto & Windus
Random House, 20 Vauxhall Bridge Road,
London SW1V 2SA

www.vintage-books.co.uk

Addresses for companies within The Random House Group Limited
can be found at: www.randomhouse.co.uk/offices.htm

The Random House Group Limited Reg. No. 954009

A CIP catalogue record for this book
is available from the British Library

ISBN 9780099507994

The Random House Group Limited supports The Forest Stewardship
Council (FSC), the leading international forest certification
organisation. All our titles that are printed on Greenpeace approved
FSC certified paper carry the FSC logo. Our paper procurement
policy can be found at www.rbooks.co.uk/environment

Printed in the UK by CPI Bookmarque, Croydon, CR0 4TD

For S, H and J; with love, as always

One realises that even in harmonious families there is this double life: the group life, which is the one we can observe, in our neighbour's household, and underneath, another – secret and passionate and intense – which is the real life that stamps the faces and gives character to the voices of our friends . . . One realises that human relationships are the tragic necessity of human life; that they can never be wholly satisfactory, that every ego is half the time greedily seeking them and half the time pulling away from them.

Willa Cather (essay on Katherine Mansfield, 1925)

'Better to fall from power, if fall we must, at the hands of a man – never be rated inferior to a woman, never.'

Creon (from Sophocles', *Antigone*)

March 2003

He had given her instructions, a few minutes earlier, on how to find the café, his voice barely audible through a sudden raging static on the mobile.

'It's on that long, ugly road that goes from King's Cross towards Farringdon. Bronze lettering. Next to a twenty-four-hour garage. I'll wait for you. Outside. I'll be there. You'll see me.'

Yes. She knows it. A workmen's café with a broad, pale-yellow front: Formica table tops, high-backed wooden chairs and ketchup oozing out of giant cherry-red plastic tomatoes.

She can see him now, pacing restlessly up and down the pavement.

His first words. 'I am so sorry.'

He ushers her into the café, empty but for a motorcycle courier, bulky in his black leathers, a thick red stripe down the arm of his jacket, drinking tea from a white cup. They sit at the back and he orders them both coffee, and a round of toast for himself.

Funny, she doesn't remember Ben Calder being this pretty. Shorn dark-brown curls and a full red-blooded mouth. He must be in his late thirties by now, but he doesn't look it. Dressed in faded jeans and trainers, carrying a large square canvas bag, he has the eerily youthful look of his tribe: male urban media professionals.

'What a disaster,' he says.

Anna nods. She is trying to remember if she has met him more than once, that time at Dan's flat a couple of years ago. It feels as if she knows him much better than that, but this may be because his picture is in the paper so often these days, his columns and features accompanied by the grainy byline image; that self-regarding turn of the head, the deliberately quizzical expression. 'Trust me, reader!'

'So are we to consider this a good old British cover-up?' he says drily.

'They actually used the term "vagrant". Twice on television. Countless times on the radio. Can you believe that?'

'Yes, I know, I checked back. A couple of the papers said, "an unidentified homeless man in his mid-forties". Look, this must be really difficult for you.' Ben pats her hand clumsily. His skin is white, his fingers as long and tapering as a girl's. She feels faintly repelled.

'Jack did what he did for a reason. It should be known.'

Their coffee arrives, scalding hot. She takes a quick sip and then another. Despite its tastelessness, the intense heat is reassuring. The woman brings back a plate of buttered toast, which Ben devours greedily, barely stopping to chew.

'It means,' he says, his mouth still full, 'I'm going to have to ask you things. About the two families. How they – you – met. About Andy Givings in particular. How you know him. How the relationship between him and your brother – well, both your brothers – developed over the years. Are you up for that?'

'Yes. Of course.'

'You know what they say about him?' Ben's eyes are alight with excitement. 'That he's considered one of a handful who might get to be . . . get right to the top. Maybe soon. If things collapse after this disastrous war.'

'Yeah. Yeah. I read the papers too, you know.'

'Just needed to check . . .' Ben is unsmiling now. From his canvas bag, he pulls out a large black notebook, a clutch of rollerball pens, a Palm Pilot, a mobile phone. He switches the phone off. Glances at his watch. 'Okay. Let's give this an hour and a half, although I'll need to be able to get hold of you later on if necessary.'

'You're planning to run it when?'

'Probably Wednesday. Depends on what else is happening. They're saving three pages. Maybe more . . . You do realise, don't you?' He hesitates, just for a second. 'It's a big story.'

'Yes.' Anna shuts her eyes, briefly. Best not to think about the consequences. Not now. Not just yet. 'Look. Just go ahead. Ask whatever.'

'Good,' he says, briskly. 'Let's get back to the beginning, to how it all started. I want you to tell me the whole story,' he says, putting heavy emphasis on the last two words. 'The story, the whole story and nothing but the story.'

'Yeah, right.' She smiles, takes a deep breath. 'Well, once upon a time . . .'

One

Once upon a time, there was a family of six, a mummy and a daddy and two boys and two girls, who lived in a tall, tidy house, with a dark-green front door and big windows, in a quiet street with tall plane trees and a bright-red postbox right outside the door.

1971

'Help lay the table, will you, Anna Lu?'

It is strange, how well she remembers the hours before the other family arrived that first summer Sunday, a sense of excitement building while she worked to help her mother get everything ready in the kitchen, her favourite room in the house, a long, cool white-painted space, the result of three scullery-style rooms knocked through years before. From here, just below street level, one got a grand view of the calves of passing pedestrians or dogs sniffing contemplatively up against the house railings.

It was a bright, sunny day. A London Sunday morning; oddly peaceful, the streets clean and clear. When she had gone out earlier to post a letter, there was no-one about apart from the rag-and-bone man slow-clattering his weekend way around the neighbour-hood, filling the road with his ringing bell and plaintive calls. In the background, tinny Radio 1, with its cheery-sounding DJs, belting out its soulful hits. Why, she wondered, do the melancholy minor chord changes of 'What's Going On?' make her shiver with happiness? It helped to have a job of work to do – her body kept usefully occupied, her mind gloriously free – as she scrubbed the long, rectangular pine kitchen table until there was not a speck or spot remaining. Shards of sunlight flooded the fruit bowl, the table's centrepiece, withdrawing without warning, like a rapid tide.

Her mother had gone upstairs to change, and fix her hair. At twelve-thirty, she came back down wearing the stiff, pouty expression that indicated she was ready to receive company. Clambering now onto a kitchen chair, opening one cupboard door after another, looking for some unspecified object, talking in that dreamy way she had when trying to do three things at once.

'He's their newest recruit. Andy . . . his name is Andy Givings. Don't know why it's not Andrew. Maybe it *is* Andrew. Came straight from doing pupillage at Geoffrey Carter's set at Gray's Inn, about six months ago. Your father says he's made quite an impact already. Hard worker. A charmer . . . Ahh! Here they are.'

She had found what she was looking for: two pale-green plastic juice beakers.

'His children are little. Two boys. So could you make a bit of an effort?'

As if Anna never does.

Her mother jumped down, the beaker handles hooked around her right thumb. Pacing the perimeter of the long kitchen table, head to one side, she scanned her daughter's handiwork, pouncing occasionally to switch a knife and fork or tidy up some spoons. Anna felt a stab of pride at the older woman's good looks: her heart-shaped face, the dark-brown eyes with high, perfectly arched brows, the slim body, in brown cords and a fitted, fawny-coloured top.

Cutlery finally arranged to her satisfaction, her mother straightened up, fingertips grazing her forehead, eyelashes flickering, a coded signal of harassment. Anna could see the delicate blue veins, thin as pencil strokes, criss-crossing the flesh of her milky-white eyelids.

Her mother was nearly forty-three; unimaginably old.

July 1971. The year of decimal money and divorce reform. Hundreds of thousands marched through the streets of New York and San Francisco in protest against the war in Vietnam, a conflict Anna's father frequently railed against, fuming at the Americans' 'criminal intervention, their colonial arrogance'. A group calling themselves the Weather Underground claimed responsibility for a bomb that had exploded in a bathroom at the White House. 'Complete idiots'; her father's equally choleric judgement on this random, threatening act. 'A ragbag mix of students and middle-class dropouts playing politics with people's lives.' So did Anna begin to recognise the contours of adult opinion, its endless shifts and subtleties, so impossible to predict.

Meanwhile, the new coins felt as smooth and meaningless in her palm as play-currency and she wanted the old blackened pennies back, gouged with the image of Boadicea in her carriage, and the thick, sharp edges of the threepenny bit. Divorce was the talk of her father's colleagues that year. In January, Victor Porter, head of chambers, left his wife of thirty-five years – handsome, worn, stay-at-home Maude – and moved in with a pointy-nosed expert in shipping law who wasn't yet thirty. Her father reported with some amusement that Victor now strutted the narrow passages and cramped, interconnecting warren of chamber's offices with a straightened back and a spring in his step, while poor abandoned Maude rang Anna's mother at least twice a week, her wail of unmitigated distress audible from the top of the hall stairs.

There, in the hallway, with the pretty turquoise, rust and gold-tiled floor (the same mosaic pattern to be found in the entrance hall of every house on their side of the street), Anna could make out the silhouette of a storybook family through the frosted glass: two tall figures framing a pair of low, bobbing heads.

'Hello. I'm Andy.'

Wavy, brown hair and an open, pleasant face.

'Anna, I presume.'

She nodded, wordlessly. The stranger took her hand. 'I'm so glad to meet you. Your father is always talking about you.' His cheeks had the rosy, mottled hue of excitement. Or nerves. He grinned, revealing a row of small, sharp, unevenly spaced teeth. 'This is Clare, my wife.' A pretty, stout, smiling woman with a short, artless haircut and smooth unblemished skin. 'And these are my boys.' Now, he couldn't keep raw pride from his voice. Pointing fondly at the head of the older one – a skinny, dark child

with a long jaw, who kept his eyes stubbornly fixed on the floor
– and then at the littler one: white blond curls like a cherub, and
a thumb jammed in his mouth.

Anna could hear her mother's footsteps coming up from the
kitchen, see her now, shaking imaginary drops of water from her
beautifully manicured hands. Walking quickly towards their guests
in her close-fitting brown clothes, a frosted lipstick freshly applied,
pout still in place, she conveyed the perfect image of the gracious
hostess: laughing just a little, at the absurdity of entertaining,
extending the generosity of her amusement to those around her.
The adults greeted each other with that honeyed emphasis that is
not quite insincerity, her father appearing like an apparition on
the front stairs, shepherding everyone through to the front living
room, the room kept for best with its long, low couches, pristine
pale armchairs and solid, close packed rows of glossy hardbacks.
There was fizzy white wine for the adults, juice for the children.
(Anna's mother kept a close eye on the little boys; she was paranoid about spillages.) Awkwardness dissolved within minutes and
it was then, memory told her, that the lunch party began in earnest.

Andy Givings was twenty-nine years old; her father forty-four, a
significant gap in age and professional experience. The younger
man was a relatively junior barrister: he had had a false start, in
career terms, with a spell in industrial management. Clearly
talented, he was, as yet, untested in the law. By comparison, Anna's
father was well established: he had a reputation. He had a *name*.
(Anna found this common term of praise puzzling: for who does
not have a *name*?) It was assumed at that first lunch – as it was
understood all during the early years of the friendship – that her
father was easily the superior of the two, in all worldly ways, at
least. He may have – secretly – loved literature more than his
work, but he was a first-class barrister, a QC since 1969, and rich
too, (now), having made a considerable amount of money from
his profession, especially gratifying for a poor boy from Essex
raised by his mother, a school teacher, alone. He had married well,
to the once-beautiful, still lovely Fiona (née Scott), a young woman
from a respectable land-owning Surrey family with whom he now,
proudly, had four children; two boys and two girls, born within

just six years, all healthy, handsome and at good schools. The family lived in a tall, comfortable, early Victorian villa in a prosperous but not, yet, fancy area. There was nothing fancy about David Adams. (God forbid, Anna's father loathed flashiness. All was solid, all was substance.)

But beneath the apparent surface of things, there were other realities. Within half an hour of Andy and Clare Givings's arrival on that July Sunday over thirty years ago, it was obvious that the young couple had a possibly much more valuable gift in their possession than wealth or conspicuous success or devotion to the outward proprieties. Human interest. Both of them possessed a contagious enthusiasm for life: the divine gift of apparent self-forgetting, as if their deepest purpose in life was pleasingly to extend themselves for the sake of others. Kind and attentive, this young man and his astute, clear-skinned wife displayed an intense and genuine curiosity in others: what they thought and felt. And why. Looking back, it was strange to Anna, both poignant and prescient, how much the older, richer, apparently more enviable family craved this simple thing: human interest. How much they all seemed to need it, each and every one of them, young and old.

Pacing the living room, a small white wine, as yet untouched, in her hand – neither of the Givings were big drinkers – Clare was bent over a display of family photos set out in stiff, brown leather frames on the marble-topped table by the French windows. 'So this must be Matt?' 'And this here is Laura? What a *pretty* girl.' (Anna, used to the familiar sting of sibling envy, could almost hear her mother purring.) Now, Clare picked up a black-and-white photograph, taken several years previously, a picture of Anna and her three siblings posed formally on the living-room couch: Matt and Jack, dressed in identical pale shirts and dark bow ties and patent brogue shoes, with broad, cheeky smiles. (With a big gap on either side of his front teeth, Jack looked like a rabbit.) Laura and Anna were wearing matching white dresses in a filmy material – organza, possibly? – their hair tied back with butterfly clips. The contrast between the girls' colouring was dramatic (it still was). Laura had fine, white blonde hair, Anna a mass of brunette curls and heavy, dark brows. ('Little Miss Serious Brow. Her father's daughter in every way', her mother would frequently sigh, it being understood within the family that Anna and her father were particularly close, and not just in the matter of their colouring: linked, too, through a shared interest in books and thinking, traits that were somehow tied up, in their mother's prosaic view, with the head and brow area.)

Anna loved this photograph, her little-girl legs ramrod-straight, blunt patent toes pointing skywards, because the photographer forgot to remind her to bend them.

'Four children. And so close together in age!' Clare Givings looked at the older woman with frank admiration. 'Two's my limit, I'm afraid. But then we did start ridiculously young. I was six months pregnant by the time I finished my finals.'

'Sometimes I hardly know how I fitted them all in.' Anna's mother was gathering up glasses in readiness to usher everyone down to the kitchen. 'Do you know? I once asked a lady who was walking behind me in Kensington Gardens if she would just take my place, for a second. I wanted to see what I looked like, a woman out, all alone, with these four children in tow.'

'And?' Clare smiled, picking up a half-empty bowl of crisps, eager to help. 'What *did* a mother and four children out all alone in a park look like from behind?'

'Exhausted, I dare say!' The older woman was leading them out of the living room now, through the hall, down the stairs into the kitchen, chucking homespun wisdoms over her shoulder, like salt, for luck. 'One makes so many awful mistakes in family life, you know. It's impossible not to.'

They ate lamb and new potatoes and tiny, sweet green peas flavoured with mint. The little Givings' boys sat quietly, wedged between their parents. Dan, the older one, brought his chair as close as possible to his mother, their elbows rubbing cosily. From time to time he would pull her to him, whisper in her ear and she would nod, smile, pat his hand, before turning back to chat to the adults. Thumb-sucking Greg had slid onto his father's lap, from where he proceeded to pick peas and scraps of meat from Andy's plate, gravy dribbling down his chin. Halfway through pudding, Anna's brothers came back from playing football in the park, muddy and perspiring. Anna felt proud of their vigour, their gleaming youth. Matt was seventeen years, slight in build, but good-looking. He took an instant interest in their visitors. ('You worked on that big case for Dad, right? Yeah. I remember – he said. Pleased to meet you.') At just fourteen, Jack was much the burlier figure, a thatch of ginger hair bonded by sweat to his lightly freckled forehead. He ate his warmed-up food at the far end of the kitchen table without saying a word.

'Now, boys. Remember!' Their mother chided when they had finished their rhubarb crumble and ice cream. 'You promised!'

'Yeah, yeah, yeah.' The boys clattered up the kitchen stairs. A few moments later they reappeared; Matt's face partially hidden by two giant cardboard packages; Jack holding a scarlet container the size of a shoe box.

'Everyone! We have a train set!' Gleefully, Anna's mother beckoned them to gather round, while Matt unpacked piles of dusty segments of track and dozens of miniature green-and-red carriages with curved roofs and tiny rectangular windows that could be opened just like real train windows, complete with 'first class' and 'no smoking' stickers.

Deftly, Matt began slotting the track together, taking the line all around the kitchen floor, out to the far edge, near the utility-room door. Jack sat in the corner, his fringe flopping over his eyes; fingers, pudgy as a child's, working intently on building the three stations, each with its own wooden hut, raised platform, benches – for waiting passengers, he explained to Dan – and signal boxes.

Anna's mother hovered over them, burbling with delight.

'You're blocking my light, Ma.'

The connection finally came good: the train signals lit up like a set of Christmas-tree lights.

'Isn't that *lovely!*' Her mother's cry.

'Fuck off, Mum.' Jack spoke in a low, even tone.

The light in the kitchen seemed suddenly to dim, as it did on late winter afternoons.

'*What* did you say?'

'It's not *that* a-mazing.' Jack did not look up; his tone remained conversational despite the church-like hush that had descended on the rest of the company. 'Electricity has been around for well over a hundred years, you know.'

Anna saw her mother's shoulders drop and, as if reading her mind, saw her decide, in a split second, that this reply might – should – had to be – permitted to approximate normality, the minor abuse of earlier set aside in the interests of a speedy resolution to her own embarrassment.

'Okay, Matt. Who's this?' Andy was speaking, trying to pierce the suddenly sombre mood.

'What do you mean?' Matt shook his head, a puzzled smile on his face.

'Just watch me.'

Andy bared his teeth in a mirthless grin and began to pump his shoulders up and down, until even Anna's father – who had been frowning, at his son's rudeness (or his own impotence perhaps; Anna could not read her father's mind) – began to smile at the younger man's passable imitation of Ted Heath.

'Hey! That's not bad,' Matt laughed in delight.

They were all doing it now, turning their heads from side to side like puppets, pumping their shoulders up and down, grinning like maniacs – even the little boys – a room full of surreally jolly, staring-eyed Prime Ministers.

Two

They had all – except Jack, who disappeared upstairs to his room within minutes of the swearing incident – remained in the kitchen long after lunch, the adults indulgently watching the little boys speed their trains back and forth across the shiny linoleum floor. It was nearly three-thirty before the adults went back up to the front room and her father, finally allowed his strong coffee and serious talk, had slipped off to his study to fetch a book he wanted to show Andy, while her mother forged ahead to plump pillows and wipe surfaces. Anna, piggy in the middle – walking up the stairs behind her parents, but ahead of their guests – heard Clare yawn rather theatrically when they got to the top. A short silence, a pregnant gap in the ordinary stream of talk. Without thinking, Anna turned. And there – she saw it – the locking of the eyes, a definite look exchanged between husband and wife in the shadows of the hallway.

There was no doubt about it. It was a smile revealing intimacy, conspiracy even. But it was not unkind. Anna's deepest instincts told her that. Andy and Clare were not the sort of people to laugh at others gratuitously, to search deliberately for the vulnerability of those who might threaten them. She did not believe they would be gossiping later about Jack's swearing, enjoying the evidence of this younger son's bad behaviour. They took no pleasure in finding fragility at the heart of the older, more established family. No, Anna groped towards a different interpretation of that brief glance of amused complicity. It was a kind of relief – yes, that was what she saw in it. As if they were saying to each other, wordlessly,

We've made it. So far. We haven't been found out. Children in the house of the grown-ups! There was something sexual in there too, Andy's eyes shining with a primitive appreciation of his smooth-skinned, stocky wife; an answering glint in hers that made Anna see them both – suddenly, disturbingly – in a different way.

Two seconds later, Andy and Clare became separate, self-possessed adults again, ambling into the living room where the cushions had been straightened, the wine and juice glasses from before lunch whipped out of sight, the coffee tray laid on the marble table. Anna's mother moved as noiselessly as a well-trained butler between the men, Anna's father settled in his usual easy chair, Andy, lounging in the middle seat of the big sofa, legs apart, arms gesticulating, already in mid-conversational flow. *More milk, yes, just a touch; no sugar, thanks, Fiona.* Having shed their family skins, the men were now more formal versions of themselves, their courtesy elaborate and distracted.

They were talking politics.

Anna sat cross-legged on the floor, near the French windows, her attention drifting towards and away from the steady masculine drone. She stared out at the blank, reflective darkness of the windows of the houses opposite. Just then, the next-door neighbour, Susan, a white-haired widow, walked past, an airmail letter in her hand. She pushed the pale-blue rectangle through the slit in the red box, and then peered over at the Adams' house, looking away quickly when she saw there were people sitting in the front room.

Anna's father was talking about trade-union rights. Anna knew a little about his work, knew that it conferred significance and respect on him, and all the family: she could see it in the way his colleagues, her friends' parents, the neighbours – like Susan – greeted him, the way they left a narrow moat of space around him out of respect or fear, or both. Younger women became arch and flirtatious in his presence. People appeared to know the names of his cases and bandied them about self-consciously. 'Porlington v. Clarkson. Terrific stuff.' Noted legal judgements, it seemed, were like a really good book or a film; they entered the blood-stream of the culture. Her father was no ordinary lawyer: she knew that, too. He took political cases which made him a hero to some, and an oddity to others. At lunch, for instance, he and Andy had been talking about one of his better-known trials, a few years back: two radicals, sent to prison for heckling the Prime Minister in a country church over the government's support for Vietnam. Anna vaguely remembered the fuss. The upstairs dining room had been commandeered as a second office, the table stacked with files a foot high. Her father's picture had even been in the paper.

Andy was saying now, 'It's a hard one to get right – this issue of trade-union power.'

Her father: 'Is power really the right word? They are entitled to the same civil liberties as other citizens, surely?'

Last summer, someone had left a leaflet about a meeting on the hall table: *Come and hear David Adams, QC, a friend of civil liberties . . .*

Now Andy was talking again – about enlightened business practices, about seeing employers as human beings.

Human beings. Yes, that made sense. She smiled at Andy. He winked at her.

The funny thing was, he seemed to be addressing her personally. Even though she knew nothing about trade unions, civil liberties, or anything very much to do with politics, he seemed to care what she thought, an eleven-year-old school girl in a burnt-orange T-shirt and cord jeans. He seemed, in fact, to be addressing everyone in the room, drawing them in; Matt, who had sneaked into the living room a few minutes ago; Clare, who was brave enough to intervene from time to time in the discussion, despite Anna's father's disdainful looks of surprise. Even Anna's mother, patently bored by serious talk, stopped and listened with an expression of the utmost willingness when Andy was speaking.

What was the name for it? Anna knew there was a particular word for what Andy had, what he was.

A woman with dark hair and pale skin came out of the house opposite.

Animal magnetism. Was that it?

The woman turned and pulled the front door closed behind her. She gave it a little shove, just to double-check, and then turned right and ran, with a deliberate lightness, along the pavement in the direction of Bayswater.

Charisma. Yes, she was almost certain, that was the word.

She had not meant to lie in wait for the boy – or anyone else – but she had not wanted to go back into the living room, either; after a while, the men's talk had sent her into a trance. For the lack of anything else to do, she had sat on the lowest step of the hall stairs, chin in her hands, wondering if Laura would be back soon from her friend's house, when she saw a pair of bare legs disappearing up the front staircase, towards the first-floor landing.

'Hello?'

Dan turned, a furtive look on his face.

'I was looking for the . . .'

'Oh, why didn't you say?' She sprinted up the stairs, overtaking him just before the landing was reached, 'Through here . . .'

'Thank you', he said stiffly.

When he came back downstairs again, she was still sitting on the step, chin in hand. He stood in front of her awkwardly, waiting for her to say something.

'There's a pool table up in Matt's room. Would you like . . . ?'

He smiled readily, a lit-up grin, all traces of sullenness wiped away. Some of his baby teeth were missing. Big gaps waiting for the adult ones to grow in. He was eight-and-a-half years old. Clare had said so at lunch. A baby, compared to her eleven years. Still, there was the tail end of a summer afternoon to kill.

'Okay.'

She noticed as they climbed the narrow staircase to the attic rooms that his navy-blue sweater was worn bare, a cat's cradle of fraying blue thread holding in his bony elbow. Her mother would never have let any of her children go out for a Sunday lunch in worn clothes: she always stressed the importance of looking your best at all times.

The rooms at the top of the house had sloping roofs and high, spherical windows that could only be looked through by adults on tiptoe. In winter it gave these top rooms a dark, atmospheric feel, like being on a ship below the water line.

Jack's door was closed. They could hear music, a soft melodic moaning. But Matt's door was ajar, welcoming them into the large L-shaped carpeted space. Anna switched on the electric light as Dan hung back for a second. 'Don't worry,' she reassured him, 'Matt says I can come up here to play any time I want.'

Her eldest brother's room was immaculately tidy, as always. A pile of school folders and textbooks were neatly stacked on a dark wooden desk. A brace of freshly sharpened pencils filled a piece of indigo perspex tubing. In the middle of the room stood the pool table, its lawn-green surface invitingly clear, a mass of coloured balls neatly stowed in the net pockets at each corner. Anna picked up a cue leaning against the wall by Matt's bed.

'Ever played?'

'Nope.'

'Come over here then.' She beckoned Dan to the side of the table. 'Stand here, in front of me.' He was tall for eight, only a head smaller than her.

She stood behind him, still holding the cue. 'Now lean over . . .' He stretched out obligingly. 'That's right. Put your arms nearer together.' She was peering round the side of his head, brushing against his dark hair, her own arms outstretched. 'Now take the cue from me . . . Hold it,' she urged, 'as if you're shooting a gun.'

'I've never shot a gun!' he said indignantly, twisting his head to try and catch her eye.

'Okay, okay.' She laughed, nudging his head back to face the green baize. 'Haven't you seen anyone do it on telly? You know how people hold a rifle, with the end up near their shoulder . . . That's better.' He was holding the length of wood awkwardly, like someone preparing to rake a lawn.

'Keep in that position for a mo . . .' Anna darted round the side of the table to fish out a couple of coloured balls and a white one, placing them a few inches away from each other on the table.

'If you want to pot the red, you must hit it just so,' and she gently pushed his cue-holding arm – rigid, still – into the white ball. 'Like that!'

And the white ball sped into the red and knocked it into a corner pocket.

'You star!' They were both laughing now. 'Now try the yellow.

Remember to hit it through the white.' She enjoyed playing the part of the kind, stern teacher.

She shifted the white ball back towards him to make it easier and he shot this one into the net, too.

'Hurrah!'

Emboldened by this second success, he looked up from the table, pushing away the hair that kept falling over his eyes, and smiled. In that moment, she had the illusion that his whole character was suspended, encapsulated in the marble-like surface of his eye, the black pupils swimming in the vein-threaded cornea, and that if she stayed very still or looked very carefully she could grasp exactly who he was and who he might become.

He was – faintly, very faintly – trembling.

'Come on,' Anna had made up her mind. 'I'll show you the Secret Room.'

They lived on a Bayswater back street; a passing-through road, it often seemed, traversed by people with their necks craned and foreheads puckered, looking for somewhere more interesting, like Whiteley's, the department store, or a tea shop someone had recommended to them on the glamorous-sounding Moscow Road. The flat-fronted, early Victorian villas were nowhere near as grand as the double-fronted houses in neighbouring streets – these with their five floors and raised, glass-covered entrances – and yet it was beautiful, she felt, her home stretch, an enchanted urban backspot in its own right, with tall plane trees widely spaced and bleached paving that gave it the smooth, hopeful gleam of a beach.

Family myth had it that this was a lucky house, the last on a long list given to her parents by the harassed estate agent, thirteen years before, when the young couple were looking to move their growing family quickly. Fiona was seven months pregnant with Laura. Their small flat in St Charles's Square, off Ladbroke Grove, couldn't possibly hold two lively little boys and a new baby. Prepared to look at any vaguely suitable property, the young couple arrived at the house in Durnford Gardens at the tail end of an August afternoon. In estate-agent speak, the house was 'full of potential', which turned out to mean it was riddled with damp, had no fence for three-quarters of the length of the back garden and had not been decorated for fifty years. It was also cheap. Lumbering from room to room, Fiona had the practical sense to see beyond the mushroom-coloured growth eating into the lower portions of the walls, the embossed dark wallpaper of another age, and instead to look up at the high ceilings and peer through the tall, rectangular windows at the front and the larger, squarer panes at the back, which gave onto a surprisingly big garden for such a central city location. 'Oh, I love it already,' Fiona whispered to herself as she walked from back to front of the property, revisiting every light-filled room two, three, even four times. Small details seemed to confirm the magic of the house. 'Look at the colours of this floor!' she said excitedly, scuffing her feet deliberately on the pretty mosaic tiling in the hallway. 'It's like a swimming pool and a farmhouse got all mixed up together.' In those days she spoke like that. Very girlish, soaring above rationality, the self-conscious opposite of her calm, precise husband.

It was Anna's father who found the Secret Room (called this only because there seemed to be no description of it in the details given to them by the estate agent). At first David had presumed the door – spied through an internal archway on the first landing, towards the back of the house – was a broom cupboard or a toilet. Instead, it opened onto a large echoey space, a giant sash window overlooking the wild garden, the late-afternoon light softening the harsh, muddy yellow of the paintwork. He decided then and there that he would make this his study, his bolthole from the all-too-apparent petty stresses and strains of family life.

Over the years the room had grown in grandeur. Anna's mother had decorated it in the heavy Victorian style she thought appropriate to the study of a serious man. The walls were papered in gold-and-cream stripes, the floor laid with thick-pile dark-red carpet. The Fifties-style tiled mantelpiece, an ugly monstrosity, was pulled out and replaced by an elegant black-marble fireplace. Anna's father had taken charge of only one part of the refurbishment. He had hired a skinny red-haired local carpenter to fit wall-to-wall shelving, giving him exact instructions on the height and depth of every row, to fit his thousands of books.

'Wow!'

'You should see it when the fire is lit in winter. It's magic.'

By the sash window, two high-backed chairs covered in dark-blue velvet were set around a low glass table. Books were piled on the transparent table top; from their pages protruded tiny white slips, notes Anna's father had made on what he was reading. Anna liked to tweak these pieces of paper from their warm vanilla interiors, to try to decipher the lines of cramped writing. They seemed to her like ancient riddles found inside fortune cookies: nuggets of predictive wisdom. The other day she had pulled out a rectangular strip of white paper from a page marked at a poem called 'The Second Coming'. Her father had underlined only three lines from the verse. *The centre cannot hold . . . The ceremony of innocence is drowned . . . Surely some revelation is at hand.* The words seemed arranged in intriguingly random order; over and over they drew her back, like a puzzle that could, with sufficient effort, be solved.

Dan had now moved over to the mantelpiece, the ledge of it taller than the top of his tousled head. He put his arm up, fingers spread wide, as if reaching for some forbidden sweet thing lodged in a high, unreachable cupboard.

'Can I?'

''Course.'

After a moment's hesitation, he carefully lowered a silver-framed photo of a young couple standing against a blank white sky and brought the picture an inch or two from his eyes, studying it intently. The young man in the picture was tall and lean with jet-black shiny hair, combed away from his forehead. He was squinting as if he had just woken up or was shielding himself from the sun. His right arm was hooked around the waist of a slim brunette, stylishly dressed in a tailored white shirt and a tight black-and-white checked skirt, her head turned away from the camera, smiling, half-shielded by an elegant, long-fingered hand.

'Who are they?'

'Those are my parents, silly.'

'Really?' Dan peered at the photo for a few more moments. She wondered if he needed glasses. 'Yes, I can see. She looks a lot like you.'

'Really?' It was Anna's turn to exclaim in mild incredulity. And blush.

'Yes. You have the same hair. Sort of tumbling down. And the smile. You smile like that.'

'I think she looks like a film star in that picture.' There was in her a need, stronger than any claim of her own, to have her mother's young beauty acknowledged by strangers.

'She looks happy.'

'Yes.' She saw it too, a young woman on the threshold of adulthood, radiant with private hopes and dreams.

He put the photo back carefully on top of the marble fireplace.

'Come over here!' Anna had crossed to the bookshelves now, and was beckoning him over to a row of orange-spined paperbacks. 'What I like to do is pick one out, read a bit, put it back, pick out another . . . I can spend ages doing that.'

She pulled out a satisfyingly thick book. '*Wuthering Heights*. I've been dipping in and out of it for weeks.'

Copying her, the boy picked out a spy novel with an alluring image of a man in a raincoat with a turned-up collar holding a gun. He opened it up and read the first page. As he read, he rubbed his cheek with a grubby, brown-skinned fist. There was a real hole in his blue jumper now. His elbow was popping out, the flesh-coloured tip of it faintly obscene.

It was here in the Secret Room that Clare Givings found them when she came searching, at the end of that first ever afternoon, for her first-born, and almost certainly her favourite, son. Sitting side by side, in the dark-blue velvet chairs, by the sash window. Dan was immersed in his spy book, flicking the fleshy tip of his nose back and forth, deep in concentration. Anna was lost in *White Boots*, which she had read twice already, wrapping a dark curl so tightly – and absent-mindedly – around her finger that the tip of it was a bloodless white.

Three

And so began the long friendship of the two families, the regular meetings of the two clans, as her brother Matt (who identified with Andy from the start) jokily called them, over the three decades that followed. The Givings became like extended family: Andy, the fond uncle; Clare, a brisk aunt; Dan and Greg, youthful relatives that Anna and her siblings had simply to tolerate. Love was not required or expected. Indeed, nothing was demanded of any of the children but that they spend a couple of hours from time to time with their counterparts in the other family, and that they receive – passively – snippets of not very important news concerning exams passed, minor injuries sustained, holidays taken. Inevitably, over time, each of them developed opinions of their clan equivalents – as it were – which remained remarkably static through the passing years. So Laura and Matt declared for Greg, because he was such a 'funny little chap' with his curly hair and his big head, a real outgoing character, while Anna and Jack preferred the shy, thoughtful Dan. Everyone adored Andy. Anna liked Clare, whom secretly she felt sure preferred her to her sister, a feeling that seemed confirmed by the fact that Laura always declared the older woman to be a 'little bit too bossy'.

She couldn't remember exactly when the ritual of the Christmas Eve dinner began: it must have been a couple of years after that first Sunday lunch. But for a long time, from 1973 or possibly 1974 – the adult Anna could not recall exact dates – the Givings family always came to the house in Durnford Gardens for Christmas Eve. They arrived at about seven in the evening, with plastic bags stuffed full of presents, many of them rather ill-chosen. (Unlike Fiona Adams, who was an inspired present buyer, Clare Givings, who was always busy, always rushing, tended to go for quantity over quality.) No matter. Both families looked forward to the moment of greeting, the ritual shout of pleasure upon the opening of the front door, the cold winter night a starry black backdrop to the lit-up faces and colourfully dressed figures. This moment – the bellowing of 'Happy Christmas' in unison – signalled the official beginning of festivities just as surely as the placing of the sprayed gold wreath on the front door, the decorating of the Christmas tree or the winding of the fairy lights along the picture rails of the front hallway had, in the weeks before, signalled the slow beginnings of the holiday season.

Over the years, Anna and her brothers and sister saw big changes in the little boys. Dan, for instance, shot up from four foot something to become over six foot (eventually). Greg was transformed from a thumb-sucking baby into a broad and shiny-faced adolescent, as cheery and confident a presence as his father. It felt a little like quick-flicking through one of those old-fashioned paper books in which someone has sketched a man running or a woman dancing or a couple kissing, each page showing the animated progression of the action in question, the entire impression one of racy, unstoppable movement.

The men were the original link of course, the ones who brought the families together, but it was the women, increasingly, who kept it all going: Anna's elegant, worldly mother who had no interest, beyond the superficial or the social, in books or in politics; and the much younger woman, a more intellectual character and a career professional. No-one ever talked about her work, but Clare Givings, known by her maiden name of Arkwright, was a respected lecturer in history and politics, first at a further-education college, then at a red-brick university. Some deep note of sympathy was struck between the older and younger women, perhaps – who knows? – because one was a working woman and the other was not, or because there was more than a decade difference in their ages, or because the children were never at similar stages, so there was limited scope for direct comparisons and rivalry. Perhaps it was Clare's ability to home in on how desperately Fiona Adams wanted, or needed, to talk about her children. And Fiona in her turn took a kind, matronly interest in the younger family's life, offering helpful hints on ordinary, practical matters that might help daily life run more smoothly, digging out recipes for quick meals or suggesting ways to steam-clean carpets or get the best deal on house insurance. She gave Clare bagloads of her boys' old clothes, without ever causing offence, and eventually passed on David's train set – the one that Matt and Jack had laid out on their kitchen floor, that first visit – in its grubby white-and-scarlet containers. Anna's mother was intensely practical, and her days long and increasingly empty as her four children grew up and away, eager to escape her kind, fussy surveillance, and her husband continued to commit himself to long days away on his legal career, and long nights shut up in his study, reading.

But there was, too, the question of Andy's new career, his third attempt, as it happened, to find a profession that was satisfying to him, a change of emphasis that intrigued all – and threatened some – who came into contact with him.

What could not have been predicted was how much this new route in life would further bind the two families, for good or ill, and not in any of the ways that might have been expected by even the most perceptive of observers.

Four

'I'm thinking of going into politics.'

As he said this quiet but momentous sentence, signifying a leap into the unknown, his going into a world beyond that of his mentor, Andy had the grace to blush, while Anna's mother gasped, as satisfyingly as a character onscreen.

Andy recovered his composure quickly and said with the utmost casualness, 'It's just a question of getting myself on various lists. No harm done in just trying, is there?'

'Do you mean *Parliament*?' Anna's mother baldly interrupted, when he was saying something about List A and List B.

'Well. It sounds crazy. *Now* . . .'

'Someone's got to do it,' Clare said stubbornly.

They were sitting in the back room of Andy and Clare's house, cream walls faintly spattered with dark stains – football? mud? hot chocolate? – the mauve carpet underfoot grubby, vaguely threatening with age. Andy had slotted in an extra leaf at the end of the dining table to accommodate the visitors and brought down two chairs from the boys' rooms. There was an upright piano in the corner, piled high with books and magazines, a film of fine dust on its walnut top.

Anna was nearly fourteen. She and her parents were on a rare visit to the Givings' house, at Clare's invitation, to celebrate Andy's birthday. Back then, in the mid-Seventies, they lived in an end-of-street cul-de-sac, with a central courtyard, fetchingly decorated with plant-filled earthenware pots, in the outer reaches of west

London. The house was pleasant but, with its narrow corridors and square, low-ceilinged rooms, it seemed on too small a scale for a man of Andy's height and exuberance. There were piles of books and folded washing on every spare step and surface. The front room was comfortably furnished with a flowery couch and armchairs, a small television and rows of practical shelving, stacked high with the boys' games and books, but there was barely space for extra visitors. Her parents sat on the main sofa, looking rather elderly, an anxious couple awaiting bad news in a doctor's surgery, while Anna squatted with the boys on the floor, pulling at her short tartan skirt, which could not quite cover her knees, and that looked to her, from the top down, as large as footballs.

To her mother, who placed such importance on the art of hostessing, this emphasis on comfort rather than style was one of the endearing oddities of the other woman's life. 'Entertaining is just not important to Clare.' She had thrown out this comment, largely for Anna's benefit, on the drive over. 'She always has a lot of different things on her mind,' she added, at that moment (rather comically) distracted herself by a complicated bit of fiddling with her fringe in the front passenger-seat mirror.

The adults toasted Andy many happy returns of the day – he was thirty-two – in sweet white wine and warm beer, while Anna and the boys clinked their glasses of orange juice. For lunch there was tinned tuna with bottled mayonnaise, green beans, boiled potatoes and salad. Slices of shop-bought chocolate cake with a gelatinous icing were handed out on paper plates stencilled with large multicoloured clowns' heads, the remainder of a job lot bought for a child's birthday.

With a mouthful of cake, Andy now said, 'Actually, I've been approached.'

'You have?' Anna's mother, responding rawly once again.

'Well, you know I've done a few meetings, mainly speaking about the Turner case.'

Anna's father nodded in that way the men had, acknowledging the claims of the outer world: *Ah, the Turner case, of course.* 'A couple of people asked me if I'd ever thought of it and I always said, "No", and then one day I thought, "Yes, why not?"'

'I think it's great.' Clare's voice was higher than usual.

'Of course, nothing might happen,' Andy said. 'There are no guarantees.'

'I'm pretty sure something *will* happen.' Clare placed her palm protectively over Andy's right hand.

'I want to be in at the real-world end of things. Doing something practical, however small. However insignificant.'

'It's an uncertain life.'

'And the law's not?' Andy snorted, good-naturedly. 'Come on, it's uncertain for those of us without obvious talent. The non-QCs of this world.'

Anna's father gave a brief, mirthless smile.

'Andy's ready,' Clare said simply, standing up to clear the table. 'To do something else. To move on.'

Then, as if roused by her defence of her husband, she lost any remaining shyness about her 'housekeeping'. One by one she threw the paper plates, still viscous with shards of uneaten cake, into a large black plastic bag she had brought in from the kitchen. She even slung in the mayonnaise jar, although there was a creamy sediment left at the bottom. At that moment Anna realised – it came to her in a rush, like a gust of wind, picking up and carrying with it all the debris of past perceptions, fragments of recognition that now made a definite impression – that Clare was a strong woman, strong in a way that her own mother was not. She had a tougher love in her, and more of the best, the most useful, kinds of anger. She could extend herself well beyond the traditional female job of caring for others and containing life's little difficulties. She was daring enough to dream. And risk.

'I'm earning more,' Clare said now, to no-one in particular, 'the boys are bigger. We can take the plunge.'

Greg beamed. Dan blinked.

David said, 'I presume we're talking about . . .'

'I couldn't join any other,' Andy replied quickly.

Party loyalty was one of the deepest bonds the two men shared. They often referred to the fact that they both came from 'solid Labour families', which made their forebears sound like chocolate teddy bears or gold coins. Granny Agnes had never voted anything else. David's only cousin was a Labour Party stalwart, had been for years. They were divided on some issues. Andy was all for the comprehensives; David was a grammar-school man. Only the middle classes could afford to support comprehensives, he said, because they could always make up for their deficiencies with their own knowledge and resources. David was from lower-middle-class Essex stock; his mother had brought him and his younger brother up alone. Exceptionally talented at maths and science, he had won a scholarship (to an excellent school) and firmly believed that only a good education had propelled him, a clever boy with no influence, away from his background, to Oxford and eventually to the Bar. Andy had been educated privately and was on the surface every inch the confident young man of the world. Yet Anna couldn't help noticing, as she looked round the Givings' small but comfortable house, that they lived a modest life that didn't even qualify as bohemian. Worldly status was clearly a complicated business.

After a few minutes, Anna's father said, with forced good grace, 'Well, the best of luck to you, if that's what you want.'

'Nothing's happened yet. It may never.'

Andy stood up, to make tea for them all. They could hear him whistling cheerfully out in the galley kitchen, waiting for the kettle to boil.

She knew – her father had told her briefly, her mother at some emotional length – the unusual circumstances of Andy's youth, how he had lost his mother and father at the age of twelve; his parents killed in a car crash one Sunday afternoon, driving back from a visit to local friends, in the Kent countryside. Andy and his younger sister were left suddenly, terrifyingly, orphaned one wintry October afternoon; within days, both of them were spirited from their comfortable home on the edge of a large town to an aunt in Haringey, London, a woman with both money and kindness, as benign a benefactor as a bereaved twelve-year-old could hope for. The aunt was a teacher, married to a relatively successful stockbroker, childless herself and so possessing sufficient wealth, plenty of free time and, it turned out, a large stock of liberal-minded good sense. In Clare's words, 'Andy and Pippa were incredibly lucky, in the circumstances.' (Fiona thought it typical of the Givings' approach to life that Clare would ever invoke the idea of 'luck' in regard to any aspect of Andy's childhood situation.)

Even so, the raw shock of it, the cold blast of mortality that blew into the young boy's life and cut through the consciousness of the young man he became, was still observable in his adult life. Andy possessed the cheerful tenacity and bullish determination found only in certain kinds of survivor: whether he was boiling eggs, making a phone call or deliberating on a big issue, he had the air of hurrying towards some pre-set deadline. The effects of early bereavement were obvious too in his adoration of, and dependence on, Clare, a rock of love and good sense (of good health, too) in a harsh world. It could be seen also in both parents' attitude to their children, their deliberate embrace of the quiet, bookish Dan and the ebullient, curly-haired Greg. The whole family displayed a special kind of devotion, almost showy in its intensity. 'That's why Clare and the boys mean so much to him, you see,' Anna's father said to her once. 'They are the first family he has ever had, in a manner of speaking. The first family he can really hold on to.'

'Yes, I see,' Anna had replied. No further response was required, or seemed necessary.

There was tragedy in her father's past, too, a thread that, just possibly – Anna sometimes speculated – bound him unnaturally close to the younger man. For he, too, had lost someone precious to him when he, too, was twelve years old: his younger brother Len, in a freak childhood accident.

He had once taken Anna to the spot where the tragedy occurred, by the banks of a shallow stream, half a mile from his childhood home, near Southend. He did not say much to her then, the visit alone a sign of the special trust he placed in her, his youngest child. As to the details of the tragedy, she had to piece these together herself, picking up scraps from her paternal grandmother, the formidable Agnes, and from her mother, to whom her father had most fully opened his heart during their early courtship.

Five

1939

This much, Anna knew: it had happened one late-summer afternoon, the horrors of the war to come pressing down like a thun-
derous grey-black sky on the first moment of the story. The two
brothers had begun their twenty-minute walk along the Essex lane
from their cottage to play, as they often did, in the makeshift playground by the shallow river. There wasn't much there, just a tyre
strung from a tree, and a crude wooden swing that had been nailed
up by somebody's father, maybe even their own, before he left for
good several years previously. That day, twelve-year-old David
breathed in the freedom of this amble up the narrow lane, hedges
high on either side – dense with juicy, finger-staining blackberries
in the early autumn months; rustling dry in late summer as now.
As they walked, the boys kicked stones, or leapfrogged over each
other. David enjoyed taking advantage of his brother's momentary inattention – Len liked to stop and peer at butterflies or ladybirds on the rocky lane – to push through to the field side of the
thick hedge, calling out his brother's name through the knotted
tangle of dry leaves, until Len, tracing the location of the teasing
call, drew parallel to him and begged him to come back out.
Approaching the shady patch of trees, at the bend in the land
where the river ran – it wasn't much more than a stream really,
about eighteen inches wide – they saw some other boys had gathered there: four brothers from the big farm a mile up the road.
David had often seen them working in the fields, had passed them
sitting atop huge tractors on these lanes, riding high like the

29

pictures he had seen of men astride decorated elephants in picture books about far-away places.

Agnes, a school teacher before she married, who still taught some children in the local area, had warned them off the farm boys. 'Those Lay brothers, they've been worked too hard for nothing very much since they were tiny, they've had no education and their father knocks them about terribly. Watch out for them, but . . .' – the rest of the sentence went unspoken. David tried to figure out what his mother meant. Watch out for them, but what? Respect their power? Watch out for them, but make sure you do not follow their example? Watch out for them, but understand that having a father at home is not everything after all? The Lay boys made him shudder. It seemed as if they were pressed from alien flesh, the possessors of malfunctioning genes; their hair was very black, their eyes a scary, unnatural cornflower blue; he was not even sure whether they were brothers, or cousins.

At first, on that warm day, the six boys played together, inner nervousness exaggerating David and Len's outward show of enjoyment. Jumping over the stream, David stumbled. He thought he'd twisted his ankle. The pain was less disturbing than the uneasy sense of something snapping out of place, a searing sensation of muscular wrongness. He sat out the game for a few minutes, rubbing his foot, breathing deeply. It was then that he noticed Len's reckless excitement, a false note in his little brother's hysteria, as he was goaded by the Lay boys. Daring him to stand up on the swing, when David knew that his brother preferred to sit with his bottom firmly stuck to the wooden slat. But Len wanted to impress, to outdo his big brother, just for once.

'All right. I will!'

Why did David not find words then, as his brother began to climb onto the swing, the Lay boys standing around, cheering him on? David could see Len was frightened. Was he frightened, too? No, it was worse than that. He was *thinking*, the passive crime of the clever, caught up in an arid internal dialogue. Asking himself: was it rational to be afraid? Little boys stood up on swings all the time. They could go high as you like and come down to earth safely. And yet, Len's fear, a visible trembling, rational or not, was a warning. Fear makes people clumsy.

His brother began to rock, faster and higher, to the jeering backdrop of the farm chorus.

'Go, Len boy! Go!'

David watched his brother fly up towards the dimensionless sky. Like Icarus, climbing foolishly towards the sun. And he, down below, rubbing his ankle, passive, nagged by the pain, failing to attend to the bigger drama unfolding before him. Glimpses of his brother's face through flashes of steely sunlight, contorted with terror and a twisted sort of pride, egged on by the boys down on the ground. 'You're brave going right up there, Lenny boy. Braver than that weedy brother of yours.'

Then, the voice of the oldest of the Lay brothers, the leader of the pack, the tallest, the blackest-haired, the bluest-eyed.

'Hey, Lenny, let go of one hand, why don't you?'

NO. David moved towards them, an attempt to cut them out of the picture, block their influence.

Shouting up, 'Don't let go! Len, those are Mum's orders!' In a moment of crisis, returning to the first and only rule of law and love they knew: Agnes.

'Mummy's orders!' laughed the leader of the pack. 'Oooh, don't let go, Mummy's boy.'

David didn't care now, although he feared a beating, was hunched in body and spirit, as he pushed himself in front of the farm boys, dragging his leg rather too dramatically. Maybe his injury (if he played it up) would be enough, would provide them with their prescribed nugget of cruel excitement for the day.

Desperately, he tried to make eye contact with his baby brother.

The last thing he remembered was the horrible jeering sound, the sight of one of the Lay boys whipping the ground with a switch of willow, beating out the rhythm of danger, and then the sickening crunch as the ropes that held the handmade swing gave way under the sheer force of Len's tumultuous effort and terror.

He saw his little brother fly, a weighty force of flesh, bone, speed and screams, through the sky. Shouting just one word. His elder brother's name.

DAV-EE!

DAV-EE!

David knew almost immediately that something terrible had

happened. Within seconds, the farm boys had scattered, taking off over the fields. His brother was lying on his side, curled up like a baby. His eyeballs were rolling in his head. His limbs were twitching. David leaned over him, called out to his seemingly lifeless little body. LEN. LEN. WAKE UP. PLEASE WAKE UP. He was too terrified to cry. Too terrified to move, and for a long time he remained bent over his brother's body, pleading with him to come back. *Come back and be yourself. Come back and walk the twenty minutes home with me. Stop as long as you like to count the black dots on the shell of the ladybirds. Run after a hundred butterflies. Come back to our mother. There'll be fruit pie for tea. This time, I promise, you can have my share, too.*

The last awful twist of fate.

His mother, he knew, had planned to keep her youngest son close to her all her life. David was the clever one; she was resigned to the fact that he must leave them when he grew up, make his way in the wider world. Len was the loving, the cheeky, one. He used to cheer her up, with his antics. Len, she was sure, could find some occupation closer to home, keep his mother company.

And so it came to pass. Len *was* kept close all his life; close as a baby after all, fed, clothed, washed by the devoted Agnes for over twenty-five years. A living vegetable, until his death at thirty-three.

Many times over the years that followed, David wished that Len had died on that September day. Because his real little brother *had* died: that cheeky boy, his companion in his lonely family struggle, his helpmeet in the giant task of comforting their proud, lonely mother; Len, who understood deeper than words what pressure there was on David, the weight of the family pressing down on his frail boy's shoulders, who could make him laugh when he was tired, from reading for too long or from helping his mother make the beds, sweep the floor, wash up. *That* Len was snuffed out for ever that September morning, the world on the brink of its own, parallel catastrophe.

With the real Len gone – a pallid, grinning, vacant creature left in his place – the hope of brotherly love was wiped out, seemingly for ever. Until that Sunday in July 1971 when the young

Andy Givings walked through the front door, eager, energetic, a spring in his step, open-hearted, so gallantly nursing the scars of his own giant wound, ready to make his more earnest mentor laugh with his imitations of stuffy politicians, willing to take up the threads of a fraternal affection that David had so painfully missed, without ever fully realising it, over the years.

Six

'Jack's still not back.'

It was a Saturday night, a few weeks after Andy's birthday meal, and Anna's mother was curled up on the sofa in the living room, watching the midnight movie. Dressed in dark sweat pants and a cream overshirt, she had put on the glasses she only ever wore to watch television, their dark rims both obscuring and revealing the elegant bone structure of her face beneath. From certain angles she looked like a sweet-natured owl; at other moments, a glamorous university professor.

Anna lingered in the doorway, waiting for her mother to say something more. But she kept staring at the screen, watching her film. It was Italian, in lurid colour, with subtitles. The male lead wore a sharp black suit and had an orange face.

'When are you expecting him?'

Her mother still did not take her eyes from the television screen. 'I mean, he hasn't come back since Thursday. That's two days and nights. And now we're going into a third. Hadn't you noticed?'

Jack was now seventeen. To Anna, both her older brothers seemed to move confidently around the wider world, independent of parental surveillance, accountable to no-one.

'He's bound to be with friends,' Anna said.

'*What* friends?' her mother now turned to look at her. 'Could you really honestly say that Jack has friends? I mean, like Matt has friends? Like Laura has friends?'

'Yes. Jack has friends,' Anna said stubbornly, 'they're just not *like* Matt or Laura's friends.' She felt a sudden spurt of hostility towards the giggling teens and brash young athletes her eldest brother brought home, and the languid bunch of girls that her sister currently hung out with, who smiled in a superior way or laughed behind their hands every time Anna came into the room.

'Well, I'm glad to hear it,' her mother sighed, uninterested in the detail, her mind moving on in its usual restless, distracted way. On the screen, the actor with the orange face was loosening his tie and looking down lasciviously at a blonde woman who was lying on a bed.

'She's pretty, isn't she?' Fiona said, conversationally. 'I like that shift thing she's wearing.' Before Anna could answer, she said, 'Do you think I should ring the police?'

'What does Dad say?'

'I don't want to bother him. Not yet. Your father leaves these things to me. He works so hard. The strain of his job, you've no idea. In return, I worry about all of you. I take care of all of you.'

'But, Mum . . .'

'*Plus,*' her mother said sharply, 'there are things about Jack that people just can't understand.' Her voice softened. 'You'll think this odd, Anna, but I think of Jack as my burden. My responsibility.'

She motioned for Anna to sit down, while she took off her glasses and started rubbing around the inner edge of her eye. Meanwhile, the couple in the film were writhing on the bed, the man trying to unzip the back of the white silk dress.

'Do you know?' Her mother's tone was dreamy. 'The moment Jack was born, I sensed that he was different.'

'Good different? Bad different?' Anna probed dutifully, although this was not a new story. Her mother often mused out loud about the circumstances of Jack's birth, as well as her more general worries about her second son.

'Different different. With Matt everything was so easy. I felt I just *knew* him from the minute he was born. He had my eyes, your father's colouring. He was our first. It was instant bonding. But with Jack, I felt I was in the room with a stranger . . .'

Anna felt goosebumps rise on her body.

'Are you cold, Sweety? Do you want this?' Her mother picked up a navy cashmere cardigan that was draped over the side of the couch.

'No, I'm fine.'

'He was a complete mystery to me. He had my brother Adam's reddish hair. And those blue eyes . . . It's crazy, I know. But Jack was so quiet and it didn't feel good, it felt wrong. He slept the first day, he hardly woke up; I had to shake him awake, which was stupid. He didn't feed well. Well, that was one thing that didn't last!'

Thank God the couple on the screen had stopped kissing. Anna tried to wrest the conversation back to the immediate problem. 'I could look in his room. For some numbers, if you want. Friends and stuff.'

'I'm not sure about that.' Her mother sounded uncertain. 'You know how obsessed your father is with everyone's *privacy*.'

'But this is an emergency, isn't it?'

'Jack's powerfully built,' her mother said, ignoring her. 'It's hard to imagine anyone taking him on and winning.'

A rare glimpse of maternal pride. Jack's solid physique was normally a source of constant nagging.

'And anyway,' her mother continued, 'he'll have to come back soon for food, I expect.'

'Mum! You make him sound like a dog!'

'Shush!' her mother said, pretending to be cross, slapping her lightly on her hand. 'All my children are equally special to me, you know that.'

Anna felt a spurt of irritation. She disliked these abstract homilies that jarred so obviously with the wholly specific ways in which each child was seen. Her mother boasted constantly about Matt, who was about to go up – or was it down? – to university, and who, it was assumed, would flourish in all he did. Laura was a beauty, sufficient in purpose, at least as far as her awestruck mother was concerned. It was as if she circled Laura, in her mind, a sculptor minutely examining her handi-work, suggesting finishing touches, but only ever to perfect the oh-so-satisfying work in progress. With Anna, 'Little Miss Serious Brow', the baby of the family, there was patronage and affection mixed, and always the tricky matter of her father's special fondness for her. And of Jack, only this constant, obsessive self-blaming, Jack-blaming worry.

'Now you go up,' her mother said, 'and I'll finish watching this. I adore Marcello Mastroianni. We'll decide what to do tomorrow.'

Audience over, Anna kissed her mother's powdery, sweet-smelling cheek and trudged up the stairs to bed, feeling, as she so often did, a vague dissatisfaction, a sense of having been marginally wronged. It would be nice to have her efforts acknowledged from time to time. God knows, Laura didn't bother. Whenever the subject of Jack came up, her sister yawned, patted her mother on the head and said, 'Forget it, Fiona. Jack's a selfish sod. Don't beat yourself up about it.' And her mother laughed. She actually *laughed*, her face smoothing itself out, grateful – incredibly enough – for her first-born daughter's lack of care. Reflecting on all this, Anna's tread was heavy. She was cross and tired. At least she had her own room, thank God, a space to herself at last, after years spent sharing a street-facing room with Laura. A few months ago, she had moved into a tiny room next to her parents' bedroom overlooking the garden. Jack teased her, calling her 'Cinderella'. Up till then, the room had been used to store clothes and bedding, the Hoover and malfunctioning household equipment.

Too tired to read, Anna crawled into bed in her T-shirt and knickers, switched off her light and almost immediately sank into a drowsiness so deep that, at first, she thought the noises she heard were coming from her own head. A deep male rumble, then a soft, satisfying thud. Phrases that sounded like *thatridiculousblacktalk* (her mother's voice) and *what would you know?* (Jack's) roused her further until, once properly awake, she heard the single sharp, unmistakable syllable 'Jack!' in her mother's equally unmistakable tone: maternal distress at its peak. Almost a scream. Anna sat bolt upright, more relieved than worried. Her brother was back. He was not dead on a street somewhere, floating down a river, burned to death in a club up in Notting Hill. (About a year ago, he had started going to clubs, not to dance, he told her, just to watch. And to talk to people. She wondered what they thought of this strange boy, in his uncomfortably tight black T-shirts, wanting to 'talk'.) She hadn't known how worried she had been until now. But it was over. This time. He was safe. This time. She could sleep. She longed to sleep. She would no doubt hear the details of his three-day absence the next morning.

March 2003

'And your brothers? Matt and Jack?' Ben asks now. 'Were they close?'

Ben knows Matt, of course he does. He has talked to him dozens of times in the lobby and corridors of the Commons and various government departments. Ben Calder and Matt Adams occupy the same world. Professionally speaking.

But this is a story about much more than the professional.

She closes her eyes, to defy the urge to sensationalism. To keep to the lines of approximate truth. Were her brothers close?

'Yes, but they were – are – very different,' she says cautiously. 'Obviously, I know Matt a bit. But more on the work side.'

Oh, it is easy to explain Matt to someone like Ben Calder. His gifts were – are – all on the surface; conventional success wedded to formidable social networking. There are thousands of Matt Adams in the political, public, media world.

'Matt was good at exams. He seemed to coast through the academic side of things. And even when he was at school, he had this knack of getting to know important people. He would get journalists and junior ministers to come to his school debating society. I remember him writing to Harold Wilson when he was about fourteen, just to let him know his opinion on some issue of the day.'

Ben smiles. 'And did the Prime Minister reply?'

'Yes. He got a very nice letter back. Correcting his spelling of "disarmament".'

'Amazing.' Ben is impressed, despite himself. And then, as if to correct any impression of undue admiration, he says quickly, 'He always strikes me as quite a cool customer.'

Quite.

'*And Jack?*'

'*Jack was clever. But he couldn't be bothered, not with school. That caused a lot of trouble at home because our father thought education was everything. But the thing was, looking back, he was always doing and thinking more interesting things than the rest of us. He was out there. In the real world.*'

She and Ben exchange an ironic little smile: ah, the real world!

How to convey truthfully that nagging sense of the teenage Jack searching, never finding? Discontent written into his very cells. How wonderful it would be – for the story, for the journalist – if he had started up his own business or travelled the world, dispensing aid to the poor and hungry. Of course, Jack had done none of these things. Instead, he learned a lot of strange-sounding poems off by heart. He read Sartre and Kerouac and Allen Ginsberg. He listened, obsessively, to Dylan and Van Morrison. He ate too much. He lay in his darkened bedroom, watching television.

The family verdict, never spoken out loud. Jack was depressed. Jack was a failure.

But you could talk to Jack. Correction. Anna could talk to Jack. They had their best conversations at night, sitting round the kitchen table. Jack would smoke, sour-smelling French cigarettes. She would be snug in her dressing gown, drinking cups of tea. They talked a lot about the family. Why their father was the way he was. She tried to get him to understand that it wasn't personal. 'Dad is an introvert. He wants to be alone, to make sense of the world, up in his head.' She would tap her skull, to make the point more forcefully. 'And Mum's trying. She tries so hard. Can't you see that?'

And Jack would say, over and over again. 'All they care about is how things seem. On the surface. They are not concerned with how things really are.'

Seven

1976

The lecture theatre was filling up quickly, the hum around her intensifying to a roar, a vast collection of stern individual judgements, terrifyingly indifferent in its intensity. Bagging two seats in the third row, Anna cooled herself with a folded *Evening Standard* while she waited for her elder brother to arrive. July 1976: the temperature had been in the high eighties for ten straight days. Anna, just sixteen, had finished her O-levels a few weeks previously: any lingering preoccupation with the exams themselves, her performance in them, had faded, transmuted into a healthy summer boredom. Seeing her drift aimlessly around the house, Matt, down from university for the long holiday, invited her to accompany him to a debate at the New Theatre in the London School of Economics. 'Seriously, Anna, you need to start taking an interest in current affairs.' He spoke with his usual air of irony. 'Plus you'll be able to see Andy do his political thing.'

She was curious about their family friend's 'political thing', she had to admit. She knew that Andy was increasingly serious about getting a parliamentary seat, that he was quietly determined to become an MP, an ambition that was proving not that easy to fulfil. Her parents blithely assumed that he would succeed and she took their word on such worldly matters. (In fact, she thought they talked about Andy and 'his plans' a lot, in tones that veered from the affectionate and the encouraging to the faintly disparaging, an attitude that she suspected concealed a dose of simple envy, a vague fear that Andy – and Clare – might one day

41

outstrip them in worldly status.) Her parents seemed to have no problem seeing Andy as a politician proper, one day in the future, whereas Anna simply couldn't imagine it. How could the man who still insisted on helping with the washing-up, wrapped in their mother's best apron, the man who was always the first to don a paper party hat at Christmas and offer his cracker to a neighbour to pull, the only adult to genuinely notice if Anna was preoccupied or worried about anything (and ever ready with the kind, brisk question, 'Now what can I do to cheer you up?'), how could that man ever turn into one of those black-and-white ghouls with five o'clock shadow and bloodshot eyes who talked on television about wage claims or the Common Market? How could someone that considerate and kind turn into someone grand and public and far removed from ordinary life? Anna thought Andy's plan unlikely. And horribly risky, she now thought – sitting in the hall that was full to overspilling, positively hissing with greedy anticipation. How could anyone bear to open themselves up to all these people and their casual, malice-filled judgements on a day too hot for rational thought?

Just then, as if confirming her fears, an older woman with shoulder-length brown hair in the seat in front of her began to talk in an intense tone to her male companion, a bald man wearing round spectacles. 'I just can't *believe* in her. She's so false. Utterly contrived. It's impossible to imagine that they'll keep her on, or let her do anything really serious.' Her companion was nodding, overemphatically. '*Richard* said he thought the party would ditch her pretty soon. He says they'll *never* let her lead the Tories into a real election. That phoney persona,' the brunette shuddered. 'All that ghastly housewifely stuff.'

Anna was distracted by the sight of Matt over on the other side of the auditorium, standing directly beneath an electric red EXIT sign, scanning the crowd anxiously. 'Matt! Matt! Over here!' She stood up and waved her arms. His face softened when he saw her. He looked different from a distance. A slim man – at five foot nine, her elder brother was not much taller than she – he had small features and neat shoulder-length hair. Close up, it was easy to be distracted by the intensity of his gaze, his self-possession. From afar, however, he looked almost frail, in need of care and protection.

He worked his way along the row, apologising courteously to each individual he disturbed, before collapsing into the free seat next to Anna with a series of burlesque exhalations; his unspoken judgement on the intense heat of the day.

'I *know*.' She confirmed his expression of cheerfully endured discomfort.

Brother and sister swapped casual observations for a few minutes about the size of the crowd, the state of the lecture theatre (it seemed rather rundown for a major London university), until Anna, wishing to enter into the spirit of the occasion, ventured a political comment. 'I overheard some people talking about Thatcher just now. About how she's just a *joke* . . .'

Matt wrinkled his nose at her credulousness, but said nothing.

'I mean, don't *you* think she seems silly?' Anna went on. 'Do you remember all that stuff about storing fish in her larder? Marking up the tins. Protecting herself against inflation? And she's so stiff and artificial.'

Matt had now put on his Extremely Patient face, blinking rapidly. 'Yes, but, Anna, you should read the speech that she made at Kensington Town Hall earlier this year on the threat posed to the free world by the Russian build-up of naval and military power.' Matt paused to wipe beads of sweat from his forehead. 'My point is, you can take any view you like of her paranoid form of free-market politics, but Margaret Thatcher is a much more substantial figure than any random member of the general public might imagine her to be.' And with a scary, instinctual precision, Matt chose that moment to point his finger at the man and woman who had made the original remarks about the Tory leader. Under Matt's sway, Anna looked on them now with borrowed pity and disdain.

'So, on to tonight,' Matt said, glancing at the watch on his thin, tanned arm. 'This is a useful gig. I suggested Andy through a student-union contact. It's a prestigious venue. There are some pretty good speakers. There will be a couple of journalists in the audience. I sent out press tickets.'

She was both impressed and a little appalled at his boasting.

'Do you go to a lot of those sorts of things then? With him?'

The question felt faintly illicit, like asking about a secret lover.

'Not that much. I keep in touch. You know.' Matt sounded evasive. 'I like to be of help.'

'Do you remember? You used to show off to all Dad's friends . . .'

'How?'

'You said you wanted to be a civil servant . . .'

'Yeah, right. And weren't you going to be lead ballerina?' He rolled his eyes, as if to say, and how likely was *that*?

She was still giggling, although his waspishness irked her, when the speakers came through a small door at the back of the stage, looking about as cheerful as a bunch of condemned prisoners; within minutes, they were seated in a row at a long table, shuffling papers, fiddling with pens. On the far left sat the Tory politician, Shadow minister for transport or roads – Matt had told her his proper title earlier, but she had promptly forgotten it; next to him, a newspaper columnist with a shiny forehead and thick glasses; then a young Cambridge philosopher often profiled in the Sunday magazines, wearing, despite the heat, a black leather jacket with innumerable zips. Right at the end sat a slightly strained-looking Andy dressed in a white cotton shirt and beige cotton trousers.

Catching Anna's eye, Andy winked. She waved back, delighting in the special attention, the ripple of interest it caused among their section of the audience.

The meeting was introduced by a beefy young man with fair hair, his nervous swallowing painfully amplified by the sound system, who raced through his introductory comments before gratefully handing over to 'my first speaker'. This was the Shadow minister for bollards, as Anna had now privately nicknamed him, a stoop-backed middle-aged man dressed in a pin-stripe suit (despite the sweltering weather), who read his speech from a wad of papers, occasionally peering at the audience over half-moon glasses, as if they were a distasteful bunch of badly behaved school children. Anna's interest was soon concentrated on predicting, from the size of the diminishing wad of pages in his hand, how long he had to go until he finished his seemingly interminable ramble about allowing 'businesses to develop unfettered'. Next up was the columnist, dressed in a banana-yellow nylon shirt, sweat soaking great swathes of his chest area, spreading like a disease under his armpits; he gabbled so fast it was hard to make sense of much, except his love of subordinate clauses and polysyllabic words. She felt relief when it was Andy's turn. As he rose, Matt hissed in her ear, 'Here we go!' as if they were all about to go on a funfair ride. Her brother had a small notebook open on his lap and a pen at the ready.

'Our subject tonight, Chair, is how do we reach the good society?'

Pause.

'That's what I'm interested in talking about. The good society.'

Pause.

'The society we need to create. Together.'

'Get on with it!' bellowed some wag at the back of the hall.

The hall erupted in laughter and Anna flushed with embarrassment for their old friend. Those dramatic hesitations. The short. Little. Stilted. Sentences. She glanced at Matt, whose eyes remained steadily fixed on the stage, an inscrutable expression on his face as Andy continued to work through one painfully clichéd phrase after another about 'the winner-takes-all jungle', the collective efforts of 'working people'.

'So why did Harold Wilson give gongs to the capitalists?' someone shouted.

'Forget Wilson,' Andy said sharply. 'I don't want to talk about the government's problems. I *do* want to stop the exceptionally frugal Mrs Thatcher from taking over.' Some of the audience tittered. 'No! Please! Checking over the contents of your larder from time to time is a very worthwhile activity. I do it frequently. I have at least *four* cans of tuna carefully marked with their respective prices at the moment of purchase . . .'

More laughter from the audience. Anna felt a silly grin spread over her face.

'I'm interested in the bigger questions.' Sensing he had won his audience over, Andy was talking faster, 'In making practical change. It's no good talking about revolution. Changing the world. None of that means anything if you have nowhere to live or nowhere to send your child to school.'

'*Go and work for the bleeding council, mate!*'

'Actually, I'd like to make it all the way to Westminster.'

'Careerist!' shouted another.

'Oh, I can think of a lot worse things one could be.' Andy was enjoying himself now, his arms pressing, fingers splayed, down on the desk. 'Listen. The progressive cause is lost if we can't stay thoughtful. If we can't remember the limitations as well as the possibilities of politics. Helping people. Making better lives. Living your own example. Forget the grand gestures, the overblown rhetoric. Take it from me,' he nodded briefly at the blond chairman, who was tapping his watch and nodding emphatically, 'the best idealism is modest, based in reality and well thought out. Thank you.'

Scattered clapping, the odd cheer, when he sat down.

'Who was that bloke again?' said a student sitting on Anna's left.

'No idea. Some campaigning fellow,' yawned her friend.

'He was . . . all right.'

'Yeah. He was okay actually.'

'Now, it's Marcus. Just look at that gorgeous leather jacket!' The pale blonde rubbed her hands together gleefully.

To her horror, Anna was dragged up to the stage by Matt, at the meeting's end, where the speakers were milling about in various states of sweaty post-speech euphoria. Andy's embrace nearly winded her. 'So what did you make of it all?'

Before she could answer, he said, 'I have to admit, Anna, I really enjoyed it. I like a *crowd*.'

But when Matt came over, it was as if Anna had never existed. The two men talked like lovers, eagerly swopping observations on Andy's speech.

'Next time it might be useful to quicken the pace a little earlier on.' This from Matt.

'You're absolutely right.'

For a moment, Anna found herself next to the celebrated philosopher.

'Well done,' she said politely, although she had understood hardly a word of his talk.

'You are a student here?' he frowned.

'No, no. I've just done my O-levels.'

'And so you come to hear meetings on politics and the economy just for fun?'

'Well, Matt – that one there, he's my brother – asked me . . .'

'Yes, you have the same *look*. There's a family look.'

'There is?'

'For sure. It's around here,' and the philosopher passed his hand across his eyes, swiftly, a pretentious exaggerated gesture, ending in a limp-wristed flourish, like a magician onstage.

'To be honest,' she blurted, 'I didn't understand much of what you said.'

'I can barely recall it myself. I speak as I write. My unconscious overtakes me.'

'I see.'

She didn't see anything at all. Mercifully, she was saved by the Tory shadow minister who was trying to get past them to reach his leather briefcase, which was still sitting on a chair behind the table on the stage.

A few seconds later, Anna heard the columnist say to the minister, 'There's a star in the making, for sure.'

'Or *two*.'

They were looking over at Andy and Matt, still deep in their debriefing.

Eight

Matt had insisted on putting her in a black cab on Kingsway, and paying for it, as he was going on to a supper with friends in town. So it was still dusk when the taxi pulled up at the house in Durnford Gardens. An empty police car was parked in the road outside their house, its driver-side door flung open so wide the top edge had caught on the paintwork of the postbox, and now looked jammed up against it. Voices from a police radio were blaring out into the street. Anna jumped out of the back of the cab and stood by the driver's window, palm jiggling with impatience, awaiting her change and spurning the taxi driver's voyeuristic concern.

'Is that your house then, love?'

'No idea,' she said illogically, digging for her house keys in her bag with her free hand.

Letting herself in the front door, she could hear raised voices down in the kitchen. The familiar sound of her mother's agitation. Deeper masculine rumbles.

As she ran down the back stairs, bathed in charcoal shadows – unusually, the bulb on the landing was out – she heard a man call out, 'Goodbye then, Mrs Adams', just as she collided with a vision in a bright-white shirt, sleeves rolled up, tanned forearms gleaming.

'*Hello*, there,' the police officer said, wide-eyed with flirtatious intent, as if they had just been introduced at a party.

'What is it? Why are you here?' She spoke more rudely than she meant to, aware, suddenly, of how sweaty she was.

'Are you family?' The officer looked sceptical now.

'It depends. I mean, I don't know what . . . why . . . you're here.'

'Just a little fracas, in a public house. Are you related to John Adams then?'

'Jack? Yes. He's my brother.'

'Well, he got himself into quite a fight. Over some *political* discussion.' The police officer allowed himself a moment of pure moral superiority, 'Luckily for him, the public house is right next to the police station and we were able to haul him out of there sharpish. And then we very kindly gave him a lift home.'

The officer's speech was such an odd mix of the threatening, the disapproving on the one hand, and the cheery, the everyday on the other, that Anna frowned and then smiled and then frowned again, trying to keep up with the changes in tone. Perhaps he too was confused: pub brawls were ten a penny in his line of work, but he had not expected to deliver tonight's scrapper to such a smart address near Hyde Park, there to be greeted by an attractive middle-aged woman wearing a flowery skirt and sleeveless white silk shirt, obviously back from some nice little supper. And the father a QC to boot! Anna could almost see the officer's mind working: *These barmy upper-middle-class people who can't keep their spoilt kids under control.*

Crossing her arms defensively – the officer was looking at her chest – Anna said, 'Was John – Jack – hurt?'

'Look, why don't you go down . . .' The officer flattened himself against the wall to let her pass, remarking casually as she began her descent, 'There was a lot of blood, but we cleared up most of it.' She felt that he enjoyed hearing her tiny gasp of fear.

'Goodbye then!'

There was no-one in the kitchen. Shrinking oil slicks of moisture on the surface of the table hinted at a recent wiping, but only the strip lighting was on, its low hum and concentrated glow giving the room an end-of-evening deserted feel. Yet she had heard agitated voices, earlier, she was sure of it. The far door leading out to the garden, via the narrow passage – you could hardly call it a room – in which the washing machine was kept, and clothes hung up to dry, was open and there she saw three figures, her mother, father and Jack, standing in the evening shadows. Her brother seemed to be wearing some sort of white headdress. Whirring around them in the darkness, like fireflies, the tiny concentrated orange glow of two cigarette tips. She guessed her mother was having one of her rare cigarettes; at nineteen Jack was already a chain smoker. It could have been one of her parents' parties of old. Groups of people laughing out in the garden. Chitchat in the warm summer dark.

Upstairs, the bang of the front door as the policeman let himself out.

Anna met Jack in the utility passage, his skull swathed in a white bandage, his bottom lip swollen and cut, his eye bruised and beginning to blacken.

'Oh, my God!'

'Don't worry,' he said, with a lopsided smile. 'It's really not as bad as it looks.' His voice sounded thick, as if he was deliberately holding liquid in his mouth, and his head was listing at a funny angle. His white T-shirt was soaked with blood. 'Mostly from the lip,' he said, gesturing downwards.

Her eyes had filled with tears, but she wasn't sure why. Jack seemed robust enough about his injuries. Without thinking, she embraced him, and he winced with pain. 'Watch my fucking shoulder!' But he didn't mind, not really. It was only gruffness.

Trusting her instinct, she kept a tight hold on him. He was broad in the shoulder and soft round the middle. If this were a different occasion, a different sort of hug, she would tease him about it, joke about the soft mass of unworked muscle, the warm, faintly sweaty flesh. No sharpness, no protruding ribs.

Close up, the salty stench of dried blood and the smell of smoke and drink – whisky? wine? – mixed.

Her parents were walking back through the garden door, her mother surprisingly sprightly, eyes alight with a mix of righteous anger and excitement. Yes, there was a definite spring in her step. Her father looked weary. He nodded at Anna, briskly, as if they had just met. His old habit of withdrawing into himself when annoyed or disturbed. Without a word, he walked past her, straight to the tap, ran himself a glass of cold water.

'Remind me again, where have you been?' Her mother, to Anna, sharp-voiced.

Anna waved the question away. 'That meeting with Matt. Remember, the one that Andy was speaking at?'

'Oh yes,' said her father, turning towards her, his face lighting up with interest. 'How was it? How was Houghton?' He was referring to the newspaper columnist, whose work he read and admired.

'Okay,' Anna said neutrally. 'He's a funny fellow.'

'He's rather creepy in person, isn't he?' her father ventured, 'I've heard him on the radio.'

'There's something slightly yucky about him, yes.'

'What was Andy like?' Jack asked, bouncing his middle finger softly against his cut lip, as if to take the measure of his own injury. 'Was he any good?'

Anna shrugged. 'He was fine. I *think*.'

'Where's Matt?' Her mother was still sounding cross.

'He went to meet up with friends. He said he'd be back late.'

Jack sat down, with a heavy sigh. Now he was fiddling with the white cloth around his head, issuing sharp exhalations of discomfort.

'You were lucky they didn't take you to hospital or keep you overnight.' This from Anna's father.

'It's only superficial – a few cuts.'

Her mother, who had been banging glasses around the draining board, turned to face Jack. Her hair was in a high bun, probably on account of the heat: it made her look rather school mistressly. A single, tiny thread of silver ran down from the crown of her hair to behind her ear.

'I want to know, did you start it? Did you provoke those men? Or were they aggressive to you?'

Jack continued to rub agitatedly at the bandaging around his head, as if he had nits.

'I told you already, Ma. They were racists. Well-dressed filth. They were laughing out loud sitting round the bar, talking about what happened in Soweto. All those children mown down. They were actually *laughing* about it. And that boy murdered in Southall, the Asian boy, outside the cinema. Stabbed to death by white racists. They thought that was funny.' Itch. Itch. 'They were filthy, ignorant scum and I challenged them.'

'What's that . . . all those things . . . that happened . . . got to do with you?' Her mother's voice was almost a whimper.

'*What?*' Jack now turned his head slowly to face his mother directly, his mood transformed in just a moment. Anna could see her flinching at the sight of his cold eyes in the heavy-set face, the gingery scrub around his chin. 'For fuck's sake, what kind of a question is that?'

'Don't swear at your mother . . .' Anna's father intervened.

'Oh, I'm sorry.' Her brother's voice was cruelly high-pitched, imitating his mother in distress. 'I mean, what do innocent people dying across the world, or even in this city, have to do with us? Us. Us. We. We. Me. Me. Comfortable ladies in our mother's Surrey pearls, human-rights lawyers in our Westbourne Grove town houses, smart little school boys heading for a Cambridge college . . . All the world's suffering, no, that's nothing to do with us.'

'I only meant . . .' her mother stuttered.

'You only meant, "Don't ruin my day, with your bad news from the big bad world." That's what you meant,' Jack sneered.

'Shut up!' Anna's father banged his fist on the table. 'Shut the hell up, you ignorant, trouble-making, foul-mouthed little *boy!*'

Anna burst into tears, the only way she knew to stop the row from escalating further. She had never heard her father shout like this before, was afraid of where such temper might lead. Her mother stood, visibly trembling, over by the draining board while Jack seemed overcome with an infuriating blankness.

'I don't care,' her brother was now speaking very slowly. 'I don't care if you don't think it's worth standing up to ignorant people. I don't *do* things your way.'

'That's really not the issue though, is it?' Having regained his self-control, Anna's father now took refuge in his courtroom voice. 'No-one disagrees with you about what you choose to call "the scum of the earth". The real question is: what good has this incident done? What good has it done the dead children of Soweto? None whatsoever. What good has it done Gurdip Singh Chaggar, murdered outside that Southall cinema by a gang of thugs? Or his family? None whatsoever.'

How typical that he should know the full – the correct – name of the murdered boy, and Jack should not; how typical that he should have all the facts, for and against the radical case, at his finger-tips, while Jack had only fistfuls of feeling. The father's precision is, in this instance, the most lethal put-down possible of the son's passion.

'None whatsoever,' the older man continued quietly. 'It has done those particular individuals no good whatsoever. No, wait!' He held up his hand. 'Let me finish, please. But I'll tell you what you have done – you have brought your mother the most intense anxiety, as usual, and yourself a great deal of unwelcome attention.'

'*Dad* . . .' Jack's voice was pleading rather than pugilistic. As always, he saved his worst fury for his worried, fearful mother. When the gloves were off, he craved his father's approval.

'No. I don't want to hear. You have brought on us the worry of a visit from the police. Possible criminal charges.'

'It wasn't me who used the bottle.'

'*Bottle?* They used a *bottle* on you?' Anna cried out, in horri-fied sympathy.

'Yes, indeed. But only after John had stood up and thrown beer all over two of them, and pulled a bar stool from under a third man.' Her father addressed her as he might a jury.

'You did?' Anna wanted to laugh and cry at the same time.

'As I was saying,' David said, glaring at Anna, 'a visit from the police, possible criminal charges, a lifelong ban, no doubt, from the pub in question.'

'Who gives a shit about that? The Ladbroke Lady is a dump anyway.'

And then, as if this was the insult to crown all insults, a last peculiarly provoking straw, their father stood and sternly announced, 'Well, I'm going to bed.' Five simple words, but they rang out like a judgement on their collective failure. Jack looked crestfallen.

'I'll be up in a second,' Anna's mother said, in a deliberately mollifying tone. 'Do you want me to bring you up a drink?'

'No, thank you.'

Her father was folding his reading glasses into the pocket of his shirt and heading up the stairs.

Anna's mother waited a few minutes, until she was sure her husband was out of earshot.

'Shall *we* have a drink of something then? We three.'

She opened the fridge and peered in, 'Yes, there's enough milk. Let's all have some hot chocolate . . . Jack?' She was speaking in her sweetest, most cajoling tones.

Anna prayed her brother would respond to their mother's peace offer. To encourage him, she said, 'Yeah, come on, boy! Tell us exactly how you took on the forces of evil and won!'

Jack grinned, and then groaned, because his lip was hurting.

'Oooh, yes,' said Anna's mother, taking out three pristine white mugs from the cupboard, 'And after that, Anna, I want to hear *all* about your night with Andy . . .'

Nine

It felt all wrong, leaving her older brother behind, holed up in his attic bedroom at Durnford Gardens, his childhood model aeroplanes dangling from the ceiling, dusty and immobile, paralysed in flight, his floor perpetually clotted with small mountains of dirty clothes. For the next three years, Jack's life visibly and painfully stagnated while his siblings made the transition from home to the wider world. Matt graduated from university with a good 2:1 (his political work taking its very minor toll after all). A week after his graduation ceremony, he packed up two giant suitcases of clothes and books and moved with a group of university friends to a flat in Earls Court. By Christmas, he had landed himself an interesting job with a reasonable starting salary at a charity connected to educational initiatives in Africa and the Middle East. Laura, who had quit school at seventeen (to no-one's great surprise), briefly flirted with a modelling career, after a married couple who ran an agency approached her one morning when she was walking down Campden Hill Road. It didn't work out – her parents overt disapproval probably stifling whatever natural inclination she had to show herself off for money – and she turned to serious partying, of which, strangely enough, they approved far more. At one large charity do, where she acted as 'hostess' as a favour for a friend, she met a tall, dark, handsome banker called Bill, who was also a part-time poet. He wooed her daily, with giant bunches of red and yellow roses. An offering of flowers arrived each morning at 8.40 a.m. at the house at Durnford Gardens. Anna often opened the door to the delivery boy, her mother clucking like an old hen in the hall behind her at the flattery and the inconvenience of this particular method of seduction. 'Go out with him, for God's sake,' she urged her eldest daughter, 'before our dining room looks like Kew Gardens.' Laura took her advice, intrigued by the combination of commerce and art on offer, and within months she, too, had left home, to live in the banker's spotless mansion flat in Battersea.

As for Anna, she found herself being driven, by her father, up the A40 one morning in early October 1978, to the same Oxford college where he had many years before studied natural sciences and where she, by dint of many late nights and hard work, had won a place to study English literature. Her father had insisted that he be allowed to take her up on this important occasion. He wanted to walk with her round the college and the town, to buy her tea, to point out some significant locations from his student days; she was happy to accompany him, although she would have welcomed her mother's more ordinary, practical help on this day of all days. With her father, she felt inclined – or obliged – to talk about the big things in life, what each thought of a recent novel, or some aspect of current affairs – his acute observations clearing pathways through her brain, helping her to 'up' her mental game, as she thought of it. But as they walked and chatted, giving all outward signs of being a contented father and daughter, arms linked, one or other of them pointing out a significant landmark, her mind felt fuzzy; she was preoccupied, experiencing a low-level worry about food and furnishings and where to do her washing and how to keep warm and not feel lonely.

There, in Anna's luggage, and one of the first items to be put up on the mantelpiece of her college room – along with her alarm clock, and some family photographs – was a card from the Givings family. '*Wishing you, dear A, the best of luck and love from us all in the beginning of this new EXCITING adventure in your life.*' Clare and Greg both had a loose, large script. The rounded sections of their 'g's' and 'o's' resembled small party balloons; spaces for human generosity and error. Andy and Dan had tighter, neater writing, their words looked darker, as if they were holding back important information.

'Have you been up to see Miss Havisham recently?' Laura asked, whenever she sashayed back home to visit Little Miss Serious Brow down from Oxford for the holidays. 'Bill says it's clear that Jack is taking Mum and Dad for a total ride.'

'Well, Bill would know, *obviously*.'

Jack was certainly in one hell of a mess and, even Anna, his greatest friend within the family, had to admit it was not an interesting mess. She worried about his situation when she was away at university, had anxiety dreams about him being found dead in his room, sheathed in a dark-green mould. It always hit her when she came back home, late on a Friday night or on a weekday afternoon, pushing through the front door into the familiar tiled hallway, breathing in the scent and stillness of home, excited at the prospect of return, knowing that her mother had made her favourite dinner – sausages, chips, red cabbage, chocolate cake, chocolate sauce and ice cream – and that her father would want to talk in detail about her essays and the latest reading list, and her sister would be on the phone or round for dinner, agog for all the gossip about the men Anna had met and the girlfriends she had made. And there, amidst all this excited anticipation, was a nagging ache in her stomach at the knowledge that Jack was lying up in his room, curtains drawn, listening to some depressing balladeer, or poring over a weighty novel about a dysfunctional family in middle Europe or a history book recounting the horrors of the Holocaust, his apparent intellectual ambition so at odds with his obvious fearfulness about the simplest of things. There was so much she would have liked to tell him, about her course, about the people she had met, her thoughts on the present, her plans for the future. She did not dare: it seemed too cruel to rub the details of her exciting new life in his unhappy face.

Ten

1980

A stroke of luck. In the Easter of her second year away, Jack, who had been half-heartedly and intermittently applying for jobs (notice of any remotely suitable post circled on the back of the evening newspaper by their mother), was offered an interview with a small west London branch of a national campaign for the homeless. Anna, down for the spring holiday, was immediately lobbied by her mother.

'Help him, Annie. Please. Do anything you can.'

Resentment mixed with a dash of pride at the old family assumption that she – and only she – could somehow fix the 'Jack problem'.

'Okay, okay.' It was always easier to agree than argue.

In the days before the interview, Anna insisted on knocking on her brother's bedroom door carrying a yellow clipboard (parodying efficiency, for his amusement) in order to run through 'key elements of the task ahead'. Anna had written down on a piece of paper four areas that needed attention: *1. Clothes. 2. General interview manner. 3. Questions on employment history so far. 4. Questions on the job itself.*

'Obviously number three is going to pose the biggest challenge,' she said, shoving his bare (and smelly) feet out of the way, so that she could get to sit down on his bed, 'but I have jotted down a few ideas on that. Personally, I think it's number four where you have to really think out your responses.'

58

Jack yawned, which was not very encouraging. His tongue was coated with what looked like glutinous white paste. She longed to get in there and scrape all that unhealthy gunk off.

'Look.' She poked him in the ribs, to get his full attention. 'This guy Tom told me this trick about job interviews. When they say, "Why do you want this job?", you don't say, "Because it's what I need now in my life" or "I thought it looked interesting". Turn the question around. Think about the organisation. What are *they* looking for?'

'What great sage told you this?' More yawns.

'I told you. This clever guy called Tom who I'm studying with.'

'Who's never had a job in his life, right?'

Unlike you, *right*. 'Jack, just listen to me. You've read the job description, haven't you? They want someone who can handle a small caseload – er . . . and what else . . . ? It says it right here; yes, someone who can help clients in a "state of transition . . . often in considerable personal distress". I think you'd be good at that, I really do.'

'You do?' Her brother beamed.

'Sure, I do.' She grabbed his hand, squeezed it. 'Listen, I've had an idea.'

'What?'

'Why don't I come to the interview with you? I'll wait for you outside.'

'Yeah?' He lifted his head off the pillow, propped himself up on his right arm. 'Would you do that for me?'

'Absolutely. The minute it's over we'll find a pub. Have a pint of cold lager. Just the way you like it.'

'Genius.' His grin split his face wide open.

Two days later, they set off for the interview mid-morning. The campaign's offices were five minutes' walk from a stop near the end of the Piccadilly line, about fifteen minutes from the dinky little cul-de-sac where Andy and Clare used to live. (They had moved, south of the river, to Vauxhall, a couple of years before: 'Higher ceilings, more crime' was Clare Givings's deft summary of the pros and cons of this change.)

'I haven't seen Andy and Clare for ages. Have you?' Anna said, making conversation.

'He comes over to see Dad sometimes. He always makes a point of coming to see me.'

'Does he?'

'He always calls up the stairs. Wants to ask me what I think about stuff. Sometimes he comes and sits on my bed. Tells me about the boys. How he thinks Greg is going to be a pop star. He's mad about music. How Dan is doing at school. I really like the way Andy talks about his sons.'

'Me, too.'

'I gave him a couple of prints of that photo I took. Do you remember, the one I took from the garden, where you can see Dad, reading at his table by the study window.'

'You caught him exactly . . . Has it been awful?' She meant: living at home, these past years, the rest of them slipping away.

Jack shrugged, just as the train plunged into a tunnel and their ghostly reflections were thrown up on the dark glass opposite. Anna saw herself, a jaundiced-looking skull with vast sockets and a mass of dark hair. Jack – head turned at that very moment, to scan the headlines on a newspaper left open on the seat next to him – looked like a Magritte painting: just a square set of shoulders, a thin line of tie, a featureless head.

The train rattled back into daylight. Back into the suburbs. They sat in companionable silence until their stop.

It was a short walk from the tube station. Half an hour early, they sat in a small café with a green-and-white-striped awning. Anna could feel her heart thumping in her chest. Jack looked like an undertaker, trussed up in his black suit, white shirt and tie. His hand shook when he brought his coffee to his mouth.

'Keep it modest,' she said reassuringly. 'Knowledgeable, but modest.'

He nodded, distracted with nerves.

Anna checked her watch every few minutes. Eventually she said, 'Time to go.'

She stood up to indicate that he should stand up too, even though she was planning to stay in the café until he returned.

Jack rose from the table, very slowly indeed.

'I forgot,' he said, 'you asked me something, on the train.'

'Yes?'

'About when I'm at home.'

'What about it?'

She was anxiously scanning her watch. *Don't be late for the interview. Please don't find a way to fail at this, now. When we're so close.*

'You asked me what Andy talks about when he comes up to my room. To visit me?'

'Yes?' She tried to conceal her impatience. Four minutes to go.

'Well, I've just remembered. We had a long talk about the trade unions the last time we spoke. About whether they are out of control. He agrees that they must protect the weak, but last time he said something like, "What happens when the weak actually become stronger than those who want to control them?" Something like that. Which is an interesting idea, if you think about it.'

'It certainly is,' she said, feeling quite panicky. Jack was quite capable of standing there for another half-hour, banging on about the Winter of Discontent and the power of the working class.

'Andy's very undecided about it. It may be something to do with a trade-union approaching him regarding sponsorship. You know . . . his parliamentary ambitions.'

'Talking of ambition,' Anna yanked her head in the direction of the street. 'Miss Yellow Clipboard thinks you'd better get out there yourself, if you're not going to be late.' She leaned over to kiss him on the cheek.

Close up, her brother smelled sour with anxiety, and for a second she wanted to put her head on his shoulder and cry, for all the difficulty he had with and in the world – and probably always would.

'I believe in you, you know.' She spoke in her steadiest voice.

'Thanks, Sis.'

And he was gone, smiling as he pushed his way out of the café door and crossed the busy side street.

'O God,' she sighed, 'please let it go well.'

Sitting back down at the table, she kept her fingers tightly crossed until they ached.

March 2003

'Did Andy fight a seat in 1979?'

Ben Calder wants facts. Dates.

1979: Thatcher's moment of glory. Think hard. Where had Andy got to by then?

'Yes, yes, he fought an unwinnable seat. Twice in fact. 1979. And 1983.'

'I can look all that up.' Ben makes a note on his legal pad. 'Where was it?'

'South London. Near where they'd moved to. He lost to a flamboyant far-right Tory. A Thatcherite.'

'It's weird, don't you think?' Ben muses out loud, 'How for so long Thatcherism had a grip on the national psyche, it seemed unassailable. And then when she went, it went. Nowadays, you can't find a Thatcherite for love or money.'

'That's because these days they're all Blairites.'

'Yeah, and one day they'll be none of them left, either.'

'If you say so.'

'So, Andy must have thought he would never make it right? Two elections lost. What happened then. Oh, I remember! It was a year or so after the 1983 election, wasn't it? Around the time of the miners' strike. That guy in Middleton East, that expert on fuels or something, died suddenly, didn't he?'

'Yes, that's right. Only he didn't die, he just stepped down. Without warning.' A flurry of speculation about a rare cancer, a depressed wife, but the true reason for his speedy retirement never came out.

'What was his name again?'
'I can't remember. Bob somebody?'
'Okay. I can look that up. Back at the office.'

Eleven

1984

Matt drove Andy and Clare up to Middleton East for the selection meeting. Andy was resigned about his chances – after all, he had tried and failed to win the nomination for several safe seats over the years. Maybe all that experience finally paid off. Maybe he just got lucky. Whatever the reason, he performed brilliantly on the night. 'Formidable,' in the words of Matt, who gave Anna a far more detailed account of the evening's proceedings than she really wanted. 'He put himself firmly in the modernising camp. Threw himself a hundred per cent behind the leader. Rational social democracy with a human heart.'

Matt's eyes were shining; Anna suppressed a yawn.

Clare's account was more down-to-earth. 'He thought it was his last real chance. He's come to hate the Bar, you know, Anna. Really loathe the law. This is what he wants to do. Politics. Whatever politics is.' She hesitated, and then laughed as she spoke. 'I've been thinking about it. All this public stuff. It's the need for attention, obviously. But it can be turned to good account. The need creates a kind of energy, a fuel that can be used. Used to do good.'

Anna admired Clare's down-to-earth detachment, even about those to whom she was most close.

Andy won the by-election easily. In his 3 a.m. speech of acceptance, delivered from the platform to an almost-empty town hall, he promised to demonstrate his gratitude to the electors of Middleton East by working harder than any MP had ever worked before. It was a pledge made in high excitement, but it was honoured honestly enough in the years that followed. Every Saturday morning, and once a month on a Wednesday night, he held a two-hour surgery at the central party offices in town. He dealt conscientiously with mounds of constituency correspondence, spoke in every local hall, pensioners' lunch club and day centre he was invited to. Within six months, he had visited every school in the area, and through the winter of 1984 he frequently came to give comfort and support to the men at the three pits on the westernmost border of his constituency, deep in the throes of battle with a hostile government. Andy wrote about this and a dozen other subjects in his weekly column in the local newspaper: 'Givings' Take' a cheerful commentary on local and national news. (Clare came up with the column's title.) In the meantime, they had come to an arrangement with the owner of a local hotel, who let the couple use two rooms as a base for their constituency lives until they had found a flat of their own.

Matt was increasingly by Andy's side. Now just thirty years old, he devoted every moment of his spare time to aiding and advising his father's old friend. Politics was his true love, he had always known that, and Andy his natural conduit onto the national scene. He had no parliamentary ambitions of his own. Matt didn't want to woo and dazzle an audience. He didn't want his name in the paper. He wanted to be a key aide to a powerful man – or woman: the indispensable back-room boy, labouring on a crucial speech in the early hours of the morning, perfecting those few sentences that summed up the message of the moment. He wanted to be the one waiting in the wings; there to encourage, to gently criticise, to applaud. To open the paper in the morning and see the results of his strategic lobbying reflected in a big splash of a story. (He didn't mind if, in the occasional broadsheet picture, he was merely a blurred dot at the back of a crowd, all clarity and focus on the man at the front.) He wanted to be on gossiping terms with all the big players. The MPs, the ministers, the columnists, the radio and television presenters, the political reporters. Those were the people he admired, the people he wanted to move among. Andy had the makings of a star, Matt knew it. In his gut.

A few nights after Andy won the nomination, the two families toasted his success in champagne at a special dinner served in the dining room. This was an occasion, like Christmas, too special for the usual comfortable meal around the rectangular kitchen table. Arriving a few moments after Andy and Clare, Anna felt momentarily star-struck, humbled by the fulfilment of Andy's long-held ambition. (She had just had a sharp personal disappointment of her own – the bitter ending of a relationship with a man she had met at university – and was feeling the relief of freedom; a more intangible uneasiness, too: recognition of the complex realities of adult existence; it was her first taste of the possible dead-ends of young adulthood.) It felt doubly odd, then, to toast such a sparkling beginning for Andy, whom she felt she'd known for ever: a fixed point in her own growing life. Matt had brought along his long-term girlfriend Janet, a pleasant-faced blonde with a pageboy haircut and a determined expression, who worked in the public-relations department at the charity where he was a department head. (Anna thought: *This is how Janet thinks our family is, at the heart of political events, when, in fact, this is the beginning of a new phase of our lives, which none of us understand.* It was on that night, too, that she first had the sense of her father being eclipsed, his superiority in professional and intellectual matters slowly chipped away by the more garish attractions of fame and power.)

The political talk that night was all about the miners. Would Thatcher beat the strikers or would Scargill and his men wrestle Thatcher to defeat? (Her mother, running up and down stairs with plates of roast chicken, buttered Brussels sprouts and honey-glazed carrots, could not have cared less about a distant industrial struggle. *Andy was an MP! How exciting! Who knew where his career would take him next.* Fiona had adjusted remarkably speedily to Andy's new status, had even determined a new role for herself in the younger couple's lives; from now on, she would act as a kind of stand-in for Andy's absent mother, become the benign provider, safe harbour in the storms to come, for their busy young friends.) The three men agreed: it was a naked power struggle, a defining moment in the politics of the country. But Matt and Andy could not unequivocally support the striking pit workers. They distrusted Scargill. They thought he was politically destructive, a madman possibly. 'Their case was fatally weakened by the refusal to hold a democratic ballot,' Andy lectured the table in a slightly irritated tone. (Did Anna imagine that this impatience was something new?) Perhaps that explained her father's exceptionally passionate defence of the miners at the table that night, the scorn he poured on Thatcher and the weak men she surrounded herself with. Anna was surprised and impressed by his passion. (And did she imagine that this, too, was something new?)

Later on in the evening, Andy jeered kindly at him, 'You're moving leftwards in your old age, David, you know that, don't you?'

'Maybe I am,' her father snapped back.

Anna – twenty-four years old and earning her own living – still felt like an eleven-year-old when she sat with the two men. She hated to see them quarrelling, however humorously. She preferred it when Andy had them roaring with laughter with the story of the selection meeting, in particular with his description of his two main rivals, a bearded local councillor, a rather hapless character who got himself into a muddle about tax policy, and a ferocious left-winger – 'a total Trot,' sneered Matt – who wanted everything in sight nationalised. Andy was equally funny about a last-minute dispute that arose when a key local party official (who had supported the incompetent bearded councillor) suddenly stood up and claimed that a group of pensioners had been bussed in to 'surreptitiously support Andrew Givings, who is clearly the London leadership choice'.

'If only!' Andy exclaimed, when he was retelling this story. 'The official buggers still don't have a clue who I am! No-one from Central Office has rung me from that moment to this. God, I wish I had been the leadership's choice, that would have been wonderful. I tell you, it was surreal to see all these old ladies, quivering in their soft pastel-coloured cardigans, and these old men with handlebar moustaches sitting to attention accused of playing some part in my Machiavellian strategy to steal the seat from its rightful owner! It was crazy. And all of this sophisticated paranoid drivel was coming from this incompetent *idiot* who didn't know the most basic thing about the tax system.'

This, too, was a new side to Andy: triumphant, unseeing.

He leaned back in his chair, tucking his shirt tighter into his trousers. 'All the old people voted for me anyway.' He smiled, immodestly.

'Not *quite*.' Clare corrected him, kindly but firmly. 'About two-thirds of them did.'

'Well, *most* of them then.' He was back in eager, good-guy pose. 'But I was bloody good, Clare, come on, you have to admit it.'

'Yes, dear,' Clare said teasingly. 'You *were* very good.'

She winked at Anna across the table.

Twelve

They arranged to meet under the rust-and-cream-striped brick arches of St Pancras station, just before 7 a.m. Waiting for Matt amid the morning bustle – the metallic ring of the train announcements, the furied solemnity of rushing commuters – Anna felt blissfully contemplative as she nursed a boiling-hot paper cup of station coffee in her hand.

'Hey!' Without warning, Matt had appeared at her side, noisily eating an apple, clutching their train tickets in his hand. It both comforted and faintly irritated her that he had already bought her a ticket (a full return, for which he would not, she knew, expect payment). He held onto it – without question, as if she were still a child – as he began to march in the direction of their platform, clearly expecting her to fall into step alongside him.

'All we have to do is a little bit of leafleting and some knocking up. Nothing too arduous.' He barked out this information as they hurried along.

'Yeah. And good morning to you, too.'

She felt shy at first, sitting directly opposite him on the train. Exposed; as if she was presenting herself for an interview (*so what makes you think I still need you to fulfil the role of youngest sister?*). There was between them the initial awkwardness of adult siblings taken away from familiar meeting grounds, a brittleness that was only emphasised by his admission during a phone call a few days previously that he would like her company on the train. Now in his early thirties, Matt looked every bit the up-and-coming executive. His thin face wore an air of elegantly endured strain. Dressed in a creaseless pale-blue shirt – Janet, now his wife, was by all accounts a ferocious ironer – and immaculate dark trousers, he had carefully hung his suit jacket on the peg provided high up on the window side, just above his left shoulder. There it gently swung, throughout the journey, a shadow figure, his cloth-and-silk double: an aide-de-camp egregiously waiting in the wings.

As the train clattered its way through the outskirts of the city, a bright rising sun pleasingly warming and revealing their tired faces, Anna idly wondered what she would think if she met Matt at a party. Came upon him as a complete stranger. Might she be a little afraid of that steely politeness, that intense self-possession? Matt could not quite conceal his impatience with those who were not 'players'. As success had come to him, and come so early, he had lost the self-deprecating top layer of his student days.

Once they had left Watford, he went to the buffet car and bought them tea and ginger biscuits wrapped in cellophane. Unwrapping these sweet gifts, they talked of Laura, partly because it was a way of not talking about Jack, and partly because there was solid news to discuss: Laura had recently left Banker Bill, with whom she had lived for nearly ten years. Poor Bill, it was his poetry which had drawn their sister to him in the first place. That and the fact that, in a suit, he looked like David Byrne of Talking Heads. The problem was, as Laura had confided to Anna recently, he looked more like Prince Charles when dressed in his rollneck and wellies, out in the country, where he most liked to be. Bill, she now claimed, with the rather irritating insistence that had crept into her character of late, was as dry as his stilted words on the page, a total bore. 'I know he's rich and handsome, and Mum and Dad adore him. But I'll curl up and die if I have to spend any more time with him.'

Anna knew all this and a great deal more (Laura was completely incontinent on the subject of sex, for instance), but she gave Matt only the barest details of the break-up, in deference to his obvious masculine nervousness about relationship matters.

'I think it just played itself out. She says, in the end, they found each other – boring.' Anna hesitated.

'He did seem to take himself very seriously.'

'Did you get to know him well?'

'We spent a bit of time with him,' Matt said, evasively. Anna knew perfectly well that Matt and Janet had been frequent visitors to the mansion block where Laura and Bill lived. They had often made up a foursome to various local restaurants. (Janet clearly thought Laura and Bill were the only sibling relations really worth bothering about.)

'You know she's met someone else?' Anna said.

It was gratifying to see the expression of astonishment on her brother's face.

'Ari. A film-maker. An Israeli. She met him at a party.' This new love was from Tel Aviv, a tall, rough-hewn man with pitted skin and the whitest smile imaginable. 'Apparently it was love at first sight.'

'Have you met this . . . *person?*' Matt sounded irritated.

'No – but I've seen pictures. He looks nice. Interesting.' Matt rolled his eyes: interesting was not a well-used term in his emotional vocabulary. 'Anyway . . . he – *Ari* – is in Jerusalem at the moment. He's back for good in a couple of weeks. He's got big plans, apparently, to make this film, this *comedy*, about an Israeli and a Palestinian family.'

Matt snorted – but she couldn't be sure if it was in reference to the idea of comedy or the suggestion of a grand political theme – as Anna further stirred his derision, partly as a way of breaking the formality between them. She lowered her voice and leaned across the white-topped table 'Oh, you know what Laura's like. Now she's talking about nothing but Woody Allen and what makes a good political comedy and Palestine, and the '67 war, and the origins of Zionism. Whereas five years ago . . .'

'It was all e.e. cummings and T.S. Eliot and modernist poetry,' said Matt, remaining straight-backed, but looking amused.

'*Plus* the size of Bill's annual bonus.'

'Yeah, right, I hear Bill did have the most enormous bonus,' Matt quipped, looking out the window, to detract from the rudeness of this last comment. Unexpected creases appeared all over his face; underused laugh lines.

'You should do that more often.'

'Do what? Make money?' He looked back at her, still grinning.

'No,' Anna bit crisply, comically, into one of the thin ginger biscuits. 'Make juvenile jokes.'

With its shabby air of grave purpose, its veiled hints of impending emergency, the campaign's headquarters bore a marked resemblance to a police incident room. A giant white board listed the key areas of the constituency. On the facing wall, a magnified section of the city map showed each ward in grainy, pastel-hued detail. And there – spread all over the gun-metal-coloured carpet, piled in corners, stacked in the corridors – dozens of cardboard boxes, overflowing with leaflets and badges and balloons. *Givings gives back! Give us Givings!* Anna winced at the populism of it all; those awful cheery exclamation marks.

Looking round at the 'team', Anna saw a familiar figure standing in the corner. Dan Givings, his face partially obscured by a giant mug (a photograph of Winston Churchill stencilled on its side). She had not seen him for over eighteen months, she quickly calculated. Two years into his doctorate, he looked even more like a student these days. Tall and spindly, he was wearing thin gold-rimmed John Lennon spectacles and a worn navy duffel coat, despite the warm weather.

There was the usual shyness in his greeting, eyes darting away and back.

Matt did not acknowledge Dan, which was rude of him. He was too busy taking over proceedings. Within five minutes he had his shirt-sleeves rolled up and was barking orders. He had arranged for Andy to do a phone interview later with one of the bigger dailies and now asked the constituency agent to set up a quiet spot for the interview to take place. This was Matt's third visit up to the campaign and, as he had told Anna on the train, he talked to Andy on the phone several times a day. 'Great, great,' Andy said now, pleased about the broadsheet interview, jotting a couple of phrases down on a blank pad – 'Thinking into the Future' and 'Keep it Real' – in front of him, nodding continually and enthusiastically as Matt spoke. Matt broke off the unofficial briefing to take the expected call. He sat at a cramped desk at the corner, finger in his ear, waving away imaginary interruptions, as he made his extended introduction to the interview proper. Fragments of his articulate, temperate enthusiasm drifted over to Anna, who was standing around like a spare part, spirits lowering by the minute. 'The point is . . . there's change on the ground. And that change will feed into the national scene . . . yes . . . exactly . . . right . . . people like Andy . . . They're what the future looks like. Well put, Larry.'

Matt gave Andy the thumbs-up sign. Andy nodded – squeezing his eldest son's arm with such buoyant delight that Dan's Winston Churchill mug wobbled and some freshly made tea splashed onto the grey carpet.

Anna felt an anxious fatigue as they were ushered out on to the streets, driven to the area they were to canvass and began the tramp from door to door, stuffing leaflets through letter boxes, evading snappy-jawed dogs, confronting suspicious, withdrawn faces. The team divided into those who did the stuffing – Anna's group, which included the constituency agent – and those who did the talking: Andy, Matt and a stout, genial local councillor called Mary. Dan Givings hovered between the two parties.

A couple of times Anna was caught by a would-be voter, her hand still trapped in the letter box. The first time, she stuttered out a few sentences on the party's tax plans, her answer based on what she had read in the paper. The middle-aged man listened to her with a patient, pitying smile – 'That's great. Thanks a lot, love' – and then closed the door in her face.

A few minutes later, Anna was quizzed by a sharp-looking woman in her late twenties, in a pink cotton blouse and grey jogging pants, about the leader's views on the Militant tendency. Taking no chances, Anna beckoned to Matt, who was 'doing' the other side of the road with Andy.

Both men came over.

'Hello,' Andy said brightly. 'I'm the candidate.'

Anna felt sorry for the young woman. Two minutes ago she had been ironing a pair of trousers in front of daytime television. Anna could still see the flat of the board, the black rectangle of trouser material, the firework-bright images on the television, through the window. Now the woman had an eager, watchful group crowding round her doorstep, wanting something from her and wanting it very quickly. She was entirely unprepared – eyes naked, face gleaming with some kind of moisturiser – for this brief and brutal political seduction.

Anna stayed to watch, partly because anything was better than pushing shiny pieces of A4 and A5 paper through snapping metal letter boxes, partly because she was genuinely curious to see Andy at work. Besides, his presence lifted her mood, made her believe good things were possible. He looked like a benign bank manager or an eager head teacher, vulnerable and eager to please. He shook the woman's hand, but then continued to hold on to it, as if desperate to ensure a transfusion of goodwill.

'So what issues are important to you right now?'

'Well, I'm a Labour woman through and through,' the young woman was smiling anxiously, 'so you don't need to worry about that.'

'Well, yes,' said Andy with a slight frown, while Matt was already looking restless. This vote was clearly in the bag.

'I know it's long over, but I just felt so sad for the miners, being beaten into the ground like that. My brother-in-law and my father, they were both . . .' For a second, the woman's eyes filmed over. 'They were done over. And no-one really stuck up for them.'

'Yes,' Andy said quietly.

'That woman is brutal and cruel. And I want a government that's going to do something for people like us.'

'Well, that I *can* reassure you on. Now we have a new leadership team . . .'

The woman's face brightened. 'I like him – the ginger nut we call him.' Her grin was quick, humour running in tiny rivulets from the corners of her eyes. 'Although he goes on too much. Personally, I'd prefer his wife to be running for office. I *like* her.'

A tiny smile played at the corner of Andy's mouth. He and Matt had been saying something similar in the car on the way from the station.

'This obsession with change,' the woman was on a roll now, captivated by Andy's gentle attention. 'That's what *she's* done. Change everything. Cut everything down. Cut away things that aren't bright and shiny and young. Why should we always want . . .' She stopped, breathless at her own poetry.

'Can we afford to be in opposition for ever?' Matt snapped.

She glanced at him, her face registering only a brief visceral distaste at his obvious courtier status. Matt took no offence, but began to pull at Andy's elbow, like a bored child, murmuring, 'We ought to be moving on now. There's a lot to do.' He was pointing to a cluster of tower blocks on the horizon, their next stop.

But Andy stayed rooted to the spot, mesmerised; continued to hold the woman's hand as if he were about to slip a ring on to her finger, his thumb stroking the third and fourth fingers, gently easing them apart. 'Look, I'm new to all this, I don't really know what I'm doing – yet.' The corny line was allowed to pass. 'But I do know I'll be nothing without the support of good, decent, well-informed people like yourself.'

For a second it looked as if the woman was going to cry, and as if Andy might join her. They were united in their sadness at the defeat of the miners, the violent determination of the Prime Minister, the corroding, low-level poverty that surrounded them, in this narrow street of tiny terraced houses.

The scene had the simplicity of a painting: she could imagine it hung on a gallery or office wall. *The Canvassing in Middleton East.* Andy, the young woman's hand still held in his, gazing into her eyes like an ardent lover. Matt standing a few steps back, frowning at his feet, one black-shod shoe raised in impatience. The unbroken azure blue of the sky, the low rust-and-ochre rooftops of this narrow row of terraced houses, its doors opening right out onto the pavement. A child's bicycle lying, as if abandoned, in the gutter. Just for a moment, it seemed to tell a tale much larger than itself, to capture the essence of democratic politics, its raw desires and its calming rituals, its small-scale dramas and supremely human disappointments.

Anna got a lift back to campaign headquarters with Dan Givings, the constituency agent and a quiet Asian student whom she had observed working tirelessly around the tower blocks. While she had loitered on the lower floors, reluctant to go any higher, she could hear the eerie bang of the metal letter boxes as the student stuffed campaign literature into door after door on higher floors.

She and Dan were squeezed in the back of the tiny car and she felt embarrassed, suddenly, being this close up to him. She ransacked her memory for snippets of information that her mother might have passed to her over the last few years. He had got a first, she remembered that. And he was now doing a PhD on some aspect of early twentieth-century liberalism. The isolation of the doctorate was getting him down – it was all coming back to her now – but he was determined to be finished in three years if he could. No girlfriend as far as she knew (her mother would pass that information along, fast enough). His face was thinner, she thought, and a little fearsome behind those horn-rimmed spectacles.

Mirroring her thoughts, he said, 'You look pretty much the same as when I last saw you.'

'I was trying to figure it out . . . was that the Christmas Eve before last, or the one before that?'

'The one before last.' He spoke crisply, 'Christmas '85. The year I did my finals.'

'Uh-huh.'

'You're teaching now?'

'Private pupils mostly.'

The car swung sharply round the corner, and she fell, briefly, onto his shoulder. ('Sorry!' 'No problem!') They were driving past dirty-looking factories, and patches of scrubland, slabs of grubby cream housing with tiny windows the shape of matchboxes. This was the rundown inner city all right. Here, she felt like a wealthy Londoner, full of shamed distaste. Did Dan wonder, as she did, at the dreariness, the pointlessness, of it? Did he think it was a strange way to have public influence, starting here, at the bottom, taking in all the miscellaneous grudges and resentments of the blank faces in the doorways, gathering them up, to speak of them, with grave authority, in a green-leathered palace? She thought of Andy's encounter earlier; of the effort he had put into one short exchange. What possible meaning could it have in the world he was going to? Being a politician seemed an odd, exhausting trade; it required of the people's representatives that they be like film stars or minor royalty, dispensing goodwill, scattering promises to the populace. Promising reform of that which cannot be reformed, surely. Or maybe that was just the way Andy, with his prodigious energy and charm, played it. She didn't know any other politicians.

'Dad said to watch out for this amazing water tower. It's somewhere along here,' Dan said.

'Do you come here often?' She smiled as she asked this.

'I've been twice this campaign.' She could feel the stubborn force of family loyalty within him.

The agent called out from the driving seat, 'I reckon Andy's going to do very well this time. He's made himself very popular in just the three years he's been here.'

'Good,' Dan said, in an unnaturally eager tone of voice. He had sat up straight like a student called to answer a question in class. Poor sod.

Anna listened as Dan and the agent rehearsed the major worries and successes of the campaign so far. She was surprised and rather impressed at how much of the detail Dan seemed to grasp. 'We should take most of the Eastern Avenue area – it depends on turnout, and the kind of campaign the Liberals decide to run in the last week.' They moved onto discussion of the national campaign. 'Good to put the dark days behind us. He's a very decent leader.' They were talking about the 'ginger nut'. She wondered whether to share that description with them, but decided against it. She had a hunch they wouldn't think it that funny.

They were laughing now, a joke about donkey jackets and the longest suicide note in history.

'What was that?' Anna asked, feeling a resentful sense of exclusion.

'What was what?' Dan turned to her.

'What is "the longest suicide note in history?"'

'Oh, it's what people called the 1983 manifesto. It was so bad . . .' Dan hesitated.

'. . . it was good?'

He frowned at her. In official party mode now, he said sternly, 'No, it was madness. A piece of total left-wing craziness.'

They were back at campaign headquarters before she could ask any more.

Thirteen

Increasingly, her own life felt secret; oddly illegitimate and insubstantive, compared to the public stories that were gathering pace all around her. She had felt invisible in the campaign offices and on the bleak streets of Middleton East, engulfed by others' plots and plans, talents that she was happy to acknowledge (Andy's energy and charm; Matt's awesome sense of strategy; Dan's loyalty and detailed knowledge). She divined that the men would not alter their course for her as she, in some minor way, clearly felt she ought to do for them (always being on hand to help, the good pliable sister, and so on). No, there they stood, quite without malice, set apart from her – creatures whom, in her better moods, she perceived as capable, kind, witty, smart, occasionally tedious, but always, unendingly, unalterably themselves, intrinsically alien and yet her own flesh and blood or near enough to it; the people she loved, the people who made her who she was.

Or wasn't.

She had to struggle, often, to put her mind to her own circumstances. She was twenty-seven years old, getting too close to thirty now for comfort. Little was happening in her life, in work or love. It did not even feel as if there was movement beneath the smooth surface, intimations of important change. In the mornings she taught English as a foreign language to au pairs and struggling businessmen; three afternoons a week she took private pupils. In her spare two afternoons and some early mornings she wrote, or tried to write, at her wooden table with the wonky leg in a corner of the dim hall of the flat she shared with her old school friend Sally.

The most significant relationship of her early adulthood had ended three years previously, yet Tom, this first and only major love, was vividly present in her mind that summer of 1987, most likely in the frustrating absence of anything or anyone to take his place.

They had met at university, where they were at first rivals, then uneasy allies and, finally, lovers. Tom was a natural academic, brilliant on sentence structure and the role of the author in the postmodern world; an intense intellectual, with a permanent five o'clock shadow; she had found his arrogance and incredible self-belief attractive at the same time as it threatened her very sense of self. In the beginning, they would have brief, intense conversations – about a book, an author, a film; she, clutching her books to her chest, balancing on one leg, biting her lip (acting out, without knowing she was doing it, a pastiche character: the feminine would-be academic, both ditzy and diligent, one of Mary McCarthy's group, perhaps?). During these conversations she would dare to offer her views, arguing with more apparent certainty than she really possessed, until at times she sounded vehement, even hysterical. Then, knowing in her heart that Tom was far cleverer than she, in a different class (as her father, a great sorter of intellects, would say), she would run away, deliberately elude him, sometimes for days, keeping her head down when he passed her desk in the library, pretending to be absorbed in *The Mill on the Floss* or *Villette*. She would have kept up this absurd dance – engage, withdraw; engage, withdraw – for ever, if he had not been the bolder one. One Saturday morning, in the spring term of their second year, they were both in the library early, standing by the photocopier on the second floor, copying endless pages of a tedious critical journal for a seminar later the next week, and he had asked her, out of the blue, if she would consider coming to Italy with him. *Yeah. Right,* she said laughing, *just like that,* pressing harder on the unyielding spine of the journal. *No, really, I mean it.* He had snatched the book away from its glass house and held it tight against his chest, taunting her to take it from him. *Come on, you know we get on so well, we could talk for ever, you and I.*

But I hardly know you, the good English girl deep inside her protested, echoes of her mother's anxieties that things should always be done 'properly'. The words that came out were much stronger, 'Well, let's start in more ordinary ways,' she said, his obvious enthusiasm now calling out of her a new sexual and intellectual confidence. She agreed to go out for a drink with him and then, two evenings later, a meal, at which both were rather formal and constrained. At the evening's end he invited her back to his flat, one large room really, with a bare kitchenette in the corner and an icy-cold mint-green bathroom. *Sit, please.* He was like the academic she believed he would become, easily commanding a room through the sheer force of his personality. He poured them both a stiff whisky even though she hated the stuff; it made her gag. *I want you to hear this. To know this book. Now, this man is a true genius.* And he began to read to her from Milan Kundera's *The Unbearable Lightness of Being.* She felt a lemon, sitting there, cross-legged on the floor, wanting to laugh, but impressed despite herself (at the book, at his audacity – reading to her as if she was a child!), looking at the dark hairs on his wrist, soft and black, sweeping up his forearm, simultaneously attracted and repelled. Shifting on her sitting bones, she was relieved to recognise that she didn't know what she wanted, but just then Tom lunged at her, with ferocious clumsiness and vulnerability. She kissed him back out of pity, trying to tunnel through to a potentially lurking desire. All through the uncomfortable fifteen minutes that followed she had an unwelcome image in her head of a woodpecker drilling at the side of a tree.

Almost immediately, the affair had turned operatic. Tom had tantrums when Anna could not see him – which was often, as she found him exhausting. He wrote her long letters on thin airmail-style paper. He was open about his 'obsession' with her. She was proud and a little frightened of her ability to draw out the passion in a man as clever and emotionally intense as this. (She had often thought their love was made of words, was both rock solid and vaporous.) They had long, intense conversations in cafés about which was the better writer, F. Scott Fitzgerald or Ernest Hemingway, heated arguments over serial curries about whether the musical was a cultural form to be respected, Mozart an intricate genius or simply sweetly superficial, Hitchcock the greatest film-maker alive. Talk, talk, talk. He dazzled her while she struggled to keep up, proud to be lusted after by someone who was so clearly going to leave his mark on the world, afraid of what would happen if she displeased him. She noticed, too, the relationship edged her out of the comfortable circle of college friends she had made up to then. Nothing was said, but she felt herself to be sitting on the other side of a wall of glass; acutely observed, mildly resented. Cut off, special.

He was sure he loved her. And his certainty, fed by her uncertainty – she was attracted to him, but did not like him as much as she wanted to like him – kept the relationship alive. Both came back to London when they had finished university. Immediately, Tom began working on a PhD, Anna to teach and start to write. They had long periods of 'cooling off'. (After his cruel condemnation of a short story she showed him, she did not speak to him for six weeks.) Several times she picked up the relationship again, missing his humour, his cleverness and his interest in her, knowing too that she was afraid to be alone. Periodically she chided herself for her inability to commit (one of his favourite criticisms of her), until one Sunday morning he settled the matter for them both once and for all when he turned up at the flat she shared with Sally, unannounced, roses in hand, an expression of anticipatory triumph on his face. Without any small talk or smooth-the-way endearments, he declared that he had come to ask her to marry him. He had just been appointed to an academic job in a town far away, the first rung on the ladder of a promising academic career, and he wanted her to join him as his wife. Just like that! As he talked, he couldn't help but smirk with pleasure at the neatness of his plan.

She felt she had a duty to usher him in, hear him out. Play for time, too. They stood awkwardly in the kitchen, talking. No, *he* talked, with his characteristic emotional and intellectual intensity, largely about himself and his needs, while she obsessively arranged and rearranged the roses he had brought in a vase on the kitchen table. As his words uncoiled, she had the oddest feeling that she could almost reach out, touch the serrated edges of control, even hatred, in his agitated lover's monologue.

Eventually she had to speak. She, too, was agitated.

'No, no. Stop now. I can't talk to you about the future because there won't be a future. Not for us.'

'*What?*'

'I don't think you love me. I don't think you even like me very much.' But who was she to tell another what they really felt?

'I know what I feel.' He banged the point home.

'I think you just want to . . . own me.'

It felt like telegrams, conversing: condensed messages of the utmost urgency, bulletins of life-changing importance. With her thoughts spoken, it was over; how quickly it was over! At the suggestion of ownership he gave her a look of the utmost contempt, which she understood immediately: *Pah, cod feminism.* His fury was icy. (It would have been the same, she consoled herself later, if she had crossed him in some major marital matter.) Some angry mutterings about working from the 'politically correct handbook' and he left with a dramatic door-slamming, while she quickly dumped the roses in the bin as if they were contaminated, filled with guilt and shame at so successfully concealing her true feelings from them both, for so long.

Since then there had been, in Sally's words, 'little action'. A few evenings in a bar with a photographer who was so handsome that when he kissed her – passionately – in the narrow green-carpeted corridor that connected the 'snug' to the room with the pool table, she was certain that she was in love, for the first time in her life. 'I think I'm going to swoon,' she said, pulling away from him, fighting the impulse to gaze into his eyes: to savour possession. 'Me, too.' To save herself, she pulled him through to the games room where they played pool for an hour – and she, for that sixty minutes, on the most intense high of her life – until, fetching in a third round of drinks, he said, oh so casually, that it 'is probably important to be honest and mention that I am married. Unhappily . . . of course.'

'Of course. What other kind is there?' She played a shot, badly, a taste of bitterness in her mouth.

But she went on seeing him and kissing him and much, much more: twice a week, in his airy studio a two-minute walk from South Kensington station, for several months. She felt ashamed. There were pictures – of his wife, a brunette beauty with sharp cheekbones, and his two beautiful children, a son and a daughter – all over the walls. But the shame didn't strangle the lust, not for a long time, not until he began to bore her with his rambling monologues.

That was the summer of 1986. More recently, one of her students had propositioned her, a plump French tax lawyer who wore pin-stripe suits and spoke excellent English (but kept taking her classes). She was sorely tempted. He looked confident: the wining, dining kind. The possibilities of a lustful, no-strings affair with an older man played out pleasantly in her imagination in those June days around the time she went with Matt to Middleton East. But on election night itself, struggling to bed at three in the morning – she had stayed up just to check that Andy had been returned to Parliament – she told herself, firmly, that she could, after all, do better. She could hold out for a more golden, deeper kind of happiness.

Fourteen

The moment she stepped into the hallway of her parents' house, the excitement was palpable. Greetings were flying at her from all directions and Anna could barely hear herself speak in the throng of the post-election gathering, a celebration of Andy's personal victory, commiseration at a third defeat for Labour; Matt's chance, too, to invite some of the bigger players in the party. The house had been transformed for the celebration: another chance for her mother to throw a party. She had even had the dining room repainted in their old friend's honour. The table had been pushed against the wall, covered with a pristine white cloth, and was now laid deep with bottles and jugs and glasses. There were cocktails with cheekily appropriate titles. The Middleton East special. The Neil and Glenys – a bright-orange umbrella poking out of every glass – and the Maggie Stinker, three kinds of spirit in a tiny glass, with pale chunks of pineapple floating on the top. The drinks were served by a team of handsome young men in white coats with black dickie bows.

She passed her father on the threshold of the dining room, on her way in to find a drink.

'Anna!' he embraced her, eyes filling with tears. 'I'm so glad you made it.'

He cried more easily these days. She didn't quite understand why.

'I wouldn't have missed it for anything.' She patted his arm, 'I'm staying over tonight, if that's okay.'

'Wonderful,' he beamed. 'We can have a good, long talk in the morning.'

'Is the leader here?' Anna heard a man say, as she moved forward to help herself to a white wine in a champagne-style glass.

'No, but I hear *Peter* may be dropping by.'

'God, I bloody well hope not, don't you?' said a familiar voice, just behind Anna's right shoulder.

'Laura!' Turning round, Anna was taken aback, as always, by her sister's beauty. Her skin was flawless, as if lit from beneath, a living cream-flesh canvas. The pristine effect was echoed in her dress: simple sleeveless black, flat black shoes, straight ironed-blonde hair. She was glowing with happiness.

The sisters hugged, then drew apart, Anna making a face of enquiry, meaning: *Is he here?* Her sister's new beau, Ari, had been due to fly in from Jerusalem that day. He and Laura were going to move into a flat together the following week.

'He's been delayed till Wednesday,' Laura said. 'Oh, Anna!' She put her fists up and waved them in the air like an excited child. 'I can't wait.'

'Is he really the one?' Here, in public, about to be interrupted any minute, things could be stated that baldly.

'Yup.' Baldly answered, too.

'Good.'

Misinterpreting Anna's briskness, her sister pinched her arm, twice, said lightly, 'Don't worry. It'll happen for you, too.'

'Right.' Anna brushed her sister's instinctive sympathy away. 'Is it only booze here?'

'No, there's *mountains* of food downstairs in the kitchen. You know Mum.'

Andy Givings was walking towards them now, miming expressions of pleasure. He looked physically bigger, shinier than he used to. 'Ah, two of my favourite women in the whole world!' He put an arm round each sister and pulled them in close, as if they had been asked to pose for a photograph.

'Congratulations!' they piped like school girls, and then laughed.

'So how does it feel?' Anna asked.

'Pretty good. Pretty good. I was mighty relieved by the end, I can tell you.'

He smelt of soap and warm water, deliciously clean and fresh. When he smiled, a look meant for Anna and no other, she felt a jolt of sexual desire, as she seemed to feel for any vaguely eligible man these days.

'You can't take anything for granted . . . not until . . . you know, the declaration.'

'Can't you tell?' said Laura. 'By the height of the piles of votes, I mean.'

'Well, yes and no. And remember, I'm a novice.'

'Hardly,' Laura drawled.

Anna wondered whether there was a way to talk to Andy without sounding the false note of flattery. She was about to say something about the campaign when Andy turned to her. 'By the way. Thanks a lot for coming up to help out. Every contribution makes a difference.'

The remark was spoken too briskly to please her. His attention had briefly wandered. A couple of MPs had arrived, and there was a group forming around them in the hall; Andy was already signalling that he would join them in a moment. The sense of intimacy with the Becoming Great Man vanished, the soap-and-water smell merely a reminder of ordinary frailty and vanity. Andy belonged to everyone now.

'Sorry to hear about the break-up with Bill,' Andy said to Laura now, as if he had a special remark to address to each one of them. 'He seemed a decent chap. But it just didn't work out, I gather?'

'Oh, forget *him*,' said Laura, with insouciant brutality.

'Of course, I'm useless at all that sort of thing. Clare and I have been together for ever. I've always been lucky that way.'

'Where is Clare, by the way?' frowned Laura, who did not want to talk of any other happiness than her own.

'Through there, with the boys. Come and say hello. They'll be dying to catch up.'

This was Andy's way of terminating their chat, moving on to the next set of pleasantries. To the knot of MPs in the hall. He was hungry for the infinite varieties of praise and admiration on offer to him, this night of all nights. He turned, his arms still stretched across both sisters' backs, so that for a couple of seconds they formed one giant creature, a vast bird of prey, with Andy as the beast's central intelligence, his host's daughters acting as his wings. There, to face a short orderly queue of fans patiently waiting to have their special moment with him.

Unconsciously obeying his earlier command that they should seek out Clare, the sisters eased out from under his protective wing and moved into the front living room. The crowd was thicker in here, but Anna immediately spied Matt over by the window, talking to another dark-haired young man in a suit, his dopplegänger in type and intensity. As a group of twenty-something national campaign workers parted, she saw Dan Givings, dressed in a crisp white shirt and black trousers, sitting on the edge of the biggest couch. He was listening in to a conversation between his mother and a slim, dark woman MP, much written about and photographed since her election in 1983. There was a quality of mildly desperate animation about both women, as if they were struggling to find common ground beyond the banalities. Clare had the slight defensiveness of the politician's spouse, the MP the ersatz humility of the more well known.

The eager brunette MP could now be heard talking about the House and its arcane rituals. 'It's a brutal place, with its own code and rules . . . Of course, Andy's doing just *fine*.'

Clare spotted the two sisters and waved, 'Would you excuse me . . . ?' She stood up and came over to Anna and Laura. Dan rose too, clearly planning to join his mother, but was caught by the MP, who began to engage him in lively conversation.

'Girls!' she hugged them both. 'And thank you, Anna.'

'What for?'

'Coming up to help. Leafleting. Doing all that boring stuff. That was so, so kind of you.'

There it was, the old Givings magic.

'You know I would have come myself, Clare, but I've fallen in love,' Laura said defensively, as if her emotional life constituted a recognisable job of work.

Clare patted her hand, answering briskly, 'And very lovely you look on it, too.'

Clare had put on weight over the years. But her skin was still clear and soft.

'You'd never have guessed it,' she turned to Anna, lowering her voice. 'I really like it. All of it. Even when I have to meet all of that lot,' and she jerked her head back, to indicate the female MP who was now flirting with Matt. 'I absolutely love the constituency stuff.'

No, Anna could not imagine it. She had not enjoyed her day out canvassing in Middleton East, but perhaps it would have been different if Clare had been there, smoothing the path of relationships, cementing human connection with her kindness and her noticing.

'I can get on with my own professional life, which no-one knows anything about. Clare Arkwright. Senior lecturer in politics and government. Who cares? Who even knows?' She laughed, self-deprecatingly. 'And then, like Superman or someone, I don this other cloak, this other identity, the one that everyone else thinks is the really important thing: politician's wife. Whereas for me, it's like a holiday.'

Twice during this little speech she had acknowledged the claims of others, squeezing the arm of one passer-by, raising her eyebrows in friendly greeting to another.

She looked at Anna as if to say, *You see.*

The three women talked on for a few minutes. Laura was eventually allowed her forty-five seconds to extol Ari's extraordinary qualities again. 'You should see this short film he's made about this market in Jerusalem. He really is amazing.'

Anna found it suddenly tiresome, her sister's insistence on projecting every half-decent human quality onto the latest man in her life. Why couldn't she develop a few skills herself? Or recognise the talents of others to whom she was not romantically drawn?

Clare Givings was nodding, eyes glazed, through Laura's little speech. ('You know, he's not conventionally handsome, but there's something *magnetic* about him.') Only once did her eyes leave Laura's face, searching out what or who? Probably Andy. Possibly Dan and Greg. In her own way, Clare was a worshipper of men: she unreservedly loved her husband and her sons. *My boys.* She would often use the term, even though they towered over her nowadays: competent separate adults.

'And what about you, Anna,' she smiled warmly. 'Everything going well?'

'Jogging along.'

Anna fished around for some way to deflect their attention. She felt reluctant to talk about herself, acutely aware that her current life couldn't be summed up in ways both truthful and appropriate to the occasion. She didn't have a funny story to tell, or a husband or boyfriend to rave about, or a job to complain of.

Luckily for her, Matt's voice was now calling for quiet, clearing a space in the centre of the room. It was time for the newly reelected MP for Middleton East to make a short, modest speech.

March 2003

Ben says, 'You're married to Chris Mason, aren't you?'

'Yes. Why?'

'No, nothing. He's briefed me a couple of times on cases. He's bloody good.'

'Yes, he's a good lawyer . . .'

Oh, and how much more complicated it gets. When Chris enters the picture.

'Excuse me a minute. I need the . . .'

The Ladies' room is not much bigger than a cupboard at the back of the café. In the cracked mirror above the sink she tries, just for a second, to see herself as the journalist might see her. Handsome, possibly, but dog-tired through distress: the skin beneath her eyes smudged charcoal with exhaustion. She has hardly slept since it all happened. Her thick curly hair is tied back, held loosely behind her head with a tortoiseshell clasp. Fine silver streaks at her temples, running like water over her ears. Dozens of tiny blood blisters, like maroon jewels, on her hairline, the coarsening of the skin with age. Handsome, possibly, but past her prime. Forty-two years old. The end of the beginning. The beginning of the end. The injustice of ageing, that those met in the second part of one's life will never truly grasp who one was, what one had, in the early years.

She paints her lips a defiant mauve and returns to the table.

Back at the table, Ben says, 'How did you two meet then?'

'Sorry? I don't get you?'

'You and Chris. Was it through your father? The whole lawyer connection?'

'No, no. Nothing to do with him. God, no. It was a party. At the Paradise Club in Camden Town.'

'Cute.' Ben nods, as if she is pitching him a film plot.

September 1989. Three months after her twenty-ninth birthday.

Ben stirs two large sugars into his tea. 'I'd love to get the whole story sometime.'

'Wouldn't we all?' Anna quips, giving him a mirthless smile.

Fifteen

Do you remember what you said?
No, tell me, what did I say?
You said: That's where your beauty is. Right there.
Well so I did. And well said too.

1989

The entrance to the Paradise Club was tucked a few feet along an unpromising-looking alley at the Mornington Crescent end of Camden High Street, marked solely by a gently swinging oblong sign of a long-stemmed cocktail glass, tilted on its side, three neon-red cherries winking on the surface of the liquid. A large, faceless grey door led to a generous-sized, dimly lit entrance lobby made over in faint homage to Art Deco: pink walls and a great deal of black lacquer; chest-high ashtrays, shaped rather like the Eiffel Tower, in which delicate, feather-light black-painted bowls perched, as snugly fitted as the pan in a commode. Several high-backed chairs, carved in the pleasing Rennie Mackintosh style, were gathered around low tables, set out for the use of exhausted clubbers wanting only quiet or to share a secret or a cigarette, or both. Empty for the moment, it had the feel of a medium-price hotel out of season, complete with the bored-looking attendant standing behind a desk; tonight, a girl with jet-black hair and kohl-rimmed eyes, her nose too strong for ordinary prettiness. With the whole club booked for a private party, there was no money to take or count, only coats and bags to check in and thin, grey raffle-style tickets to hand out.

Sally checked in their coats and scarves – it was cold for a September night – while Anna surveyed the club art. Large silver-framed prints of stars from the movies, mostly. Clark Gable, Vivien Leigh, Spencer Tracy and Katharine Hepburn. Writers, too: Hemingway looking ruggedly arrogant, F. Scott Fitzgerald arrogantly spindly. Picasso was there, with his domed head and big, round staring eyes. She was also gratified to see a print, high up on the wall, above an elaborate plant pot, of her heroine, Martha Gellhorn, dressed in a fatigue jacket, looking rather cross.

'Come on!'

Sally beckoned her through another grey metal door into the club proper, a long low-ceilinged cavernous space with a circular bar and two dance floors. Some chairs and tables were set out along a narrow balcony running the length of the side of the bigger dance space. (Anna could dimly make out some of the same prints from the lobby hanging on the walls: she wasn't sure she wanted to dance under Clark Gable's seductive grimace or her heroine's gimlet eyes.) Pink, yellow and green strobe lights moved with a menacingly steady measure across the room, which was pleasingly full but not packed, the advantage of a private party. Jazz music was playing softly, and most of the guests were clearly still in arrival mode, their greetings and laughter daubed with self-consciousness. On the smaller of the two dance floors a tiny woman with a shaved head was dancing languidly, eagerly watched by a knot of cool young men. From time to time, a concentrated blast of pale-green or pink light picked out her swaying figure. Dressed in a low-cut black gown, she had an elaborate tattoo of a serpent snaking and shimmering its way down her bare, narrow back.

A motley metropolitan bunch had gathered to celebrate this, the thirtieth birthday of Oscar, Sally's closest friend at Roof, the housing charity where she ran the publicity department. Sally pointed out all the various groupings, simplifying and exaggerating her descriptions, for entertainment's sake. 'There are the butch dykes and lipstick lesbians,' she whispered, pointing to a gaggle at the far end of the main dance floor, pals of Oscar's older sister, a twice-published poet. These young women divided just as Sally had indicated, into the boy-like women dressed in baggy-legged trouser suits and trilby hats and a cluster of bobbed blondes and sleek brunettes, in a variety of short tight dresses, with cherry-red lips and lashings of mascara.

Over near the back dance floor, mesmerised by the swaying pixie figure with the shaved head, were 'the groovy post-modernists', a group Oscar had met at a creative writing class, which, according to Sally, he had joined 'mainly because he's got to keep up with his arty sister'. These classes were run by a famous punk novelist, the swaying serpent-backed lady, whose acolytes surrounded her, a gang of pretty-looking boys in their mid- to late-twenties. With razor-short hair and thin ties of varying lengths, they looked like Fifties Teddy boys or country-and-western stars.

The largest group at the party was the 'work gang – all this lot'. Sally pointed to the groups milling right around them. A lot of the women were dressed in variants of the little black cocktail dress or silky see-through blouses and dark trousers. A group from accounts stood near the fire exit, smoking furiously. The more senior figures of the organisation struck an incongruous note in the dim, sweaty crush. Most of them had dressed down for the evening, and were now looking rather insecure.

Sally went to look for a free table, while Anna queued up at the bar. Her friend temporarily out of sight, she felt the mild pangs of loneliness that always came upon her in a crowd, the pointless envy of other people's intimacies and apparently infinite capacities for enjoyment. It was at times like this that she wished she had someone of her own. (A partner: that awful word.) Her photographer lover would have liked this underground place; Anna could easily imagine the two of them, exchanging swift, sardonic observations about the poets and the wannabe punk novelists, the men from accounts and the edgy-looking bosses.

Sally waved to her from the narrow balcony raised above the dance floor, where she was sitting at a table with two men she seemed to know.

Over here, she mimed, patting an empty chair next to her.

Coming, Anna mouthed back, treading a careful path, drinks in hand, round the side of the dance floor, in passing admiring a bunch of Oscar's sister's friends who, now the music had started in earnest, were dancing in formation, clicking their fingers, swaying their hips and laughing fondly, as if at a child, at their collective feet – a long row of polished black shoes: brogues, spiky heels, ballet flats, Dr Martens – moving as one, as if independent of the bodies and brains that directed them.

Reaching the balcony, Anna handed her friend her drink and nodded to the men, a guy with ginger hair and a sweet, slightly flabby face, and a striking man with hawk-like features and light-blue eyes, wearing a fitted dark shirt. She felt the lovely indifference of first acquaintance, the freedom of not knowing, not caring, who these people were.

'Can I . . . ?' she pointed to a chair next to the handsome one. He would have to shift his seat a fraction if she was to sit down.

'Oh sure, yes.'

He stood to free the leg of the chair, his exaggerated courtesy a mirror of her own indifference of a few seconds earlier. She was a stranger, his gestures said. Where she sat didn't matter to him.

He was tall even in the dim light, and she could see the outlines of a lean, hard torso underneath his shirt.

Sally made the introductions, turning first to the ginger-haired man. 'Anna, this is Pete . . . Pete works with me in the press office . . . And . . . this is . . . Chrissie . . .'

Sally, Pete and the handsome man brayed heartily.

'What's so funny?' Anna took a sip of her drink to disguise her irritation.

'Well, clearly, my name is not Chrissie,' said the handsome man, but offered no more information.

'Well, *obviously*,' said Sally, annoyingly prolonging the joke. 'Anna, this is Chris. Plain old Chris.' ('Ha-ha,' broke in the ginger-haired Pete.) 'Who works in *campaigns*.'

Pete added, 'Chris is our star advocate.'

'So what do you advocate exactly?' Anna barked. In a speedy reversal of her earlier feeling, she realised that she found the man in the dark shirt attractive. It made her anxious to feel desire this immediately, a feeling that dredged up in its wake the usual profound defeatist conviction of what other, more lovely women possessed and what she lacked. The old sense, *Ah, if only I were Laura. This part would be easy.*

'Not talking about work at parties?' he smiled.

She saw him look down: swiftly, a barely discernible glance at her legs. Let him stare. Her legs were good, and tonight sheathed, rather fetchingly, in sheer black tights.

'Sorry,' he continued, 'my proper job title is campaign worker, which means I try to get stories into the press about rotten landlords.'

He sounded more normal, more approachable now.

'I see,' she said, wondering whether he had ever come across Jack, who was, after all, in the same business in his Jack-like way. Guiltily, she found herself wishing that he hadn't.

Pete said genially, 'Whenever Chris comes in the press office, we groan. He's always got some grand plan up his sleeve, or some new piece of research he wants us to get the *Guardian* to do a two-page feature on.'

'And does it?'

'Rarely,' he grinned. This time, the smile was for her alone; it demanded her complicity. A surge of excitement went through her, such as she had not felt since the photographer French-kissed her in the bar.

'And you are?' he said.

'Anna.'

'A friend of the lovely Sally, I presume.'

Flattered, Sally burbled excitedly, 'Anna's a writer.'

'Really?'

'Oh, don't listen to her,' Anna said, glad that the darkness disguised her blush.

'Rubbish, Anna!' Sally was generously insistent on her right to have a talented friend. 'Seriously, you guys. Don't forget her name. Anna. Anna Adams. You heard it here first.'

'Stop, will ya, Sal?' Anna leaned over and flicked her fingers perilously near her friend's face.

Chris looked on, clearly intrigued.

Anna turned towards the dance floor just as the opening bars of 'Young Hearts Run Free' came on the sound system: a sweet, instantly catchy melody. Anna felt her spirits rise, her nerve ends tingle. A couple of the women from accounts were now jigging about self-consciously. She watched them, her thoughts spinning pleasantly. She had heard recently that Tom was already making a big splash at his new university, was about to publish his first book on the challenge of the neglected author. Only this afternoon her mother had told her that Dan Givings, having given up his doctorate the year before, had started working for a big national newspaper. And this guy Chris was clearly pushing his way in the world too. *Star advocate,* whatever that meant, she thought meanly.

Yet, here she was, turning her face away from her friend's loyal insistence of her own skills, refusing the public confirmation of her ambition yet again. Maybe those glamorous continental philosophers, the ones with names like Helene and Julia, were right after all – the ones who talked about how the core of the female, enwrapped in mysterious folds, was hidden away, while men's physicality explained their need to display themselves like peacocks, to push themselves forward in the world. Did anatomy really explain these things? Was that why she always found it so hard to boast or even speak a simple truth – *I write, I would like to write* – punished by her own sense of hubris, painfully aware of the value her father placed on modesty, while always pushing forward, in his own quiet, utterly forceful way, and her mother placed on female compliance to the male will, while so clearly resenting it?

A group on the main dance floor were now doing the twist and she watched a lovely girl with white-blonde hair, a host of delicate butterflies swooping across her golden-skinned shoulder, twist to the floor, keeping her balance perfectly, while her dance partner, a short squat figure dressed in a baggy men's suit, with a fresh rosy face, gyrated expertly around her crouched figure. They were laughing as they moved, exuding controlled but exuberant pleasure. No unnecessary reserve here, Anna noted wryly.

Chris touched her shoulder, 'A penny for your thoughts.'

She didn't enjoy sitting on the sidelines like this, with Sally and the two men, watching others dance, laugh, drink, live. Casual conversation was becoming harder as the volume was ratcheted up to match the rise in alcohol-fuelled excitement down in the club proper. It was impossible to bellow out anything truly felt or subtle.

But there were compensations to their little group. Genial Pete had nobly offered to go to the bar, to get the four of them a second round; Sally was full of jokes and good humour, her neck flushed as if with high fever. (Anna wondered if her friend had a crush on Chris, although she had never mentioned him by name, in their several discussions about the men she liked at work.) Was Anna herself just imagining a spark of interest from the man with the surprisingly toned muscles?

'Thanks. It seems weird, all these film stars looking down on us,' Anna said, when Pete came back from the bar and was handing out the glasses. 'Look at Bette Davis . . . Isn't she great?' The actress wore a fur hat and a typical mischievous expression.

'I just love her,' Sally sighed. '*All About Eve*. Fantastic film.'

'Now *she's* the one I like,' Anna said, pointing directly above them, to another framed shot of a grave and pale-skinned Martha Gellhorn, dressed in a slash-necked black sweater, staring coolly into the middle distance. 'It's my favourite picture ever taken of her. She looks so calm and pretty. That was taken when she was married to Hemingway.'

Chris turned to stare, rather ostentatiously, at the portrait.

'She's beautiful.'

It was odd to feel a frisson of sexual rivalry with Martha Gellhorn.

'And you'll tell me . . .' Chris said, turning back.

'Tell you what?'

'You'll tell me who she is. Won't you? Later.'

'Perhaps.' She teased.

'I went to Cuba,' he called into her ear, information for her and her alone. 'Just recently.'

'And . . . ?' she blew her question back.

'Interesting. Complicated.'

'Oh, right.'

It was as if they were waving posters at each other. Phrases or single words having to do the job of proper talk. There were subtitles in there too. *You interest me. You scare me. Just a little.*

The dance floor was filling up, and Anna was afraid that Chris would ask her to come down with him. It wasn't that she didn't like dancing; she loved it on the rare occasions when she could forget herself. But suppose the handsome stranger didn't? Suppose he turned out to be cripplingly self-conscious or, just as bad, embarrassingly free? She didn't mind a man who couldn't move, but she would very much mind a man who didn't have the grace to realise it.

Sally stood up. 'Come on, Pete', she said. 'Let's get on down there.'

Chris leaned over towards her, and she tensed herself for his question.

'Do you want to go and get something to eat, Anna Adams?' he whispered in her ear. 'This is really not my thing.'

Sixteen

They had met just forty-five minutes earlier, she thought, glancing at her watch in the entrance lobby, waiting for him to fetch his jacket, which he had left over the back of his chair on the balcony, in their rather indecent haste to leave the party. (Sally, bopping on the dance floor to Jocelyn Brown's 'Somebody Else's Guy' with Pete, who turned out to be quite a nifty little mover, had given her an unfathomable look: pride and a distinct disappointment mixed.) If it was true, as she had recently read in a book on relationships, speedily consumed near the psychology shelf in a large West End bookshop, that everything you need to know about someone is revealed in the first hour you ever spend with them, then she had just fifteen minutes left.

As if on cue, Chris came through the grey door from the club proper, a look of childish concentration on his face. As he came near, he reached out to touch her shoulder, a proprietorial touch that thrilled her.

'Found it,' he said to the girl, who had just come on shift at the coat checkout, a pretty petite blonde, in a red silk bustier. 'Thanks for all your help.'

He flashed the checkout girl one of of his shy-but-not-really-shy dazzling smiles (odd, how it already felt familiar) as they pushed out the main door into the cool night air.

'So what do would-be writers read then?' he asked, as they walked along Camden High Street towards their agreed destination, a pizza parlour in Parkway. 'I presume you like Hemingway?'

'Not much.'

'Oh, why not?' He sounded rather crestfallen.

'Do you know what honestly happens to me when I read Hemingway?' (Perhaps it was the sense of release after leaving the club, the chance, finally, to speak normally, but she could feel herself launch into a long, slightly didactic answer – more, anyway, than was required, her voice still pitched at an unnaturally high volume.) 'It's like I've been introduced to the most confident, objectively accomplished man in the room, and all I feel is a sort of profound *phoneyness*. I just can't get beneath the flashy, hard surface of his words. I know we're supposed to divine tender emotions, a sense of vulnerability beneath the hero's exploits. To me, it's just showing off. As if he's borrowing knowledge from some more genuinely sensitive source. Or trying to have his cake and eat it.'

'Jesus!' he whistled, sounding both impressed and appalled.

'Plus, I *hate* the way he treated Fitzgerald.'

'Who was Fitzgerald? His butler?'

'F. Scott Fitzgerald? The *world-famous* author?' Too late, she realised he had been teasing her. 'Whom I just happen to think is much the greater writer.'

'Whatever you say.'

'But you do obviously? Like Hemingway, I mean,' she said, in a more emollient tone.

'Oh, forget all that.' He was laughing. 'I'd be much too frightened to argue about literature with you. No, it's just that I went to his house.'

'What? The Finca Vigía?'

'The one outside Havana.'

'I've seen it in books. It looks magical.'

'The grounds are fantastic, but they won't let you in the house. You're kept back by a silken rope. Tourists are only allowed to creep round the edges and peer in. It's very strange. As if he's still living there. You can see his riding boots, his books. There's even mail left unopened on the desk. Like he's gone out and will come back at any moment.'

'Did you like Cuba?' she asked, as they began the walk up Parkway, past the Spreadeagle pub.

'Not as much as I thought I would.'

'I saw a TV programme about it once,' Anna said, 'and all I remember are all the huge billboards along the roadside . . .'

'"Be productive", "Be principled", "Remember those who sacrificed themselves." Yeah, yeah. They are all still there.'

She liked walking along the street with him, weaving in and out among the drunks and punks, the office girls out for the night in tittering, teetering gangs and the handsome, middle-aged couples, dressed in well-cut European-style coats in bottle-green or burgundy wool, strolling arm in arm. People looked at them: she, with her long curly hair, sheer black tights and heels, and he, tall, blond and blue-eyed, handsome in his dark shirt and lighter linen jacket.

'So why go? To Cuba, I mean?'

'I wanted to see it for myself. Caribbean Communism.'

'Really?'

'Really *really*? I had just split up with a woman, someone important, and I wanted to get right away.' He grinned, without a dash of shyness now.

The lights in the pizza parlour were too harsh and they ate and drank quickly, the mood dipping and soaring. Anna was uncomfortably aware of the dark rings under her eyes, found his constant fiddling with the salt and pepper pots distracting. She wasn't hungry, and had to force herself to eat. Easy to drink, though. Glass tumblers of a sweet Italian white kept the flame of possibility alive.

He was telling her about how he came to London, seven years ago.

'You can't imagine what it felt like, driving down the M1, in a rented van, all my stuff piled up behind me. I knew only two people in the whole city.'

'So why did you move down here?'

'That's what people do, isn't it? Come and make a new life for themselves in the capital. I didn't want to spend the rest of my life living round the corner from my mother, feeling guilty if I hadn't gone out for tea and cake on a Saturday afternoon.'

Anna was thinking of her father, and how he, too, had broken away from an overprotective parent, come to London to make his fortune. How lonely he must have been, in his one-room flat in Bermondsey, scraping a living as a bright pupil in barrister's chambers, knowing no-one, not intimately, until the night he spied the lovely twenty-three-year-old Fiona Scott across a room at a party and began to woo her in earnest.

'My mother's a nurse, totally self-educated, a tough character,' Chris sounded proud. 'She had to be. Brought me up pretty much without help.'

'What's her name?'

'Rosemary.'

'Ah.' He seemed less threatening all of a sudden. Just a boy, once upon a time. The only child of a tough, lonely mother.

'I don't want you to think that I'm not grateful to her. I ring her every Sunday. Whatever's going on in my life.'

'I'm sure you're a wonderful son,' Anna teased him, forking up a piece of uneaten salad from his plate.

'But I've never been able to tell her anything important. Ever. It's like a wall between us. That high.'

'A lot of people feel like that, don't they? With their parents. Or with their siblings or spouses. They want to be close, to share everything. Too often, they end up simply doing their duty.'

'It doesn't have to be like that.' Chris was insistent.

'I suppose not,' Anna replied. She was thinking of her own mother, whom she had come across only the other day waiting like a child outside her father's study. Strains of discordant, beautiful string music coming from within. (Bartók? Shostakovich?) And her mother: hovering, hand grazing the door knob; wanting, but not quite daring, to go in. That particular night Anna had gone back home for dinner, with her parents – Matt had been round, too, but without Janet, for some reason – and they had had a jolly meal, the four of them, teasing her father about his Reading Obsession (a game they would never have embarked upon if Jack or Laura had been there, she wasn't quite sure why; perhaps because she and Matt were the more bookish of the children, in her father's view). Her mother was slightly tipsy and excessively flirty, laying her hand on her husband's arm, laughing in an exaggerated way at whatever he said. Uncomfortable as it made Anna, it was possible, at moments like this, to see the glimmer of her parents' famous early passion, in her mother's girlishness, an answering steely glint in her father's eye.

Her mother had been unusually quiet when Anna helped her clear up afterwards. When every dish was put away, all surfaces wiped, she had said, winsomely, 'You know, Anna. I get lonely in the evenings, when your father goes upstairs, shuts his study door. Sometimes I would like a little bit of conversation . . . especially now you've all fled the nest.' A telltale wobble in her voice.

'I suppose,' she hesitated, 'I could go and interrupt him tonight. Just for once. After thirty-something years. What do you think?' Her tone was forced, jocular.

'Go for it, Ma.' Anna had waved a dishcloth in the air, playing the cheerleader. But, truthfully, she felt a pang of pity.

Had her mother interrupted her father that night? Or any other night? She couldn't remember. Or even imagine it. The fixed image in her mind was all of the waiting, the fearing: the faint clash and bang of music in the background, the sudden soaring sweetness of the violins. Her mother, a still figure on the landing, dressed in tailored black trousers and a fitted scarlet-and-black silk shirt, drop earrings. (She took immense care of her appearance, still; kept her weight down, her nails long and beautifully manicured, her hair dyed and cut regularly.) There, she stood, patting the back of her carefully coiled hair, smoothing down the flat front of her trousers, trying to disguise the inevitable loose swell of late middle age.

'What is it?' Chris was leaning towards her. 'You look so sad!'

'It's nothing. I was just thinking about marriage, that's all.' She smiled, for now she was remembering Andy and Clare, last Christmas, giggling like a couple of school children, poking each other in the ribs. Completely at ease with each other.

'My father was a complete waster, walked out on my mother when I was only two,' Chris said angrily. 'I don't know why my mother picked *him*.'

He shook his head, as if trying to get water out of his ears. She could see he didn't like the melancholic turn in the conversation, was already rifling through his pockets feeling for the right amount of loose change. Putting a generous tip on the table as he stood up, he said, 'Shall we walk for a bit?'

There, out in the Camden dark, she felt hopeful again. They walked down wide roads fringed by warehouses and rural-looking pubs, festooned with hanging baskets and window boxes crammed with tiny-petalled, velvety purple and red flowers. The dark mound of Primrose Hill rose before them like a rain cloud. 'Let's go this way,' he steered her by the elbow, down towards a wide cross-roads. 'I love it round here. I used to come here during my early years in London. When I was lonely or sad or bored. I'd just walk around exploring the quirky squares and cul-de-sacs, looking at the different colours of the rich people's houses up on Regent's Park Road. Then I'd go sit at the top of the hill. I could breathe there. See the future.'

'And what did you see?'

'Nothing, in particular. But it was reassuring to think there might be something or someone out there for me. There were times I wasn't at all sure.'

'Do you feel that still?'

'No.' He gave her a sideways smile, 'I do know, though, that I've reached the end of the line with the work I do. The housing-charity stuff. It's too bitty, too reactive. Dealing with little pockets of bureaucracy. Getting the press interested in worthy causes. I've decided to train as a lawyer.'

She took a sharp intake of breath. Was that what underlay the excitement she felt, her barely conscious sense of 'fit' between them? She, seeking a father substitute; he, too, divining something eminently suitable in her.

'I've got a place on a course to study law starting in September.'

'Terrific,' she said neutrally.

'I'm thirty years old. I've got to get on with it.'

Thirty years old. The age thing was perfect, too.

They stopped and sat on the low, brick wall of a church on a corner. Side by side. Not touching. His profile, illuminated by a street light, was as sharp and defined as a statue. For a few moments she had the illusion that he was not made of flesh and blood, but of a fine impermeable rock, like marble. Glittering and hard.

'I want to do something solid and decent. And to be honest, I can imagine myself, briefing some pompous barrister or even' – he gave a small, immodest smile – 'standing up in court. *Performing.*'

Yes, she thought; yes, you would, you could, for she was soaked in years of a daughterly, instinctive knowing about this particular profession.

'. . . but I fear, I don't know, the loss of other dreams.'

Yes, she thought, you are right there, too.

'Once I go down that route, it will all be about money and colleagues and success. Worldly stuff.'

'Not necessarily,' she said, her coolness of tone a determined refusal to take up the full burden of his dilemma. She felt momentarily weary; here was yet another ambitious and demanding man in her orbit, just like her father. Like Andy. Like Matt. Maybe these were the only kind of men she knew how to deal with.

'I think that people have difficulty accepting their limitations, the fact of their sheer bloody ordinariness.' Chris was leaning back, looking up at the stars in the inky late-summer sky. 'That's why I went to Cuba. I wanted to see if society could have a different feel. But all I saw were people desperate to get their hands on American dollars. Boys in the street hissing: *Cambiere? Cambiere?*' He hesitated, 'You know what Cuba turned me into? A materialist. It made me dream of those little shops in European airports, the ones that sell a dozen different varieties of the same handbag. Or the chocolate shops, rows and rows of luxurious sweets, sealed in cellophane, with scarlet and lilac bows. Enforced principles make me want *things.*'

'That doesn't make you a bad person.'

'No. But we're a spoiled generation, us Eighties lot. Don't you think?'

'Speak for yourself,' she said, lightly.

He jumped off the wall and turned to face her, her knees pressing gently against his thighs.

'I like the way you half-close your eyes when you talk about things that matter to you. When you were talking about Hemingway . . .'

'I told you, I'm a Fitzgerald girl . . .' She spoke quickly, out of embarrassment. '*The Last Tycoon*. Best book every written. Even though he never finished it.'

He seemed to be studying her, as if she were a drawing.

'I knew almost straight away.'

She didn't mean to nod, but she did, a tiny affirming shake of the head: *yes, I knew, too.*

He was still scanning her face, intently.

'It's here. And here.'

With his index finger, he traced a path from the corner of her left eye to the top of her cheekbone, lingering there for a moment, pressing his forefinger into her skin, she could register the pressure; then, fast and light as a breeze, trailing his finger down to her bottom lip. In preparation, she thought, for a kiss, half-closing her eyes in readiness, nervousness and desire mixed. But he made no move towards her. Instead, he continued to stand close to her, his body's pressure subtly insistent, simply looking.

'You know, you have wonderful genes . . .'

'Thanks a lot!' She laughingly protested.

'Oh no!' He seemed anguished at the possible misunderstanding, placing his hands on her shoulders to emphasise his sincerity. 'I only meant, I find you beautiful.'

Seventeen

The following Sunday, in the early evening, he came to *claim* her: his choice of words. The tail end of a September day that had turned freakishly warm. Anna had been sitting out in her tiny back yard – face turned skywards – soaking up the warmth of the sun, talking and laughing with Sally and Laura. Her sister had left to meet Ari mid-afternoon; an hour later, Sally had gone out to the cinema. Now Anna was alone, looking forward to a tranquil evening in on her own, when the brisk knock on the door came.

There he stood, wearing an unexpectedly loud red-and-white shirt, holding flowers – shades of Tom's disastrous proposal, five years previously – and a big box of chocolates.

'How did you know my address?'

'Sally.' He grinned.

They talked in the kitchen for what seemed like hours, with the concentrated languidness of those who know for sure that they will soon make love.

He would decide the exact timing of that crucial moment, as he would decide so much in their life together. The sky was darkening when she went to the fridge to take out some beers; when she moved back to the table, he stood up and blocked her way, indicating that she should put the cans down on the table – he patted the table top twice, sharply, with the soft ends of his fingers – before placing his hands on her shoulders just as he had done on the Paradise Club night.

Then, without saying a word, he began to kiss her.

* * *

It was past midnight, when she saw him steal away from the bedroom, dressed in her lilac bathrobe, which only just covered his knees; even in her slightly swoony state, propped up on a bunch of pillows, she could register that he looked ridiculous, like a transvestite in a skirt, the muscly tendons and hairiness of his calves absurdly exaggerated by the girlish garb. After a couple of minutes, guessing that his absence indicated something other than a bathroom stop, she went to look for him, found him standing before a display of family photographs mounted on the hall wall.

'Hey!' she said.

He turned and kissed her bare shoulder; she was wrapped only in a bath towel.

'I'm finding things out. Or being a voyeur. Take your pick.' He turned back to look at the photographs.

'What do you mean?'

'I realised when I was lying there that I'm in love with you, but I know so very little about you. Ssssh . . .' he would not let her speak, only squeeze his arm, her way of saying: me, too, 'So . . . I decided to come and do a bit of independent research.' He indicated the display of photographs. 'I saw these earlier.'

He kept hold of her hand as he studied the pictures. (The light in this hallway was particularly dim; she had not been able to find a hundred-watt bulb at the supermarket the other day.) There was Granny Agnes, her father's mother, in a prim white pin-tucked shirt, with those fierce eyebrows that Anna had inherited (but long ago shaped and plucked, under Laura's lovingly skilful instruction). Just below that, the picture of her parents as young lovers, the photograph that had once been on her father's mantelpiece in the Secret Room; her mother had, obligingly, had it copied for each of her children. There were some more recent group shots, which included Matt's wife Janet, and then Matt and Janet cradling their baby son Bo, born last year; Ari and Laura, embracing like teenage sweethearts. Looking at these images as he, a stranger, might, Anna thought how golden and untouchable they all seemed. Even Jack, of whom there was a single black-and-white headshot, a cigarette rakishly protruding from his mouth, looked like an intriguing French existentialist writer.

Anna said, quickly, 'Perhaps I should have told you, I come from a legal background. Yes, I *should* have told you.'

'I knew you were holding something back,' he laughed. 'To be honest, I thought you were married.'

'Christopher!'

'David Adams, I'll be damned,' he said a few moments later, 'Chambers v. Gibson. Went right up to the House of Lords.'

She groaned as he reeled off the names of more cases, quoting short passages from judgements. For someone who had barely started out on his training, he knew a lot more about the law than he had at first let on.

'Is that him?' Chris said, pointing to a picture of her father, dressed in his Sunday gear of sweater and slacks.

'Uh-huh.'

'And this elegant lady, your mother?'

'Correct.'

'And this, your sister?'

'Yup. That's Laura. The beauty of the family.'

'Not to me. *Ever.*' He turned around to emphasise the compliment, wrapping his arms around her, kissing her bare shoulder again. Twice. He looked at her mischievously, a look deliberately designed to recall the passion of barely an hour before.

'Come back to bed.' She tugged on the arm of the bathrobe.

'Yes. Yes. Just give me a moment to take it all in. The fact that my future wife is such a wondrous archetype . . .'

'What are you talking about?'

'But you are. The perfect product of a middle-class London family. An impeccably liberal upbringing and all that. Lucky old you,' he finished off wistfully.

'Oh, puh-leese,' she said, sticking out her tongue, 'that poor-boy-from-the-sticks guff won't work on me.'

Eighteen

1990

From the beginning she felt a bone-deep certainty about this new man in her life. ('Christopher Mason. Christopher Mason.' She skipped down the road, rolling his name around her mouth and her mind, wondering how its complete ordinariness could sound so thrilling.) Within a few weeks of that first night they had decided to move into a flat; within a year of meeting (in fact, with just two days to spare) they were married. The wedding was far grander than they meant it to be; Anna was caught up in her mother's fantasies, her dedication to high standards regarding all matters decorative or social, especially as it looked as if Laura and Ari would never marry. (Her sister's Israeli lover did not approve of the 'institution'.) Anna's mother was ridiculously excited about the match; within weeks of meeting Chris, all her conventional ambition had shifted from her beautiful daughter to her interesting daughter – the unconscious distinction she had always made between her two girls. Chris was everything she could have wished for in a son-in-law; ambitious and ruggedly handsome: his strong nose and those pellucid blue eyes saved him from mere prettiness. It even pleased her that he did not come from a well-off family, as if, in choosing this worldly young man from a modest background, Anna was confirming Fiona's own choice, decades before, to pluck the determined but socially awkward David Adams out of a crowd and make him hers; when everyone knew that she, a gorgeous twenty-three-year-old with a twenty-four-inch waist, could have had anyone!

Anna was willing to go along with her mother's social pretensions, to gossip idly with her of possible futures, to participate in the sheer thrill of being a *girl* (although she was very nearly thirty), just as she had seen her mother and Laura do throughout adolescence. When it came to wedding plans she agreed, with just a touch of reluctance, to complicated flower arrangements, the addition of this guest or that guest to the wedding list, acknowledging a host of long-lost relatives' presumed disappointment at being excluded from this key occasion. It was only on the big day itself that she sensed the full consequences of her exuberant casualness. At moments she felt fraudulent, sanctifying her most personal decision before so many virtual strangers, trying hard to shut out the alienating element, to immerse herself in the moment ('my moment' she tried to say to herself, fluttering with nerves as she waited for their half-hour slot in the cool, dark passages of the municipal building where the actual ceremony took place). Chris was jumpy too; here, at least, she had a job to do, could help him negotiate the reflexive politeness, the hungry curiosity, the deep, complicated kindnesses of her parents' social world. It seemed to go on for hours, the grasping of hands, the murmuring of gracious banalities.

The reception took place in a fashionable restaurant, a glass-ceilinged palace flooded with natural light so bright and pure on the day it made jagged scars of the older women's laugh lines. From the raised plinth on which the principal persons sat – herself, Chris, her parents, Andy and Clare, Chris's mother, Rosemary (a surprisingly ebullient woman with cropped grey hair and her son's lovely wide mouth) – she could survey the entire social landscape created by their union. Her extended family dominated the occasion; Chris had barely any family, but this was amply made up for by a large, lively contingent of guests from the housing charity. She was proud of how popular he clearly was with all his – erstwhile – work colleagues; at the same time she tried not to think about how many of the attractive young women of a certain age in this big vivacious party were ex-girlfriends.

There was only one blip throughout the long, warm afternoon, involving Jack. Despite having been placed, very carefully, at a congenial table with Sally, Dan Givings and a second cousin called Miranda, a rather stiff-looking brunette of about forty, Jack fell into an inebriated (champagne-fed) stupor before the pudding was served, his large head nodding low over the white damask-covered table, occasionally rearing back with considerable force, as if suddenly awakened in front of a television screen. 'Oh, for God's sake!' Anna's mother slammed down her napkin and sprang into action, signalling imperiously to Dan that he should walk her second son – discreetly, of course – out of the restaurant.

Anna followed them down the narrow aisle between the snowy-white tables, nodding and smiling to right and left, a concentrated shot of sympathy for poor Miranda, who had clearly found Jack a trial, but was now laughing quite happily about the incident with Sally. This procession felt oddly similar to the journey she had made earlier in the day through the packed first-floor room at the town hall, gliding – she hoped! – from the gilt-edged double doors at the back to the registrar's large mahogany table at the front, acutely conscious of how filmy and essentially insubstantive was her cream-and-blue dress, a spray of blue, violet and white flowers in her hand. (For somewhere to look, she kept her eyes fixed on Dan Givings, who was perched at the furthest edge of the front row, next to his mother, and was staring at her with a stern, unfathomable expression.) Now she was glad to scuttle after his tall, reassuring back and the bent body of her errant brother. Out in the vestibule, loosening his black tie with his left hand, Dan was phoning for a taxi while Jack lay slumped on an antique, rich red-velvet love-seat. With his scrappy ginger beard and moustache, he looked like one of the hard drinkers living rough on the Strand whom it was his day-job to help back on their feet. Today, he was wearing a shiny silver suit that was at least a size too small. The overstretched waistband had rolled over under the pressure, revealing a ruched strip of stained white cloth. He had tied his own tie, rather inexpertly.

'Hello, Anna,' his voice was slurred, but very jolly. 'I'm shorry to go, but I've . . .'

'That's fine, Jack. You go and get some rest.'

Dan, still negotiating some detail over the taxi, smiled at her.

'I've got a busting headache and I'm not really 'njoying myself any more. That's always the time to go, don'yewthink? When it's no fun.'

Anna made a face at Dan, as if to say: *See! You lot failed! You're just no fun!* He mimed a comic desolation, shrugging his shoulders, pursing his lips.

'No worries,' she said to her brother. 'Ring me tomorrow.'

'Will do. I certainly will . . .'

'Okay. I'd better get back.' She patted his shoulder.

'And, Anna?'

'Yes?'

'I'm really proud of you. Looking lovely and all that. You *know*, speshal on your speshal day.'

Dan was giving her the thumbs up, wearing the same stern expression as earlier, at the registry office. She wasn't sure if the raised digit and/or that look merely meant business – the taxi was ordered – or if he was confirming her brother's message and that he, too, found her lovely and all that, you *know*, speshal on her speshal day.

Nineteen

The mail came early that Saturday morning, crashing through the letter box well before 9 a.m. Anna, four months pregnant, stood by the front door, dressed only in an oversized white T-shirt, a ripped-open cardboard package in one hand, a smooth square book with a shiny cover in the other. The Spring 1991 issue of the prestigious quarterly literary magazine took *Betrayal* as its theme; there, as its third item, was an extract from her story 'Last Days in Havana'. (The title pleased her, every time she saw it written down.) Thirty years old: her first-ever appearance in print! Happiness had worked like an engine on her in the early months of courtship; in a few short weeks she had penned this tale of a middle-aged journalist and his wife whose twelve-year-old marriage disintegrates on a trip to Cuba, the final scenes of their relationship being played out over six days on the tourist beaches, and in the hotel lounges of late-1980s Havana; (her subject matter, she realised, a distorted mirror image of the steady euphoria she was experiencing, that golden happiness she had yearned for, for so long). The last scene was set at Hemingway's villa at the Finca Vigía and involved a cryptic, embittered conversation about the final failure of the marriage of Ernest Hemingway and Martha Gellhorn, in particular the competing claims of each one's work.

Chris, her first reader, was generous and enthusiastic. He did not seem to mind – or indeed even to notice – that she had stolen, word for word, several exchanges they had had in the early months of their relationship on the Hemingway/Gellhorn marriage. (He had read more about the journalist, while she, on his urging, had tried the major fiction works one more time; they had, at least, the advantage of being relatively slim volumes.) Brimming with belief in her 'talent', he encouraged Anna to send off her story to magazines and literary agents, had even offered to go down to the local print shop, there waiting patiently for the bored brunette at the counter to make five photocopies of the story while Anna pored over the *Writers' & Artists' Yearbook*, copying out the relevant names and addresses. Together, they stuffed the stapled sheets into large, plain brown envelopes. Within days she had sent off a final typewritten copy: forty pages long, double-spaced; within weeks, the magazine had written to signify acceptance of her story.

Now she held the final product of all her hard work, proof of her very existence (or so it felt) in her hand, trembling with delight. Her story took up just six pages of the quarterly magazine, but it was enough; here it sat snugly, and wholly gratifyingly, between a famous novelist's elegiac piece on the dying days of Thatcherism and a glossy American's rant against the shallowness of post-feminism.

Chris was standing next to her. Now, like a town crier, he hollered out the story title and her name. 'Read all about it! "Last Days in Havana"! By the utterly fantastic Ms Anna Adams!' Thrusting the book above his head, whooping for joy, he did a little war dance around the narrow hallway.

'Now we must spend the whole day celebrating.'

'Later, please,' she groaned good-humouredly, for she wanted to do nothing more than retreat to the living room couch, put on some music and read her story over in absolute peace.

She put Miles Davis on the headphones and sat back with a sigh. It was strange. Try as she might, she could not recapture that first moment of intense pleasure, the fierce sensation of pride at seeing her name in type on the front cover.

Twenty minutes later, Chris walked in to the living room, freshly showered and dressed, just at the moment she chose to fling the magazine across the floor with a comic cry of frustration.

'What is it?' He looked alarmed, striding over to crouch by her side. 'Is there a mistake in it?'

'I hate it!' she said, beating her fists on a cushion like a two-year-old. 'It doesn't do what it should!'

She knew he was smiling, his warm breath tickling the lobe of her right ear. But he did not speak. Lifting her head up, she squinted at him. 'What?'

There it was, that sly grin that still gave her a short, sharp electric shock of lust, deep in the pit of her stomach.

'Nothing,' he began and then said quickly, 'It's just nice for me to feel, at last, that I'm getting to know you.'

'What's that mean?' she said grumpily,

'You want to know the truth? I was intimidated when I first met you. I thought you were lovely, but high-cheekboned scary.'

'Really?' Anna struggled upright, smiling wearily, like someone who had just recovered from a high fever. Like all lovers, they had gone over their first impressions of each other a dozen times, but he had never said anything quite like this.

'I just didn't *get* you, you see,' he continued, 'and I certainly couldn't understand why someone like you would be interested in a pig-ignorant, pushy boy like me. I was sure it was all some sort of ghastly mistake, that you'd change your mind.'

'The fact that I married you must have been just a *little* bit of a clue.'

'And that sharp tongue!' He stopped her mouth with a kiss.

'And now you see,' she struggled to speak as he kept on kissing her, 'that I'm just a . . . silly . . . uncertain . . .' Between kisses, he mimicked her, pretending to gulp his own singular words, 'lovely', 'ordinary human being' , 'thank God'.

Thank God for sex, she thought, falling back on the pillows, as her greedy husband put his hand up her T-shirt and began to rub her swollen belly, to edge her knickers gently down over the ridge of her hipbone. (Their baby had been conceived some months earlier on that same battered, second-hand rose-coloured couch.) Thank God for sex and its power to pull us right back to the present; to wipe away all our petty failures; to pull us into the future; to create new things.

In the weeks after Harry was born, their bedroom permanently illuminated by a corner night light, she felt as if she dwelled nightly in a painting by Vermeer. The old oak desk in the corner was piled high with papers, drafts of the novel she was struggling to write. Frequently Anna woke to the sight of Chris's tall, strong figure, crouching over the changing mat, tenderly cleaning and powdering the tiny figure, limbs flailing, pressing down the sides of the nappy. With infinite tenderness, he would pass this human parcel across the bed, little Harry's fists clenched in hungry protest. A large, soft pillow placed across her lap, Anna would bring the baby up to her breast, relishing the muted glugging of satisfied need.

Lola was born almost two years later. The first night they brought her daughter home from the hospital, she placed the scrawny newborn in a basket, next to her side of the bed, half-mad with the weary alertness of the new mother. Chris collapsed into bed next to her. 'Thank God, it's over,' he muttered, kissing her left ear. Within seconds he was asleep, his breathing slow and regular, while she lay, rigid with tension, and a sensation close to hatred, staring at the shadowy patterns on the night ceiling. Predictably, the tender midnight ritual established between husband, wife and newborn baby son did not continue; Chris slept through his daughter's mewling cries. He had recently joined a high-profile firm over in east London, and was beginning to take on a few cases of his own. He was putting in the kind of hours her father used to work, his whole being infused with hurry, intensified by his desire to make up for what he considered the lost years of his twenties. It was now his conviction that the law was his true vocation.

Like snow, the burden of domestic life fell slowly and silently on Anna; despite her best intentions, she felt buried beneath it. On top of the daily round, they soon realised that their one-bedroom flat was far too cramped for two adults and two children. For months, Anna tramped along treeless avenues of terraced housing, pushing the buggy, the baby strapped to her chest, looking at dozens of poor conversions, crumbling hallways, rodent-infested kitchens, and the occasional dream house right out of a magazine – calm, cream-coloured kitchens, lovely landscaped gardens – that they could never afford. Finally, she came upon a two-down, three-up house, riddled with damp, unpainted for decades (echoes, here, of her parents' purchase of Durnford Gardens, back in the late Fifties), but with a small yard for a garden. After their tiny flat, which she had loved so much, it felt as spacious and echoey as a palace.

They moved on a crisp, cool January day, camping out for months, as the builders worked around them.

'Bye-bye, Daddio,' two-and-a-half-year-old Harry cooed solemnly every morning as Chris kissed each of them goodbye in turn, a giant figure in his dark suit with his large oblong bag, eager to escape the chaos of home for the ever fresh challenges of work. Anna was usually propped up in bed feeding the baby (and coughing from the dust that seemed to rise perpetually through the house), while Harry played with his toys nearby. Or she was downstairs, huddled on the couch with her son in the still-undecorated living room – bare boards, thin, grubby curtains – watching television, reading a book or building a tower, while the baby slept, arms above her head, nostrils quivering, in her Moses basket upstairs. Since his baby sister's birth, Harry had taken to waking at 5 a.m. insisting on his mother's dawn company.

'Say hello to the real world,' she would sometimes call after her departing husband, with mock cheer. Then, when the front door had slammed shut and she knew she was alone for the rest of the day, and quite possibly for the whole of the evening too, she would burst into tired, self-pitying tears.

'I'm Matt to your Andy,' she used to say, half-jokingly, to her new husband, who had decided soon after their first meeting to train as a solicitor, not a barrister. 'Your very own special adviser.'

It was true. She *was* like Matt, in many ways: a natural strategist. 'I think you should approach Brian (one of the firm's partners) pretty soon about that case,' she would say over breakfast or when they were sharing a late-night glass of wine; or 'What about writing a piece for that journal on the wider ramifications of the Lincoln Seven case?' She was also skilled on all the more personal stuff. 'Not that tie. Definitely *not* that tie' or 'Don't forget to eat breakfast!'

'I'm the luckiest bastard alive,' Chris often said, pinching the flesh of her upper arm, like a child in the playground.

Whenever he had a spare moment during the day, he telephoned her: to report, to rehearse, to rage. 'The barrister was totally useless today. I could have done it a lot better. After all my careful preparation.'

In the beginning, she found his calls reassuring, a sign of his wish to keep their intimate connection alive during the long days away. She would set aside whatever sorting, painting, cleaning or sanding she was doing – the house had, for the moment, become her pet project, a kind of job – and put her mind to the problem at hand. But after a while she noticed an impersonal element creep into these conversations. She might as well have been anyone, hanging on the end of the line; impatient to get back to the dripping paintbrush, the calming rhythm of the roller moving over the bigger walls or her class preparation. (With the new mortgage, she had had to take on some more private teaching, set her own writing to one side for a while.)

Less and less was needed of her in these thrice-daily conversations, intricate reports of failed expert witnesses, intractable coroners or corrupt police officers. They would often laugh at the lack of equivalence in their days. Anna liked to draw the comedy out, if only because it gave her something to say, 'Well, yes, it's been pretty busy here as well. The post and the milk came, although I have to say that postman is completely useless. I have to keep telling him to put the bigger letters in sideways.' (He never got her gentle jokes, her parody of his intense irritation at the other professionals in his life.) 'And we were late for drop-in club. Lola's gone down for her morning nap and I'm hoping Harry will go to sleep after lunch.'

'Make sure you get a sleep yourself, Anski' (his pet nickname for her). 'You're doing such a brilliant job.'

There was a subtext to all his husbandly approval; both knew it. Chris was reluctant to have his children 'farmed out' to anyone else, as he had been as a child.

'No-one could do what you're doing.' He spoke like an automaton on this subject, his choice of phrase never varying. 'We'll reap the benefits of it for decades,' he added.

'You make Harry and Lo sound like a business proposition!'

'Never.'

'I have to leave them sometimes . . .'

'I know. Just not too often.'

He sounded distracted; she could hear voices in the background. 'Look, I've got to go. I'm going for a drink with some work people. Stuff to discuss. I'll be back at eight, I promise.'

'I was hoping to try and write for a while after supper.' Already, she felt dejection, a sense of doomed enterprise.

'I know. And I won't be back any later than eight. We'll wolf it down and I'll deal with the kids so you can get going. You've got to plug on, Anna.'

'Yes. Yes.' She spoke testily because she disliked his penchant for catchphrases: a symptom, in her view, of a lack of the particular, in thought and action. 'Fish all right?'

'Fish is frigging fantastic. As long as it's not salmon. It's not salmon, is it?'

'No, prawns. Stir-fry.'

'*Anything*. Anything is perfect.' His briskness an indication, she knew, of his disdain for domestic detail.

'Just don't be surprised if you have a tired toddler sitting on your lap and a fractious baby to walk up and down the kitchen.'

'I do have to work later' – he sounded worried – 'but I'm sure they'll have gone down by then.'

And if they're not, guess who'll be jiggling the baby up and down the hallway, her four hundred words a day abandoned at the corner of the desk in the marital bedroom?

'My family,' he said; spoken like a politician, acknowledging victory in a crucial election.

She was easily roused – still – by her tall, handsome husband's appreciation; could live without seeing him much in the week, knowing that he was working so hard on their behalf. *My family*. Could toil herself, happily, in return for the gift of certainty; her children provided for and she, safe in the knowledge that she was loved and desired, at the centre of this infinitely delicate, infinitely precious creature called 'us'.

Twenty

1994

The real world was still out there, that much she knew. Every so often, during those early years of marriage and the exhaustion of young children, she caught sight of Andy Givings being interviewed on a news or current-affairs programme or heard him on the radio, when she was brushing her teeth or preparing the children's lunch. Often she would recognise his voice just in time to focus on the tail end of a grilling by an enthusiastic or wearily arrogant presenter. She still got news of him through the family grapevine, met up with him and the rest of his family at Christmas Eve and the occasional two-family reunions, but increasingly *that* Andy – the Andy of her childhood, the Andy of her family self – was divorced from the public man, the Becoming Great Man (shortened to BGM, the nickname that she and Jack would use, in private) and she could not put the two together.

Soon after the election of 1987, he had been appointed to a junior job at transport on the opposition team. Eighteen months later, he was given some worthy-sounding post relating to Europe (Anna could never keep the exact details of these political positions in her mind). He survived the debacle of the party's 1992 election slaughter, which finally killed off the loquacious, eminently decent 'ginger nut' and ushered in the brief reign of the portly, equally decent Scot, who gave Andy a junior job in education; all was settled, or so it seemed. Anna watched the news bulletins about Smith's sudden death when she was at home alone, the children at nursery, fingers laced over her face as if it was a distressing scene in a soap opera, pitying the brutally bereaved but impressively stoical wife and daughters. Within days of his election, the young Blair promoted Andy to Shadow minister for education. It was then, and only then, she thought – nearly twenty years after that first announcement, round his dining-room table, of his intention to 'go into' politics – that Andy, a remarkably youthful fifty-one years old, who had in fact been around for years, was firmly established as one of the 'new' figures of the new-model party (as Matt insisted on calling it) an up-and-coming star on the national stage. 'So, that is how long it takes to make your name in that game,' Anna mused out loud one evening, just after Andy had been interviewed briefly on the BBC on the party's opposition to city technology colleges. 'Yeah, but it takes only a day to lose it,' Chris observed drily, flicking through a pile of papers on his lap. When Matt rang her, a few days later, his first words, without accompanying explanation, were, 'Well . . . what do you think?' She knew exactly what he meant. 'Yes. Well done. You've done it.'

It was obvious, right from the beginning, that Andy 'had' it. He could do the media thing. He looked good on television, was attractive, buoyant, sure of himself, if occasionally a little too grave. He had put on weight during his time in Parliament and it suited him. 'He sounds like a human being,' Chris said – approvingly – one Friday evening, when, the children put to bed, they were eating a take-away curry and drinking beer, *Any Questions* playing at low volume in the background. This was a major compliment coming from him; Chris had scant time for most politicians and was only polite about Andy on account of the family connection. 'Yes, somehow he talks about the world as we know it. Blair, too,' Anna said, with her mouth full of spongy garlic naan. That long-ago teenage question of hers – how could friendly Andy ever be authoritative Andy? – now seemed irrelevant. Andy had grown in stature just as politics had become less formal: they met perfectly in the middle, she could see that.

She also knew enough to understand – largely from conversa-tions with Matt, with Chris and occasionally with her father, who liked to keep a lofty distance from the daily political round – that the next stage of Andy's career depended on how well he did *this*,

this *Today* programme/*Newsnight*/*Guardian* briefing behind-the-scenes thing, what blend of human warmth and authority he brought to his particular brief. The voters of Middleton East would be rooting for him from now on; he was their man. Their judgement would matter, but not as much as that of the dozens of professional political watchers – journalists, opinion formers, senior civil servants – who were looking for evidence of flair and wit and knowledge and integrity in the grinding game of parliamentary politics.

Light relief, then, to glimpse Matt on television too. Just a couple of background, bag-carrying seconds. Shaking hands energetically, his dark fringe flopping; listening intently, his head tilted to one side; jumping out of the front seat of an official black car, in one swift movement. A mere extra, except to those in the know, those who understood that Matt Adams – part-time special adviser (his proper title) – was best political friend to the fast-rising opposition star Andy Givings. As she watched him striding along a corridor in a modern European building, a structure made up of what looked like delicate silver tubes and glass (attending a symposium on Education in the Global Economy), or walking along a London pavement a few steps behind his apparent political master, she thought how odd it was that in private the relationship seemed reversed; there, Matt was the potent one, Andy the apparent supplicant.

There were occasional references to Matt in the newspapers.

> *Clever Andy Givings has chosen one of the most talented of a new young breed of political sophisticates to help guide him through his Commons career. Matthew Adams, a high-profile charity worker, is giving half his working week over to support the up-and-coming Givings, and the politician is reaping all the benefits.*

Amazing how an intriguing, semi-public character could be moulded out of a few stray facts.

Her mother marked these newspaper items in pink or green highlighter, then sent them in brown A4 envelopes through the post to her daughters and other assorted relatives, like ransom notes.

Twenty-one

It was a dark, rain-whipped November night, the children sleeping
upstairs. Chris was away in Leeds, on a case that was scheduled
to go on for several days. The television news had just begun, full
of reports about peace talks at Dayton, the shocking hanging of
Ken Saro-Wiwa. She planned to watch the headlines, then drag
herself upstairs to the desk in her bedroom to write. It was odd,
how much easier the children were to manage when Chris was
away: she kept them to a strict routine, which gave her hours of
free time in the evenings. That and the absence of a second evening
meal to cook, or at least always arrange: the list of local take-away
numbers was the most frequently consulted list on the cork board
in the kitchen.

Within two minutes of sitting down in front of the television
she was fast asleep. She awoke with a start – her chin wet with
drool – to the sound of rustling, directly outside the front bay.
There was no mistaking the nearness of the noise. Somebody or
something was rooting around the dustbins, in the front patio,
just a few feet away from where she was sitting. Luckily, the
curtains were drawn.

Her heart was banging but she could not move. Wiping the
wetness from her mouth, she tried to clear a pathway through her
panic. The children. The children were upstairs.

A muffled voice called out. 'Anna? Anna?'

Relief, followed by a surge of anger. Her face still stiff with fear,
she got up, strode through the hall, pulled open the front door.

'What the fuck do you think you're *doing*?'

There was Jack – dressed in just a T-shirt and jeans and scarf, despite the wet and the bitter cold – smiling in his most infuriating, detached manner.

'I didn't want to frighten you by knocking'.

'Ever tried using a telephone? Announcing your arrival like ordinary mortals?'

'I lost your number. I got your address from Fiona a while ago and I just happened to be in the area. I've had a couple of clients resettled round here.'

This juvenile insistence on calling their parents by their first names, a clear statement of disassociation.

'Okay, okay.' She hugged him, briefly.

'Do you have any cigarettes?'

'Nope.' Anna was an occasional smoker only, and tried to keep temptation away from the house.

'Wait for me,' he said, 'there's a garage round the corner.' And he disappeared into the darkness once again. Fifteen minutes later he was back, with two packs of cigarettes. One for him, the other a brand that she used to smoke as a teenager.

'Want one?' He taunted her with the pack, waving it in front of her face.

'Oh, why not?' Smoking was one way of exacting harmless, petty revenge against her occasionally controlling husband; he didn't like 'women who smelt of smoke'.

Back in the living room, Anna turned the television off and the side lights on; recently painted, the room glowed with cosiness. Calmer now, after the earlier shock, she was relieved rather than pleased to see Jack (no-one in the family had heard from him for several months), who sat smoking, a saucer, taken from the kitchen, at his feet, spattered with ash.

He offered monosyllabic answers to her questions. No, he hadn't seen David and Fiona for some months. Yes, he talked to them on the phone from time to time.

'I'm just not interested,' he said with the unnatural calmness that Anna found peculiarly provocative, but which always threw her back on herself; might her own precious children one day regard her with such contempt?

'I came here tonight to show you something.' He spoke as if they were in a business meeting, reaching into his jeans pocket and carefully extracting a crumpled piece of paper. 'Thought you might want to know what I've been up to in recent months.'

It was a news article. She held it carefully, smoothing out its sooty crinkles; it described developments in a long-running high-court case involving two political activists who had challenged the claims of a giant burger chain. There was a large black-and-white photo of the two defendants, a young woman with dark hair and a fringe and a studious-looking man wearing glasses, defiantly holding up the offending leaflet, surrounded by a blurred crowd of supporters.

'Is that you in there?' Anna knew that it must be (he wouldn't have handed her the article otherwise). She squinted at the pale mass of faces, but it was impossible to make out any individual features.

'I've been involved for a few months now.'

'I won't be taking the kids there any more then.' Anna smiled.

'One has to start somewhere,' he said, as if she had not spoken. 'And I decided I had to pick. Some place. Some thing. Just to start with.'

'You don't worry about it being a hopeless case?' In her head, she could hear the cynical worldly voices of Chris and Matt. Taking a fast-food chain to court over the quality of its meat. Mere gesture politics. Lighten up! Get a life! Get a burger!

'That's all there is. Gestures. Really.' He spoke as if he had read her mind.

'And are you still working? At the housing place?'

'Yeah. Why?'

'No, nothing. You just haven't mentioned it recently.'

'Twelve years, Anna,' he said, as if the length of his employment was her fault.

'Well, you've taken on more responsibility, haven't you?' she responded defensively, as if he was right to blame her. He had been given a central London patch a few years back, and Anna had heard through Sally, who knew people who knew people who worked with Jack, that he was excellent at the streetwork side of things. His 'clients' were devoted to him. 'So you think you'll get more involved . . . in this sort of thing?' She waved the press cutting gingerly in the air.

'Maybe.'

My God! Her irritation flared up again. *You come round here, nearly frighten me half to death, take away two precious hours of free writing time and you're treating me like an intrusive tabloid journalist!* She stood up, ostensibly to stretch her legs and arms, scrutinising him carefully as she jiggled her legs, eased her neck round and back. He was greying around the temples and thickening around the waist. How old was he now? Thirty-eight? Thirty-nine? He had an unhealthy pallor that suggested not enough fresh air or fun, too many cigarettes.

'I've met someone.' Jack's voice broke into her unkind train of thought.

'Oh. Is she involved in the burger trial?'

'No. She's a kind of administrator. At this office we've all had to move to in Borough. We might go to Paris together. We've talked about it a lot.' Again, that unnatural provoking self-possession. She wondered if he was on some form of medication.

'So what's she like?'

'Very pretty,' he said triumphantly. 'Very very *very* pretty.'

'*And?*' Anna mimicked his emphasis, made a beckoning gesture with her right hand, as if to say: Come on, give me something more substantial, less teenage than that.

'She's smart. In a practical kind of way.'

'Good. Yes, that sounds good.' Anna spoke slowly, like a patient primary-school teacher, aware of sounding less enthusiastic than she was supposed to.

'We don't meet that often. But when we do, we have a really good time.'

'But does she have a name?'

'She does.'

'And?'

Anna could see how hard he found it to name this paragon, although there was no doubting the animation, the blaze of feeling that had briefly illuminated his pasty face. There was some tinny element, a discrepant note in his unusually ebullient account. Perhaps it was the odd phrase inserted here and there: 'We might go to Paris together.' 'We don't meet that often.' She felt a sisterly impatience with the very very *very* pretty girl, willing her to return her brother's affection. *Please, God, make him happy.* Jack was the only member of the family who had no partner or special friend. It would surely make all the difference. She felt like her mother, phrases running through her head like: *He needs to have a normal life. To be brought out of himself.*

'I'm really happy for you,' she said, thinking it best to act with hope. She put her hand on her brother's shoulder.

It was kindness, then, without an ulterior motive, that did it: the key to unlock the most intractable of locks.

'Lucia,' he said, as grave-faced as ever. 'Her name is Lucia.'

'So, how late did the mad monk stay?' Chris asked when he returned home on the Friday night, and she was filling him in on everything that had happened while he was away. Even though he had won the case, he was still edgy; he kept his distance from her, as if he was still up in Leeds, talking work, not quite yet home. Standing by the fridge, beer can in hand, his face was creased with fatigue.

'Two in the morning, can you believe it?' She relished the idea of telling Chris the whole story. 'He just pitched up about nine. I heard him rooting around in the bins outside the house.'

'Madman.'

'No, it was really odd, Chris.' She still didn't have her husband's full attention, tried again to draw him into her tale. 'He arrived at the door, coatless, bagless, even though it was wet and freezing. And when he came in, there was clearly something on his mind. And that he wasn't going to go until he could tell me *all* about it.'

'Poor you.' It was beginning to infuriate her, that careless, disengaged note in her husband's voice, as if he were on automatic pilot.

'He told me about being involved in this burger case. Showed me this newsclip thing, a picture of a crowd of people outside a court. He was supposed to be one of them, not that I could make out any specific faces. And then he starts telling me about this girl at work.'

'He's in love, you say?' Chris was interested in this detail, at least.

'It seems so.'

'Has the lucky lady got all *her* marbles?'

'That's not fair.'

'Anna, if you would just stop being so blindly loyal for a moment . . .'

'And if you would stop being so bloody rude.'

He smiled his edgy, sorry-I'm-just-so-great-I-can't-help-it grin. The scent of battle between them, with its sexual undertones, warmed her to him again. A Grace Paley line nudging round the edge of her consciousness, something about how *a certain amount of intransigence was nice in almost any lover.* Yes.

'He's going to have to fight for this girl,' she said, glad to have his attention, 'and I don't think any of it will come easy. God, how do I know? I'm just going on what he tells me.'

Chris snorted with derision. 'Yeah, right. I bet you any money you like, she's not that interested. I mean, no offence, but would you want to hook up with a nearly forty-year-old man, living in a grim one-room flat, who has a problem about his family, doesn't dress properly, eats crap food all day long, but campaigns tirelessly against a perfectly decent fast-food chain?'

'There's a lot more to Jack than meets the eye, you know, Chris.'

'Yeah? Like liver disease?' Her defiant husband took a swig of his beer as if to say: Case closed.

'Go away, you horrible cynic.' Anna made a shooing motion as she would to a spiteful cat. 'Good for him, I say, pursuing true love against the odds.'

Chris gave a heavy, amused sigh. 'You always did love a loser, Anna.'

March 2003

'Hey! I remember, the first time I ever heard about you. It's just come back to me,' Anna says to Ben now.

'When was that?' He looks alarmed.

'I met Dan Givings in the street. Remember, soon after he'd given up that big job on your paper.'

'Fool that he was.' Ben spoke with feeling.

'He came round to see me, soon after. That's when your name came up.'

'I tried to stop him leaving. I thought he was chucking away his future.'

'Dan wasn't – isn't – a journalist. You know that.'

'Come on. You can say it. I can take it. You-think-he's-so-much-better-than-that.' Ben, supremely comfortable in his own skin, triumphantly secure in his chosen profession, is smiling.

'No comment.' Anna grins.

Twenty-two

1996

She had arrived well before the lunchtime rush, she noted with relief, coming out of the tube station. She loved Victoria Street: its anonymity, the bustle around the clock tower. And then the walk up broad, shop-lined pavements towards the river: it was as though the city itself was opening up ahead, laying out its best before and beside her; the glimpse of leafy side streets, lined with mansion blocks or vast grass-lined courtyards through which prep-school boys passed with a sure sense of possession; the European-style piazza that lay before a ginger-and-white-striped Westminster Cathedral. (Even the McDonald's on its far right-hand corner could not ruin it.) Nearing Parliament Square, the sense of sky expanded and the grand silhouettes of state and church, to dominate: Big Ben and the Houses of Parliament, Westminster Abbey and St Margaret's. Her simplest thoughts were imbued with a queer – almost transcendent – significance.

Today, Anna was having a rare day out, leading a group session on 'writing skills' at the headquarters of Roof, Chris's old employer, where Sally remained, as head of publicity and communications. The money earned would buy her a week of writing time, once she had paid her share of the mortgage and food bills. (Such calculations ran constantly, like a looped tape, in her head.) Her session at Roof, whose offices were a couple of hundred yards along Horseferry Road, was due to start at two-thirty; she had arrived early because she wanted to stroll alone, looking in shop windows, have lunch, enjoying this short period of freedom from the demands of young children.

She had just reached the far edge of the Army & Navy store, was wondering whether to nip into Westminster Cathedral for a rejuvenating quick-fix of holy high ceilings and incense, when she became aware of a dark figure, hovering next to her.

'Yes, it is you.'

It was the voice that first registered: it was so similar to Andy's. Dan and Greg Givings had both inherited their father's pleasant bass tones; she would have trouble distinguishing between the three of them on the telephone.

'Do you recognise me?' he said, head cocked to one side. He was dressed in a smart dark suit, no tie, and had a short, dark coat draped over one arm, like a waiter.

'Well, well, well.' It took a moment to surface from her reverie. 'Of course I do!' Of all the crossings on all the roads in London!

'What are *you* doing here?' They spoke the same words, in unison. Then, both laughed.

'Making my way back to my office, after a morning interviewing mad professors,' Dan replied genially. 'And you?'

'Looking to buy a sandwich before going to teach a roomful of housing advice workers the proper use of the colon and semi-colon.'

'Whew!' Dan whistled. 'I could do with some of that.'

'And you – I hear – you changed jobs?' She put a questioning intonation in her voice, even though she knew more than she was letting on.

'Plunged off the promising career ladder into oblivion,' he said cheerfully. She nodded briskly as if to confirm: yes, that was, more or less, what she heard. Dan had recently given up a prestigious reporter's job on one of the big national dailies. According to Anna's mother, whose account could not always be fully trusted, he had simply walked out one morning without explanation.

'A long story.' He seemed reluctant to say more.

They stood, wordless, for a moment or two: a peaceful human island among the urban bustle, as shoppers and office workers poured past them on this autumn lunchtime. Both knew that they could easily carry on swapping pieces of news for five polite minutes. ('And Greg? Still doing his music? And Laura, still with the Israeli film-maker?') The silence confirmed a mutual sense that some more meaningful exchange was possible, if only they could reach beyond this odd category of intimate strangers. They had never had more than a half-hour's conversation in all the years they had known each other, and yet she felt – was it always? or had she only just recognised it? – a deeper bond. A connection that went beyond family habit and history, although all her siblings and parents, even her children, had a 'special feeling' for the Givings. (Only the other day, five-year-old Harry had asked, 'Is Andy my uncle or sort of grandfather?' and she had not known what to answer: 'More of an uncle really,' she had said, eventually.)

But this feeling, out in the autumn daylight, was different. She felt at ease with Dan, could speak to him as a real, sympathetic friend.

'I was rereading "Last Days in Havana" not long ago,' he said now. 'I keep all the back issues of the magazine. I just happened to pick up Spring 1991. I'd forgotten how good it was.'

'Thanks,' she said, wondering if he mentioned this only to be kind. That was five years ago now and she had published nothing since.

'Are you working on anything right now?'

'Funny you should ask. I've just finished writing . . . something much longer. My third child!' she joked.

'Yes, how is the family?' he said quickly, looking embarrassed. Over the years she had figured out the meaning of that stern expression he had worn throughout her wedding ceremony and occasionally at subsequent family gatherings; Dan Givings didn't like Chris. In fact, all the evidence suggested, he disliked him intensely.

'All great,' she waved this side of her life away. And his. (It is not possible to ask a man of any age if he has a girlfriend without seeming both intrusive and critical.)

'I'd love to read it. Your – er – novel? It is a novel, right?' He still had this disconcerting habit of staring at her – down at her, in fact, since he was a good five inches taller – as if she was the most absorbing sight in the world.

Yes, she confirmed, it was a novel.

'But . . . if you'd rather not,' he said quickly.

'Let me think about it.' She had become used to the intense privacy of her writing. Too used to it perhaps.

Dan was fumbling for his wallet. From one of its smaller pockets he pulled out a plain white business card, turned it over and scribbled some lines on the back.

'Here,' he said, thrusting it into her hand as they kissed each other goodbye; polite pecks on the cheek. 'I've put my home address on there.'

She waited until the man in the coffee shop had placed her sandwich and coffee down in front of her before she took out the business card. *Dan Givings. Features writer. Science Today.* Ah, so this was what he was doing now. Her mother, of course, had neglected to pass on the more prosaic details of life after the rejection of Conventional Success.

Interesting.

She put the card down, took a bite of her sandwich, gazing out at the human traffic passing beyond the glass of the café window, thinking about Dan. He had the loveliest eyes. Nothing complicated in that. She could make up their loveliness like a recipe: the dark-eyed gene from his mother (he looked nothing like his father), plus a substantial measure of intelligence and sensitivity of his own. Add to this, a dash of fear. Yes, that was part of the loveliness, too. Because he hadn't stamped on it, pushed it down. Dan Givings had a proper righteous fear of other human beings.

She turned the business card over. Beneath his home address, he had written a few words in an elegant black script. '*I mean it about your book. I would love to read it. And then perhaps we could meet up?*'

She smiled.

Looking again at his address, she did a double-take. Had she known that Dan Givings lived on the same road as her brother Jack?

Twenty-three

'I thought I'd deliver this back in person.'

His first words, standing at the front door, dressed in the same conservative navy suit he had been wearing that day on Victoria Street and rectangular black, heavy-framed glasses, which gave him a spuriously fashionable air. He was holding a parcel containing the manuscript of her novel (which she had sent him in the post, rather reluctantly, a few days after that central London encounter). It always surprised her, his olive skin, the hint of non-Englishness about him – there must be Mediterranean blood somewhere in Clare's ancestry – and that enduring air of vulnerability, which drew her in more than it would once have done. She had had her fill of arrogant, high-achieving men.

'Come in the kitchen,' she said, masking her awkwardness with maternal bossiness.

Obediently, he followed.

While she was filling the kettle at the sink, he said, 'I liked it a lot.'

'Thank you.' She was glad her back was turned, concealing her blush. 'I'm going to try a few publishers and see what they say. It's a total addiction, this writing business. Well, you'd know that.'

'Hardly,' he said, 'being a journalist is different. And I'm not even sure if I *am* that any more.'

'Come through and tell me all about it.'

'By the way, I made a few comments – on a separate sheet of paper. Nothing very significant. Just things that occurred to me as I went along.'

'Thanks,' she said, picking up the two mugs of tea and inclining her head towards the door, indicating that he should follow, adding wistfully, 'I worked bloody hard on those early chapters, trying to get them right.'

'And I think you did,' he said with genuine warmth, 'I stayed up till three in the morning, I couldn't sleep until I had finished it. That's quite an achievement.'

He looked embarrassed at his sudden outburst of enthusiasm.

She led Dan into the living room. They had recently had the wall knocked down between the two front rooms and every time she walked over the threshold, she revelled in the fresh sense of space and light. There was no carpet, just bare floorboards, some cheap pink-and-green rugs covering the bigger gaps that tempted the stray mice that visited them from time to time. All was sweet, dusty chaos as it had been, years ago, in the days after they had first moved in. A small couch, an empty bookcase and a couple of lamps were piled higgledy-piggledy at the garden-end corner.

'Music!' she said, suddenly aware of her bare feet and the silence. 'Do you have any Sam Cooke – or something on the violin?'

Perfect. It was exactly what she would have chosen. It often saddened her that she and Chris didn't much care for the same music. The last track they had both loved was an obscure Tim Buckley song; before that, John Cale's version of Leonard Cohen's *Hallelujah*. These days, it felt too much of an effort to appreciate the singers or groups her husband liked; an extension of wifely duties; as if it was all about *him*. Instead, she permitted herself the luxury of enjoying and expanding her own tastes, CDs she had bought half-price in high-street stores, building up a stack of wholly private preferences.

'Okay,' she said briskly. 'This is my current favourite. It crackles a bit, it's my original record.'

'Called?'

'"A Change is Gonna Come",' she said, dropping the needle onto the black vinyl.

Dan sat on the TV couch, as it was called, the battered, old rose three-seater near the front window. It was strange to see him there. She did not associate him with this life of children and marriage and friends and neighbourhood. Odder still, to see him in the place where Chris sat every evening, and most weekend afternoons, legs sprawled before him, beer in hand, the children crawling on or around him; his regular TV-watching spot. Both men were tall, but Chris was broader, moved more swiftly, with an edge of carelessness. He was a man used to getting his own way, to making an impression. Marriage had enlarged his sexual confidence, made him more, rather than less, conscious of women's attraction to him. Dan was not only younger, and single (as far as she knew). He was an entirely different breed of being: leaner in body, far less sure of himself.

The introduction to the Sam Cooke track was rather grandiose – lush and orchestral – suggesting a big theatrical number. But once he started to sing, the mood changed; what *was* that quality in his thin, reedy voice that nearly reduced her to tears? It was so powerful; this one man – singing, consciously, for his race: denied, pummelled by malign forces, laid low by neglect. Yet even so, he – and they – could rise up (a very Sam Cooke lyric, this). Overcome their fate.

She could see that Dan, too, was moved by the key chord changes, the jagged melody. (In his place, Chris would have mocked her predilection for what he called *sentimental tosh*.)

'So, Dan, I want to know *all*.' She was longing to hear the story of why and how he had quit his job on the famous newspaper. She wanted all the 'gory details', as she and Laura liked to say; to enjoy too, utter self-forgetfulness; the sensation of immersing herself entirely in someone else's tale.

He began falteringly as if to check that yes, she really was interested, she really did want the detail. (She did, she did.) Well . . . he began . . . it had taken most of the three years he spent on the newspaper – his last and most prestigious job in journalism – to work out what felt so wrong. About the job. Or about him in the job. He had come to understand that this was work best suited to someone with a natural scepticism – 'or possibly cynicism,' he added wryly – someone fresh to the world of politics, with no ties and attachments. Andy's prominence, and the connections it brought, had not helped, but hindered him. Everyone on the paper had treated him as if he were an insider, assumed he had a storehouse of political knowledge, an organic connection to all the 'issues'. It was true, he could read political situations accurately; more often than not he knew what was going on, who was saying what and why, both in public and behind the scenes. But it frequently felt like more of a personal knowledge; 'almost psychological,' he said to Anna now with a confiding shyness as if she, the writer, could understand the human dimension better than he. His employers and colleagues had also assumed he had easy access to the powerful within the party. Again, this was true up to a point. It was easy enough for him to get the inside story on whatever was going on over a particular policy argument. He need only listen in to a few conversations between Andy and Matt (who seemed to spend every spare minute at his parents' house these fevered political days) to get the gist of the state of most of the key relationships at the top of the party. Most of his father's colleagues would talk to him off-the-record, trusted him enough to distinguish between what could be reported from what could not, and were happy for him to display some of his privileged knowledge in acceptable ways. *Party insiders suggest . . .*

Dan reaped the benefit of his father's popularity, the long years of his skilled work as a team player. Andy was liked; he was seen as straight, as principled. That Dan could not deploy this inside knowledge to good journalistic effect was entirely down to his personal inhibitions and limitations; increasingly, each conversation he participated in, be it on the performance of a particular politician or a proposed policy, left him exhausted and worn down. He felt he was fast using up personal credit, and for what?

And, there, always, roaring behind his back like an open furnace, were the insatiable demands of the paper, day after day: the demand for news, for analysis, for comment, for contacts, the pressure for that special something which he might bring back – a snippet of gossip, a new angle on an old story, a new story entirely – which, too often, he failed to do. He didn't imagine it, did he, the paper's disappointment at what appeared to be his fatal passivity, compared with the naked hunger, the incredible productivity of his more restless colleagues? He had lost his judgement about that, even.

Ben Calder, his old university friend who worked on the same paper and with far greater success, tried, in clumsy fashion, to psychoanalyse him. 'Stop feeling guilty,' he kept saying, 'about this privilege that's been handed you. By chance, the luck of your genes, you have landed at the centre of public life. You won't be there for ever. Make the most of it. You can get to the real heart of any half-decent political story quicker than the rest of us, if you only want to. Okay, it has its awkward moments. No-one can be completely objective. Andy is a rising star. We all know that. Just don't get so fucking *neurotic* about it.'

On and on Ben went, Dan told Anna now, offering his helpful, utterly useless advice, which only served to emphasise what it took to make a success of such a job – the human detachment that goes hand in hand with true driving ambition – and the fact that he, Dan, did not have it.

'But Ben is the real thing, you see,' Dan told Anna. 'One hundred per cent the real thing. Will do anything for a good story. Charm the birds off the trees to get it. Et cetera, et cetera. All that corny stuff people say about journalists is true about him. He's a lovely guy, but totally driven, a political animal through and through in the sense that he adores the intrigue and the plotting of high politics. He is fascinated by the personalities, but is never fatally drawn to them, except perhaps for the odd passing crush – political crush, I mean – that all good journalists have, they *have* to have, at some time, on a really impressive political figure. Because they are so few and far between. Ben admires Andy, for instance. He really looks up to him. Which of course helps me *enormously.*' Dan smiled sorrowfully.

So here he was, pitched against his good old friend, his old university mate, who could grasp each new configuration of personality, policy and political moment, and could write it all up in lucid, moving or amusing prose as the case required. They loved him at the newspaper; his stock had soared as Dan's had plummeted.

Dan's moment of epiphany came one spring afternoon, earlier that year, walking across Westminster Bridge, nose dripping with the cold. He had just come from a particularly miserable briefing on health policy, unhappy only because he was thinking about its implications for the future; what it would be like if and when the Labour Party got back into power? The Major administration was limping along; it looked perfectly possible that there would be a Labour government before too long. How would he feel when he had to report on government from his own side? Forever torn apart, wooed and wooing, and all for what?

He had long ago lost sight of what he, himself, believed. This he realised standing on Westminster Bridge, the coffee-coloured water moving in foamy torrents beneath his feet, the northern shore of the Thames spread out before him, the dazzling array of black modernist towers, ugly sandy-coloured office blocks, neo-Roman structures, complete with ten-foot-tall pillars, the dome of St Paul's shining solid in the distance, like a benign big brother. If someone had stopped him there and then, asked him whether he thought it was right to raise taxes to fund public services, or in what ways the criminal justice system should be reformed, the kind of news stories he was wearily tapping out on his computer, day after day (stories about what others thought, or pretended they thought), he would not have been able to utter a single word; instead, he would have spoken knowledgeably and fluently (as Ben Calder would speak) of the positions of four or five of the leading members of the Shadow – or real – Cabinet, and what it meant that this one emphasised that aspect of taxation, or that another had not spoken of the importance of jury trials for the past three years. On and on he would have – *could* have – spieled about what other people thought and why, and how they trimmed for the sake of their career or were, not, fundamentally that bright. Judgements of the human jungle that were so easy to make. But of his own views? Nothing! He had been neutered, the best parts of him suppressed. He didn't believe in anything.

And so, about halfway across the bridge – halfway across his very life, it felt at that moment – he took out his mobile and keyed in Ben's number.

'I'm quitting.'

'Are you fucking mad?' Ben, a famously cool character, did not sound that surprised.

'I've worked it out. It's like I'm walking around with a huge great sign on my back. "Connected to . . . Close, but not too close." And there's something else. You're the amateur shrink, Ben, you'll understand this. Some part of my unconscious is furthering my genetic interests. I can't help it. I'm never going to insult a man in print that Andy thinks is a good colleague, or even a lousy one, or write a story that might sink the government. And that makes me useless to Watkins and the paper.'

Sandy Watkins was their news editor, an inspiration to some, but the man they all feared. Except Ben, who did not seem to care a jot what the older man thought. In return, Watkins adored Ben. Treated him like a son.

'Hmmm.'

'You see!'

'I'm thinking.'

'What?'

'Your family – you're not dysfunctional enough – you all like and respect each other – it's unhealthy – shouldn't you be trying to do your old man down?'

'Yeah . . . right.' Dan felt too weary even to convey sarcasm effectively.

'Usurp his power, that sort of thing?'

'Come on, Ben.'

'No, I mean it. You lack the killer instinct, Daniel Givings. You lack the killer instinct.'

It was true. Dan did lack that key, noxious element in ambition. He did not want to cut throats or corners; he prized the delicate threads of human connection, the humour and history he shared with his mother, his father and his brother, the careful relations he had built up with both family and friends. He would rather not work at all than casually or ruthlessly throw over the ties that bind (especially for something as trivial as a good news story). That these emotions felt like failure was all part of the madness of ambition, the craving for professional glory. If that was the killer instinct, he could not pretend to possess it. He had made his mind up.

The next day, he handed in his notice. Watkins clucked at him, with contempt. Ben shook his head, kindly. His parents grieved for him, he knew, but gave him every support. Andy looked stricken, as if this career crisis was somehow his fault.

For the past four months Dan had been working three days a week on a popular weekly scientific journal, writing features on Marie Curie, the history of the discovery of DNA, the inner workings of a locust.

'At least I don't feel tainted. I have my dignity restored.' But, he looked troubled.

'And nobody understands, right? How you could give up the so-called big job?'

Dan shrugged. 'You know what I realised the other day? I was thinking about Ben's point, you know, about the slaying of the metaphorical father. I was thinking, how could I, of all people, ever contemplate slaying my father – metaphorically or otherwise – when I know that he lost his *real* father? I mean, there's death and there's *death*. Andy found out much too young what the real thing felt like. And at some level, I'm still helping him to come through that. I mean, that's quite common, isn't it? A kind of second-generation, survivor guilt.'

'The burden of the eldest son, too.'

'Yes, you're right. Greg seems freer.'

'I mean, look at Matt,' Anna said, glad there was someone with whom she could at last frankly discuss these things; her mother and sister were oblivious to either the politics or psychology of it; Jack, too bitter, too embroiled, too strange. 'Who does he end up making the centre of his professional life? Only his father's great friend. That's weird, too, when you come to think of it.'

'Ah yes, The Terrible Twins,' Dan said, smiling, before explaining 'That's what Mum and I call Matt and Dad: The Terrible Twins.'

'Laura and I call them The Inseparables.' What she didn't add was: *And when Matt's being too full of himself, we call them The Intolerables.*

'Well, they're going to do it. I really think Labour are going to do it.'

Yes, there would be a change of government. Soon. Within the year. And Andy was headed right for the top. Her mother has sent her cuttings about that, too, sombre newsprint lit up by the daffodil-yellow and mint-green highlighters; torn-out strips from Sunday features that tipped him for one of the big jobs some day: Chancellor, Home Secretary, Foreign Secretary. Some even suggested that, one day, he might even become Prime Minister.

'What about Andy? Does *he* have the killer instinct?' She couldn't help asking him.

'Dad? I'm not sure. What do you think?'

She hesitated. Dark thoughts rose up in her, unbidden, and she said, quickly, 'I really don't know.'

'Do you have *The Four Seasons?*' Dan asked, a moment later. 'I feel like listening to a piece of good old-fashioned, corny classical music.'

She went to the mantelpiece where there was a stack of old cassettes lined up. She would recognise the tape as soon as she saw it: she had played the Vivaldi a lot in her mid-to-late-twenties when she was unhappy in a mid-to-late-twenties way.

'Here it is. Sweet, uplifting Vivaldi.'

He smiled. The heavy black frames of his glasses were too domin-ant for his face, she thought. Disconnected sentences floated into her head. *And I saw this man who looked like Yves Saint Laurent. Well, perhaps Philip Larkin is closer to the truth. He was standing by a mantelpiece, and he was staring at me. Eyes boring into me . . .* Words spoken by her mother, long ago. The story of when she first saw Anna's father, across the room at a party in Notting Hill.

'What is it? You look like you've seen a ghost.'

'It's nothing.'

They were listening to the opening bars of Vivaldi's Spring, when the phone started to ring in the kitchen; its insistence somehow increased by being so far away.

'Shouldn't you get that?'

She pretended not to hear him as she came back to sit on the couch. She guessed it was Chris. *Let it ring. I deserve some time off.*

'So how's *your* life going?' he took his cue from her and ignored the persistent trill of the phone.

'Well, it's hard work.'

'That's to be expected, I suppose.'

The phone had stopped, then started up again, the caller's im-patience echoing her own feelings about how relentless her life was, meeting the same demands, day in, day out, leaving her so little time to do the things that mattered.

'It does make me laugh, all that slogging over irony in Jane Austen and the development of Henry James's late prose style at university, when *really* I should have been pumping iron to prepare for all the carrying and lifting, or done a catering course in order to learn how to churn out the same meal six different ways.'

She was trying for a note of levity, but not managing it. Dan sensed that easily, had picked up on the intimation of a far deeper disturbance in her life. It did not displease him. She could see the happy gleam in his eye. *Ah, so you're not so content with the handsome, arrogant Christopher Mason after all.*

'It's really not that simple . . .'

In her guilt at denying Chris and the children, she reached for Dan's hand, in preparation for a short but definitive statement on the compromises of marriage. (She loved Chris, there was no question of that.) Dan's hand was warm and broad in hers; she just had time to register that fact before he gave a shout and jumped away from her, as if he had been electrocuted. His face flushed a dark red.

'Sorry. I . . .' She stuttered.

'No, no, it's nothing.' He turned his head away, like a child, refusing to join in a game.

They sat in silence for a full, agonising minute. The violins were soaring in the background; she gazed at the most perfect azure-blue sky through the front bay, the tree outside their front door waving gently in an unseen, unheard, unfelt breeze. She recalled the sadness of her late twenties, her despairing conviction that nothing would come right for her in love or life. Those days of uncertainty were, surely, long over: the big questions settled for good. Weren't they?

Dan had turned back to face her, his eyes on a fixed far-away point, his tone tremulous, 'You probably have no idea . . .'

The phone had started ringing again.

'Dan, hold on to the thought . . .' she said, kindly. 'It could be – the phone, I mean – something to do with the children.'

The hall tiles felt cool beneath her bare feet; her kitchen, a sharp reminder of a previous life.

Chris sounded irritated. 'You'll never guess what just happened to me . . .'

'No, I guess I won't.'

Did he spot the reluctance in her voice? Her husband had no idea what he had intruded upon, most likely because he assumed there *was* nothing to intrude upon, except, possibly, in his imagination, gangs of tired mothers, chatting and giggling in this same kitchen, in perpetual covert competition over sleep or school places, the look of their houses or their post-natal tummies. In his innermost core he assumed – or wanted, not the same thing, of course – his wife to be waiting there, day in, day out, in a state of suspended animation, anticipating the next exciting bulletin from the embattled front line. But now, she thought, rubbing her thumb over the coiled grey telephone wire, glancing nervously through the open kitchen door down the hall (dreading the bang of the door; her new friend gone): *I am embroiled in a drama of my own. And your phone call, all six minutes of it* – she timed it by the kitchen clock – *is taking me away from an important moment in this story.*

Dan would not stalk out of the house: he was not that sort. He was brisk and impersonal instead, rising almost immediately when she came back in the room, pleading a crucial work appointment. A layer of flesh had been stripped away; glimpses of blood and gristle underneath. Yet the moment, whatever the moment was, had passed. In taking Chris's call she had reminded them both of where her true loyalty lay. Dan, too, had other priorities. Right now, he had to make his way to Euston, where he was expected to file a report on an important conference on current developments in the cure for colon cancer.

Twenty-four

1997

The small, local grocery where she used to buy milk, baked beans, detergent powder and the like was only three streets away, but the walk there and back could be spun out if she was in the mood, peering into other people's front windows, checking out the varying layouts of their front gardens. She much preferred the wilder front spaces sporting a cottage-garden look – tiny, delicate violet and ultramarine-blue flowers, tall pale reeds, waving in the breeze – over the arid paved frontages laid with shop-bought pebbles, a giant beige urn placed neatly middle of the designer rectangle. At this time of the morning there was a steady stream of human traffic heading down towards the Tube station that connected this close-in north-west London suburb with town proper. Anxious-looking young men in suits passed her at unseeing high speed. Women in high heels, dark skirts and red lipstick clattered past her ambling figure. Every other day she passed an intriguingly hybrid figure: a distracted-looking brunette, in her late twenties; dressed in smart dark clothes and low court heels, pushing a buggy helter-skelter down the road. Privately, Anna nicknamed her Sina Thetymes, for she was either a working mother rushing her baby to the childminder or a desperate upmarket nanny out on the first of several manic walks with her charge. Whatever or whoever she was, Sina blanked Anna's rueful smiles, as if threatened by someone so clearly on the downward slide into full-time parenthood.

Five years before, most of the houses in this maze of Kilburn back streets were unfêted, functional. Families, Irish mostly, had lived in these properties for decades, and passed them down to the next generation. In recent years, new money had moved in, taking over whole chunks of the area; not the media millions or trust-fund hundreds and thousands that took up residence in the double-fronted houses round the park, but ambitious young professionals, moving in their droves into these still-modest streets. Many of the squat terraced houses had been split into flats. Anna glimpsed low, pale couches through wood-slatted blinds, manicured gardens beyond. Stuccoed fronts were being stripped away, brick rendered and painted pale blue, lilac, primrose-yellow, the doors a rich plum or navy gloss. The young women who came out of these houses were glossy and well cared for, their children dressed from shiny catalogues. These were the people, she thought, this April morning, that Matt and Andy needed to reach in order to win the general election that was coming in just under a fortnight.

She turned into the parade of shops, a mini high street – but without, yet, either bank or bookshop – dithering between the rundown grocery owned by the bad-tempered old man, wrapped up in a muffler winter and summer, and the brand new delicatessen, with its black marble frontage and the giant glass counter spread with freshly made organic salads, cheeses and meats. Without her make-up and dressed in an old winter coat over her baggy tracksuit, she decided in favour of the grocery.

She took two pints of milk from the humming cold of the back fridge, and a sesame snap for herself. Fumbling in her purse for extra change, she heard an amused voice.

'Is that my sister I see before me?'

She turned, awkwardly, to see Matt, clean-shaven, smiling, the skin beneath his eyes a telltale grape. Tiny silver threads at his temples, a scattering of iron filings.

He was holding two giant shiny-white packets of crisps with a lurid image of a scarlet dried chilli stamped on the front.

'My new addiction,' he said, with a shrug. 'They're ridiculously pricey, but they bring them out in these fantastic flavours. Seaweed and rosemary, cream cheese and coriander . . .' He smiled. 'I must need the salt.'

It was strange; she and Chris lived just ten minutes' walk from

Matt and Janet's house, but they rarely bumped into them. Occasionally the two aunties, Anna and Laura, would take their nephews – Bo and George – out to the cinema or the park or make up a foursome with Anna's two, Harry and Lola, who were a little younger. Late in the day, they would bring them back to the large, perfectly maintained house on the north side of the park. Did it matter, Anna often thought, as she was led into the minimalist living room, offered a glass of mint tea, if she thought the whole house a palace of bad taste? Laura was much less kind. Whenever Janet was out in the kitchen, she hissed critical comments across the room about the fake black-leather sofas or the glass tables with ornate legs, the enormous wall hangings, or rolled her eyes, the Adams' way of indicating sarcasm, at the quasi-royal life-size photographic portraits of the two boys that took up half the living-room wall.

Anna asked now after Janet, Bo and George.

'They're great. Fine. And Chris and . . . the children?'

Could her harassed brother really not remember Harry and Lola's names? She patted him on the shoulder, reassuring him – or maybe herself – that it really didn't matter; he had other things on his mind, they all understood.

'How's it all going?'

This question was the only possible enquiry she could have made or he could have answered on this day. With fewer than fourteen days to go, the ups and downs of the daily battle absorbed him completely. His eyelid began to quiver, a mix of impatience and pure excitement.

'It's going well – don't you think? I think we're in with a real chance. It's incredible to think we might actually *do* it.'

That was the mantra: she suspected he said it a hundred times a day. *It's incredible to think we might actually do it.* As he talked, he paid for his crisps, then ushered his sister out into the street in the manner of a spy thriller. They stood on the pavement; Matt a man of the world with his large de-luxe leather holdall, Anna acutely aware of her saggy-kneed trousers.

'I would have thought,' Matt continued, indicating the shop fronts all around them, 'that it's all wrapped up round here.'

'And on streets like yours?' She couldn't help it; a little sisterly dig at Matt and Janet's grandness.

'Well,' he frowned, 'there too, I guess. A lot of people are putting up posters for us. But it's in the counties and the shires, that's where our credibility will be tested. He's good, don't you think?' He meant Blair now, not Andy. 'He's so straight. He's so *nice*.'

'He looks bloody terrified,' Anna said, and then thought better of it. In Matt's eyes, Blair was God. 'Which you would be. There's so much at stake.'

The pavement was filling up now, with people stopping off on their way to work, to buy cigarettes, train cards, bars of chocolate. Matt edged Anna a few feet along, out of the main stream.

'Have you seen Jack?'

'Not for a bit. I went for lunch with him a while ago. Down at Borough. He's in love, you know.'

'Well, it's not doing him any good.' Matt looked sombre.

'What do you mean?' She felt alarm.

'I had the weirdest visit from him. Seriously *weird*. Honestly, Anna, you might have to look into it.'

There it was again, the old, unexamined assumption within the family that she was something between a detective and a psychiatric nurse; Jack somehow *her* concern.

'What are you talking about?'

Matt glanced at his watch. '*Very* quickly,' he said, if she were detaining him, not the other way round. 'Last Sunday, I held a sort of briefing over at my house. Andy and some journalists. On the school plans we have, should we make it into . . .' – he couldn't quite say the word government or power – 'but a more general get-together. You know, meet and greet. These people are so important to us, Anna.' He named a couple of newspapers, then a columnist Anna had heard of – Susanna Seargent – and an editor Anna had not.

'Anyway, just when the conversation was really getting going, the doorbell goes. Janet gets it, but she doesn't come back for ages. When she comes back in, she mouths "Jack" at me.'

Anna could picture the scene: Janet in her Sunday-lunch, dressed-down political hostess outfit: the stretchy patterned top, her best black trousers, the same clothes possibly that she wore to Anna and Chris's wedding. Fresh highlights in her hair, a pale-pink lipstick. The camel-coloured high heels, the ones with little pointy toes that make her roundness more pronounced. She could see her now, putting delicious little trays of snacks down on the table, refilling glasses of wine, making fresh cups of tea. Smiley.

'She came up and whispered in my ear. Something about how Jack needed to talk to me. About some CDs.'

Matt was munching on his crisps now, cheeks bulging like a hamster.

'What CDs?'

'George Buckley? Jack Buckles? Remember, we used to like some of the same sort of stuff. Years ago, when I actually listened to music.' Matt smiled ruefully.

Anna nodded.

'My first mistake. Not to go out to him. But this briefing was really important. Andy needed me there. So I told Janet to ask him to come back later . . . I *know*.'

Matt gave her at look as if to say: how stupid is that? Anna's heart contracted for him.

'Janet goes out of the room. I hear a door banging, but some-where far away. I know he's left. I don't feel good about it, but I think, "I'm going to ring him later. I'm really going to talk to Jack. Find out what's going on with him." Despite all this . . . political madness in my life. And it is mad, Anna, you've no idea. It's just taken over my life. *I have no life.*' His smile was triumphal. 'Anyway, that's when I hear something out in the garden. This noise. You know that balcony bit at the back?'

Yes, Anna nodded. She knew it: a pair of elegant French windows that opened onto a small wrought-iron balcony overlooking a side alley that ran for about twenty feet along the side of their house, before joining with the (giant) garden proper.

'Susanna Seargent was sitting nearest the window. She leaned back in her chair and said, "I think you've got an intruder in your back yard." And there was Jack at the end of the alleyway bit. Standing there. Doing nothing. It was like we were facing each other in a gun fight. He had the oddest expression on his face. A little smile. You know the annoying Jesusy, martyred smile?'

Anna nodded. She knew the annoying Jesusy, martyred smile.

'You know what he did next? You won't believe this, Anna. He picked up a handful of stones and he *threw* them at the window. Jesus, I did *not* know what to do then. "What the fuck was *that*?" Susanna Seargent jumped up out of her chair. She was really scared. Then Andy got up. He was behind me, looking over my shoulder. He could sense my panic. I was frozen, waiting for a second pebble or, God knows, even a rock.'

Matt hesitated, eyelids half-closing, a shudder running through him.

'Thank Christ for Andy. He was very solid, very calm, turned to everyone in the room. "Would you excuse me for a moment? This is important." And he walks over to the windows, opens them, climbs out onto the balcony, jumps down from there to the ground. It's quite an awkward jump, about four, five feet? He walks along to where Jack is standing and I see them embrace, as if this is the most normal thing in the world, and then he steers Jack around the corner . . . and they're out of sight. And then, only then, do I snap out of it, turn and say, "Look, shall we have a break for just a sec?" And everyone lets out their breath, total relief all round, because they thought, well, you know, it was going to be a *situation*. And we start to gossip, the usual gossip, talk about the latest poll figures.'

Here, Matt trailed off, his eyes filled with tears. He was exhausted.

Now he grabbed his sister's arm, his distress oddly impersonal. 'Any *other* Sunday, I'd have welcomed Jack with open arms . . .' His grip was painful, terribly strong. 'The truth is, we haven't been able to talk politics for years. He's out there. On the street. Out in the cold. Literally. And I'm in here, behind the French windows, cosying up to the rich and powerful.'

He was satirising himself, yet he was deadly serious, too.

'What happened at the end?'

Matt shrugged, a touch hopelessly. 'Andy came back in after ten minutes. We carried on. He told me later he had walked round and round the garden with Jack. Just talking. He told Jack, "I'm sorry. I've kept you away from your brother. Everyone needs their family. I will get Matt to ring you tonight. That's a promise."'

'And did you?'
'Of course I did. I rang him twenty times. Thirty times?'
'And?'
'The usual thing. He never answered.'

March 2003

'Did you stay up all night? On May 1st? You know, in 1997?'

'Well, till dawn . . . just after. Did you?'

'You bet,' he says, smiling. 'I was down on the South Bank, there when Gordon Brown arrived. It was incredible. Every time, I hear that song "Things Can Only Get Better" I get goosebumps. Even now.'

'I took the children with me. To vote.' She had cried, taking her children with her into the polling booth, marking her cross with that stubby pencil on a string. She met a neighbour on the way to the polling booth and he was tearful, too. After eighteen years: a new dawn. That's what it felt like.

Chris had been more sanguine: 'It won't be utopia, you know. It's just another Labour government. And we all know what happens to them.'

'And you're just jealous,' she had fired back, 'because it's someone else's moment, the fruit of their hard work, their risk-taking.' She knew it. He was jealous of Matt. And Andy. This was their moment.

Ben says, 'And Jack, what was he doing?'

'Well, that was the year of the love crisis.'

'What, with the lovely Lucia?'

'Yes — she married someone else. May 1997, as it happened.'

'And was he heartbroken?' Ben smiles, as if to say: We've all been there.

'He was stupefied by it.' She speaks sternly.

'Stupefied?'

Yes, stupefied. The end of Lucia was the end of hope.

Twenty-five

1997

The moment Anna had set eyes on Lucia – a couple of years earlier, on a visit down to the Borough office – she had understood. Jack hadn't a hope in hell with this wide-eyed, curly-haired Anglo-Italian, with her beautiful olive skin and her impressive bosom, dressed in tight-fitting tops and fetching A-line skirts, a high but not too-high heel. Lucia was the kind of young woman supremely, and rightly, confident of her sexual power; she was femininity incarnate, the dream female, immortalised by writers like Philip Roth or Henry Miller, an object surely of perpetual sexual infatuation rather than daily, earth-bound engagement. Men were clearly mesmerised by that full, smooth-skinned body; those bewitching dark eyes, their seductiveness subtly enhanced by the severe tortoiseshell glasses she wore when in work mode. In that drab, depressing building, dedicated to good works, she was the nearest thing to a goddess that existed.

Everyone at the office knew that she was engaged to a dentist in Edmonton and that she was going to quit her job, as soon as she could, settle down and have 'lotsabeautifulbambinos'. (She would pretend to stir a giant saucepan of pasta when she said this, making fun of her own longed-for future.) But in his myopic arrogance, Jack did not seem to absorb this fact so widely known among his workmates. It did not help that he was something of a loner at work; oblivious to much of the daily gossip. He could register only the intensity of his own feelings, was completely hooked on this alluring beauty who possessed a supreme talent –

Anna saw this straight away – for spotting and exploiting the weakness of those around her.

She had to acknowledge, her brother had some grounds for his pathetic hopes. He and Lucia lunched every Friday (an established habit he was reluctant to break, even for Anna). He and Lucia 'frequently' went for a drink after work, but how 'frequently' it was not possible to establish. Jack insisted their contact was 'fevered', a mutual understanding quickly established, constantly developing. He thought her potentially brilliant, but totally untutored, and had therefore prescribed her a daily diet of broadsheets to further sharpen her native wits. He had drawn up long lists of books, fiction and non-fiction that he considered required reading (shades of his father, here, the didactic intellectual). No, he did not know if she actually read any of this stuff; she never said; he never asked. Instead, she preferred to talk, rather wistfully, of her grandparents, whom she adored, and of her mother and father and her two brothers, and of her dreams for the future, omitting, obviously, the most crucial pieces of personal information: her relations with the faithful dentist and their wedding plans, which included a huge party in a restaurant near her parental home and a honeymoon in the Canaries.

But what was behind Lucia's attraction to Jack? Anna's mother and sister, hearing about the affair through Anna, simply could not understand why any woman, let alone an attractive one, would be drawn to someone whom, in his absence from their daily life, they caricatured as overweight, antisocial, crude and rude. They did not understand that Lucia touched a masculine nerve in him, brought out – finally! – the showier, peacock side of his personality. Plus, as Anna reminded them, there is always something compelling about a man who is in love, or lust, or both, especially a man of such intellectual certainty and emotional intensity.

His mother and sister also knew little of his reputation at work. Jack was respected for the way he handled people on the street. Anna had seen it for herself when he had taken her out a couple of times, late at night, to meet the rough sleepers he worked with in the Strand or round the Bullring. Like a kind, attentive uncle, his pockets were always full of treats: the right newspaper, a favourite brand of cigarettes or bar of chocolate, cans of beer, although this was strictly against the rules. Here, in this other world, he displayed skills he so deliberately refused to employ in the ordinary, daylight world. Here, he could judge exactly who people were and what they needed; under cover of night, he was a man of exquisite, tender manners, a seemingly inexhaustible well of human kindness. During those evenings – shaking with cold, even though she was wrapped up in Chris's massive fur-lined parka – Anna developed a much deeper understanding of, and respect for, her brother. She fervently hoped he could channel the pointless anger directed at so-called 'middle-class values' and build a life for himself based on his own, rougher-hewn talents. Small chance. For back inside the housing charity's office, south of the river (a sick building if ever there was one, a concrete structure that seemed to leach the life out of whoever had the misfortune to work there), he once again lost his touch. That Lucia became increasingly unavailable to meet outside work time was – bizarrely, infuriatingly – taken as proof of her growing involvement with him, rather than a clear sign that the relationship was severely limited from her point of view. Not once, right up until the last moment, would he have dreamed of seeing her 'as a two-timing little vixen, stringing along a doting idiot' – Laura's typically charitable description of the unhappy love triangle of Lucia, the Edmonton dentist and their brother.

The predictable climax to this unfortunate office affair came in April, two days before the stone-throwing incident at Matt's house, and clearly the direct cause of that strange, sad episode.

The end – as Jack took to calling it with portentous drama, in later years – came on a Friday afternoon, around three o'clock. (Although it was a couple of years before he told Anna the full details of what happened.) Jack and Lucia had had their weekly lunch and she, as usual, had delighted him with her sharp observations of everyone in the office, especially the managers, whom they both despised. There were her familiar, funny stories about her parents, who still behaved as if they were living in a southern Italian village.

'But,' Jack told Anna, much later, 'I could tell something was up. She was unusually hesitant. Uncomfortable about something.'

Back at the office, Jack sat at his desk, trying not to fall asleep. Drowsing, he saw Lucia get up and cross the floor, to talk to a colleague seated a few desks away. Surreptitiously, she handed over a long, slim white envelope. His curiosity aroused, he pretended he had not seen anything while Lucia went back to her desk, turning and putting a finger to her lips, to warn her friend. But Lucia's friend was already ripping open the envelope; a soft, cooing sound issued from her lips, 'the kind of soppy noise stupid people make about kittens or babies,' said Jack. Soon after, she propped the white card up against her keyboard.

'Seventeen minutes,' Jack told Anna, 'seventeen minutes I had to wait, until this bloody woman went to the toilet, or whatever it was that took her away from her work station, and I could walk past her desk and see what was on that white card.'

It said everything about Jack that he had not guessed after seventeen seconds what was on that card. (Anna had understood the significance of the white envelope straight away.) Sure enough, the card had serrated edges and embossed gold writing on it. In fancy lettering it said, 'Lucia and Michael request the pleasure of your company at a lunch to celebrate their wedding.' Followed by the address of a nice Italian restaurant in Islington, run by a friend of Lucia's aunt by marriage. 'And do you know what I did?' Jack told Anna, 'I picked up the card, and I tore it in half. And then I tore it in quarters. And then I took all the pieces, cradled in the palm of my hand, and I went over to her desk and I gave her each piece. One by one. Little frayed pieces of white card . . . And then I walked out of the building.'

And never went back.

Two days later, he went to visit Matt, taking his older brother the Jeff Buckley *Grace* CD. The day after, he disappeared, although the family did not discover this until later in the week, when the head of human resources rang Anna's mother at home.

There was nothing anyone could do. He was a forty-year-old man, who had voluntarily left his job and his home. He could be anywhere. Or nowhere.

Time passed. Ordinary time. Political time. Labour won a landslide victory. Andy regained his seat, with a massively increased majority. His count was featured live on both ITV and BBC; he did a tour of the TV studios, at dawn, laughing with the Dimblebies and the Paxmans, the most relaxed that Anna had ever seen him onscreen. Later that morning, Tony and Cherie – she dressed in a wide-collared rust two-piece – shook party workers' hands with affectionate enthusiasm on an unseasonably warm Friday, as they took the short walk from Whitehall to the door of Number Ten.

Anna stayed up most of the night, hoping Jack might ring and they could laugh in that way only they did – if Jack was in the right mood – about the pretensions of the public world.

Matt telephoned in a state of high excitement, from the South Bank. The next day he began his new job as senior special adviser to the new minister for education. She congratulated him warmly.

When, in early summer, Harry celebrated his sixth birthday, there was no word from his uncle. A few weeks later Lola turned four. Still, no word from Jack.

Autumn passed.

By now Anna was convinced that her brother was dead. She felt sick when the phone or the doorbell rang. She could barely work. Waiting: for the shadow of a policeman at the door. (In dreams, he looked like Andy, rosy-cheeked with nerves on that first-ever visit, back in 1971, merging sometimes with the face of the handsome young officer who had brought her swollen-lipped brother back from The Ladbroke Lady all those years ago) She tried not to think of him, laid out somewhere, on a railway line, sheltering from the rain or cold.

From the sound of her mother's voice on the telephone – they spoke daily during these months, bound closer by their mutual fear – she knew that she, too, awaited bad news. Over and over her mother fretted, 'I could accept the worst, you know. It's the not knowing I can't stand.'

The trees were stripped of their leaves and the sky a blank paper-white on the November day that the phone rang. Anna was folding laundry in her bedroom while Harry and Lola watched television in the front room.

When she picked up the phone she thought of the day Chris

interrupted her talk with Dan Givings, how unresolved that still felt, how sad she was that he had not visited again, how much she wished it was him, calling now.

'Hello?'

'Anna. It's me.'

Soon after, the e-mails began.

November 26 1997
from: Jack777@callme.dot.com
to: AAdams.@worldonline.co.uk
subject: direct action

Now that the end has come, I am going to set aside the personal. You must remind me if I weaken.

I went to see Peter T. talk the other day. He has given his adult life, twenty years of it, no, more, to direct action. He's a good speaker. A bit of a ranter. Square, clean-cut. Much too thin. He looks like a puppet, a cartoon version of himself. You cannot wait, he said, for those in power to give to those without power. Everything must be taken, fought for. All that time I was working with people on the street, I could never work out really why they didn't take something for themselves. RISE UP like the revolutionary mob of old. At least terrorise the comfortable class. But the language of the entire enterprise was passive. It infected them. It was bound to. We will help the poor dirty ragged ones. To get some shitty job. To live some small unthreatening contained life somewhere. Challenging nothing and no-one. It's like my eyes are opening.

I felt a bit of an impostor at the meeting. I feel a bit of an impostor at every meeting. A couple of hatchet-faced far-left types dominated the discussion afterwards. Why do these people not smile more? And why is their language so impoverished? Everyone is a traitor. Governments by definition are betrayers. Their hatred of Blair and Co. unbounded. Already. They would lynch Matt and Andy without a second thought. And they've hardly been in the job for a few months. Idly wondered if I should mention what Matt does, to annoy them. Wanted to annoy them. Then decided, it's not really relevant. How important are any of us, in the great scheme of things?

November 28 1997
from: Jack777@callme.dot.com
to: AAdams@worldonline.co.uk
subject: neighbour noise

Domestic problems. The upstairs neighbours – the flats so close in this building you can hear everything. Used to hear them SEXING – do you remember that's what we used to call it as children??? – and now could hear them battling. The young wife was screaming. YOU'RE FUCKING SUSIE AREN'T YOU? YOU'RE FUCKING HER AREN'T YOU? She was screaming the same sentence over and over again, it was like a back beat to a disco track. You could tell he was guilty, his voice was dripping with the stuff, full of evasions and suppressed guilt. I wanted to go upstairs and say: 'Look. Everyone in this building must know it by now. You clearly *are* fucking Susie. Just come clean and admit it. It will be easier in the long run.' They argued almost the whole night, and all the way through I was just afraid that one would kill the other and I was going to have to give evidence in a court – I swear, by almighty God, blah-blah – and then it went silent at dawn, with the twittery birds, and I was afraid that it had happened. One of them was dead. Him, most likely. She sounded homicidal.

December 10 1997
from: Jack777@callme.dot.com
to: AAdams@worldonline.co.uk
subject: of all the joints in all the world

You WON'T believe it, Anna. You won't believe it. I went to the doctor's today and anyway . . . wait, a bit of back story. I told you, didn't I, that she has put me on medication. On and off for some time now. The sleeplessness. All the crazy L. stuff, she said, just get some help, get through it. Sensible I suppose. I have been seeing the same GP for twenty years because I am essentially so unadventurous. (Matt would instruct me to shop around, to set my local doctors against each other, in this vast competition that is called life . . .) Her name is Audrey. She is large, beady-eyed, deep-voiced, tries to be kind, probably a dyke. What I like about her is that for years she used to tell me to read books, not pills, she used to say, This is a problem with the way you think about life, not a problem with you. OK, OK, her book choice is a bit crappy, seeing as she is part of the vast softcounselling brigade that march across our nation. Make me long for élitist Viennese professors with a couch covered in a carpet, a true Freudian. Five sessions a week until you're sinking in the unconscious stuff. Better that than these, think-positively, turn-the-situation-around types. They make me want to scream. (More plans to create little lives that threaten no-one. LEARN HOW TO ENJOY YOURSELF! WHY ARE YOU SO ANGRY WITH YOUR HUSBAND/YOUR EMPLOYER? YOUR PARENTS? WITH GOOD REASON I SAY.) Anyway back story over . . . I was there to get my next issue of pills, to talk over how things were. And Dr Audrey was a bit distracted and a bit dressed up, in a pale trouser suit, and she said, Look, you'll laugh at this, but we're having the new wing of our surgery opened today, and the Prime Minister and his wife are touring the surgery. They'll be here . . . they'll be here . . . She looked at her watch, and just then, we heard voices out in the corridor and she said, without missing a beat, Well, that will be them then! I said, You are kidding me. She said, No, we wrote to them, the practice manager wrote to Cherie I think, and they replied within forty-eight hours, saying, Yes, we will come and cut the ribbon. I said, Hasn't he got a country to run? Dr Audrey said, straight-faced?, Allegedly (But I could see that she was excited, really). I said, It's the cut in single parent benefit, isn't it? The vote is today. They'll want to be seen talking to a single parent who doesn't look cut-back. She said, I couldn't possibly comment. But film cameras will be down in the reception, in about – she looked at her watch again – twenty minutes. If you want to hang around and shake hands. I said, I'm not a single parent. But I AM single . . .

Cut to the chase . . . I did hang around, reading leaflets on testicular cancer and how to give up smoking, and eventually, Les Blairos came down the stairs like Fred and Ginger. You know what struck me, the only thing, apart from the rictal grins, was how orange they both looked. They were positively tangerine. Like Liberace. (Is that necessary? For the TV and all that?) And then they start nodding-dog their way round the reception. Straight to a young black woman with a child, asleep in a pram. And then I scarpered.

Forget Matt. Who among us all is always at the heart of political events????????????

March 2003

'He didn't go back to work. Any sort of work. He lived off benefits – which disgusted Dad – and some savings. I think he had saved a bit of money. And he became more involved in direct action. It was like . . .' She hesitates.

'Yes?'

'It was like, Matt had embarked on this exciting political venture. Was at the heart of things. And Jack wanted to be at the heart of things, too. In his own way.'

'Simple sibling competition.'

'Well, I would never the use word "simple",' she snaps. 'Nor go in for any easy psychology. Whatever the motivation, he decided to give everything over to his "gestures". To making a difference. And that's when the e-mails began.'

'Yes, you said.'

'I brought some for you to see.'

'Great.'

'They were funny, actually.'

'What funny ha-ha? Or funny peculiar?'

'Both.'

Yes, that's exactly what they were.

Twenty-six

They were all there, apart from Jack, that Christmas Eve: the original two families plus girlfriends, wives, husbands, grand-children; gathered for present-opening in the front living room, then moving through to the dining room proper, to sit, grouped around the grand oak table festooned with holly, a large shiny red or green cracker at every place setting. Anna felt herself nudged by the complex claims of the past – relief at Jack's return had given way to emotional exhaustion; she could see that her father, too, felt alienation from the high spirits of this evening, ensconced in the large cream armchair he had made his own, still sprightly despite his advancing age, dressed in a beautifully pressed pale-blue shirt and black trousers.

Anna stopped in front of his chair, from where he was benignly watching his four grandchildren – Harry and Lola, Matt and Janet's boys – joyfully ripping open the presents left beneath the tree.

'Refill, Dad?' He liked his gin and tonic.

He had refused, his look of fondness almost conspiratorial; as if to say: *You and I, Anna, we understand too many things to partici-pate with unambiguous joy, with no irony, in an occasion like this.*

But he was wrong to assume her complicity in family matters. Marriage had changed Anna. Her mother's vain attempts at marital closeness struck her as poignant, even heroic, rather than silly; she was more critical, these days, of her father's withdrawal, the way he recoiled from his wife's loving touch. Any show of husbandly coolness infuriated her. She wanted to take him aside, lecture him gently: *Can't you see, a family only ever works if the original couple are united, the first pairing stronger in some way than all the relations spawned from it?* Her father's immersion in his books was another part of the puzzle. How often had he lent Anna a novel or wanted to read her a poem brimming with a human feeling and understanding that he so signally failed to convey in his own, most intimate relations? Only the other day, he had told her she must read, or reread (if she knew it already), the Henry James story 'The Middle Years'. She had been happy to oblige – his recommendations were always good – and had picked up the book when she was in the mood for a bit of Jamesian prose. There, on the second page, she had read of the young man walking the beach, immersed in a book, oblivious to the apparent drama of a young woman just ahead. 'So that while the romance of life stood neglected at his side he lost himself in that of the circulating library.' Reading that sentence – twice, quickly – Anna sat up straight, thinking: *How true that is of my father, not over a minute or two, but over a whole lifetime. His soul, buried in the storehouse of his library, oblivious to the treasure of human relations. Blindly unseeing of his wife's desperate jollity, her deep need, her deep sadness.*

With compassion, she watched her mother working the room. She was dressed in a fitted dark-green silk dress with a bow at the neck (a tiny triangle of sweat beneath her arms: the result of her usual tireless Christmas labours), and wearing a scarlet party hat that matched the unnaturally high colour of her cheeks. She was still lovely, with her dyed chestnut-brown hair, her heart-shaped face, her high cheekbones, her make-up damp in the overheated house. Quietly happy (at Jack's safe return) and delighted tonight at the presence of the minister and his wife, *our old dear friends the Givings*. There was a gentle snobbery and general foolishness in her hostess's pleasure, yes, but there was also deep generosity there in the constant provision of food and drink, in her fastidious care for the way everything looked, in the steady stream of conversation, however light; in her approval, however indiscriminate, of the vast majority of her family. If Anna's father had supplied a greater share of generosity, it might have freed his wife to irony, ribaldry, sharper perceptions. Had that ever occurred to the man who adored the dense, high art of Henry James?

At dinner, Andy sat at her father's right-hand side, deferring with an almost saccharine sweetness to his old friend, asking pointed questions about cases and ex-colleagues: forever playing the reverent junior to the experienced master.

She had heard Andy tell her father earlier that Matt was 'extremely highly regarded . . . He's got excellent political judgement. First-class. He doesn't want the limelight, which is extremely refreshing. He wants to get the thing right.'

And she had seen her father smile, a small, irritatingly mysterious Jack-like smile as if to say (she knew): *Like father, like son.*

Up until his late forties, Andy had had a full head of light-chestnut hair. After his election to Parliament it had become flecked with grey; the light spittle of ageing. Now in government, the grey had mysteriously vanished: Andy's hair was once more a gleaming, warm brown. Anna peered at the hairline, trying to spot the greying roots. No luck. It had been recently, and professionally, done, and must be retouched regularly, she guessed: efforts that signified an extraordinary, determined vanity she would once have thought quite out of character.

Another thing she noticed. Twice during the meal Andy leaned back rather perilously, in his chair, stretching his arm across the back of it in order to stroke the arm of his wife, who was sitting two places away from him. Such shows of affection, undoubtedly genuine, were also just that: shows. Was it the first time she had noticed this? Or was she getting cynical in her own middle years? Andy often winked at Clare across a room, or hooked his arm around her waist, when they were standing together, or planted a noisy kiss on her cheek. 'A smacker' as he called it.

'Hey!' he said now, leaning his chair back for a third time, trying to catch her attention, 'Remember! I want my moment under the mistletoe.'

'You'll be lucky,' she laughed, catching his hand on her shoulder, holding it there for just a couple of seconds.

Clare was positively stout. She wore a frumpy black frock and there was, these days, an inch-wide white streak down her centre parting. It made her look like a friendly badger. A senior lecturer in politics at a London university, her professional achievements were barely mentioned, few questions asked directly of her. Andy's growing fame was now the clear, if unspoken, focus of these family occasions.

Yet her good humour remained unflagging, her affection for her husband apparently undimmed. Anna guessed that it came down to one simple fact: show or not, she clearly knew that she was loved. And they must all – Anna's mother included – bear witness to this grand, enduring love affair.

'What is this gin rummy stuff your mother gives me?' Ari, her sister's partner, barked at Anna early in the evening. 'It's like drinking petrol.'

Anna liked Ari: he eschewed conventional politeness, and there was something primitive in his use of the English language, which often sat comically with the sophisticated nature of his observations.

'It's a gin and tonic. Not gin rummy. Gin rummy is a *card* game.'

'Gin makes people sad. Why do English people always want to be sad?'

'Something to do with the weather?'

'Oh, the weather! Another thing they'd rather go on about. The weather and how to make a good cream sauce. Anything rather than talk about politics or ideas.'

'You think?'

'I adore your mother, Anna, but she would do anything to avoid a serious conversation. Food, furnishings, fornication . . .'

'Fornication? Now you are joking!'

'All right. Not sex. Never sex. But still, she loves the trivia, your mother. I say this to Laura and she says, "I know, it drives us all mad." . . . But you know, Laura, she is a little bit the same.'

It was the first time Anna had ever heard Ari criticise her sister.

Slivers of pale turkey meat were handed round on a giant silver platter.

'So tell me, guys,' Chris said, as he held the dish steady for

Greg's girlfriend, a pretty brunette who worked at Greg's record company, 'I mean, *really* tell me. That was a huge mistake, you must admit, cutting benefit to single mothers?'

Anna had not seen this coming, although it did not entirely surprise her. Her husband had been incensed at the government's stand on single parents, had hinted earlier that he planned to raise the matter in some form.

'In what sense an error?' Matt, sitting directly opposite Chris, responded with icy politeness, taking a spoonful of glistening peas from an earthenware bowl at the centre of the table.

'I know you had to reassure Middle England, but really . . .'

'It was a manifesto promise,' Andy intervened with good-humoured sternness from his end of the table. 'We promised not to exceed existing government spending limits. For two years. To be credible, we must honour that promise.'

'Yes. Yes. We get it.' Ari was waving his fork in the air. 'You people need to look like the evil old rightist government, so no-one thinks you are an evil old leftist regime.'

A collective pause, a silent sigh, at the foreigner's gross exaggeration.

'*Evil?*' Matt said irritably.

'It's absolutely crazy!' Chris was crosser now. 'Taking money away from poor mothers, just to keep a spending promise?'

'It is fairly important that this government, of all governments, honours its election commitments, actually,' Matt said carefully. 'It's a matter of trust.'

'I have wondered,' Anna's father said, in a carefully neutral tone, 'is this really going to be the general direction of your economic policy?'

Anna's mother rose, muttering lightly, to fetch more turkey from a sideboard, while Andy, turned to Anna's father, said, 'It's so easy to take a romantic position on the welfare state. Tax and spend. The Old Labour problem. We're trying to do something different. To build a sound welfare state around the idea of the work ethic.'

'But that's what I mean. It's so insulting. It's just so incredibly insulting.' Chris was almost shouting now. 'To suggest that single parents, of all people, do not understand the work ethic.'

His own personal history was in here, of course it was. But

Anna wondered if her father and brother – and Andy – had ever taken in this information. After all, she was only Anna, and he, just her husband.

'All right, Chris,' her father said firmly but kindly. (Yes – he had remembered; she felt a rush of gratitude.) For a moment it was like the old days, her father's authority restored.

Chris was calmer now. 'Perhaps a lone parent does have to be reliant on the state from time to time – so what? That's what the state's *for*.'

'It's certainly not there to punish,' David added.

'We're not punishing anyone, Dad,' Matt said drily.

'Hear, hear!' said Janet, who was cutting up her children's meat into cubes the size of postage stamps.

'We're really trying to do things differently,' Matt went on, ignoring his wife's cheerleading. 'It's about the reciprocity between government and citizen.'

Andy was nodding, solemnly.

Chris said, '*Responsibility. Reciprocity.* These words are f—— meaningless.' (Thank God he had edited out a 'fucking', at the very last moment.) 'Set against a cut of eleven pounds a week.'

'Oh, come on,' Andy was roused to anger now, 'this is just pure romanticism. Or passivity. "Let the state pay out for everything. We deserve it." There's a contract underlying the relationship between every citizen and the government and, like all contracts, there are conditions attached.'

'And there's a contract underlying the relationship between a mother and her child and, like all contracts, there are conditions attached. And one of those conditions is that the parent, particularly the parent who is the *only* parent, be allowed to spend time with their children in their early years. God knows, the rich can do it. In fact, we positively laud the mothers of Middle England who stay at home.'

'Good point,' said Ari, nodding enthusiastically.

Andy looked at Chris with a cold, irritated expression. But Chris was on a roll, failing to notice any change in the other men's mood. 'Frankly, you'd be better off chasing the deadbeat dads who aren't supporting their offspring than punishing the mothers who stayed put.'

'The hand that rocks the cradles,' sighed Ari.

'Ah!' said Andy, with a patronising jocularity forced from the iciness. 'Ah! Now *there's* a good idea.'

He turned to David, a deliberate move to block further interventions from Chris, to cut the argument off at its source. 'Now, David, what would you think of a policy that concentrated on the father's contribution to family life, but wasn't the disastrous Child Support Agency? How might we make *that* work?'

'More meat anyone?' Fiona firmly finished off the dispute by thrusting two more platters into the middle of the table. 'Please, everyone, there's so much!'

Getting up to help her mother, Laura wrested the silver dish from her hands too forcefully, turned her heel on the shiny floor and executed a distorted, wild little dance of survival before losing her grasp of the plate. Fiona gave a high-pitched shriek, but saved the platter at just a foot from the floor, like a fielder making a fine catch.

'Don't worry everyone,' Laura said, rather too emphatically, struggling up to standing position, 'I'm absolutely fine.'

But Anna could see her wince with pain when she sat back down at the table. Ari patted her arm without conviction, then poured out a large glass of spring water, which he handed over to her, like a parent soothing a child. She smiled edgily, and gulped it down. When she had finished her water, he patted her arm again, and raised his eyebrow in the directon of the wine bottle: meaning, *no more*. Ari had strong views on women and alcohol, as strong as Chris's views on women and smoking.

For a minute, Anna saw her sister and herself, from above, as if bound by a tiny, vibrating wire, incarcerated within neighbouring, invisible cages.

Twenty-seven

All evening, Anna's mind kept returning to that half-ignited argument, reflecting not on those who had spoken, but on those who had kept silent. The women. The mothers. Herself, Janet, Fiona, busy attending to their children's plates or nervously measuring the subtle changes in the emotional temperature while the men slugged it out, largely unconscious of the effect on the others. And all over the public politics of the family! It annoyed her, more than she felt it should. Moving now, at the evening's end, to gather up the children's stray belongings, she felt resentment which she tried internally to recast as amusement.

She was acutely aware of Chris, still sitting in the living room, sprawled on the largest couch, listening to Ari talk about the struggles he was having to get his magnum opus made.

Odd words and phrases drifted out from the front room into the hall where she was piling the children's Christmas presents into a plastic bag, ready to take home.

'. . . A domestic comedy – illustrating the ridiculousness of family relations – in a political context.' This, from Ari.

The next thing she heard was 'showing up . . . matriarchal controlling behaviour'.

'Tell me about it,' Chris said with a laugh.

Outside, alone in the hall, Anna made a face of exaggerated fury and irritation. '*Arsehole.*'

Suddenly, Dan appeared out of nowhere. She had the distinct impression he had been waiting for her, lurking in the shadows, near the top of the stairs that led down to the kitchen.

'That was a close thing.' She was embarrassed at being caught out abusing her husband out of earshot.

But Dan assumed she was referring to the bad-tempered squabble during dinner.

'It's pretty late,' she said lamely, 'I've got to get our stuff from upstairs.'

'I'll come up with you.'

He walked up the staircase behind her, humming gently. Everyone had left their coats and bags in her parents' bedroom. A low side light threw out a diffused honey glow. It reminded her of parties when she was a teenager, dark rooms filled with mysterious heaving life, bodies entwined under the dark covers, teenagers 'getting off together'. Tonight, the bed was swamped with nothing more than sensible outdoor clothes: coats, raincoats, scarves and bags. Anna began rooting through the mass for her family's belongings, recounting (to Dan, who seemed interested) the detail of a recent letter of rejection from a publisher, her last attempt, she told him now, to send out the novel he had read in manuscript form.

'I'm reconciled to it now,' she said, pushing a heavy leather jacket (Greg's) aside, in order to dig for her children's coats beneath. 'I really am. I'm well into the next one. Time to move on.'

'Anna, I love you.'

He spoke these words in such an ordinary voice, she did not take in their meaning for a few seconds. She turned, still holding the children's coats, just to check that he had spoken after all. His face was contorted with such anguished uncertainty that she knew he had.

He added hurriedly, 'You did know that, didn't you?'

An image suddenly entered her head.

'*Betrayal.*'

'*What?*'

'That scene in *Betrayal.* The film of the Pinter play? Haven't you seen it? The story of the love affair, which begins at the end of the story, and ends at the beginning.'

'What about it?'

'Don't you remember? Jeremy Irons comes into the bedroom where wotshername is brushing her hair while the party is going on downstairs, and he says, "You know I adore you." Or words to that effect. And we already know that they will have a long affair and that it will end in disaster.'

'I'm not asking anything of you.'

'Yes, I know,' she said kindly. For she did know that. Just as she had known, for a long time really, that Dan Givings loved her, certainly since that day he had come to return the manuscript. Perhaps much longer.

'I loved that film,' she said now, conscious of a low flame of happiness, burning inside her. 'Do you remember that bit where the lovers are talking about throwing a child up into the air in a kitchen, but because they are so fuddled by deceit they can't remember whose child it was, and whose kitchen?' She was gabbling now. 'And that time when her husband discovers that her lover has been writing to her, when they are on holiday in Venice, and she tries to pretend they are just friends? What was the name of that actress?'

'Hodge. Patricia Hodge.' Dan sounded sullen.

'Yes, and Ben Kingsley plays the deceived husband. Ben Kingsley is *brilliant*.'

The sound of feet – heavy feet – coming up the stairs. Thud. Thud. Anna and Dan stepped apart as the door was pushed open.

It was Janet.

'Hello, all,' she said, yawning. 'I'm going to take mine off. Stockings to stuff. Reindeers to feed. It's always a long night.'

'Yes, it is, isn't it?' Anna said, mother to mother.

Janet started digging for her belongings while Dan and Anna stood back, smiling at each other across the bed. After a few minutes Janet staggered out under the weight of four sets of outdoor clothes, topped by her own white-wool winter coat and a tartan throw.

'Night, all,' she said cheerily, 'have a really good one.'

When she had gone, Anna turned to Dan and said, 'Please don't not visit. I mean, please come and see me again. You will, won't you?'

'Yes, all right.' He looked defeated.

'Good. Then. That will do. For now.'

Downstairs, Chris and Ari were still sprawled on the living room couch. Anna was wearily aware of the amount Chris had drunk that night: a bottle and a half of wine at least. He could not possibly drive. She worked quietly around them, gathering up the remains of the presents (her mother always gave the children far too much), stuffing the wrapping paper into empty plastic bags she had fetched earlier from the kitchen.

Lola sat glassy-eyed, thumb in mouth, on her father's lap.

Harry, playing on the floor near the Christmas tree, was sulking; she could see it in the set of his jaw.

'Chris,' she said, 'we should probably take the kids home now.'

Dan said from behind her, 'Do you want a hand with taking stuff out to the car?'

'Thanks,' she said quickly. Then, to Chris again, in a stagey voice, 'Chris – I'm – putting – the children – in – the – car – now.'

'Yeah, okay.' He barely looked up, was deep in his conversation with Ari, a discussion brimming with black-and-white certainties and complaints, about politicians and peace settlements, tax policies and income inequalities. Fucking this, fucking that. Corruption. Betrayal. Useless bunch.

It took Anna and Dan a full five minutes going back and forth to load up the car. Dan held the door while she put the children in their car seats, and leaned over to strap them in. She found them especially lovable when they were this tired. Lola had her thumb in her mouth before the buckle had even engaged, her eyelids drooping.

'Christmas tomorrow, Mummy,' she said, before falling fast asleep.

'Now, what are you *really* hoping for tomorrow, Hal?' she said to her angry-looking six-and-a-half-year old son, who was on the brink of exhausted tears. 'Give me a list. In order. What you'd like *most*.'

'Difficult, Mummy,' he answered seriously, his good temper temporarily restored by the challenge. 'You go get Daddy and I'll tell you both when you get back in the car.'

'Will do,' she said, dashing back through her parents' front door. Just then, Chris emerged from the living room looking rumpled.

'God, I'm completely exhausted,' he said, chucking her the car keys.

They said their goodbyes to all the family – although Anna could not find Dan anywhere; he seemed to have disappeared – and walked back out to their car, Anna keenly aware of the distance she was keeping from her yawning, drunken spouse. She felt masterful, vaguely deceitful, excited, a little sad.

Harry's wide eyes watched them from the back of the car.

'And it all starts up again at dawn,' Chris sighed, yawning again.

Anna placed the key into the driver's side door. But before she could climb in the car, Chris pulled her close, arms wrapped around her body, and murmured, 'Don't think I don't realise how lucky I am to have all this. To have *you*.'

Instantly, her heart melted and her anger blew away. At the same time, her mental picture of Dan's anguished look of love – so comforting up to now – dimmed: just a fraction.

'Love you, Anna,' Chris mumbled.

'I love you too,' she said crisply, although she hated it when he omitted the personal pronoun, that all important 'I': the most crucial part of that age-old three-word sentence. For without it, what is there? No subject, no emotion; no subject, no real object. Her brisk tone was the only clue to such angry thoughts, but it was wasted on Chris – tonight – who failed to notice the slightest difficulty and merely held her tighter, belching with marital contentment.

Twenty-eight

They sat and talked quietly, husband and wife, hands loosely linked across the table: a rare weekday lunch in a small French restaurant in Marylebone: to mark the tenth anniversary of their meeting in the Paradise Club, an anniversary of equal, if not greater importance (in their personal mythology) than their wedding day. The tables were spread with a rose-and-white checked tablecloth ; the wine came in rich blue earthenware jugs. Their table was snug, in a corner, beneath criss-crossing dark wooden beams. The restaurant was a low-ceilinged series of interconnecting rooms, the kind of place, Anna joked when they first walked in, that a man should bring his mistress, not his wife.

Afterwards they strolled hand in hand along Marylebone High Street, idling before shop windows, taking their time.

Anna, light-headed, euphoric, squeezed Chris's hand. 'I feel so happy.'

It was understood – or so she thought – that this was a moment of mutual acknowledgement and appreciation. Stop the clocks; this is who we are, this is who we have become.

'Now there's an emotion I can share.'

His stilted tone riled her. *Lawyerspeak. Mannishness. The way my father was, is, will always, be to my mother.*

Just at that moment an elfin creature, a slim beauty with long narrow eyes and a pouting bottom lip, walked past them. A teenager, possibly, only a decade or so older than their own children. A look passed between her and Chris – more than momentary, less than lingering – lasting for how long: four? five seconds at most? Long enough for Anna to experience it as a minor discourtesy to herself. Her thoughts were a wine-stained jumble and she, a little tipsy, was willing herself to be happy. *Of course, Chris still operates as a man and there are laws governing these things, which make such mating signals acceptable, but which put limits on them, too.*

Maybe it was the wine, but her sadness expanded further. She was thirty-nine, her children growing older. It felt as if she had been away on a long holiday, somewhere warm but confining, returning slowly now to the world of work and street flirting, politics and new technology, only to find that both she and that world were irrevocably changed, everything and everyone operating by new rules. Chris, too. She felt it most at times like this: here, in the world, removed from home, where so much was unexamined, briskly taken for granted in the daily round.

She thought back to that chilly evening ten years ago when they wandered around the streets of Primrose Hill. True strangers to each other. Two young people, with vague plans; she, to write; he, to become a lawyer. Both had honoured their ambitions, with varying degrees of success. Despite the promising start of 'Last Days in Havana', Anna had had no luck with her novel, in spite of a couple of enthusiastic letters from publishers. 'The market is bad for this kind of serious work,' said one. 'This is the era of light fiction.' She had had no choice but to put the manuscript away. For a long while, she wrote nothing out of an irritated despair, but for the past couple of years she had been working, very slowly, on another book. She had no intention of going down the light fiction route – she didn't even know what it meant; there was a deep layer of stubbornness in her that would never give up, or do what she was told. Still, it felt hard, to keep writing her four hundred words a day, with publication just a vague hope, a shimmer on the horizon.

As for the children, she oscillated between regarding them as her saviours, the one unambiguous pleasure in her life, and as the biggest road block to true independence. As she complained to Sally, 'It's so hard to find uninterrupted time. Okay, they are both at school now, but I have to earn money. So, I can only work in the evening and I get so . . . tired.' But there was a limit to how much Sally, who had one failed relationship behind her and would probably now never have children, could bear of her domestic difficulties. Better to suggest with dark humour that the children 'hold *some* of us back more than others'.

She meant Chris, of course, who had every reason to be pleased with himself, professionally speaking. In the intervening ten years he had grown in professional stature, become exactly the man he dreamed out loud of being in those autumn London streets. Taken on by a good firm, he had become known, particularly over the last year, as a solicitor who worked hard on difficult and important cases, a reputation sealed last summer when he had represented a family whose teenage son, Terry Atkins, died in custody in a north-London police station. All during the weeks of the inquest Chris had put in twelve-, even fourteen-hour days (or so it felt to her, the domestic widow) in order to secure justice; or so it felt to him. Convinced that Terry Atkins had been unlawfully restrained and almost certainly maltreated in an underground cell, Chris burned with a wholly authentic passion about the case. Eventually, the coroner's jury at St Pancras had brought in a verdict of unlawful killing, which caused a sensation in the national press.

Chris was – in the jargon – good with people. Terry's distraught mother rang him daily; he talked her calmly through the inquest procedure in court, never crossing the boundary between the professional and the personal. He was there at court an hour early, every morning: ready to greet Terry's three sisters and two brothers as they arrived, dressed always in their dignified, funereal black. After the dramatic verdict, the family directed every request for radio and television and newspaper interviews to their handsome, articulate solicitor, with whom they had temporarily, and collectively, become infatuated. They looked on, marvelling, as he conducted a series of brief, sober interviews in the ornamental gardens outside the court entrance, walking between the small hand-held tape recorder held by the young reporter from the local paper to the large fuzzy boom-mike of national television news, knowing exactly what each of them needed from him. When the evening bulletin wanted to interview him, exclusively, on the wider significance of the case, he was ready. 'This story is hugely important,' he said in a calm and measured tone. 'It shows once again how the coroners' system can ask important questions of our police force and our prison authorities. It puts flesh on the idea of accountability. Which is good for democracy. And, painful as it seems, good for all of us.' Afterwards, the home phone rang for an hour: friends, family, colleagues calling to pass on praise.

Yes, the Atkins case was the moment when hard-working, anxious Chris (for he took all his cases to heart, was never casual about his work) became this hybrid creature; a third party; a *name*. Christopher Mason, committed, radical solicitor.

His gain, Anna thought ruefully now, may be their loss. She and he were far from the carefree strangers who paced the back streets of Camden ten years ago, linked by an intense mutual curiosity. How could it be otherwise? They were an established married couple, well into their life together. Yes, and so? (She was quizzing herself, conducting an interrogation of her own mild feeling of disappointment, as they walked, hands still clasped but loosely, without ease: in her momentary alienation, his hand felt like a stranger's paw or claw: lumpen, and strangely chilly.) It's just . . . she found it hard to admit to herself; must now imagine herself talking to Sally or her sister, who might coax the expression of these difficult feelings from her with sympathy and genuine kindness . . . *well, you know, it's as if marriage and parenthood have diminished me and emboldened him. The idea that we're equal, he and I against the world, in the world, it just hasn't worked out like that. At times, I feel more like his PA . . .*

Stop! She had spied her reflection in a supermarket window, a half-inch gash of worry between her brows. Taking her hand from Chris's – a murmured explanation about an itch on her head – she rubbed her index finger at the point between her eyebrows, trying to smooth away the surely unnecessary anxiety.

Over the next few months she dreamed the same scene repeatedly. *She is walking along Marylebone High Street. A sharp object is flying through the skies, heading towards her. If she doesn't look up, get out of the way, it will crash down and pierce her, right between the eyes. But she can't stop to look and see where it is coming from, because she is too busy trying to find the elfin girl with the jutting lower lip who is here somewhere in the crowd. She needs to speak to her: the girl is in possession of crucial life and death information. Anna never finds the girl; she always wakes up, crying soundlessly in terror, as she is just about to be crushed by the object hurtling down from the sky.*

Twenty-nine

'It's like a cathedral!' Anna cried, as she and the children gawped, arching their necks to peer up to the roof, silenced by the grandeur of the central lobby. They were waiting for Matt, who was already ten minutes late. Lola, nearly six, was playing an impromptu game of hopscotch on the richly tiled floor. Eight-year-old Harry was watching the men in their various guises: police officers, Commons messengers in black breeches, the endless waves of men in suits. Anna spied a lone figure in a smart pin-stripe outfit approaching briskly from one of the wide hallways that led into the central lobby. As he crossed the floor, she recognised him as a Tory ex-Chancellor, famous in his day, but rarely heard of now. He must be seventy now, she thought: his hair was a glossy white, his expression confident and benign. She felt as if she was watching a waxwork come to life, a statue who has decided to play at being a living, breathing human for a day.

Matt suddenly appeared, walking, very fast, down a long hall directly opposite. He and the ex-Chancellor met crossing the lobby. Matt nodded. The ex-Chancellor smiled genially. Masculine murmurs were exchanged.

'Genuinely nice bloke,' Matt's first words, his greeting to his sister. Anna made the face that was expected of her. The one that said: *I'm impressed.*

'So how are you?' Matt gave her a warm hug. 'Everything okay? Kids look great. You look great. And Chris?'

These last two words, uttered lightly, but with a rather more deadly precision than his enquiries about her or the children. Since the Atkins case – and Chris's new-found, minor fame as a critic of the government, on certain legal matters – there had been a subtle shift in family relations. Not a word said, but it was now understood that Chris did not quite belong to *this* part of the family, the easy underbelly of the group, the people who do the nice stuff, the soft stuff, the tea-on-the-terrace stuff. (Anna, of course, was different. Anna was flesh and blood. First and foremost a sister, a daughter, a mother. In the real world, Anna didn't count.)

'Fine. Great. Fine.' Anna's standard let's-get-this-out-the-way answer.

Even Matt seemed vulnerable in this grand place, the long shadow of real power falling across his sharp, well-defined features. She felt sisterly love and a dash of genuine concern each time they met and she saw that thin face and burning dark eyes.

'Fantastic news,' he said, as they walked along the corridor. 'We've just heard. The money for school building is going to double this year. We've had a hell of a fight over it, but I think we've won. This is great news for us.' He meant him and Andy.

'Great!' Anna clapped him on the back.

Her children, real flesh-and-blood creatures with disappointingly little interest in the projected increase in the capital budget for school building, were now trying to catch Matt's attention.

'Uncle Matt! Uncle Matt, we saw a policeman with a gun!'

'And did he try to shoot you? I hope not.'

'No, of course he didn't!'

They walked, through the richly decorated halls with ceilings high as houses (Anna was left with the impression of burnished gold), past the statues of former great Parliamentarians and knots of men and women, very much alive, conferring in corners, down thick-carpeted stairs, through darker more oppressive corridors, back up a few stone steps, into the bright light of the summer day. As they walked, Matt fed them digestible scraps of parliamentary history, enjoying showing off his knowledge, his intimate acquaintance with power. In the past couple of years, both Andy and Matt, she thought, had become larger than life – no, *harder* than life: Matt, in particular, who has no need to wrap himself in the public cloak of charm. He seemed to know everything and everybody; no fact, no human being, was a surprise to him; nothing could make him stop and say: *oh, really?* Trying to talk to Matt was like trying to hold a conversation with a marathon runner; the whole exercise had an air of acknowledged futility about it. At best, one could only trot along, as Anna did now, breathless with sympathy, as he reeled off anecdotes about the first woman ever to take her seat in the House of Commons, or statistics about literacy and numeracy, school admissions and the national curriculum.

On the terrace, bathed in a warm autumn sunshine, Harry sat quietly at his mother's side while Lola ran along the narrow strip of terrace, slaloming between the tables and chairs. Several times Anna had to warn her away from the low parapet wall that separated the civilised tea-drinkers from the fast-flowing grey water down below. After a few minutes Andy came out onto the terrace. He was noticeably bulkier now – Clare jokily claimed he had put on a stone for every year he had been in government – but moved towards them with the old, apparently relaxed charm. Rounder and sleeker, with his improbably brown hair, he reminded Anna of the German politician Gerhard Schroeder.

'Good to find you out here already.'

He felt safe with her and the children, visibly relaxed. They couldn't embarrass him or catch him out, demand something impossible to deliver. When she stood to greet him, he gave her a bear hug that nearly crushed her. 'Harry and Lo . . . come here, you two scoundrels.' But Lo ran off, bored, in a benign sort of way, after thirty seconds, while Harry tried to answer Andy's rather general questions about school and friends and sport. 'Good boy!' Andy patted Harry on the top of his head when the conversation ran out of steam. Effort made; audience over. Anna noticed other visitors, a scattering of fellow MPs smiling fondly at their group, as if they knew something intriguing about them all. Andy had now become what Jack, in one of his recent e-mails, jokily described as national-TV-famous ('No longer the Becoming Great Man, but the Nearly Very Great Man'). In his company now, Anna felt uncomfortably impressed by a sense of her own significance.

Matt brought out a tray of orange juices for the children, tea for the three adults, a plate of biscuits. As the cups were being handed out, Andy asked the same question that Matt had posed earlier. 'And how is Chris? Busy, I hope?'

'Good. Yes.' Anna threw caution to the winds. 'They might be making a half-hour documentary about the Atkins case.'

But Andy was distracted, already, by some internal preoccupation. 'Good. Splendid. Half an hour, you say?'

Then, just as suddenly, his attention returned, razor-sharp. 'There's really no question that the police were guilty of any substantial brutality? Insensitivity, yes, I gather. But more than that?'

Matt jumped in: a clear attempt to change the subject. 'God, Lola looks *just* like her father, doesn't she? Chris in a frock.'

They all ha-ha laughed at the absurd thought. Andy nodded briskly, distracted, then engaged again. 'Although I expect people don't say it enough, do they? That a daughter who looks like a father is always, or should be said to look like, a very *pretty* version of her father.'

Anna smiled, grateful for the acknowledgement of Lola's charms.

Andy bit into a biscuit. He said wistfully, 'I was always sorry we never had a daughter, but Clare was adamant, two was enough, and there was no arguing with her, then or now. You and Laura are the nearest I have to daughters, you know, Anna.'

'Ahh.' She leaned over and touched his hand, moved by this unexpected declaration.

Just then, a scary-looking young woman in a charcoal-grey pencil skirt and scarlet square-framed glasses came out onto the terrace. She stood at the top of the stone steps leading out from the riverside corridor, looking around.

Matt jumped up, waving a wadge of files. 'Hey! Hey! Martina! Over here.'

Arriving at their table, the brisk young woman apologised formally to Anna. 'So sorry to interrupt.' Anna felt insubstantial and unworldly in this determined presence.

'Everything okay?' Andy squinted up at her against the bright sun.

'Fine,' she said quickly. 'But this may need immediate attention.'

'Fire ahead.'

Martina explained that a prominent head teacher of a comprehensive in the North-East had just resigned in protest over the most recent government initiative. 'He *says*,' and Martina began to read from a piece of paper in her hand, putting an ironic distance between herself and the words, 'Wait a second. Yes, here it is. Yes. In his words, "He is tired" . . . yes here it is, "tired of tedious paper-pushing, ridiculous form-filling. I would simply like to be left to get on with the important job of educating the next generation of citizens."'

Matt rolled his eyes in irritation.

'As if we're stopping him,' Andy murmured harshly.

'He's given quite a lengthy interview to the six o'clock news,' Martina said, crinkling up her nose in distaste. 'Lots of the usual Wraggian stuff about disappointment in a Labour government, where's the genuine freedom to innovate, could do better, etc. Personally' – now she made a wry face, suggesting apology, to Anna – 'I think this needs a pretty immediate response. Just to stem some of the expected reaction, negative comment, and so on.' She tapped her foot, sharply, twice, as if to emphasise the urgency of action.

'Right,' Matt stood up, 'let's get to it.' He looked sprightly. Andy, however, lowered his head and rubbed his hand back and forth over his forehead. He appeared – briefly – haggard. 'I'm so sorry, Anna. Needs must and all that.'

Now he rose. The three of them talked – rapidly – across each other. A statement should be drafted. Nothing too defensive. Or offensive. Matt had some ideas about wording already. He was pretty sure that the head in question had a history of far-left activity, which might be useful, 'Let's put it no stronger than that' (a glance at Anna, representative of the outside world), in any rebuttals of his position. They also needed to get another head teacher to go on the media, to put a contrary view.

'The local MP could be helpful to us here, too,' Matt said. He was enjoying this minor crisis, Anna could see.

'Is he one of us?' Andy was brushing crumbs from his trousers.

'He's pretty reliable, I'd say.'

Andy kissed Anna and the children goodbye and then stood, his back already turned to his guests, waiting for Matt to join him for the walk back inside the building. Be at his side.

Matt squeezed Anna's shoulder. 'I'll ring you later. Sorry about this. Martina will arrange for you and the kids to be taken back to the central lobby.'

And then both men were gone: Anna was left, on the terrace, next to the scary-looking woman, feeling emptied out and exhausted.

No-one was looking at them now. They were ordinary mortals, finishing up their tea, on a moderately warm day.

Thirty

For over five years her middle brother's e-mails frame her every day. From late November 1997 to early March 2003, he writes to her at least twice a day. Streams of consciousness. A bombardment. An eccentric record of the politics of the time. A certain kind of politics, anyway: street politics; angry politics. Inevitably, these messages become a record of his fluctuating emotional state. He must have written during the night, for she often had one or two messages – sometimes even three – sitting in her in-box first thing in the morning. And there would be another, written during the day in a break from agitation, which she would receive when she went up to the attic to try to write late at night.

April 26 1999
from: Jack777@callme.dot.com
to: AAdams@worldonline.co.uk
subject: heart disease

Did you see the Crt of Appeal verdict on the burger case. Vindication Total. Baldly stated that staff 'do badly in terms of pay and conditions'. And on content. Confirmed without doubt that eat enough of that kind of food the risk of heart disease is 'very real'. Glad for the original two. They fought so hard. Saw L. in the street near the court, standing like she was just hanging about . . . MY GUESS . . . she knew that I would be there, the only place she might find me given all that went on – she wants to tell me she's not happy with the dentist, now realises that I ws the only person who ever really saw her – saw through her more like –

and she wants to talk to me. Yet she pretended she did not see me so cannot want that or anything that much. I wanted her to know that I hd seen her pretending not to see me, and then I wanted to walk away very obviously. All the time I was busy telling myself that I felt nothing, absolutely nothing.

Unforgivingness. Non-forgiveness. The most EXQUISITE OF SENSATIONS.

May 9 1999

from: Jack777@callme.dot.com
to: AAdams@worldonline.co.uk
subject: what the passage of time reveals

Watching television in the early hours, some programme about Sixties Britain. It horrified me, actually, to see that black-and-white world that we grew up in . . . look back on it like that and all its rigidities and certainties. There was Enoch Powell with his cat's eyes and working-class women interviewed in the street encouraged by the moronic interviewer to parrot their common-sense view 'that a black man and a white woman can go out together but they must never have children – ever. That would be their big mistake.' And then – and then – it was incredible – to see – footage – live footage of Malcolm X speaking at a debate at the Oxford Union, some time in the late Sixties. Cld have reduced me to tears; the pride of the man, his dignity at a time when black men delivered coal and the post, and doffed their caps or were assigned cheerful-chappie roles in black-and-white minstrel shows or in a black-and-white minstrel role in the public services, and here was a black man standing among the braying white upper classes; a slim, proud, clear-voiced man saying: *If you do not fight back against what is morally wrong, you are defeated.* In your soul. That's what I understood him to say, which is exactly the same argument that propelled Britain and the allies into war against Germany (I know, I know, nations do not have souls, war creates employment); it's essentially the same argument, only incendiary, because it's words in the mouth of a young proud black man, and Malcolm X was not talking about obvious evil, but apparent good. He was talking about post-war white America and white Britain, with its appalling ignorance and stupidity and double standards and violence posing as exquisite mannered politeness.

May 10 1999
from: Jack777@callme.dot.com
to: AAdams@worldonline.co.uk
subject: sleeplessness

The neighbours, the young couple upstairs, have been reconciled. Clearly the Infidel, the Dangerous Other, Evil Susie has been slayed in the name of marital harmony. Now we are back to SEXING, and playing rap and God knows what music with a thumping back-beat on a continuous-loop tape till two or three in the morning. When I ask them to turn it off, they turn it down for twenty minutes and then turn it up loud as they can again. Must be recognised as a form of torture surely in some European Convention, some Bill of Rights that no-one pays any attention to? Now I have fantasies of murdering both of them. So I stay at the library as late as I can, you can stay till ten at Holborn, and then I come back and read through the night. History and politics mostly. History mostly. Iraq, Israel, Palestine, Ireland, India. Essays about politics. Orwell sometimes, just for fun. Gramsci. I realised the other day, in some ways, I am like our father, a semi-recluse surrounded by books, obsessed with the human attempt to make sense of the senseless. The noise, my thoughts, I cannot sleep, I manage barely a couple of hours a night. Actually, it's not the hours awake at night that bother me, I enjoy them apart from the sadists' music. It's the daytime following I find so difficult: EXHAUSTION MEANS IT'S IMPOSSIBLE TO LIVE IN THE PRESENT. FATIGUE IS DISTRACTING, MENTALLY. Extraordinary, however, what you CAN do . . . odd what functions stay and what go. I find it hard to spell and can barely put together coherent sentences. But I can walk for miles and miles until I feel the soreness in my muscles, and feel I can keep going for a dozen more. I NOW TALK TO MYSELF. IT'S OFFICIAL. I was walking past a huge glass-plate building in town somewhere. I thought: Who is that madman walking just in front of me talking to himself?

May 11 1999
from: Jack777@callme.dot.com
to: AAdams@worldonline.co.uk
subject: lists and Lucia

Sometimes when I can't sleep, I write lists, lists of the women I have fancied, not very long, the women I have liked, longer, the women I have loved. Non-existent. Funnily enough, L. does not now make it into lists two or three. SHE HAD BEAUTIFUL HAIR AND EYES. I DO REMEMBER THAT. BUT would you believe me if I said now that those eyes always bothered me. Not bothered me THAT way. Bothered me morally. It was as if I needed always to gauge the exact depth of cruelty contained within them. Often used to wonder whether love (or sexing) would soften her expression in any way. That was my obsession. To make the meanness go away or maybe to get the meanness on my side. Fatal. I wonder – what do you think, Anna, you understand women better, obviously – if there would have been a moment when we were sitting on a park bench or standing together in a kitchen, talking, and I would have looked at her, and seen through the physical self into her soul and felt repelled?

October 13 1999
from: Jack777@callme.dot.com
to: AAdams@worldonline.co.uk
subject: government

The VNGM on TV tonight. He looks like a waxwork. Almost as bad as the big Tone himself. And all this bone-dry chatter about statistics. Exam results. Targets. Tables. The sheer bloody violence of the atti-tude underlying all of it, as if everything is teacher's fault. Sackings. Closing downs. Good schools. Bad schools. Do you think he believes all that guff? And then he and our brother come up with these execrable, cheap ideas. Talent Academies! The promotion of so-called excellence in all things intellectual or artistic. Taking the money from corrupt millionaires to help fast-track the haves into better schools. The new grammars – but with a dash of celeb backing – for people like our father who never stopped mourning the loss of them . . . Oh and don't forget, the importance of school uniform. Do u think Matt ever finds playing the support role boring? Constraining? No, no, I know he doesn't. He's a wonk at heart, isn't he? Loves all the policy detail. Less people, more policy, the better, and the seminars I bet and the press stuff . . . huddling with the young men with pencils, who treat all of us with such contempt . . . Something funny for you . . . the other day I got a round-robin letter which said: So-and-so has been respon-sible for some 'seminar thinking' on such-and-such an issue. I choked myself laughing. Seminar thinking. Perfect!

from: Jack777@callme.dot.com
to: AAdams@worldonline.co.uk
subject: Seattle

We have done it. Shut the whole fucking thing down. You must have read about it. And they made it out to be mad hippies. Crazy anti-glob-alisers, etc., etc. Fine people in fact. Brave people. Anna, what I have gone through here, what I have witnessed, finally proved to me that I am a coward. Not just in my physical self, which I am. I am scared of confrontation. Blood. Anger. The real thing. The stuff that edges near annihilation and death terrifies me. I do not want to face police in riot gear. I do not want to be beaten over the head. I do not want to die. But I am a coward in my deeper self. I do not want to tell people what I feel. My whole life about hiding. See that now. This, the lesson of our upbringing, Anna, the ordinary burdens it has brought down on you and on Matt and on Laura; we were all raised not to speak of what was in our hearts and we were socialised into politeness, into a steely front, and that is a killer too and I see now that the love I thought I had for Lucia was not an opening up but a closing down, because she was cold and smart and pretty, yes, but cold and smart, rather like our father, and pretty like our mother (I am not going in for cheap psychology here, but a genuine truth as I see it) and I went for the purest representation possible of that which I despised. I should have been trying to throw it off, not merge with. And you saw that, I'm sure you saw that, in your own way – Anna, you are the most open of the four of us – and I knew you didn't like her and you never said because you were trying to help me, but now I see what you saw and that is a RELIEF. But the people here are brave. I have not met people like this. Much younger than me. They sit and talk, face each other, talk for hours, passionate about poli-tics, open about their fear. What's the big deal? I'm afraid? What's the big deal? And at the same time there is a carnival atmosphere and samba bands, and people dress up and there is plotting and there is strategy. It is exhilarating. Like nothing I have ever known. A kind of coming home. This group called the Infernal Noise Brigade walk through the streets. They are a mix of a marching-drum orchestra and street performers, 'a tactical mobile rhythmic unit', consisting of majorettes, doctors, strat-egists, gun-toting members and drum-bashers. There are armies of people with spray paint and stencils and wheat paste and posters, and at night they fly-post, one neighbourhood at a time. For the first time, here, I have made sense of my sleeplessness. In two ways. Understanding that there was a purpose to it, back in Essex Road, in the old flat. I was not sleeping because I was not doing the right things in the day. Sleep, gd sleep, is a kind of reward, for right living? Right? Here, if I am not sleeping, at least I am doing something good. I am doing. I am not lying stiff. TRYING to be like everyone else. I am being myself. Tired and beautifully myself . . . Yesterday, I decided to help out at something called the Independent Media Centre, which was trying to get information about the WTO summit, and the protestors, out. I did that because at least I have some skills that way, from my years working at the campaign. I was better at that, better than being out on the streets. Cowardice again. It was scary. Outside the window, we could see the so-called Peacekeepers, the armed militia of the National Guard with huge mounted guns, driving past. And people around us were getting arrested and we at the IMC were right in the middle of it. In this zone, they suspended 'constitutional rights', which means, basically, that the government can do exactly what they want. It's frightening. At some point a National Guard officer pushed through our door and someone said: We better get out of there. We had to climb out of a back window, clamber over a burning rubbish dump. Police blocking our way, everywhere we turned. Each alleyway, each street down and away to freedom, police were blocking. My heart was thumping. I was shit-scared. We turn, there is a third alleyway. Clear. And we got away. It felt so gd, running away. I ran fifteen blocks. Not looking back. And I realised then what the force of the state means. What it means to be terrified by armies and tanks and men whose faces you cannot see with enough weaponry in thr hands to kill ten of u.

He was at his best then. Far-away. Involved. Sleepless for a purpose. Full of words. Such times were followed by long periods back in his flat, his messages dwindling to dawn one-liners and he, back in the agony of eternal, vigilant, purposeless self-consciousness, agony about 'the L. crisis', the curse of the second son, torrents of fury directed at 'our father, our mother, our siblings'. Anna waited for the day when he turned on her, never quite understood why she had been exempt from this wholesale rejection of 'where I came from. THE PAST'. She dreamed often of herself and Jack talking in the kitchen back in the old house; perhaps his indulgence of her went back to those days. The simple fact of time given, time taken. Or maybe it was the long embrace she had given him, that night of The Ladbroke Lady, his head bandaged, his lip cut, that night when her parents were so incensed at what he had done. They had not meant to condemn, Anna knew that; they had simply thought they were setting rules and standards for the giant struggle of adult life to come. Now, they were at sea in their relations with their second son, had long ago given up hope of restoring 'normal relations'. Two frail old people, they looked to Anna to provide just a morsel of news now and then: this burden, if it could be called that, fell on her, and she accepted it, because she had no choice.

Thirty-one

2001

'Excuse me . . . it's Anna Mason, isn't it?' The woman behind the counter of the bookshop, a cheerful, smiley woman of indeterminate middle age, dressed in a green rollneck, was straining over a pile of cut-price poetry volumes, trying to catch her attention.

'Yes.'

Anna looked up from the new-fiction table with a smile. A well-regarded agent had recently shown some real interest in her new manuscript, had already drawn up a list of possible publishers to approach; he and Anna mulling over three alternative titles (which was great fun, the icing on the cake after all the lonely work of writing). At last it was possible to come into bookshops, to browse once again without the old, sick feeling of failure.

'Mrs *Christopher* Mason.'

'*Yes.*'

'Right, I have a couple of books here.'

'Sorry?'

'Books that your husband ordered?'

'He did?'

'If you wait just one second.' The woman in the rollneck turned to the long shelf of reserved books behind the counter and took down two paperbacks, sheathed in plain white paper.' Here we are. *Farewell to Arms, American Pastoral.*'

'But we already have a copy of the Roth, and I think we have *two* of the Hemingway,' Anna protested, more irritably than she meant to.

The woman behind the counter smiled with a forced brightness, books still in hand. 'Shall I . . . ?' She made a swivelling movement as if to indicate that she could – should – put the books back.

'Sorry. I'm forgetting myself,' Anna opened her bag, rooting around for her cheque book. 'No, no, of course I'll take them. They've been ordered by one of us.'

As she wrote out her cheque, the woman was sliding the books into a paper bag decorated with pink-and-white stripes, tiny strawberries around the borders.

'Pretty paper.'

'Thanks. I chose these bags myself. I like a cheerful pattern.'

'Very important,' Anna assented, extra-pleasantly. 'Right. Lola! We're off!' Anna called over to the children's section, where Lola was sprawled on a giant cushion, thumb in her mouth, reading *Charlie and the Chocolate Factory.*

'Is that your daughter?'

Was there a note of surprise in the woman's voice, at how little mother and daughter resembled each other? Lola, with her straight blonde hair, small features, fearless blue eyes; Anna, with her dark ringlets, wide mouth and brown eyes.

'She's lovely.'

'Thanks. Yes. She looks very like my husband. And my sister actually.' As soon as she said it, she began to laugh, and then to redden. 'Well, that sounds odd!'

The bookshop woman was blushing too as Anna backed out towards the door, emitting embarrassed gobbets of talk, desperate to make her escape into the street.

Later that night – the books still lying in their candy-striped, strawberry-stencilled paper bag – Anna has a powerful feeling of foreboding, the irrational sense that she is in imminent danger. Eight-fifteen: she and Chris – he, brimming with excitable energy, she can't help but notice, rather resentfully – climb a flight of steep stone steps, stand and wait before a richly decorated door, sinuous plants and flowers stained into the glass in vivid blues, reds and greens; this, the home of fellow solicitor Kevin Brown, with whom Chris occasionally works, a large late-Victorian house at the end of an empty, ill-lit street near Hackney marshes.

A middle-aged woman wearing a formal mask of delight comes to the door. 'Chris! My favourite troublemaker!' (This means what?) The woman embraces him warmly, then clutches at Anna, largely, it is obvious, in the interests of fair play; this is Lisa, the solicitor's wife, some kind of psychotherapist – Kleinian? Reichian? – with unnaturally large square teeth, wearing wooden jewellery over a black polo neck. Coats disposed of, she leads them, with rapid-fire talk, requiring no response, down the hallway towards the dinner party proper, where Kevin stands on the threshold of a large room, bottle of white wine gripped between his thighs, strain bulging the veins on his forehead.

'Ahhh!' he exclaims, just as the cork pops.

More shaking and gripping. More bonhomie. Taller and thinner than his wife, Kevin has small, beady eyes and round spectacles. He steers Chris and Anna towards a large pale-skinned middle-aged blonde wearing a padded, jewelled jacket as regal and comfortable-looking as a throne. Anna recognises her immediately: Susanna Seargent, the regular columnist on a centre-right newspaper. A few feet away, a man with a large floppy fringe and a brilliant white T-shirt pulled tight across a well-developed chest is talking fervently to a pretty blonde girl with a rather deliberately blank expression. Fragments of their talk float over to Anna: 'years since I last saw his work . . . and then I walked in. Those giant canvases . . . once meant so much. But I felt nothing . . .'

'Listen up!' Lisa, the hostess, calls across the room. 'You all know Chris. And this is . . . Anna.' A slight hesitation. 'I'm ashamed to say, Anna, I have no idea what you *do*.'

'Well, I . . .'

Kevin nudges Lisa: she has forgotten to hand out the pre-dinner nibbles. A half-dozen bowls of curly edged rust and pea-green coloured crisps, olives and salted nuts are sitting on the sideboard, undevoured. Mercifully, Anna is saved from the public ordeal of having to explain herself.

During the pre-dinner chat that follows, Anna has a sense of both being watched and avoided by the pretty blonde. She has caught her name earlier: Katie Robinson. Robertson? Yes, she remembers Katie; she was – is? – a pupil at the chambers of one of the barristers with whom Chris works most closely. Her husband's words come back to her. 'Graduated top in her year. Awesomely thorough preparation. Given time, she will be formidable.' (But this sort of description – full of hyperbole – was, Anna noticed, common in Chris's line of work. The favoured novices were always going to be awesome, formidable, etc. Anna had long ago decided to wait and see how real life panned out.) This Katie is also the niece of an eminent scholar and the sister of Helen Something-or-Other (the MP goes by her married name), one of the '97 intake of women MPs. All these connections give her an additional glow, a borrowed patina of celebrity and intellectual substance. For a moment Anna feels a defensive arrogance; she, too, the child, the sister, the wife of self-made and successful men, but this adopted hauteur does not endure. The young blonde exists within her own universe, after all. A pale beauty, she radiates an appealing stillness, standing a little apart from the rest of the company, talking, now, with Lisa, Kevin's toothy wife. Behind coiled rings of smoke, they seem to be observing the others. Anna senses that she is being judged, the two other women assessing, in one deeply unkind instant, her social background, sexual allure, likely intelligence and emotional toughness. And her best jacket, which, she realises with a rush of shame, has been her best jacket for seven years.

Did she really hear their names? *ChrisandAnna.* Muttered over in the corner. Like a child in a game, she turns quickly, a clumsy attempt to catch them at it. Either she is mistaken or the women are better than her at this sort of thing. (It is the latter, she is certain of it.) Eyes averted, they are now diligently grinding their cigarettes into the tray scattered with olive stones.

Anna joins a conversation with Susanna Seargent and the man in the white T-shirt with the fringe, who is called John. He is describing a trip to a Paris art gallery where he queued for three hours to see some of the early paintings of Mark Rothko. 'It surprised me, the intense detail of the pictures. Stick figures scurrying through the New York subway. Nothing like the vast washes of the later canvases.'

'I think he – the later work – is completely overrated,' Susanna Seargent says pleasantly, while Anna tries to remember what she knows about her. A fervent Catholic as a young woman, a passionate radical feminist in her twenties and early thirties, Seargent is now a born-again militant social conservative with an acid tongue, at least in print. In the flesh, she looks rather fragile, puffy around the eyelids. Some other fact is nagging at Anna's brain; an unrelated piece of information about the columnist that feels relevant.

'He didn't start doing those – the big blocks of colour – until he was forty,' says John.

'I love them,' Anna, who turned forty the year before, sounds apologetic. 'Their size and the depth of the colour.'

'Forty seems very late.' Susanna cuts across her. 'Are you sure?'

'Absolutely.'

Twenty minutes later they are shepherded, up a few stairs, through to a dining room, beyond the kitchen. A vast conservatory with a glass roof and interior walls of rust brickwork, hung with tasteful prints and filled with the melancholy blue glow of a summer night. Dozens of tiny candles are set along the centre of the main table, a glowing spine of fire. To the side, set against one of the naked brick walls, another table, on which sit two vast green glazed bowls, stuffed with white and black grapes, papayas, bunches of cherries and a silver plate laden with varieties of soft cheese.

'How lovely!' exclaims Susanna Seargent, her eyes briefly blurring with emotion.

Anna is relieved to be put next to the apparently mild Kevin – Chris is seated at the other end of the table, between Katie and Lisa – who has obviously been briefed to talk to her on some domestic-related topic. As she picks up her spoon to try out the soup, a chilled vanilla liquid dotted with dark-green-and-red chips of pepper, he asks, 'So, Anna, do you do paid work?'

'I teach part-time, and the rest of the time I write.'

Kevin nods, rather overenthusiastically. 'Yes, I see. Well, of course, Lisa has found it all very hard. She has her practice during the day, the children after school. I do my best to help, but I'm afraid – work – you know.'

'Ah, yes, of course.'

'Yes.' Kevin has an odd way of talking. He stops and starts, like a car that can't get into gear. 'You should be proud of that man of yours. He did a brilliant job on the Atkins case. Good barrister, Stephen Stepney – do you know him? Well, that always helps. And with the additional loan of Katie . . . well, they were unbeatable. She's only a junior, I know, but you should have seen her and Chris – and Stephen, of course – in action. Heads together, over the paperwork. A pretty formidable team.'

'So I hear,' Anna lies – badly, she thinks – no longer able to taste the soup, which she had only seconds earlier registered as delicious.

Chris and 'the additional loan' of Katie. 'Part of a formidable team.' Memories of the Atkins case are beginning to come back to her, small pieces of information she could never fit in the whole jigsaw, until now. Panic tasting like acid in her mouth as she looks down the table. Katie, wearing a plain rust shift and a cream long-sleeved T-shirt, talking quietly with Chris – Lisa has dashed back into the kitchen in a fish-related panic – glows like a novice nun in the candlelight.

Kevin has been speaking for a few seconds. 'I'm sorry,' Anna turns back towards him.

'I only asked, what do you write, when you can?'

'Oh. Stories. Mostly.' She knows she is being vague.

'Any plans for publication?' he asks jovially.

'Well, actually,' she begins, trying desperately to concentrate, 'I have got an agent interested in something I've just finished.'

A shout from the kitchen. 'Excuse me, won't you?' Kevin jumps up and disappears through the archway into the kitchen. Surreptitiously, Anna glances down the table, deploys all her will power to screen out the words of the acerbic journalist and the art lover, who take up the central portion of the table.

Katie Robinson is saying, 'That Lessing – you – gave – me – profound – amazing.'

Thank God for double hard consonants. 'Lessing' comes across loud and hissing-clear.

Books it is, then. And two more books, further gifts for the formidable beautiful junior, are waiting at home in the pretty pink bag. Collected by none other than herself: Chris Mason's domestic PA.

Just then Susanna says, very loudly, to John, 'People are so afraid to express emotion in art these days. It's all so clever-clever.'

Chris looks startled, says something that sounds like, 'Wrath is good.'

Nearer to, John sneers, 'Emotion is not confined to the figurative forms, you know, Susanna.'

Katie giggles audibly and everyone at the table turns her way, wearing friendly, faintly curious expressions. Anna watches her husband watching the younger woman. That look; she has seen it many times before. Sitting on a wall near a church in Primrose Hill; answering a summer-evening knock on the door; looking up to offer or receive a kiss, a thousand times, down the years.

A few moments later, Lisa comes back in the room carrying a vast white plate aloft, laid with a very dead fish with some kind of soft fruit stuffed in its prised-apart mouth.

'At last!' she neighs.

There is a brief round of applause. Kevin glides round the table, refilling everybody's glasses.

Anna, distracted and distressed, plays with the stem of her wine glass At the far end of the table, Chris is trying to catch her eye, but she refuses to meet his gaze.

'So, everyone,' Susanna barks, clearly bored of her talk with John, turning her head from side to side, so that the whole party should understand that a general conversation is now required. 'What do we make of the renewed mandate for this government? A convincing majority for a confident second term, yes? I'll tell you one thing. They are serious about protecting the family. And we need that.'

'It's an It,' says John, an anxious crease across his brow. 'Governments are Its, not Theys.'

'Maybe they – sorry, "It" – is pretending to be something else,' snaps Chris, irritably. 'All that family stuff, it's a kind of cover. If *it* was really serious about enforcing family values, I mean really enforcing them, then surely it should prohibit and punish single parents, the gay unions, the long-term cohabitees. They don't dare.'

'Yes.' Kevin slides back into the seat next to Anna. 'Just as, if they were really serious about radical change of another kind, there's a well-developed agenda there that could be picked up in a moment.'

'And that is?' asks a wide-eyed Katie.

Chris addresses the whole table. 'Oh, come on. We all know it backwards. We're way behind Europe in our uncivilised working habits.' He pauses to swallow his food, waves his fork in the air. 'In fact, I'd wager the government will do quite well on all that. Fiddling around the edges, helping working women in the name of modernity. Thanks, yes,' Lisa has put some extra fish on his plate. 'But on the big questions, it will be the same old reactionary stuff. Pandering to corporate interests, naked greed. Let's face it. The signs aren't good.'

Susanna sighs audibly, 'Do you know how many evenings I've sat through over the years, listening to delightful, handsome, clever radicals like you, dear Chris, talking about corporate this, multinational that? No thanks, Lisa.' She refuses the new potatoes briskly. 'In the meantime, I have become a menopausal old lady who's finally getting up the courage to admit to a table full of good lefty people like yourself that maybe, just maybe, the redistributionist, greater-equality, change-the-whole-fucking-world-and-why-stop-there agenda is a busted flush.'

She picks up her wine glass, draining it with deliberate bravado. 'Perhaps most people only want – what did you call it, Chris? – a well-meaning "fiddling around the edges".'

Anna can tell by Lisa's expression of deep, but rather fake, absorption that it was for just this kind of mutual provocation that Susanna and Chris were brought together.

Her husband would certainly not disappoint his hosts, is already shifting his body weight in his chair, getting ready for the next round. In the last couple of years, provocation has become his standard party piece. If anyone is going to tackle the British liberal Jew about Israel, or the private-school parent about the inequalities of the education system, or lay into the feminist about twin studies and biology versus nurture, it is going to be Chris. Calm and measured in his professional world, he is increasingly waspish in his private life, free with his scathing opinions. Recently they had gone to see a gently escapist comedy with Sally and her new husband, gentle, thoughtful Don (to whom Anna felt a quiet gratitude, for making her friend happy). On the phone beforehand, Anna and Sally had agreed it was just what they needed, something amusing, light, at the end of a busy week. In the pub afterwards, the first round bought, Chris had said, with some belligerence, 'What complete and utter *crap*. Whose idea was that?' And Anna saw the light go out of Sally's eyes, and Don sigh and suppress a yawn, look quickly at his watch. Anna knew that afterwards he and Sally would talk disparagingly of Chris's 'bloody-mindedness', speak sympathetically of Anna and what she had to 'put up' with.

'Well, I'm sorry, Susanna,' Chris says now. 'In awe as I am of every single middle-aged woman on this planet' – he glances at Anna, wondering whether to risk a joke at her expense, but deciding against it – 'but I want a bloody lot more.'

His old trick of sounding more northern than he really is.

Susanna smiles coyly; she, too, is enjoying the spat. 'Come *on*, here is a credible, electable mainstream party that has made it to government. One term and they've proved themselves. They have an *agenda*. To use the jargon. Even more important, these are seriously impressive people. We all *recognise* them. Blair is a human being. One of us. The kind of father, husband, friend we all have. Or would like to have. He could sit right here and take you on, Chris, that's for sure. There's a whole host of them. Andy Givings . . . Jack Straw.'

Suddenly, Anna recalls the stray fact that has eluded her all evening: Susanna Seargent was one of the journalists and editors present at the strategy meeting at Matt's house a couple of weeks before the 1997 election; she was there when Jack started to throw stones at his brother's window.

Susanna leans forward and says with heavy emphasis, 'I am telling you. These are good men.'

'And what does good actually mean?' Chris snaps.

'Straightforward? Not deceiving?' Anna's voice comes out low and tremulous, eyes cast down.

'But – if I get your meaning,' – Katie is all sharp edges now, the awesome barrister-to-be – 'you think we will see no substantive change? With this government?'

'I'll tell you what we will see.' Chris turns to her, entirely impersonal in his political passion. 'There will be years of obfuscating, well-meaning talk, and things will remain more or less the same. The rich will get richer and the poor poorer. Not obscenely so. But enough for us to note the change. There may even be some serious evil committed.'

Anna's husband is at that point where slight drunkenness is a glorious brain-sharpening, mood-enhancing experience. 'Thatcherism went too far, you see. New Labour is considered a safe bet to administer capital for the capitalists. To use the *jargon.*' He is openly mocking Susanna now.

Katie's hair is the colour of wheat; her mouth, just the shape Anna's husband would sketch out as his perfect receptacle for the gaze of love, the hungry lunges of lust. *How do we know these things. We just do.* She is twenty-six, if that. Childless. Unattached. Brimming with well-managed energy.

Lessing and Hemingway. They will not go away. *Wrath is good. Roth is good.* Yes, surely, that is what he meant. The complex sickness that is justified distrust has invaded her brain.

'Would you excuse me?' Anna mutters, still not able to meet anyone's eyes directly, 'I just need the . . .'

'Oh, of course. Upstairs, second right.'

She can feel Chris's gaze on her as she stands up, stumbling a little as she edges her way round the table. He is willing her, not to disgrace him, not here in front of important colleagues, people who matter; but he is also worried, she knows, by her downcast expression, concerned at her manifest (to him) distress. It is this demonstration of care, his expression of genuine concern, that she is so keen to avoid at this minute. For underneath the glittering surface, beneath even the flirtations and entanglements that so brutally exclude her, is his love for her, private knowledge that they share alone, too deep to deceive. Tonight, dragged to a place where she must sit and bear silent witness to his vanity and foolishness, it is this fact, above all facts, she finds the hardest to bear.

It is just possible that she might disgrace him, she thinks in the hall. *After all, there's nothing to stop me walking out the front door.* No, she cannot do it. Years of her mother's training have suffused the fibres of her very being. One suffers silently in company. (One suffers silently alone, too.) She walks up the stairs, gripping the banister tightly, wondering why a place in which one is profoundly unhappy feels so intrinsically alienating, as if the wallpaper itself was designed to make us feel a stranger to our deepest selves?

The bathroom is large, light and warm, a sunken bath at its middle. There, in the mirror, a vast showy affair, its pale-green frame embedded with seashells, is an exhausted white-faced woman with high cheekbones. Anna feels pity for her, crouched on the closed toilet seat; making balled fists of her veined forty-year-old hands.

Opening and closing.

Opening and closing.

Things fall apart: the centre cannot hold. These words of old return to her as she squats on the cool seat, tearing off pieces of soft toilet paper – a pale bluey-green, to match the walls – trying to dab at her eyes, without smudging her mascara.

Thirty-two

Surely some revelation is at hand.

They drive home in icy silence through the neon-splashed night streets. And then, as if out of nowhere, there is a squall so vicious she is amazed that the car isn't pulled over by a passing police officer and both of them arrested.

The books? How do you know about the books? . . . Well, they're no secret. They're just birthday presents, for a hard-working colleague. We worked well on a case together . . . Get a life, Anna. Sort out your pathetic paranoia.

Yes, and you spoil it. You have to bloody well spoil it. Years and years of work and loyal support and blah-blah wifeliness, and then you have to go and do something bloody stupid with a twenty-six-year-old-girl at work . . . How original is that?

You're mad.

I think you'll find that I am perfectly sane.

The facts finally emerge at a set of traffic lights, directly opposite the lurid lights of a burger restaurant in Swiss Cottage. (Their ersatz flame etched into her memory for years afterwards.) He collapses under the weight of her utter, by-now-murderous determination to live in truth, whatever the cost.

'Okay, so perhaps there is more to it than an exchange of birthday presents, yes, perhaps she is rather more than a close colleague. Yes, something has gone on. Yes, with Her.'

'And did it mean anything?' She cannot believe she is using these banal, borrowed terms, engaging this way, with an alien object that has flown in, to the centre of her life, smashing it to pieces without warning.

Chris hesitates, half of him still sitting in the glow of candle-light of earlier on, an appreciative, beautiful young woman at his side, a woman who understands how good he is at what he does, how hard he works, how hard it is, the risks he takes; none of which his hatchet-faced wife, forever exhausted, surrounded by clinging children, now banging her fists against the dashboard of their car, seems to grasp.

In place of an answer, he begins to shout. To outdo the drumming of her fists. Guilt and bad faith fill the car like noxious fumes.

Later, she has no recollection of jumping out of the car upon reaching their house, of leaving the key in the engine, opening the door, paying the babysitter or driving her home, making distracted – absurdly distracted – small talk about A-levels and college courses. She does remember a short stretch of the car trip back home, a large roundabout near Carlton Vale, empty at this time of night. For it is here, steering the car around this vast circle of concrete, three times in all, that she considers the option of not going home at all.

But there are the children. Always the children. She is in shock, and such a state creates its own velocity, propelling her back to the place where her tormentor waits for her anxiously, pacing the kitchen, a bottle of beer in hand.

Here, his mood has shifted from defensive fury to vulnerable gravity.

'I don't . . .' he begins, when she walks in the kitchen, car keys in hand, brandishing them like a weapon.

Even he cannot complete the long-planned opening sentence of his defence.

A little later on, he talks about his need for Freedom.

Freedom? She marvels at the appalled fury in her own voice. *Freedom?* But you, she screams (in her head: only in her head; all night, she speaks in a low, controlled voice that terrifies him, she knows), you have had nothing but freedom throughout our life together. It is I who faced the mountain of crockery in the sink every dawn morning, who rose for the babies every night once your brief flirtation with involved fatherhood came to an end; it was I who was left morning after morning with the patronising kiss on the head, while you went out into the world to make your reputation and complicated love with another woman. What more freedom, bar a return to the single state, could a man want?

'I fucked up, Anski.'

'Don't call me that.' Her voice is trembling. 'That was a nick-name from a loving, committed marriage. I don't want to hear you speak that name. Ever again.'

He is seated now, an empty beer bottle between his feet, holding his head in his hands. Groaning.

'Are you in some sort of pain?' she asks coldly.

A long silence. How long? Two minutes possibly. A gigantically long absence of talk. A stretch of time as long as counting out tooth-brushing time with children: one elephant, two elephants, three elephants – *get right in the back there, and don't forget the front gums!* One hundred and twenty tooth-brushing elephants.

During this marathon run of quiet, she thinks: So this, then, is how these things end; everything that has been so painfully constructed has to be dismantled. The feelings. The furniture. Yes, I can see myself, removing each of the drawers of the Victorian bureau, folding up all the contents within, unhooking the pictures from the wall outside our bedroom, taking down my treasured photographs, my mother smiling in her tailored white shirt and check skirt, my father's arm hooked around her waist; proof that the past is never any guide to the present, whatever our vain illu-sions. And how will I get that Chinese screen down from the attic? I will need *his* help then. And how will I ask for that, after this?

'I've fucked up, Anna. Completely fucked up.'

'Spare me, please.'

But she is also thinking, with a shamed relief, that maybe this is not the end after all. And thank God, in one sense; for she does not know if she has the energy to dismantle a life of a decade-plus, lacks the courage, or foolishness, to deprive the children of their father. But how can they possibly survive this? (For who tolerates betrayal, really, whatever the relationship handbooks say? Look how much she, the great truth seeker, longs, like deceived wives throughout time, for silence and comforting lies.)

He is not prepared for the silence, must unpick the lies, expiate his sins at some length; he is the kind of man, having done wrong, who must be punished by baring the mess that is his soul. Anna, stern priest, school teacher, steely mother rolled into one, must stay and listen. She must understand what has happened; he insists on it, like a condemned prisoner calling for his right to proclaim his last words and wishes. They must, he insist, 'come to terms with what has happened'. (Her lip curls at the cheap phrase-making of the damaged relationship.) Yet even before he has embarked on his soul-baring, truth-telling session, she, the tired wife, knows exactly what he is going to say. She has heard the substance of the monologue that now emerges from that lovely mouth, with its fine crenellated edges, in one form or another, albeit in different moods, shades, tones of voice, for years. The familiar riff about how the coming of children altered everything, about their being no time for 'us', the pressures of work, the ways in which Anna seemed to have changed, to have gone into herself, imperceptibly, and it was hard to talk, in the old way, about the old things – ideas, books, films; even the simplest thing was so fucking hard to arrange; just a walk or a bit of sex; it was a major strategic operation; how he felt the need to earn, make money, do well, to pay for things, to secure a future for his family, and while he had known this was the deal, he hadn't known that this was what the deal would *feel* like; somehow, at some point, being out there became more interesting, more enticing than being at home.

(There was a time four years ago when she had boldly offered the odd scrap of dissatisfaction herself: Dan's declaration and the deep response it called out of her forcing herself to recognise, to speak, just a little, of the resentments she felt. It had made hardly any difference: temperaments are unchangeable, essentially. She had learned that now.)

Now Chris is openly pleading with her, 'But all of that is crap, too. I love you. Ansk . . . Anna . . . you're the one I want to be with, get old with.'

'Really?'

His nod is so childishly eager, a weak ray of hope returns.

'Everything else is fundamentally irrelevant, beside the point, you know that.'

Poor Katie, Anna thought. Dispatched in such a brutal manner and without her birthday presents.

'I must go to bed.' She stands up, refusing to look him in the eye. It is nearly dawn. The sky outside is a dark, washed grey; the bird song, comically loud.

Thirty-three

May 14 2001
from: Jack777@callme.dot.com
to: AAdams@worldonline.co.uk
subject: direct action

This has been one of my better days. You will read about it tomorrow.
I hope. We jumped out in front of the car of that visiting fascist? I was
really trembling, before. I thought they weren't going to let me do it
because I might let them down. But I was determined. I had my slogans
rolled up in my jacket, ready to run forward. It is not natural, to run
towards danger. You do know that, Anna, don't you? But there were
ten of us coming from all different sides. The car was stopped. A couple
of his heavies jumped out and started laying into us. Thank God for the
British bobby who came in and saved us, roughly of course, but they
got us away from a terrible mauling. Of course, the news made us out
to be mad men who couldn't use proper channels of democratic protest.
I feel so fucking exhilarated now.

We were kept at the station for hours. But then most of us let go.
The beers afterwards tasted amazing and I think I will sleep properly for
the first time in years.

Yes, this has been a good night.

Thirty-four

She reads in the pages of a favourite novel of the passion a married man has for his lover, of the ways in which 'his hunger wishes to burn down all social rules, all courtesy', of how 'his life with others no longer interests him', and she thinks: Were any of that to have been true with Chris and this Katie girl, true even for a second, were such sentiments spoken (and what was Anna doing, at the exact moment those things were spoken: ironing? talking on the telephone to her mother? reading *The English Patient*?), how could she ever find any real meaning in her future life with her husband? And if there could be real meaning, after such a breach, what would that say about love? And where does Dan Givings's declaration, and her knowledge that she could, in a different life, have reciprocated it, but did not choose to do so, fit into any of this?

She is as confused as she is bitter.

'Where are you going?'
  'Out? Is that allowed?'
  'You can't be this angry, not for ever?'
  'I'm not going anywhere, Chris. My children are here.'
  'Don't talk in riddles. Talk to me as a human being.'
  'As you did? To me? All through the Atkins case?'
  'When will you be back?'
  'I don't know.'
  'You're wearing new shoes.'
  'And?'

'You look great.'
'Thanks.'
'Anna?'
'Yes?'
'Please come back.'

It felt strange – almost illicit – walking down the road where her brother lived, on her way to see someone else entirely. She walked fast in the charcoal summer dusk, loving the sharp clickety-click of her new shoes on the paving stones, moving in rhythm with her obsessive thoughts. Two-inch heels – she couldn't wear higher: black leather, a recent bargain buy. Freedom: it was all she could dream of now, like an escape artist coming loose from a complex set of binding knots. Her father had just been diagnosed with an aggressive form of lung cancer: a lifetime without ever touching a cigarette, or even indulging in many pleasures, and he was going the hedonist's way. Why be good? Twelve years of giving and receiving love, and her husband unthinkingly (worse, thinkingly) beds a younger woman in his office. Why be good?

Above her, the mild night was like an unconditional offer. Briefly, she stopped to stare up at the sky, searching for familiar shapes. It always delighted her as a child, those random bright jewels which could be drawn by the eye into the shape of a saucepan or a bear. But tonight she couldn't see anything but a milky veil drawn across the impending darkness; city pollution blocking the beauty of nature.

She continued walking, enjoying the threatening quiet of this long street. Out of nowhere came the dazzle of car headlights.

He lived on the top floor of a large, modern block, his name the last of a long list, scrawls mostly, appended to the right of the bell. (**Jim and Alice**, written in red pen. The next one, neatly typed: **The GULLINSONS**. The next two, blank. And the top bell. **D.G.** As if he were a spy or head of the BBC!) He answered almost immediately, his voice scratchy and far-away: *Top floor – I'll be waiting for you.* As she climbed the three flights of stairs, she could hear him opening his front door; he was there, above her, calling down cheerfully from the top landing – 'Keep going!' – dressed in a baggy old brown wool sweater, and a pair of round spectacles, like a university don.

'I forgot to mention it to you on the phone,' his first words, when she came level to him, 'Ben Calder – remember I told you about him? My friend at the paper? The guy I went to university with?'

Anna, still catching her breath, took a moment to remember. 'Oh, yes. The amateur psychiatrist.'

'Right. Well, he's staying here for a few weeks . . . Until his own place gets fixed up. He's not back yet, but he might be.'

'Fine,' she said, feeling as disappointed as a teenager discovering that her parents were not going out after all. She followed Dan through a narrow hallway into a spacious white living room with a wooden floor. Magazines, books, CDs, stray pens and pencils, scraps of paper, half-empty beer bottles, ashtrays filled with cigarette stubs were scattered across the floor. (She guessed, somehow, that most of this mess belonged to Ben Calder, the visitor: Dan had always struck her as rather tidy.) A long, low white couch and a couple of IKEA armchairs – she recognised them from last year's catalogue – faced a wide-screen TV. A large black sound system squatted in the corner. Through an archway, she could see a galley kitchen.

'Nice.'

'Thanks.' Dan was in the kitchen, leaning over the fridge. He called out, 'Ben's obsessive about music. He sits in that big chair for hours, headphones clamped on his head. Tea? Or something to drink?'

'Beer would be nice.'

'So how's David?' he asked, when he brought her out a bottle.

'You know, then?'

'Mum told me the other day. Anna, I'm really sorry. But it's treatable, isn't it?'

'Aggressive chemo and then wait and see. Between you and me, I don't hold out much hope.'

'I'm really sorry,' he said again, 'that's tough on you all.'

'And Andy and Clare? How are they?' Anna didn't want to talk about illness and death; not now; not tonight.

He looked embarrassed all of a sudden. 'Fine, yes. Fine . . .'

'Are you sure?' He was hesitating, holding something back.

'Apparently, Dad was called in this afternoon. He's been offered . . . well, he's accepted . . .'

'*What?* You're holding something back.'

'Didn't you hear it on the news? He's been sent to the Foreign Office.'

'Jesus Christ. That's . . . incredible!'

'Anna, I'm sorry.' Now she understood his embarrassment of earlier. He felt bad about the stark contrast between the fate of the fathers; thirty years on since the first meeting of the families, the clearest reversal of fortune possible.

'Why?' She refused comparisons, however covert, however deeply and kindly felt. 'Is Andy pleased?'

'I guess so,' Dan shrugged. 'It'll be on the news. I'll need to watch it.'

'Of course. You must. We both must. Turn it on now.'

Just then, the front door banged. Dan made a face of reluctance, even distaste. A scuffling noise in the hall. Ben Calder burst in, dressed in a black jacket, black jeans and a pale-yellow open-necked shirt, a vision of rumpled masculine beauty.

'Why didn't you tell me?' his first words, before turning to Anna, eyes rolling. 'Hi, whoever you are – nice to meet you. You need to know that your friend has kept back some *very important information* from me.' He turned back to Dan, 'I mean, come *on*, everyone at the paper expects me to know that extra little thing about high-up stuff, to have that extra special leading edge, because I know *you*, am, in fact, currently living with *you* – and then *you*, of all people, don't give me the big story.'

He was pretending to be angry, but he was angry, too.

'This is Anna. Anna Adams.'

'No kidding? As in Matt Adams? Seriously, your brother is fantastic. Without people like him, I would never find *anything* out.' And Ben glowered comically at Dan, before shaking Anna's hand with enormous enthusiasm. 'You and Dan, the two families, you go way back?'

'Yes – and Dan didn't know anything, you know. Not until today. If that makes any difference,' Anna said loyally.

'Really. I'm joking. Sort of. Anyway, Dan's used to me. He

knows I know he's useless. At all this kind of thing. He always has been. That's why he couldn't hack it in a real journalist's job. Right?' Dan pulled a face at this, 'But you know the weirdest thing, Anna? Well, you will know. You think, maybe it's because he hates his family, maybe that's the problem. But then you see them all together – Mom, Pop, the two boys – and there's this love between them all that beats anything I ever grew up with. They're all so incredibly close, it would be creepy if it wasn't a little bit touching.'

She wondered if Ben was drunk.

'Yeah, yeah.' Dan had obviously heard all this a dozen times before.

Ben shrugged, pleased by his own comedy and perception. Now he stood before the couch, looking aggressively at the blank television screen.

'*Come on, Dan.* Turn it on! I ran all the way from the station for the pleasure of watching this with you.'

He groped for the remote control. The news had just begun: it was the second item and lasted about thirty seconds . . . In the long-expected summer reshuffle, Andrew Givings had been appointed the new Foreign Secretary. John Gray was to go to education. There were a few minor changes lower down the government . . . And there was Andy, grinning and waving as he walked out of the familiar black door.

Ben, leaning forward eagerly, said, 'Is he going to say something about the foreign-policy issues looming? Nope, apparently not. No, just a statesman-like smile. And yes, here it is. Thank you, look forward to the challenges of this huge job. Blah-Blah.' Ben really was drunk: he was talking over Andy now. 'That's quite enough. Sensible boy. Car's waiting. Hey, Anna, look really closely, you can see your bro in the back there . . .'

'Oh, yeah!' The briefest shadowy glimpse of Matt's profile. Anna went pink with delight and pride.

'Fucking brilliant,' Ben said, flicking the remote control to off when the item was over, 'Andy's a total star. A future leader, I'd put money on it. He's got the gravitas. And the charm. You've got to call him, Danny boy.'

Just then, the phone rang. Ben jumped to answer it.

'Greg, you scoundrel! Yes, I know! So what do you think of *that*? Milk it, man, for all it's worth. No, seriously. Pretty amazing, eh? Yes, yes. He's right here.'

'I'll take it in the bedroom,' Dan said crossly.

Ben followed Anna's concerned gaze. When Dan had shut the door, Ben said thoughtfully, 'You want my opinion?'

She looked at him with an expression of surprise.

'He's far, far too loyal to that old man of his.'

They both shrugged, unsure what to say next.

Half an hour later Ben left them, taking the phone, a packet of unopened cigarettes and an ashtray into his bedroom. He was in love with a young Polish sub-editor on the paper; they often had long phone conversations late at night.

Sitting cross-legged on the floor, Anna told Dan about the agent who had shown interest in her book. 'He really likes it. He thinks, with a bit of work, he might be able to sell it.'

'That's fantastic, Anna. At last!'

'Well, who knows what will happen? Nothing yet. But I'm keeping my fingers crossed.'

Dan was the second person, apart from Sally, to whom she had told the good news about her book. She had not mentioned it to Chris, whom she now treated with chilly politeness at all times.

'I'm enjoying myself, working on a short-story plot right now.'

'Tell me.' Dan had taken one of Ben's cigarettes. He lit it, inhaled with steady deliberation, his attention focused inwards, on the pleasurable sensation of sucking the smoke in. 'Please.'

'Really?'

'Really. I need the distraction.'

'Okay.' Easy to talk if it was for kindness's sake. 'You asked for it! Well, it begins at a party. A young man is standing by the mantelpiece, bored, and he spies this pretty young girl across the room, laughing with another man, and he realises, then and there, that he wants her and he's going to get her. This guy, who is steely and determined, goes in hard: lots of crafted compliments, observations of her uniqueness. He gets his girl. They fall in love. They get married, big wedding, have a family.' Anna is speaking very fast, 'All this is told very quickly, summarised, quite brutally, in a sort of Doris Lessingish way. So far, so good.'

She could hear the sharp inhalation of cigarette smoke.

'Then something funny happens. We switch to seeing things from her perspective only. It's as if the romantic myth of their courtship has grown rather than diminished in her head. Even when she is worn out, with the demands of the children, the tedium of domesticity – no, *especially* because she is worn out with the demands of children and domesticity – some part of her clings on to 'their' story, its apparent uniqueness. It becomes her greatest fantasy. She remembers it all with a glow of tenderness and excitement, the dress she was wearing when he first looked at her across the room – even though she didn't even notice him, did not like him much the first time they spoke. The way she felt when he first came to declare his love, the private jokes they shared, about the ley lines linking his home to hers, the way he used to talk about wanting to kiss her neck, when there were other people present.' Anna paused. 'Okay, so now they are married. For a long time. Eight years, ten years, they are well into the long haul. It's all real, often dreary. You know, its *life*. But what sustains her are those memories, and what they mean. About how cherished she is. How much he wanted her. And fought to get her. She feels chosen. Then, one night, she goes to a party, a work party of her husband's. It's at this place called the Paradise Club – music blaring out, a lot of drunken men, women in dresses that are far too short and men in sweaty shirts. Everyone is much younger than her. But with her usual good grace she, being the wife, knows that this is what you're *supposed* to feel at your husband's office party. She is here to support him. All she has to do is smile, and chat to some of the other people whom she knows a little better – a couple who have been to the house for dinner, the young secretary she sometimes leaves messages with, and so on. This, she is perfectly happy to do, until, until, until . . .'

'Yes?' Dan's voice had an urgency she did not quite trust. 'Yes, what happens then?'

'Then she hears her husband's voice – it is unmistakably his – he is a large man, and his voice has a certain booming quality – and it is coming from around a corner, so that she can hear him, but he cannot see her. And what she hears is quite extraordinary – this man, *her husband*, is speaking almost exactly the same words he spoke to her during their courtship! Those special words, those particular compliments, that she thought unique to her. She simply cannot believe it; she hears exactly the same line from his mouth, something like, "Here's where the line of your beauty is. Here and here." And then something mock-ironic about her fantastic genes . . .'

'Jeans or genes?' Dan interrupted.

'What kind of a scientific writer are you?' Anna smiled. 'It's genes, for God's sake. Keep up! And then she overhears another line, lifted direct from her own courtship, and she cannot stand it. Ten years into marriage she realises she has been *cheated. Cheated of her own sense of utter uniqueness.* For she realises now that her husband's seduction of her was just a *rap*. A glorified chat-up line. Still with me?'

'Uh-huh. The poor woman married a creep. Oldest story in the world.'

'No, no, no. Dan. What you don't see,' and she raised her eyebrows, warning him off partisanship, 'is that for the story to work, you're not to think he is merely a creep. What I mean is, what really shatters her is *not* the fact that the man she chose to be her life partner is seducing another woman right under her nose. No, what's really cutting her up is the realisation of the emptiness on which she has built the meaning of her *own* life.'

By now Anna was talking so fast, so low, he could barely hear her.

'I'm still with you.'

'Thanks.' She shot him a grateful look. 'So what then? That's what I keep thinking. What happens then? You see, this is actually a story about *biology*, not love. Because all love stories are in a sense a story of biology rather than feeling. That's really what I'm trying to say.'

'So what is the *biological* answer to betrayal?'

Was he laughing at her? She couldn't be sure.

'This is how I see it ending in my head. She leaves the pub and she starts walking, randomly. She's a mad woman, obviously. She's in so much pain. She starts to walk down by the river.

Across Westminster Bridge. Life-changing Westminster Bridge. Remember?' (She throws him a smile, homage to his own crisis, five years before.) 'And she stops to look, because the view, the perspective, the lights and the darkness, the buildings, the water, it's all so completely beautiful, St Paul's lit up over there, and the House of Commons glowing auburn and green-tinted over there, and the darkness of the river . . . but she's all crazy and obsessive up in her head. And with the clarity of the temporarily insane, she sees that she should have paid more attention to the content of her husband's original remarks, all those years ago. She should not have let romance, which is essentially an irrelevance, obscure what was really going on. But now she sees; the clues were there all along. Now she understands that when he made that comment to her about her genes, he was talking literally. He was saying: Yes, you, lady, have the right cheekbones, eyes, whatever, to make nice babies with me. He was dissecting her like an animal, choosing her like a breeding cow. And so it was – is – with the woman at the party, who is, inevitably, younger – with creamy skin and smooth eyelids and glossy hair.'

'Ah, so we have seen the girlfriend, have we? We know what she looks like?'

'Yes. Well, let's just presume that our heroine knows who the most likely contender for the post of her husband's mistress might be, based on her knowledge of his workplace. Okay?'

'Logical.' He conceded the point, as he took out another cigarette.

'So this woman, the inevitable younger woman, the woman who looks up to him, through thick lashes, in awe of his proven worldly skills and power – well, there's a biological drive in here, too. Mid-life crisis. The need for renewal. Out with old flaky cells: in with the new. Don't you see? The first time round, he was choosing a partner, in order to reproduce. Fairly straightforward. The second time round, he is choosing someone to ward off the intimations of mortality.'

'There could be other times the heroine of your story doesn't know about?'

Anna frowned, ignoring him. 'I thought it could be called something like "Biology Lessons".'

'What about "The Paradise Club"?'

'Possibly . . .'

'And the husband? Is he to remain unpunished?'

'God, no. But he needs to be to the story what he has become to her: irrelevant. Biologically speaking, of course, he is. Her family is complete. The job is finished. She no longer needs his sperm.'

'But presumably she needs his continuing protection? His money maybe?'

'When she stands looking over the river that night, she understands that whatever happens, she mustn't keep her attention riveted on him as she has done throughout their marriage. Love, romance, anger, bitterness. Essentially they're all doing the same thing, which is diverting attention from *her* life to *his*.'

Dan said, 'I think she should stop being brave and so detached. I think she should kill him, slowly, painfully, with a screwdriver. And chuck his body in the river.'

'Seriously?' Her own voice came out like a squeak.

'Why not?' He was looking at her so intently, his eyes so full of sympathy, that she had to turn her head away, pretend to scratch her foot: a totally fabricated irritation.

'It's rotten luck, Anna.'

He stood up, walked across the room, to get a cushion for his back. He spoke at first with his back to her, his voice muffled. 'The world is full of men like that.' He turned round, and his voice was clearer. 'Tall, successful, good at their jobs. Marry well. Have kids. Dress well. Do all the outward stuff. But, you know what? Deep down in their soul, they're frauds. And they know it. Preening, self-regarding, inauthentic *phonies*.'

Such irritation suited him. He had more colour in his face. At the same time, she thought: but this is envy speaking: of what you have not had.

Now, she chided him. 'Hey, you of all people are supposed to know the difference between fiction and non-fiction.'

'Oh, but I do,' he said, turning back to look at her, this time with an unfathomable, almost hostile expression on his face. 'Believe me, I do.'

Thirty-five

On the way home, reflecting on their conversation, she thought, fondly: *But Dan cannot possibly understand.* She liked it, his partisanship, the way he saw things in black-and-white, just as her brothers would, had they known of Chris's betrayal. (For Dan had guessed: of course he had.) At some level, she wanted that: simple finger-pointing at simple bad behaviour. The problem for her was that an accusation of wrongdoing or even of middle-aged banality did not nudge close to the agony she was enduring, an agony Dan could not understand only because he had not yet taken that giant, foolish, extraordinary step, of trusting and translating feeling into more solid form – the committed relationship, the marriage – that the pain of betrayal is not merely a feeling of foolishness, not primarily; it is the pain of absolute and utter exclusion. Infidelity, like a slow-acting, invisible poison, sour-sweet to one; vast in its unglimpsed, but guessed-at dimensions, to another. Hence the perpetual shadow of distrust. Who knows what gesture, what joke, what snatch of song or poetry, what promise – broken, but still spoken out loud, in the real world, once upon a time – has entered the bloodstream of the betrayer? There, to be spirited into consciousness at random future moments for evermore, part of a silent, fully realised language – the language of the past, the language of secret love, the language of hope itself – swelling with clandestine meaning, forever unknown and unknowable to the betrayed?

Even now she could not allow herself to conjure up images of her husband, so utterly familiar, so newly strange, lying with the pale fragile blonde from the dinner party, the woman with the small smile and the powerful family (interesting, how she could not hold the woman's name in her head, had expunged it from the moment she knew of real wrongdoing). It was quite simply an outrage. Lying with, yes. Lying with. (That came close to the real truth of the matter.) Laughing with . . . no, in the interests of sensible self-preservation she bats the scrap of an emerging picture away. What damage, she thinks, did Chris have to do his idea of her soul, her living, breathing, loving soul; what mechanism allowed him to obliterate all those years of knowledge, in order to lie with, laugh with, create a private language with, a sometime stranger? Was it pure vanity, as some element of her story suggested? A panic about fading youth? Perhaps Dan grasps these banalities better than she. Sees them for what they really are.

But no, he cannot know.

One thing she has to concede. Dan understands enough to feel a deep sadness for her, a feeling she has not yet experienced, not since the first moment at the dinner party, when her head seemed bursting with a torrent of tears, ready to break. But since, then? Nothing. It was her most bitter discovery yet, the aridity of the pain of betrayal. A feeling that drove deep down, into the hard, unyielding earth of self, far beneath sadness.

At home, everyone was asleep. There was a loving note from Chris in the hall. She smiled, but screwed it up into a tight ball and threw it in the living room bin. She hoped he would find it there. Discarded.

She was not tired. She poured herself a glass of wine and climbed the ladder that led up into the attic as quietly as she could and turned on her word processor. She had decided how she would end her story, what would happen to the husband. She was keen to get on with the writing.

Her screen flashed up: three e-mail messages. One wanted to sell her software, the second offered to extend her penis by a full four inches.

The third was from Jack.

June 20 2001
from: Jack777@callme.dot.com
to: AAdams@worldonline.co.uk
re: fame at last!

Thank you for telling me about our father. It does not surprise me, cancer the return of the repressed in the form of bad dancing cells. Is it treatable? (See – I am trying to ask the neutral questions?) News not sunk in. Nor the news about Andy. From the VNGM to the Nearly Great Man. NGM. Andy Nearly There Givings. Did you see it on the news? I try not to be impressed. It's only power after all. Temporal. Meaningless. A job. Right now, there is a book being written that will have far greater impact on the future of our world than Andy Givings becoming Foreign Secretary. His name, a footnote in history. Can you remember the names of any Prime Ministers, let alone Foreign Secretaries or Chancellors of the past? How quickly they become yesterday's men. Waxworks. You have to represent a powerful idea, not a state, a set of armies, an economy, to be truly remembered. Hard not to remember right now, the other Andy, the one in the red-paper hat, the thinner, smilier man of all those years ago – do you remember how he would insist on doing the washing, putting on our mother's yellow rubber gloves? Well, you know I always liked him the minute I first saw him in the kitchen. He took an interest in me. And not false. Andy had a talent for people. Such a talent should never be derided, but should be spread more thinly through the population, in my humble opinion.

March 2003

'He was one of those, wasn't he? Activists waging the war against the war against terrorism . . .' Ben is scribbling fast now. 'There's the odd reference to his activities from 2001 onwards. On the Net and stuff. But surprisingly little, actually.'

Anna says, 'He became obsessed. After September 11th, then the invasion of Afghanistan. He began to sit out at that encampment opposite the entrance to the House of Commons.'

Ben nods; sees it almost daily.

'He was there day and night.'

'So there was Andy,' Ben muses, 'the new Foreign Secretary. Flying back and forth to America. Doing the Americans' bidding. Part of the build-up to war. And there was Jack . . .

'Yes — Jack — out on the streets.' Like all his old clients, in fact. Yes, she hadn't thought of that. All those years getting people off the street and he ends up on it. And then the politics. It was that stark, his opposition to power. Everything black-and-white with Jack. As if he was personally taking up a position of opposition to Andy. What he represented.

'I think that was Jack's idea, conscious or unconscious. To stare the powerful in the eye.'

And yet, at the same time, it wasn't personal. Jack loved Andy. More than he loved his own father.

Ben says, 'Hang on a minute. Andy must have seen him, every time he sped out of the Commons in his big black car. Did he know Jack was there?'

'Yes, he did. And yes. He went to talk to him. Just once,' Anna *says, reading the journalist's thoughts. Late one night, after a vote in the House. Early on, during the war in Afghanistan. He had gone over, to talk to Jack and the young woman standing out there with him, a woman holding a white banner proclaiming* NO MORE BLOOD TO BE SPILLED IN OUR NAME.

'I don't think he went again,' she says.

'And when did you . . . last see Jack?'

'Just before . . . our father died. A week or so before. I wanted him to come and say a proper goodbye. Despite everything.'

'And? Did you succeed?'

'What do you think?'

Thirty-six

Jack might not have buzzed her in if he'd had a chance to think about it. The street entrance worked on an answerphone system; she was relieved to find the door swinging open. The internal stairwell was light and airy, the walls painted a chilly ice-blue, but the stairs were scattered with rubbish. The acid smell of human piss on the second-floor landing.

'Jack. Jack!' she called through the letter box. 'It's Anna. Don't worry. No emergency. No-one's dead. I was just passing.'

Her words echoed around the empty landing, a commentary on her lack of frankness.

'Are Harry and Lo with you?' His voice sounded muffled, a little frightened.

'No, it's just me. Sorry.'

She felt ashamed that she had never visited the flat before. He had never invited her, and she had never asked to be asked. For a long time it had seemed enough to meet him on neutral territory, to encourage him to visit her and the children at home, when Chris was out.

It was the smell that hit her first. A sweet musty smell; the odour of enforced enclosure; of tinned food; long-unwashed clothes.

'It's a mess. You don't mind?'

She followed him now through the tiny vestibule into a room no bigger than twelve feet by twelve, painted an oppressively dark turquoise-blue. Along one wall ran a cooker, sink unit and fridge.

'Welcome to my humble abode.'

'Well, thanks. You have a bedroom too, I presume?' She kept her comments factual while she absorbed the shock of this squalid accommodation, tried to resist comparisons with Dan's airy front room just a hundred yards down the road, to not register the painful contrast between the two men's lives.

'Yeah, the bedroom's about this size again.'

There were books everywhere, spilling out from cardboard boxes, stacked in precarious-looking towers on the floor. In her confusion and rank upset that her brother should live like this, the room briefly appeared to her as a distorted dream-like version of their father's study back at the old house. A square, self-contained space, stuffed with words. The Secret Room; shutting the world out.

Brother and sister faced each other. Two middle-aged people. The dark curly-haired sister, with her tote bag stuffed with tissues, combs, spare change, a bottle of water, house keys, book, newspaper, notebook (in case a useful thought should come to her, while she was out and about). And the brother, in T-shirt and shorts, stomach protruding, the ageing face framed by a greying ginger beard.

'Ol' blue eyes,' she said, punching his stomach lightly, teasingly. Still recognisably Jack. Still alive. 'Your e-mails are amazing,' she said, conversationally, turning her back to pace round the room, looking for signs of life apart from political activity. There were piles of paper everywhere that looked vaguely official. 'So is this where you fire them all off from?' She walked over to an old computer terminal sitting on a rickety four-legged desk.

'The Americans are dangerous,' Jack said, equally casually. 'They're going to take us into a third world war if they're not careful. *Empires* are dangerous. Any kind of empire.'

She wondered whether to sit on the hideous mustard-coloured couch, but it was spread with a grubby-looking blanket, and, here too, there were clothes and books piled on top of it.

Jack misinterpreted her look of enquiry; answered with typical solipsism. 'Yeah. I often just lie down there. If I'm having trouble getting off. Something about the bedroom depresses me. The law of paradoxical intention. If I think I'm supposed to sleep, I don't. I can't.'

'So you're not sleeping much better then?'

He shrugged.

'But in *general*, you're okay?' She sat down on the furthest edge of the couch. 'Got any tea?'

'Tea, no milk. Yeah?'

'I just wanted to see you. I never really *see* you. Everyone asks about you.'

He had pressed the button on the base of the kettle. A roaring sound filled the small, sickly, sweet-smelling space, rather like an aeroplane taking off. The noise drowned out everything except his shouted 'They worry about me, do they?'

'You know they do. Mum and Dad. I wish you'd come and see them. Just once,' she bellowed back.

He turned off the kettle, leaving her last two words reverberating around the room, while he poured water into a white mug. (Did she trust the cleanliness of the cups here? She felt ashamed of her suspicion.)

'Dad's sick,' she said, very quietly. 'He's probably near the end . . .'

'They don't need me,' Jack spoke with the old infuriating coolness, so different from his e-mails. 'They've got Matt. And pretty-as-a-picture Laura. And brave, campaigning Christopher. You married well there. Successful hubby. Son. Daughter. And then look at *you*. Publishing a book to good reviews.'

'Yeah, yeah.' He had never mentioned it before, even though she had sent him a copy of the book, invited him to the launch. She had even sent him a couple of press cuttings – Fiona-fashion – so that he would not feel out of the loop. But he had never responded.

'You're talented, no doubt about that.' He was struggling, not to attack her, of all people. But he could not quite succeed: 'Your *father* must have been extremely proud of you.'

She winced at his use of the past tense, more than the brutal rejection implicit in the term 'your father'. Once more, she set any hurt firmly aside in the interests of her one aim: to get her brother home, to Durnford Gardens, one more time.

'That's families, Jack. That's just how it is. Parents are proud of their children. Grandparents adore their grandchildren. Everyone does their best with their in-laws. We all learn by our mistakes. You know that perfectly well. You have to have a measure of detachment. To understand the extent to which we were . . . *practised* on. That's families.'

She was choosing her words very carefully.

'No, that's families of a certain kind.' Jack was bullish now. 'The kind that can tolerate anything but worldly failure or the refusal to reproduce.'

Are you telling me that if Lucia had thrown herself at you and wanted to have your babies, you'd have said no? And if she had then said: Get a job, get a haircut, stop the politicking, you'd have refused her that, too?

One doesn't say the obvious to Jack.

'Refusal? Or just the fact of never getting round to it?'

'Anyway,' he said, shaking his head like someone climbing out of a swimming pool, 'all that is irrelevant. It really is. I've chosen my path. Different drummer and all that.'

'But they want to meet you halfway.'

'Have they sent you? They *have* sent you.' He handed her a cup. It looked clean enough. She took a sip. Weak milk-free tea.

'This is not a thriller, Jack. I'm a mother myself now. I understand how easy it is to get it all wrong. I'm simply trying to get you to undertake a kind act in regard to two elderly people who recognise they may have been a little harsh, a little too conventional.'

Her parents had admitted nothing of the sort: such self-criticism was beyond them. But, Anna had decided, a certain emotional licence was permissible in emergencies. The truth was, her mother was so exhausted these days, she uncharacteristically exploded whenever Jack's name was mentioned. *Such total, utter selfishness.* Her father lay under cover of terminal illness; unreachable in new ways.

Jack looked momentarily confused, 'Yes, but . . . You were always kind, Anna. "Kindness, the ruling principle of nowhere." Do you know that line?'

'No.'

'You're the writer in the family. You should know who I mean. That bloke who became a woman, the travel writer. Jan somebody. I forget his . . . er, her name . . .' He grinned, briefly embarrassed.

'I know who you mean . . .' she said quickly. 'Were they – are they – *so* bad?' She meant their parents.

The odd thing was, the death of their father would hit him hardest of all. Couldn't he see that?

Jack was shaking his head again, more violently this time. 'No. No. No,' he kept saying those words, very quietly. 'No. No. No. No.'

'All right,' she said, impatience giving way to concern, leaning down to reach into her bag, searching for her wallet. It was a few months since she'd last seen him and she sensed a discernible change; whatever it was, lodged in his head, that made him Jack, that made him angry, that kept him isolated, had been whittled down, even further. He was, now, in an almost animal state, a place of primal reaction. She was worried that he might have a fit or lose control. For the first time in her life, she was physically afraid of him, unsure of what he might do. He had a powerful physique and enough fury to fuel an army.

'Can I show you – I know it's crazy – a picture of Lola at her assembly?' Anna was talking quickly, 'taken last week. You see she's in a samba band. Look, Jack! Lo and a drum. Different drummer. Like those people you mentioned – what was the name of that band, the street band?'

Hold his eye steady so he can't go into one. *Remind him who I am. Anna. Your sister.*

He was blinking at her, blue eyes bright, as if he had just come awake. 'What band?'

'You wrote to me about them. Years ago. When you went to Seattle.'

'The Infernal Noise Brigade!' His face lit up with a childish smile.

'*Yes! Yes!* That's it exactly. Here, come see your niece, carrying on the family tradition. Making noise for a constructive, meaningful end.' Anna was chattering like a parakeet.

It took a moment, but she saw his chest collapse, his body calm. Then, he smiled; a stiff smile, at first, broadening into a real grin (he adored his niece and nephew) as he came to perch next to her on the couch, peering over at first, then taking the photo out of her hand.

'Good. Yeah. Good. Wow. Lo looks *exactly* like Laura . . . That's weird,' he said good-naturedly.

This close, she could hear his breathing. It was a rasp: fast, panicky. A rattle in his chest.

Thirty-seven

She had maintained a vigil throughout the night, dozing on and off through the early hours. As the dawn light began to push through the ward's thin, navy curtains, the body on the bed sat bolt upright, a stream of brownish-black liquid spewing from his mouth. Shaken, she searched round for something to stem the flow. Jutting out from beneath the end of the bed she found a stack of stiff grey-cardboard, kidney-shaped dishes. Just in time, she managed to catch the next emission, a large teaspoon's worth of the thick treacle, before her father slumped back on the bed.

'Is there anyone there?' she turned her body towards the door, hoping to attract the attention of a passing nurse.

Within seconds the ward sister, a kind middle-aged black woman with round, gold-framed spectacles, had come into the room. 'Wash there.' She directed Anna to a small sink over by the window, pulling open the curtain to let in the gritty light.

On the television, high above the ward sister's head – bobbing up and down as she briskly cleaned up the sticky black mess on the white sheets – images of world conflict flickered in lurid primary colours. Image succeeded image with dizzying speed: Blair and Bush standing side by side at waist-level podiums; Hans Blix speaking before a bank of microphones; Andy, running down a short set of aeroplane steps, hand extended in readiness to shake those of the dignitaries awaiting him on the tarmac.

Washing her hands twice, Anna gazed out of the window, down at the sprawling city far below, still wreathed in a dawn mist with its pearly-grey buildings, putty-coloured mash of roads, the tranquil band of blue-grey ribbon of the Thames. She could see the light strip of terrace where she had sat on that warm afternoon at the House of Commons three and a half years ago, she, Matt, Andy and the children, having tea, briefly, before they were interrupted by a minor political emergency. From here, it looked like a detachable piece of a children's train set. Things fall apart, that's for sure, she thought, drying her hands on a stiff grey-white towel hanging below the sink. Marriages. Love. Life. Countries. Governments. Even the special relationship between Matt and Andy had disintegrated over the past year. To everyone's surprise, Matt had been uneasy about the strikes in Afghanistan, America and Britain's response to the Twin Towers disaster, was firmly against the invasion of Iraq; unthinkable, he insisted, without a second United Nations resolution. Increasingly, he was a lone voice among Andy's circle at the heart of government. Loyal as ever, he had spoken to no-one bar his parents and wife (and Andy, of course) about his reservations; had not once briefed a journalist, or hinted publicly at his unease over the direction of government policy. As the months passed and the prospect of an all-out attack on Baghdad grew stronger, the strain had begun to show. He had come often, in the past few weeks, to see his ailing father, who, they all knew, had only weeks to live, to seek his advice. Should he quit entirely? Should he stay and continue to try and persuade Andy, who was increasingly hawkish, to another view? Anna had run into Matt a couple of times in the hall at Durnford Gardens, coming down the stairs from her parents' bedroom where her father, before this final move to hospital, had been confined to bed, cared for round the clock by two nurses and his wife; Anna had been struck by how drawn, almost gaunt, her elder brother had become.

'It's exhausting your father, this Matt/Andy crisis . . .' her mother had said after one such visit. 'Matt keeps going round and round the same difficulties.'

'But what does Dad advise?' Surely he of all people would know how to reconcile his dearest friend and his eldest son.

Her mother, whose authority had seemed to swell as her husband's was slipping, said briskly, 'He told him to follow his conscience. Not power. If he thinks what's being contemplated is wrong, he should not support it. Regardless of what anyone else thinks. It's as simple as that.' She added, 'He's against this government, you know. What they're planning.'

'But Matt and Andy. They've been inseparable. For so long.' Anna spoke as plaintively as a child.

'This is not the school playground, Anna.'

And her mother swept on, down through the kitchen to the laundry room, her arms full of soiled sheets, her back bowed by these final, draining wifely duties.

There was no dramatic break; no big falling out; neither man would allow it. As the build up to war began, Matt was simply pushed, gently, to the outer edge of the advisers' circle. (Anna had the same dream, three nights in a row: her eldest brother, standing in the garden of his house up on the park, looking back up at the French windows of the house, the room where he had held that briefing meeting, on the Sunday, in spring 1997, the meeting that Jack had interrupted, the one at which Susanna Seargent was present and had witnessed the rock-throwing. There at the window stands Andy, his hand resting on the shoulders of the brisk adviser in the square red-framed glasses, Martina Cartwright, the woman who had broken into their family group on the terrace that afternoon at the House of Commons with the news of the head teacher who had resigned.) Martina was a key part of Andy's expanding circle of policy advisers; he relied on her more and more. A graduate of Cambridge and Harvard, this handsome young woman was one of the leaders of the faction who supported swift, severe military action. While Matt sat – quiet, not quite defeated, simmering with fury and confusion, in meeting after meeting – he heard Martina argue that not only would action against Saddam Hussein end the reign of an appalling despot, and so honour the millions of his victims; it would cauterise the growing cancer of world terrorism. This, she said, frequently, with the utmost sincerity, will be our ineradicable, long-lasting contribution to the spread of democracy throughout the world.

'Are you comfortable? Can I get you anything?'

Back at the sink, she soaked a flannel in cold water, brought it, dripping, over to the bed; pressed it to her father's dry, lined forehead. It was hard to know what to do to help him; he was barely responding. Tiny droplets of water trickled down his face, caught in the hard waxy flap of his ear. She stemmed the flow with her forefinger, scooping up the cool water, drying her finger on a towel.

After a few minutes she unpeeled the flannel from his forehead, put it down carefully on the squat side locker. Still standing, she took her father's hand in hers.

'I saw Jack a couple of weeks ago.'

Her father squeezed her hand so hard, she winced in pain.

'Dad? You'd like Jack to be here?'

Another hard squeeze.

The words began to tumble out of her. 'You know, don't you? Things went wrong for him. He loved a woman, but she married someone else. He couldn't tell anyone. He felt humiliated. And then he was jealous of Matt. Well, that's what I think. Jack didn't know just how to be good at the things *he* thought *you* thought were worth being good at, so he never learned how to stick up for his own talents. He'd always been so busy telling himself other people didn't matter, when in fact they matter too much.'

What is this thing called life or death? Consciousness, here, now, perhaps total, and then, all dark; the brain such a beautiful, sophisticated instrument, in service for such a short amount of time. She couldn't imagine her father's consciousness no longer existing in the world, containing all the experience he had had, all the knowledge he had absorbed; his care for those he loved. For Anna. He had loved Anna. She knew that; it was a blanket she could wrap round herself, warm herself within, endlessly.

This was her last chance. To tell a truth, or two. To protect her father, too.

'I used to think Jack was made up of all the awkward bits of a person, all the parts everyone else tries to hide. Especially his refusal to compromise. That refusal. It's so juvenile and yet it's awesome, too. Do you know what I mean? Remember, we've often said, how every quality has two sides to it? Flexibility is weakness in another context? Determination, an amoral rigidity?'

For this was how they did talk, at their best; father and daughter.

235

Slowly, the dying man's lips began to move, an animal noise emerging. She could not make out what he was saying, leaned in closer, to try and disentangle the words. He had enough power left in his muscles to wrench at her arm; now, he pulled at her so hard she nearly toppled onto his chest. There was something repugnant, almost sexual, in the force and intimacy of the gesture. On and on his mouth formed agitated shapes; a discernible sentence hovering there, she knew, tantalisingly beyond her hearing.

'What is it? What is it?'

Once more, a string of hoarse words, fragments of incomprehensible sentences. Anna was near to tears at her failure to understand what he was saying. These were his last words, she was sure of it.

A stab in the dark.

'Do you want me to tell Jack that you love him. Is that it, Dad? I can do that. *Will* do that. I promise you. I will let him know that.'

Her father's head was now turned towards her, the bones of his skull visible in his emaciation, dry lips opening and closing, like a fish out of water. After a while he stopped, the intensive effort exhausting the thin, shrivelled frame.

'Hello, darling.'

Her mother, a few minutes later, brushing past her shoulder, returning from a rare night away from the hospital, catching up on sleep. For a moment, she seemed both utterly alien and completely fresh; moving, Anna noticed, rather like the busy nurses moved, her actions part of one continuous fluid, purposive movement. Laying her flame-red coat over a chair, draping her patterned silk scarf over it, she immediately turned towards the bed and rolled up the sleeves of her shirt.

'Where have the sponges gone? Did the nurse bring a new batch? He needs moisture, Anna. Can't you see? His lips are cracking!'

'I didn't realise . . . He was trying to say something.'

She felt eleven years old all over again, a child acting under more competent instruction.

Her mother moved the damp sponge around the inside of her

husband's mouth. He sucked wildly at it like a newborn baby rooting for the nipple. '*That's* probably what he was trying to tell you,' she said sternly.

'I hate what this has done . . . is doing . . .' Anna collapsed on a chair by the locker and tried to control her tears.

'I know, darling,' her mother rubbed the top of her head, gently, 'you're exhausted. And it's horrible. For us all. But you of all people mustn't get overwhelmed by it. You have your own family to look after. Chris and the kids.'

'Yes.' At this moment, even her precious children seemed remote.

'It won't be long now. Matt and Laura will be here any moment.'

'I . . . I was just telling Dad . . .' Anna found it hard to get the words out; her mother's version of reality had always overwhelmed her, she realised. She would not want Anna to say what she was about to say. An invisible barrier needed to be broken through. 'About Jack. And why he is not here. And how it doesn't mean Jack isn't thinking of him.'

Frowning, her mother took the sponge out of her father's mouth, laying it in the dish by his bedside. She said nothing.

'We don't *know* that, Anna,' she said eventually, with the harshness of earlier.

'Oh, but I think I do.' Anna wailed, suddenly child-like, 'Why didn't we sort all this out before? Why could we never talk about it – Jack – whatever it was, before it was too late? Now I can't reach him. I can't reach him.'

She grabbed her mother's arm and shook it, while the older woman, her face surprisingly smooth and young-looking after a good night's rest, looked at her with an unfathomable expression. 'Perhaps,' her mother lowered her voice, spoke between gritted teeth, 'your father could *never* be reached. By some of us. About certain things.'

'I don't understand you.' Anna backed off, shocked at the violence of her reaction.

Seeing her disturbance, her mother adopted a more emollient tone of voice, 'I just mean, don't upset yourself, you of all people, Anna, about two stubborn men, who couldn't find a simple way through the difficult matter of human relations. Perhaps your father and Jack are – were – too alike. Unreachable, as you say. Arrogant.'

Anna felt surprise, again, and a touch of pity, for her mother's late-burning anger. Remembered her, a lone figure, standing outside the Secret Room, her hand on the study-door handle, wanting but not daring to go in. Afraid to disturb her busy husband. Wanting, waiting, yet somehow not ever daring to act.

And she *should* have acted. That's what Anna is thinking now, still gripping her mother's arm, feeling a new power coursing through her. Too little too late! Her mother should have insisted on her right to be heard, to be treated with more affection; long ago, she should have usurped her overbearing mother-in-law Agnes, whose grief over Len, her own second-born son, stalked their whole family, whose passion and ambition for David, her successful first-born, shaped all their relations without their truly realising it; she, Fiona, Anna's mother, should have insisted on her husband gently loving his own second son, whoever he was, however much he angered and annoyed him. No, they were not 'two stubborn men' who were forever squaring up to each other. Jack was the child: David was the father. Jack had the childish right to reject everything his parents stood for, and still be kept close.

Her mother had failed to stand by her own, more emotional truths; to honour her own instinctual belief in the importance of encouragement, tolerance and forgiveness. Instead, all was covert; she, herself, a fifth child: suggesting secret hot chocolates when the angry patriarch had gone to bed; sending money, no note attached, to the flat in Essex Road (a dozen times: Jack never acknowledging these gifts), making pleading phone calls that demanded a change of life course. No, she had deferred always to the high standards of her solitary, brilliant husband. Matt, too (lucky enough, one might say, to be born with a temperament that allowed him to do what was expected of him, make a success of his life, drive himself to ever greater achievement; a course that had taken him through right to this late mid-stage of life, when he, too, was suddenly lost). But Jack? What had happened to Jack in all this? Her mother had collapsed before her husband's stubborn power. For the love of David, never won (or not in the way she wanted it), she, too, had sacrificed her awkward second-born son.

That was why Jack was not here: they both knew it.

And it was – very nearly – too late.

'Promise me one thing, Anna.' Her mother, tidying up one of the locker's drawers, stood with her back to her. Laura had just phoned from the hospital shop to say Matt was parking the car, and she was on her way up in the lift.

'What?'

'No sacrifices, Anna. No martyrdom.'

For the second time that day, Anna looked at her mother – the silky back of her, with just a hint of the curvature of the spine to come – with complete incomprehension.

'What do you mean?'

Her mother turned round, unwillingly, reddening slightly as she spoke.

'Look out for yourself. Promise me that you'll look out for yourself.'

Anna could hear Laura's voice in the hall, speaking to Ari on her mobile. *Yes, yes, any time now. Yes, I'll ring you as soon as . . .*

So this was where the web of family, stretching over the generations, drawing everyone in to its complex connections, might end after all; no all-embracing we, no all-forgiving us; just the plaintive cry, beneath all surfaces, of me, myself, I.

Thirty-eight

I have to see you.

In the six days between her father's death and the funeral, she and Dan meet every day. They did not know that this was what they craved or had to do. The sequence of meetings just happened. (He rang her, in the hours after her father's death, awkward condolences offered on her eldest brother's mobile, the phone passed around the living room, where she, her mother, Matt and Laura sat, with cups of tea, companionable silence broken up by tears, excited chatter, gales of laughter; when it was her turn to take the phone, he said very little, except, *I have to see you*, and then, bowing to the practical necessity of making arrangements: *Can I speak to you later about where and when we might meet?* His tone was low, and urgent, his request exact. He knew what he was doing and also, so it happened, what she needed; and so, at that urgent, exact moment, she fell in love.) Each morning she wakes, full of longing for him; each night she calms herself, picturing his face before falling into a deep, dreamless sleep. She is in the grip of a grieving infatuation; unreal; intensely felt; a substitute; a thing in itself; she knows all this. They meet at a different location around the city, agreed the day before: at a small Italian café in a passageway near Lincoln's Inn; in the foyer of the cinema on Islington Green; at a bench on the top of Primrose Hill; at a pre-assigned room at the National Gallery. Sometimes they have only an hour together; at other times, they are together for most of the day.

Anna is often late; she arrives, half-running, hair flying behind her. Seeing his tall, reassuring figure – newspaper open before him, or head to one side, scrutinising a painting, film poster or the view sloping away from him – she leans against him, wordless, eyes half-closed. Neither asks the other how they managed this time away, nor to whom – employer, spouse, child, parent – they lied or said nothing, which amounts to the same thing. They speak very little. They walk a great deal. Arm in arm.

On the third day, Anna tells Dan about the way the consultant, a small, squat woman of about fifty years of age, dressed in a white coat, with a ferociously tight brunette perm, talked, very kindly, about her father's 'progress towards death'.

'What an amazing phrase. I didn't know whether to be impressed or appalled.'

'Sounds pretty much like Andy's world, too.'

She smiles in melancholy understanding of his position. Could anyone have predicted how much Andy's public stance would have shifted, subtly at first, with increasing vociferousness over the past year, so that he is known now as one of the most bullish of the Cabinet, urging full-scale invasion? 'Time to take a stand' the motto by which he has become known. Newspaper billboards offer capitalised summaries of his latest speech on the 'just war'.

Today, in one of the liberal broadsheets, he is interviewed by Ben Calder on the necessity of standing up to evil, whatever the consequences. Calder notes his new 'tough demeanour, the famed charm decisively set aside, as if the life-and-death decisions that face him demand it'.

'Does Andy *really* believe all this?' she asks, genuinely curious.

'When Colin Powell spoke to the United Nations, well . . . I think I shifted a bit,' Dan, loyal as ever, answers her question obliquely.

She and Chris had watched Powell on the news making his speech to the United Nations. Afterwards, her husband had taken her hand in his – she did not resist – and said, 'Looks like the Third World War is really going to come, Anski.' (She did not protest at his use of her nickname, either; he took it, she knew, as a small victory in the long campaign to win her love back.)

'But then I see Bush,' Dan continued, 'that stupid face. And the terrifying people around him. And I don't believe any of it. I don't trust them. I don't trust that this is the right thing to do. Harold Wilson didn't get pulled into Vietnam. Why are we following the Americans so blindly?'

This is the stuff, she tells him, of Jack's relentless torrent of e-mails over the past few weeks, pages and pages on the delicate negotiations in the United Nations, the bullishness of the Americans at the UN, the 'spineless craven behaviour' of the British, the sufferings that the Iraqis have already endured. He writes nothing personal any more. He does not mention his father's death. (She had telephoned the flat several times, in order to give him the news; either he was not there or he did not pick up the receiver, knowing perhaps who or what it might be. In the end, she drove over to his flat; the street door had been mended, and there was no answer when she pressed the bell. She left a short, loving note, written earlier at home, because she had predicted his absence, had hoped for it, in truth.)

The e-mails refer only to his desperation at the sight of powerful men playing at international conflict. *We have to stop them before it is too late, Anna.*

As if she has any power.

'I'm beginning to wonder if I'm being tailed,' Dan says, rather bemused, on the fourth day. 'That man in the brown jacket over there – or there – that pizza-delivery guy. They worry, you know, that we – Greg and I – will be targets for kidnapping. Or random attacks.'

They: Andy and Clare: Andy's people: Andy's *new* people. Martina, perhaps?

'Have you been offered any protection?'

'Well, no. But that's why I wonder. If they don't bother to ask. They just do it.'

'I wonder what they'd make of us?' She smiled. 'Meeting like this, day after day.'

'I can just see the headlines. WIFE OF LEFTY LAWYER IN ILLICIT LOVE TRYST WITH WARMONGER'S SON.'

'Sounds fun,' she giggled. 'Perhaps we should try it.'

On the sixth day, the day before the funeral, they meet in the middle of Waterloo Bridge. For once she is early, a lone figure with blown-about hair on a London bridge looking down into the grey sludge of the Thames.

They wander down by the bookstalls on the South Bank, separating for a few minutes, as they stroll along the aisles of second-hand volumes. She likes to glance up, see his tall figure, dressed in a long black-wool coat, standing at a stall just twenty feet away, his face intent on a slim book of scientific essays, unaware of her watching him. There, in the long rows of paperbacks, she spies three copies of Hemingway's *To Have and Have Not*, the battered black, gold and red cover of Lessing's *The Golden Notebook*, a run of recent Philip Roths, the later, greater works. Even a few weeks ago, the sight of those particular volumes, the unhappy associations, would have momentarily pulled her back into the bleak territory of betrayal, a place of sterile, unchanging loss. Only now does she realise that the cord is cut. Time and circumstance have played their part; they have given her new and greater losses; they have deepened other connections. With a shock, she realises Chris is no longer at the heart of her life, although she is not, yet, sure what this means.

'Shall we go for a coffee?'

Dan takes her arm, companionably, and she thinks how sad she will be to let go of this particular kind of solicitousness. Since the moment of death – 10.19 p.m., this last Wednesday night; her mother, calmly holding her father's wizened hand – she has felt the absence of a solid, unquestioning male figure in her life, like a wound.

They go into the NFT canteen, but take their drinks back outside, to the outdoor tables. Stirring two lumps of white sugar into her coffee, Anna says, 'Jack never came.'

'You told me.'

'Do you know what I kept wishing, on the last day? I had this fantasy that he would arrive, with a cassette player. And a tape of Dad's favourite music. Schubert, the violin concerto in C major. I imagined him coming in, plugging in the cassette player, putting on the music and just sitting there. And everything would be healed, in that moment.' The tears were pouring down her face, dripping onto her lap.

Dan leaned over, stemming the salty flow with his fingers.

'Hey, you!' he said gently, reaching into his coat pocket for a tissue, 'you've done all you could. For all of them. You really have.'

While she blew her nose and patted her cheeks dry, he said, 'The worst is over now. It really is.'

Thirty-nine

She can feel it: the collective excitement at the presence of power, fresh-minted fame. Here, in the church filled with the soaring voices, a choir of adolescent boys singing Fauré's Requiem, she can hear the whispers: *The Foreign Secretary is here. Old family friend. He may become Prime Minister if the war goes wrong.* A gathering of lawyers, professional people. Their curiosity is not overt: it expresses itself as a kind of restiveness. Time and again she spots it; the brief, hard stare, emptied of deliberate intent. Feral.

Even she has to fight the endless echoing thrill within herself, the wish to edge near to the charmed circle, the source of light to which everyone's eye is drawn. How it rubs off on her – the curiosity, of a second-hand kind, and a touch of resentment. *Who are you to make me need to look twice at you? The ties of friendship alone? Come off it.* She sees how Clare stoically accepts it; Dan shies away from it; Greg soaks it up.

The long, pale-wood coffin at the centre of the church is both a reminder and a rebuke. This is where all life ends; preserve it, enjoy it.

Heads bent. Mutterings of prayer. Discordant confident voices – high-court judges, retired head teachers, senior barristers – swelling the hymn's chorus. There's an old man dozing at the back; his wife is wearing a huge, stiff black hat.

Matt squeezes Anna's hand, her own curled tight around a ball of damp, disintegrating white tissue. Every so often Anna turns, searching for her missing brother's face among the congregation.

When the time comes for them to leave the church, Andy walks with Anna's mother behind the coffin. Clare walks with Matt, followed by Anna and Laura. Then Dan and Greg. Janet and the boys. Chris and Harry. Ari, holding Lola's hand.

For once, Dan takes precedence over Chris, his rival in love.

The two families.

The special relationship.

At the wake, Anna hears a middle-aged couple talking in low, intense tones to each other.

'Just go up to him.'

'It's silly. I *can't*.'

'But what? *What?*'

'I do just want to hear his voice. Just once. Close up.'

'Do it then. Go up to him.'

'Okay. I will.'

They are talking about Andy.

Forty

Perhaps he took a small radio with him, just to make sure of his timings, and dropped it along the way. A radio then, and a lighter, a small can of fuel and his deadly intention. So much they would never know.

What they did piece together, much later, was this: some time between the announcement that an invasion has been launched and the first recorded fatality on foreign soil – a taxi driver killed by enemy fire on the road to Basra – Jack stopped at a piece of pavement on Whitehall, twenty seconds' walk at most from the sentry posts that guard the entrance to Downing Street. He probably sat down, although they could not even be sure of that. What they could be sure of was that within seconds he had doused himself with the entire contents of the can of petrol, found turned on its side minutes later, then flicked open the square head of a small lighter and torched himself alive.

'NO!' A deep male voice (never identified) was heard calling that single word out, over and over again. An anguished holler of deep-throated dismay and fear from the person unlucky enough to be the nearest human to the conflagration, who witnessed the flames shoot up and the cross-legged figure, shimmering, behind the wall of fire; a mirage of unnatural agony.

The lighter must have been thrown clear. This, too, was found later. It was small, square and red, emblazoned with the head of Mao Tse-tung. A novelty, a joke, brought back from Hong Kong by a fellow peace campaigner.

Five seconds perhaps before the mass of orange flame staggered up and began to run. A moving ball of fire. The sister at the hospital told Matt later: That's what the body tells you to do, to run from the pain and the horror.

The ball of flame was keening, issuing a high single note of animal pain, trying to tear the fire from his arms, his leg, his torso, to wrench his head high above the heat. Float away towards the blue ether.

So, it – he – Jack – ran in the direction of Parliament, cars swerving and people screaming. Women covered their faces with their hands, then lifted the weight of their heads very slowly, fingers spreading; this, after all, their only chance to peer at unmitigated horror. To experience war. Men stared open-mouthed, muttering to themselves, soundlessly.

He ran towards the river, the cool of the water. Maybe he was trying to run back in time, one last chance to save himself.

Because they were under the strictest of instructions not to leave the entrance to Downing Street unattended whatever the circumstances, it took time for the police to organise themselves. A few minutes at most, but long enough for it to be too late. A knot of officers gathered and then, on a single shouted command, ran full pelt towards the fearsome, frenzied freak on fire in their midst. They ringed him, threw blankets – one, two, three – over the blaze, felling the human fireball brutally to the ground. They rolled his squiggling mass over, twice, three times, like a giant carpet, stamping out the rogue firecracker flames licking out from the corners.

Everyone knew; it was over. The men in uniform knew that, too, when the small crowd – rustling, whispering – was shooed away and they began to peel back the protective covering to investigate the sticky mess at their feet.

The man had been on fire for an eternity.

Forty-one

Anna, at home, knew nothing.

Later that same night, she was blithely wiping surfaces – getting the kitchen ready for breakfast the next day while Chris finished up some work in the small back bedroom he used as his study – when she noticed the blinking of the answering machine.

It was probably Matt. There had been some brief allusion on the news that night – a political correspondent talking in passing about the deep divisions caused by the war, a throwaway reference to 'Andy Givings's breach with his closest adviser, Matt Adams'. There, at last, it was out in the open, her brother's vulnerable position now made public. It was probably for the best. But she could not think about it. Not this late. Not on an ordinary Wednesday evening.

She looked at the kitchen clock. Ten-forty. (Twenty-one minutes after the moment her father had died: she thought like this all the time these days.) She would ring him in the morning.

Her last act of the evening: to switch off the ringer on the phone.

Twenty minutes later, Harry and Lola's bags for school ready in the shadowy hallway, she climbed the stairs. She brushed her teeth, splashed her face, checked on the children, then undressed speedily and silently in the darkened bedroom. Chris was already fast asleep, his head peeping out from beneath the feathery mound of the duvet.

She turned the duvet cover back carefully and climbed into bed, savouring the delicious anticipation of surrender to oblivion. It was a cold night. She edged closer to the warmth of Chris's body. Even in her loneliest, angriest moments, his body heat had been a source of comfort, a reminder of what it felt like to belong.

They had not touched properly, beyond a peck on the cheek, a squeeze of the hand, brief hugs, for over two years.

She didn't know why, tonight of all nights – the night that a war was launched; perhaps it was that – she edged closer to him, rolling towards his curved body, putting her hand on his leg. Her own fingers felt long, elegant and cool, spread over the heat of his flesh.

He woke with a start.

'Anna? What's happened? What is it?'

'Nothing. It's you. I mean, it's me.'

He turned to face her, uncertainly at first, and then with a spreading smile. He had been waiting for this moment, the acknowledged moment of reprieve, for a long time. His patience, she had to admit, was impressive. The price it had exacted from them both was obvious in the speed, the greed, with which they began to make love, Chris struggling out of his grey sleep shirt, his chest a wall of white flesh rising above her in the porous dark of the night. He felt like a stranger. Pictures of them both, a series of flickering images of the people they had been, the couple they once were, danced inside her head. The way he had reached out to touch her arm in the lobby of the Paradise Club. The sight of him, standing by the fridge, being rude about someone. Laughing. The two of them walking together down a road. Somehow, the pain was drained from these mental pictures. For now. Time stilled by pleasure, she felt only a great tenderness for the ordinary mess they had made of their marriage.

When she came, Chris put his hand over her mouth, like a hostage taker.

'Sssh. You'll wake *them*.'

She was crying with relief, and laughing at this benign reference to their beloved children. She was luxuriating in the bliss of her returned sense of that other 'them' which was truly 'us': Chris and Anna, the original couple, restored to their once-entwined glory. And then, just at that moment of reflection, she teetered helplessly over the edge of remembrance, his fateful hesitation on that awful Hackney night – *did it mean anything?* – and black-ness filled her again. It could never work. The aridity was back. He sensed it.

'I – am – so – sorry,' Chris said, sensing her withdrawal, empha-sising each word like someone reading from a telegram, lowering his head, in shame. At that moment, she believed him. Even while knowing it was possible to feel shame in one place, and utter forgetfulness in another.

'Oh, there are worse things,' she said, reclaiming the hardness she had learned with such difficulty over the past two years.

'Yes, there are much worse things,' Chris agreed with obvious relief, kissing her tenderly on the end of her nose. He thought, perhaps, she was referring to her father's death. Or the outbreak of war.

Chris must have played the message and turned the ringer back on first thing in the morning, when he went down to the kitchen to make them both a cup of coffee, for she heard the harsh bell of the telephone when she was in the shower. It was early and she had slept badly, uneasiness pervading her consciousness all night. Rising reluctantly, she had run, still naked, on tiptoe down to the bathroom, to the shower: hot water would wake her up, release her from this strange, edgy sensation.

She had just stepped out of the creaky glass cabinet, pulled on her robe and was sitting, dizzy with heat and fatigue, on the edge of the bath, when Chris came into the room.

She knew straight away.

'Matt's message last night,' he began.

'Yes?' she said, looking up. 'Has he been sacked?'

'It's worse.'

'Much worse?'

'Much worse.'

Forty-two

After that, everything began to happen very quickly.

As soon as Chris told her Jack was dead, she went down to the living room in a somnambulant trance to switch on the television, searching for some public confirmation of her private terror. The death by self-immolation of a middle-aged man in the centre of London would surely be big news, even on the first day of the invasion of Iraq. She sat as Harry and Lola did, legs crossed, right in front of the screen, putting her hand up to touch the glass. Keeping it there, flat palm across flat screen, as the images flashed beneath her flesh and bone.

But there was nothing. All the news was of the war: first bombings, first casualties, military leaders in khaki standing in empty blue-green spaces, giving an account of the first twenty-four hours of 'the campaign'. Some shots of demonstrations throughout Europe. Hopeful faces, tilted skywards, illuminated by candlelight. Slow-moving processions of protest through the capitals of Europe. Then, a report of a minor train crash – five people hurt, none seriously – and a predicted further fall in the stock market.

Chris was in the kitchen, standing by the toaster, listening to the radio. 'Anything?' he asked.

'Nothing. Zilch. On the radio?'

'Nothing. Maybe there'll be something in later bulletins.'

She walked over to him and they embraced; her body still stiff with the horror, unable to take in what had happened. Out in the garden she could see the children's bicycles, abandoned in the centre of the dry winter grass. Half a picnic basket was scattered around the base of a swing, left out from a game that Lola and some of her friends had been playing yesterday in their gloves and hats.

'I've got to ring Laura. She'll want to be with us . . . with me.'

'She called already. She's coming over.'

Chris was looking at her, anxiously. He was cutting up pieces of fruit into bite-sized chunks, to feed her, she knew. Already, she could see decay at work, the flesh of the apple browning under the harsh halogen lights of the kitchen.

A series of rapid, light knocks at the front door. Anna answered the door. Her sister's lips were colourless, her eyes bloodshot. She clung to Anna, shaking her head. 'I was ringing you. Where were you?'

Here. Making love. Sleeping.

The sisters walked, arms around each other's backs, into the kitchen; a slow, awkward, sorrowful procession. Chris was holding out the phone.

'Matt for you,' he said to Anna.

As she took the phone, Anna realised she was afraid. A brother losing a brother, that felt the worst blow.

'Matt?'

'Are you all okay?' He was in head-of-the-family mode. His severity was not unkindness. He was in shock. He was in a room with a lot of other people. She could hear them murmuring in the background. 'Who's with you?'

'Laura and Chris. What about Mum?'

'Janet's with her for the moment,' Matt said. 'Listen, I've already spoken to the undertakers. He'll be taken there later on. They can do a little, but they don't recommend . . .'

'I don't care about that. I just don't understand . . .'

'Balance of the mind disturbed, Anna. It's pretty clear. It seems Jack was on heavy medication, and then had come off it suddenly. I hadn't realised quite how bad it had got. I can't go into it all now, but he was in a right mess. If we can just keep it contained.'

'I meant, I don't understand why there's nothing on the news. This happened in central London, for God's sake. Last night.'

Laura was pacing up and down the kitchen, smoking furiously. She kept passing the cigarette to Chris, and he kept passing it back. They looked like they were rehearsing a complex sequence of dance steps. When Laura turned her head away, to knock ash into the sink, the line of her chin was so sharp her head looked like a skull.

'There will be information released. But it will be kept low-key. And no connections will be made – you know – *apparent*. Andy and I spoke a couple of minutes ago.' Still, after all these years, after all that has happened, the proximity to power lifts his voice, soothes him. 'They will protect us, Anna.'

'Protect us from what?'

'Please, Anna. This is not the time.' Matt sounded as if he was about to burst into tears. '*Really.*'

'But what good does it do, to keep it quiet? *Really.*' She couldn't help the mimicry, the little sibling dig, even though she wanted to be kind to Matt above everybody, even their mother, because she felt such deep sadness for him, losing his little brother. 'Jack did what he did for a reason. You know that. He made it his life's business . . .'

'To make trouble. To draw attention to himself. So *terribly* effective, don't you think? The rebellious forty-six-year old.' Matt's voice cracked.

'But what he's done, what he's *tried* to do, will come to nothing. Don't you see? It will be a complete waste if no-one knows what or why he has done it.'

'Anna.' Matt was almost shouting now. 'I have to go. I've got things to arrange. Seriously. I'll speak to you later.'

The line went dead. Anna looked at her husband and sister. They were looking at her strangely, shocked by her bullish determination.

Chris made a conciliatory gesture. Laura began to talk very fast.

'Anna, come on. If we can just get through the next couple of days, then we have a chance to come to terms with it.'

'I don't want to *come to terms* with it.' Anna spat the words out.

'*Anna!*' Laura began to plead. 'What good would making a fuss do? Think of Matt.'

'Matt's finished, Laura. Don't you know that? They even mentioned it on the television yesterday. What were the words the commentator used, Chris? "Matt Adams has been given a burial with honour." Some tricky cocktail of words like that. Andy's people would have released that statement. Andy's *new* people. In other words, our faithful, loyal, clever elder brother, who has given every waking hour of his life to furthering Andrew Givings's glorious career, has been moved to an office off a main corridor that no-one walks down, set to work on devising a policy for Burma, which we must apparently now call Myanmar, that no-one in the Foreign Office will pay the blindest bit of attention to – all because for once he showed some independence, because he had guts. Why Matt's still doing Andy's bidding I've no idea.'

'How did you know about the Myanmar thing?' Chris said.

Dan had told her, a few days ago.

'Forget it . . . I just do.'

A flicker of admiration in Chris's eyes. He understood the politics. And now, at last, so did she.

'So what are you going to do?'

'I don't know. But I'm going to do *something*. Tell Jack's side of the story. Why shouldn't he, too, have some sort of "burial with honour"?'

'This isn't a fucking Greek tragedy, you know, Anna,' Laura snapped.

It was still only 8.30 in the morning.

Chris had taken Laura's cigarette out of her hand; he was drawing on it heavily, looking down at his shoes, trying to decide how to play this; the scenario of the rebellious wife, wondering how far she was prepared to go and whether he should try to stop her. Whether he *wanted* to stop her. He didn't know the whole story, of course; he didn't have the patience for complex human narratives, even – no, especially – for the ones that involved him. But something had changed in him, too, over the past few years. The Chris Mason of that dinner in Hackney in early 2001, hard and ambitious and unforgiving, eager to impress at all costs, had faded. There were glimmers of the old vanity, his childish determination to make a splash. But he had pulled back, put away reckless illusions. As the world had become a more dangerous place, he had become calmer, steadier. The trauma of revealed infidelity and Anna's response – neither to leave, nor to stay and condone – had made him over into a man more solid, more interested; more interesting. As if, through the medium of marriage, he had glimpsed the danger he was capable of inflicting on his own soul.

'Look, we're talking about Jack here . . .' he began.

'Yes. Don't be a martyr to Jack of all people,' Laura interrupted, unconsciously echoing their mother's words to Anna on the day their father died.

'Jack is a loving person.' Anna used the present tense deliberately, determined now not to give ground. 'He's been good to me, Laura.' At the same time she was pinching a flap of skin on the inside of her hand, to stop her turning on her sister, hurting her in return for all the years of low-level meanness and neglect of their middle brother. *It was you, Laura, who never showed much love to him.*

'Well, there wasn't much left for the rest of us,' Laura rejoined bitterly.

Hard to know if she was talking now about their brother or their father.

Chris was looking at her with intense curiosity. Yet there was a note of scepticism in his voice, or did she just imagine that?

'What are you going to do, Anna? What *can* you do?'

After she had dressed, she climbed up to her attic office, sat at her desk and turned on the computer, hungry for any new information. There might be news of her brother's death on the Net.

Her e-mail counter told her she had several messages. She scrolled down the in-box, her heart hammering to see, it was just possible . . . yes, her worst fear, her greatest hope, had come true. Jack had not forgotten her. He had left her a message from beyond the grave.

March 19 2003
from: Jack777@callme.dot.com
to: AAdams@worldonline.co.uk
subject: the fog of war

In a society where it is normal for human beings to drop bombs on human targets, where it is normal to spend 50 per cent of the individual's tax dollar on war, where it is normal . . . to have twelve times overkill capacity, Norman Morrison was not normal. He said, 'Let it stop.'

Annna Annnna Annnna Thanks for looking after me Anna. What would I ever have done without my little sister?????

'Don't make Jack out to be mad, bad or sad, will you?' she says as Ben begins to tidy up his papers. 'That whole medication thing. It's irrelevant really. Show him as a person of principle.'

'Don't worry, the principle will scrub up well. How can it not?'

She thinks now: Dan was right when he told her earlier: Go with my mate Ben. He can be trusted, within certain limits.

'The extraordinary thing,' Ben says, 'is that more questions weren't asked, that someone there, one of the witnesses, didn't question the official version, that whoever in the press knew about it allowed it to be written off as the act of a homeless madman. That no-one guessed that there was a political motive. And on the night of the invasion itself. Incredible!'

He glances at his phone, checking the number of messages – and texts – that have come in over the last few minutes. 'Even more extraordinary,' he murmurs, 'that none of my esteemed colleagues discovered the connection between Jack and Andy.'

'He left a note, by the way,' Anna says. 'That Norman Morrison quote. You know, the man . . . the one who . . . made a protest at the time of the Vietnam War?' (Anna cannot, yet, use the words that actually describe what has happened; she prefers comforting generalities.) 'Left it scrawled on a piece of paper on his table in his flat. Matt found it – and – they found it near his body. But the police took it away.'

'I can get it off the Net.'

Not for the first time, she thought wryly: Jack never did possess any public-relations skills. If that had been Matt, the whole world would have known what he was doing and why.

'There's another thing I don't get,' says Ben thoughtfully. 'Why Andy has not asked to see you. He must know what a huge thing this is for you.'

'He has seen Matt, of course. And our mother.'

'But not you?'

'No.' Even from this distance, she can feel the steeliness of his anger, at what she is about to do.

They say goodbye outside the café. This is her last chance to retract. Even now, at this last minute, she could presume on his goodwill, the connection with Dan, and plead with him to drop the whole thing. Her breathing is shallow and rapid.

'Well . . .'

'It's not too late . . . you know.' His expression is kind.

'No,' she shakes her head. 'No, I have to do this. For him.'

Ben nods. A single nod, acknowledging the difficulty. But he is also relieved, she can see that.

'Do you remember the time we met?' he asks her, with a smile. 'It was the night Andy became Foreign Secretary and I burst into the flat. Dan was furious. You probably never realised it, but he always had a thing for you. And I think he was hoping to seduce you that night.'

'Really?'

'You're shocked. And happily married, of course. Forget it. I shouldn't have said anything.'

'No – don't worry. It's just that compared to this . . .'

'You're right. Jack's what matters right now.'

Forty-three

She watched Ben Calder walk away, over the brow of the hill, striding in the direction of his paper's offices. She could tell: he knew he had a good story. A story that would work.

Only then did she check her mobile.

There were messages from Chris (three in all: increasingly impatient) and Matt ('Ring me now, Anna. I mean *now*.')

And a text from Dan.

> *Andy knows s-thing up. Some mole from the paper in touch with his people. Wants to see u. Alone. This pm. Ring me asa u get this. Danx.*

A thin rope connected to a succession of shiny, white poles marked the portion of Whitehall pavement where Jack's death began. Anna was glad that some evidence remained of the momentous event that had occurred on this spot, although now she was standing here it seemed more extraordinary than ever that they – whoever they were – had managed to keep the identity of the 'unidentified homeless man' out of the news. For days now. It felt increasingly sinister.

She wished she were religious, that there was some sign she could make, some prayer she could speak out loud. Instead, as she stood with her head bowed, Antigone's cry of pain came to her, unbidden. 'Where can I find another brother, ever?' She could not have Jack back, the pudgy-fingered red-headed teenager or the kind, excessively troubled middle-aged man. Swiftly, a few nights ago, an essential part of her life, her deepest memories, her very self had been burned away.

She stood there, head bowed, for ten minutes.

It was almost rural, the peace and quiet of this part of central London. She pushed through an old-fashioned black iron turn-stile, waiting patiently while her bag was searched, then walked fast across a wide courtyard. The entrance hall was painted an ugly, dark salmon-pink, dominated by a grand story-book stair-case that swept up to the first floor. A camp young civil servant in a blue V-neck sweater and a bright-pink tie was there to meet her at the door. 'Do you mind?' he put his hand out; he needed to take her mobile. She watched him scribble on a Post-it note, *Anna Adams, seeing AG*, fix it on the phone, then slip it into his pocket.

They made small talk as they walked up the grand stairs. The civil servant was a South-East Asia expert; he spoke highly of Matt and his recent work on human rights in Burma.

'We're in here. The ambassador's waiting room,' he said in a hushed voice, thrilled, it was obvious, at his access to these grand rooms of state. She low-whistled in an answering appreciation as he ushered her into a room the size of a school hall with floor-to-ceiling windows, overlooking Horse Guards Parade. 'Yes, it's lovely, isn't it?'

'He won't be long.' Did she imagine a sneer, a shadow of disap-proval across the young man's face. '*Do* browse through the papers if you want.' He gestured to a low table covered with all the main daily broadsheets and tabloids, plus a couple of country lifestyle magazines.

'Thanks.'

She couldn't sit still, nor could she concentrate on newsprint. (No, certainly not that.) Instead, she wandered restlessly around the room, stopping before a large painting hung above the mantel-piece, showing a medieval female figure with waist-length golden hair, in decidedly celestial surroundings, sitting straight-backed before a black-and-gold organ; in the foreground, a cluster of female musicians sang, played the violin and the harp. *The Martyrdom of St Cecilia*. What captured Anna's attention was not the quality or even the subject of the painting – she found it absurdly baroque – but rather its misty, transcendental atmosphere, all eyes riveted on a young woman at its centre with the strong suggestion, not of worship, but of imminent self-sacrifice.

The menacing sound of sharp footsteps out in the hallway. Then a familiar male voice.

'Ah, good old St Cecilia. Patron saint of musicians. We've put her on some twenty-pound notes, so the Treasury tell me. She's been paired with Elgar, lucky old thing.'

He stood alone in the doorway – although she had the impression that his officials had walked along the hall with him, were hovering, just out of sight – holding out his hand, as one would to someone suicidal teetering on a ledge, ready to talk her down. For a few seconds she felt herself to be in mortal peril, a sense of acute vulnerability now she had climbed this high, with such a clear mission.

She was struck, as always, by how much healthier he looked in the flesh than he did on television. The effect of power was tangible. His back was straight. His dark-brown hair was smooth and well brushed. He looked fitter than he had on that day on the terrace four years ago, although the effect of fatigue was now elegantly etched into his features, part of the innate structure of his face, going far deeper than mere markings on the flesh.

For a few seconds she was unable to move, incapable of either taking his hand or refusing it. He was the first adult who ever shook her hand; she, barely out of childhood.

Anna. I'm so glad to meet you. Your father is always talking about you.

He took several steps forward, wrapped his arms around her, held her close for nearly half a minute. 'No-one should go through what you have been through.' His voice was muffled. When he pulled away, his eyes were full of tears. 'I'm just so glad that David is not here to see any of this.'

He beckoned her to sit in a chair, drawn up next to the low table spread with newspapers, which lay there taunting her with the power of their raw immediacy, their incipient moral shoddiness. As soon as he was seated, he leaned forward and took her hands in his. She felt uncomfortable touching him – his hands were warm and surprisingly smooth. But he was no longer in any discernible emotional category; neither family, nor friend. It felt as if she had known him for ever, yet she understood him no better than she had on that July day back in 1971 when he burst into their lives with his engaging smile, his endless questions, his boundless energy. It was odd, how alien he seemed to her now. Looking at his hands, Anna thought of Ben Calder's cool pencil-slim fingers; the contrast between them. Andy had good, solid men's hands. Surely, that meant something?

The thought of Ben Calder was a sharp reminder of what she had set in train; internally, she reared back in fear. Andy had been her father's best friend. The grieving daughter in her wanted to weep and talk; the child in her to please him, win back his approval.

She closed her eyes as a child might. To shut out reality, the claims of the past. To resist the temptations of intimacy.

'I'm going to get straight to the point, Anna. I have some idea of what you think needs doing . . . let's put it no stronger than that. And I understand the impulse. But it's simply not wise.'

'Wise?' Her voice sounded tinny, alien to herself.

'Can I just talk to you for a bit about what's going on, from my point of view?'

She nodded, relieved at the idea of a few seconds' reprieve. Andy inclined his head briskly in return, like a headmaster, un-willingly licensed to administer punishment. Almost immediately a far-away look came into his eyes.

'Anna, you're a brilliant girl, and I know you understand what a threat we face. A tyrant who has already slaughtered hundreds and thousands of his own people. Over the past few years the world has changed beyond recognition, I believe. These changes seemed to happen, almost overnight. Whatever . . . the analysis . . .' he hesitated, clearly deciding to change track, 'Anna, the choice we face is simple. Could you live with what happened in New York? Could you forgive yourself if that – a 9/11 scenario – were to happen here? Your family destroyed. By madmen.'

'My family has been destroyed already.' Immediately, she was aware of her gross exaggeration. It was not the way she meant to talk to him. Knew too: she never would find the right way, not here, in these grand rooms of state, surrounded by so many suave soldiers of power. His persuasive ability was awesome. In contrast, her own voice was weak, her spine bent with uncertainty. She glanced over at St Cecilia, proud and straight-backed, sitting at her impressive black-and-gold instrument.

Briefly she backtracked, in typical English understated fashion. 'Well, in a way, it has.' She was thinking not just of Jack, but of Matt, too; his messy, ambiguous fate hung in the air between her and Andy.

He said now, 'Anna, I don't need to tell you, it's been agony for me. Knowing what Jack did. What David would have felt. What your mother *does* feel.'

Now he withdrew his hands from hers. For some reason, it gave Anna the courage to speak once again. 'I can't answer all your political points. Not directly. But I know Jack like – others – hundreds of thousands of others – saw it differently. He saw this action – what you have done – as directly aggressive. An invasion of another land. Without good cause.'

A spasm of irritation crossed Andy's face. His eyelid twitched; weariness at the familiar arguments with which he felt nothing but a brutal impatience. Power demanded difficult, agonising decisions; how could she, an ordinary citizen, with no access to the terrifying information with which he was plied, day after day, night after night, filling up his red boxes, its classified nature cutting him off from true contact with all those close to him – except perhaps Clare – possibly understand? Besides, the decision had been taken. It was too late now. Couldn't she see that? Now, of all moments, he could not listen to reasoned arguments, to take in a contrary point of view; he was isolated by the high stakes, by the certainty he had no choice but to feel.

Anna tried another tack. 'But you knew what Jack . . . what he had been up to, how he was involved in direct action for years. You knew that, didn't you?'

'Of course I was kept up to date on all his activity.' The voice of officialdom.

'Jack had a right to do what he did. And he had a right to be heard beyond the community of his family and friends.'

There, she had said it. Heat coursed through her body; her neck was flushed with her own daring.

'Anna, you're getting into something bigger than you know.'

'Jack sacrificed *himself* . . .'

'But he was mistaken.'

'Who knows that we're not *all* mistaken? Who can ever know for sure that they are right?'

She was surprised at how cleanly she had hit her mark. Andy looked startled, momentarily defeated. She pressed home her advantage.

'Whatever you think of what Jack has done, he has a right to be heard.'

She had brought the Norman Morrison quote in her bag; at this moment, it gave her strength. The unspoken accusation hung in the air between them: *That's what we're fighting for, isn't it? In the end? The right for the views of our opponents to be heard, not to be stifled?*

Andy had placed both his palms on his thighs – slowly, deliberately – a prelude perhaps to rising, cutting their interview short. 'You're meddling, Anna. Forgive me, but you're meddling. *You don't know what you're doing.* You understand very little about politics and, if you'll pardon me for saying this, very little about the world. The real world. Your brother – Matt – who knows more about both, more than probably anyone I know, has told you, I understand, how wrong he thinks you are. To contemplate – to even *imagine* – that you might speak to someone in the press. How damaging that would be, to the family, the link . . . to here . . . to draw out, to draw upon, the long family connection.'

He was so angry, suddenly, she began to tremble. At the same time, she tried to say calmly to herself: *I am not a girl. I am forty-two years old.*

Seeing her tremor, his voice softened. 'Dan understands the pressures you are under. Of course.'

She nodded, and turned her head towards the window. The sky was a thin, definite grey. Stick figures were walking across the sandy expanse of the Parade, like holidaymakers, picnicking on an empty winter beach.

'He loves me.' She turned back to look at Andy.

'Yes. I know.' He spoke with a matching equanimity. 'His mother and I have known that for many years.'

She hated feeling this love. For him. His son. His wife. Here, last-minute, it came coursing through her. Hated the imaginings already crowding out her brain, pictures of how different it might have been; she, a part of this most loving group, not a pariah standing outside it, pressing her nose up close at the window of family happiness.

While she still had the strength, she stood up, quickly, abruptly, in order to be looking down on Her Majesty's Foreign Secretary when she said the words, 'I'm sorry. But it's already too late.'

Her audience was over.

Forty-four

Betrayal comes in many forms. There's the obvious stuff: sex, lies and secret phone calls. Then there are the ambiguous, the everyday betrayals: loving a child, a friend, a sibling more than a spouse. Or laughing behind someone's back when, faced with them, you seem to address them only and ever with steady, strong-hearted frankness. Beneath this, the subterranean webs of minor daily dishonesties, such as editing an account of events so subtly that while what is relayed may be wholly accurate, the full picture is not given, so the truth not told.

The truth, the whole truth and nothing but the truth.

Anna had often thought about this kind of lying when she talked to Dan about her marriage. A small sign of her mendacity: she could never say the name *Chris* in Dan's presence. Never. It was always *him*. Or the quickly uttered *us*. This was not because she no longer loved her husband – it was because she did – and she was denying him to a man whom she knew loved her as much as he did in the hope that she did not love her husband that same way. Was not *in love* with him.

Some of the facts of love, not touched upon, not spoken of: the depth of laughter round the supper table when Harry does a cruelly accurate imitation of his best friend's mother at the school gates, or when Lo pulls that indefinable comic face of hers, which makes the three of them, fond older brother and parents, smile in the same way: *That's just so Lo!* The countless mornings of their marriage, long before the betrayal, and in the week or two after Jack's death, the earlier breach seeming finally to have healed, when Chris wakes slowly, pulling Anna towards him, a primitive form of greeting and claiming; making love with a continuing greed, a seemingly endless gratitude.

Ben Calder had warned her, just before they left the Farringdon café:

'They won't let you get away with this, you know. You'd better not have any weak points.'

'Like what?'

'Oh, I don't know,' the journalist said insouciantly, 'first marriages, gay love affairs, money offshore, criminal convictions . . . Take your pick.'

'I'll pass, thanks,' she said, grimacing.

Ben was right to be pleased with what he had. A pull-out quote, from an anonymous source: 'He was like a son to Andy Givings.' The resulting story was beautifully judged. *'He sacrificed his life to stop the war. The family friend who would not stay silent.'* She had to admit, Ben had found exactly the right tone in which to write of the family connection, its strength, its meaning. He had brilliantly linked the spare facts of Jack's life and death to wider events, to national politics, the horror of war. He had found some telling photographs, too. (Where from? She had refused to give him any.) They humanised the whole tale. A great shot taken of Jack one summer morning in the years when he still had hope for Lucia. He was smoking a cigarette, his eyes screwed up against the sun.

Ben Calder had done her brother justice; he could rest in peace.

If she hadn't known better, she would have sworn she could detect the highly professional hand of Matt in the suave official rebuttal that followed, a flurried series of briefings and counter-briefings, which, in one form or another, found their way into several television and news reports over the following days.

The essential message of these briefings being as follows:

The Foreign Secretary is perfectly well aware, and has been for several days, of the identity of the man who committed suicide in Whitehall on the March night in question and the reasons for it. The public will understand, however, that, out of respect to the family, whom the Foreign Secretary has known for decades, it was decided, perhaps rashly, to suppress the man's true identity. Andy Givings was in close touch with the family throughout this horrendous incident and its aftermath. Indeed, he was grieving himself, John Adams being – as one newspaper report suggested – like a son to him. However, now this information has been released, by an unknown source clearly hostile to the government concerning its foreign policy, it should also be known that the deceased, John Adams, had a history of mental problems, and the balance of his mind was clearly disturbed on the day in question, etc., etc.

The Foreign Secretary would like to emphasise once again that, above all, this incident was a terrible tragedy for all concerned.

Anna's punishment came just a few days later, in a Sunday tabloid. This, too, a double-page spread with full-colour photographs. A lovely shot of her and Chris at their wedding; she, in her clinging cream and pale-blue dress. (It hung still in her cupboard, swathed in its protective, crackling plastic.) Andy and her father, at the christening of Bo, Matt's eldest son. A small head-shot of Katie Robinson, with her golden hair and grey eyes; reference made to her famous uncle, her sister, the MP. There were details of other women too, women of whom Anna had never heard: a red-headed barrister on the Leeds circuit, a brunette who lived in Oslo. Later, Anna was to peer closely at the pretty, dark, small-featured face, a large mole on the top right-hand edge of her mouth. The double-page spread was rich with incidental detail: the nights spent in assorted hotels, largely around the North-East, but some London locations, too. (An upmarket establishment in Primrose Hill. A fake-Tudor inn somewhere near Mayfair.) A sidebar helpfully set out the exact amounts spent on alcohol, restaurants, gifts, clubs, and so on.

It was Laura who telephoned first, that Sunday morning.

Anna, still in her dressing gown, was fiddling about in her kitchen, blissfully unaware, as yet, of the paper sitting on doorsteps all over Britain (but not hers: they did not subscribe to a 'rag' like that – Chris would not even have it in the house; was scathing when Anna brought it home sometimes, 'just for fun'). Waiting for the coffee to percolate, so that she could take two cups back upstairs to bed for her and Chris.

'Hello?' she answered cheerfully, keeping one eye on the blue flame licking around the silver base of the coffee pot.

Her sister spoke so carefully, so lovingly, as if she feared Anna might break into a million pieces.

'Shall I read you the headline first? Or do you want the whole thing straight off?'

'You better just read it to me.' Anna could feel the body-blow of it, knew it would take her months, if not years, to truly recover. This first pummelling was just that, only an opener; best to get used to it.

So she stood, facing the cooker, the telephone clamped to her ear, the tensed fingertips of her left hand rubbing her forehead, bouncing gently up and down on the balls of her feet. Listening to her sister read out the details of her handsome husband's various assignations across cities and countries: hotel rooms booked over lunchtimes and weekends, e-mails back and forth across cities, letters picked up from poste-restante addresses.

At the end Laura said, in a strangled voice, 'Anna. Oh, Anna. Are you still there?'

'I'm not sure . . .'

This is how I am to be killed off then. It's like a public lynching.

After a moment, she added, 'And after all our hard work. Putting back the pieces of our marriage. After all that. *This.*'

'Anna, are you saying you *knew* about . . . these people?'

'Actually, not. Well, I knew some of it.' She felt guilty, for a moment, that she had never let her sister in on the pain of Chris's betrayal; Laura's love and concern for her were so comforting. 'Look, I have to go, right now.'

'Okay, okay. But Ari and I. We are here for you. We will come round later. Anna? I mean it . . .'

Her sister was still speaking as she put the phone down and began the long journey upstairs, thinking: So this is what Ben Calder meant; *they'd better not have anything on you.* This was what

Andy had meant when he said: *You don't know what you are doing.* The men's warnings, their deep unease, made sense. They must have thought her so naive! Andy must have known: his *people* must have known: there were already plans afoot to disgrace the disgracer. Chris had long been a minor nuisance to them. He spoke so well, with such graceful, still-youthful authority of the state's transgressions, its continuing injustices. To them, he was a showy lawyer, high on his own principle and radical certainties.

How clever, she thought. Slaying them both at once, with the same newspaper article. Two for the price of one.

Realising, as she walked through the hall of her family home, turning to walk up the stairs: so this is the killer instinct.

Andy, it seemed, had had it all along.

Chris was still in bed. Hearing her come upstairs, he opened his eyes and smiled sleepily.

'Hello, *you.*'

For a moment, she felt real pity for him.

A few weeks later, on the very same morning that a large, white van pulled up before their beloved terraced house, taking Chris's belongings away (although it was hard, after fifteen years, to know exactly what belonged to whom), Dan Givings was checked into an expensive private hospital. Diagnosis: clinical depression. Amazingly, there was no publicity about it in the weeks to come, almost certainly because Matt, skilled old hand that he was, was asked by Andy and Clare Givings to handle the public side of things, which he did, with his usual thoroughness.

Anna's mother tells her, much later, that Dan blamed his father, and his father's people, for what had happened to Anna (he didn't care about her husband, but he cared about the public humiliation of the man to whom she was married and the subsequent ruination of her marriage). In some nightmare chain of retribution and non-forgiveness, he could not forgive his father, and Clare could not forgive Andy for what had happened to her precious first-born son. Her grief was visible to all who saw her in the years to come. Her hair went snowy-white overnight, her body swelled with fat. Anna's mother, who saw her from time to time, said her ebullience had evaporated. She was quiet. Brisk. Sad. In the rare public pictures of the couple, there was no frown, no apparent anger or bitterness. Just an official smile, and blank eyes. Strangers said, 'She looks like Andy Givings's mother.'

Anna has one photograph of Dan, which she keeps hidden in the back of a drawer. The picture makes her want to weep every time she looks at it, partly, she guesses, because it was taken by her father. Dan is in his late teens, already a beanpole. He is standing in the living room of the old south London house. Young and pretty (had she realised how pretty he was as a boy? no, she hadn't), his right arm draped, lovingly, teasingly, around his mother's shoulder.

His expression has the vulnerability of the just-woken: stripped of worldly props and mannered grace.

One summer, long ago, soon after they had completed their finals, she and her first big love Tom took a trip to North America together; on the return flight, they were marooned for a few hours, while their plane refuelled, ushered into a tiny terminal the size of a large hut in the frozen wastes of northern Canada. On the wall were three giant clocks, telling the time in New York, London and Tokyo. An exhausted Anna sat, intrigued by the existential strangeness of the sight of time moving across the world. That it should be morning in one place, the middle of the night in another, the onset of dusk in a third.

Now, remembering that bleak stopover, she feels such fluid connections to be a form of burdensome indivisibility. For what difference is there really between one life and another? Jack's death feels unique, and terrible; but so is every life unique, every death terrible; each one momentous in its way; each one reducible to a fleeting statistic, a matter of indifference to a stranger. There is no difference between what has happened to her and what has happened to hundreds and thousands of the bereaved around the globe, their loved ones slaughtered in a hundred different ways, one at dusk, one at dawn, a third in the dead of night.

She often dreams of her brother, lying in a bed with high sides, a mummified figure swathed in white bandages. As she walks towards him, she can see that he is smiling. He wants to tell her something.

To begin with, she cannot hear what he says, must lean in close to catch the whispered fragments of last words.

'Anna. You've come.'

'Oh, Jack! Why didn't you tell me what you were planning to do? I could have done something.'

He tries to raise his left arm, as if he wants to embrace her, but the arm is too solid, too stiff with thick bandages. For a second, the white stump grazes her shoulder and then falls back onto the covers.

She wakes, crying.

Forty-five

He is waiting for her, wearing that same black coat – frayed at the cuffs and collar now – that he wore on the windy day before her father's funeral, when they strolled along the South Bank. He sits alone on a bench on the slope leading down towards the pond on the Heath on a chill, clear autumn morning, the water before them as glassy as a mirror.

'Hey.'

'Hey.'

On hearing her approach, he turns, but very gingerly, as if he has recently been injured.

'No, don't get up.' She pats his shoulder from behind, then slips round and sits down next to him, touches his hand in greeting once again; in part, to mask her shock at his bulk, how rapidly he has aged. Streaks of silvery-grey running through his dark hair. His weight has ballooned; even his knuckles are puffy with extra flesh.

'How peaceful it is here,' she says, as casually as she can manage. 'Been here long?'

'Twenty minutes maybe. I couldn't remember if we said eight or half-past. That happens to me a lot these days. The details. They slip away remarkably easily.' His only allusion to depression.

'I'm pretty sure we said half-past.'

She has not seen him for more than three years, not since his first, dramatic hospitalisation, in the weeks after Jack's death. (Clare had telephoned her then, in desperation, asked her to come to

274

the clinic; but Dan had cried, painful sobs, wrenched from deep inside him, when Anna entered the room; had turned his face away from her and soon afterwards sunk into wordless gloom, and Clare had ushered her out the room, apologising profusely, her neck taut with distress.) He had been taken into hospital twice since then, but had been out, living at his flat, for a year now. Clare hopes, desperately – Anna's mother has told her this – that Dan will find a way to survive out in the world. She is most anxious that he should survive the next step in their family's life: Andy's expected accession to the leadership of party and country. (There is to be a contest in a month's time and he is the clear favourite to win.)

At this moment, Anna feels the discrepancy in fate between father and son as a rank injustice, a reversal of the natural order of things. The father, in his mid sixties, with a full head of chestnut-brown hair and boundless energy. The son, in his early forties, his black hair streaked with silver, weighed down by sadness, a paralysis of the will.

'Look at us!' she pretends to light-heartedness. 'We're like refugees in our dark clothes, sitting on a park bench!' Or like an old married couple, worn out by experience itself.

'Look over there,' he says, his voice lower, tighter in his throat. 'That man in the motorbike gear. In the black-and-red leathers. He's here to keep an eye on me, you know. This will all get reported back.'

'Are you sure?' she tries to keep the scepticism out of her voice.

The man in the biking gear is sitting on the grass, eating a white bread sandwich, apparently oblivious to his surroundings, a tabloid spread out before him on the damp earth.

'Do you think of him much?' Dan says.

'Who?'

'Your brother. Jack.'

(No, he would not ask about Matt. Her eldest brother threatened Dan because, at some level, Matt Adams was who Dan thought he himself ought to be.)

'I dream of him. I dream of everyone. I have more time to dream now.'

To her left, on the broad concrete walkway that cuts across the pond, she can see the half-naked figures of early morning joggers, the light-footed wiry ones who run with swift ease; the huffing and puffing ones who stagger like drunks out of a pub at closing time.

'Actually, everyone's doing okay, all things considered,' Anna muses out loud, trying, against her better judgement, to cheer him. 'Matt is still using his considerable PR talents to wage a one-man war against smoking in all public places. Nearly won now. He spends a lot of time with his boys, which, as you know, he couldn't, in the old life. And Laura has become a photographer.'

'Clare said, she had some kind of show?'

'Yes.'

Laura began to take photographs in earnest soon after her split from Ari, a year after Jack's death. Good photographs, which, in time, have become exceptional images.

'Her show was excellent,' Anna says to Dan now. At last, her sister had made something of her own, begun to use her own talents.

And you? Are you managing to be happy, just sometimes? This is what she longs to ask, but dare not. Her fear, Clare's fear, his own unarticulated terror: that he will not make a life for himself. That he cannot endure the long haul, not in the semi-public world that he inhabits, where success belongs to the likes of Ben Calder (whose star has continued to rise) or Martina Cartwright (never far from Andy Givings's side these days) or Andy himself, soon to be a leader of the free world; all those who possess the killer instinct, she sees that now; those who know how to move other people around the chessboard of their minds and hearts, disentangle themselves from the kinds of human commitment that hold them back. Such men and women, she realises, teach themselves how to turn away – gracefully – from pain, the inevitably compromised past; they learn – slowly perhaps – how to patch up their own wounds and, most crucially, to abandon those who are more badly injured. To demonstrate, over and over again, that they are not ruined or even deeply affected by those both stronger and weaker than themselves. Anna understands now: at both the lowest and highest levels of worldly endeavour, success is not the issue. It is much more bloody than that. It is simply about survival.

'But you write?' he asks now, with as much interest as heavy medication will allow.

'I have the time now, for sure,' she jokes, touching the hard edges of paper beneath the leather carrier on her lap, reassurance of a more solid reality. On the days when her children are staying over, she watches them, curled up on the sofa, deep in a book, their mouths working in silent concentration. She has often wondered: could she make up a story that would one day draw them in, show them some of what has made her who she is?

> *Once upon a time, there was a family of six, a mummy and a daddy and two boys and two girls, who lived in a tall, tidy house, with a dark-green front door and big windows, in a quiet street with tall plane trees and a bright-red postbox right outside the door.*

'Tell me,' he says, turning his neck stiffly, to look at her directly for the first time. 'Do you regret . . . any of it?'

Does he mean going to Ben Calder with the story about Jack? Perhaps he means the afternoon they spent together – the day before her father's funeral – at his flat in the Essex Road, his cry of intense anguish when he came inside her, her own brief but powerful conviction that he was her soulmate, after all. Before, that is, she went home to continue the long, doomed battle to save her marriage and her family.

And yet once Chris had left, she did not run to Dan. She did her duty, when asked by Clare – that awful half-hour, in the private clinic with its beige walls and grey institutionalised carpet, its fruit bowl filled with waxy apples and bananas, peaches out of season; later, passing the psychiatrist in the hall, recognising him as a regular on some late-night TV show on which he counselled distressed minor celebrities about their eating disorders. Yes, she had gone to see Dan when he was in trouble. But the old life was over, they both knew that. The war and Jack's death changed everything.

And now? What matters to her now? The healthy pallor of her children; a new friendship made, or an old friendship sustained; another day successfully survived, without too much struggle, too many mishaps. The writing. *This* writing, here on her lap, done; finished, a piece of art, outside her now. But how can she tell him any of this, when he – white-skinned, sluggish, buried deep within himself – finds even the smallest life tasks too momentous to contemplate?

She is being disingenuous when she answers, briskly, 'Do I regret going to Ben Calder? No. How could I?'

That part is certainly true. As the years roll on, Jack's death has become legendary, is talked of in the same breath as Jan Palach's protest against the Russian army invading Czechoslovakia in 1968, or Norman Morrison's last stand against Vietnam in 1965, throwing his baby daughter Emily to a bystander before he set fire to himself outside the office of Robert McNamara, Secretary of Defense under Kennedy and Johnson, chief architect of the Vietnam war; a life sacrificed in protest at the hundreds and thousands of lives lost since. Her troubled middle brother has already emerged as a hero of the anti-war movement, his name invoked on platforms around the country, the outlines of his face printed onto a thousand mass-produced black-and-white posters, held aloft, waved angrily, jauntily, on countless demonstrations.

And those who sought to write her brother off as a drugged vagrant, a mentally ill trouble-maker, to deny him integrity and purpose? She doubts that time will be as kind to those more worldly, that they will be granted the same moral authority, presumed virtuous by future generations. It is impossible to know – yet – whether Andy will be seen by future generations as a tawdry figure, guilty of gross misjudgement, or a hero, one of a handful of leaders who possessed the vision and judgement to stem the advance of the barbarians. The account of history may well be written and rewritten many times; she understands that, too; there are few absolutely final judgements. Either way – she knows – the public portrait of public men can never encompass the full complex, human picture: the truth, the whole truth, nothing but the truth.

But no, she is not sorry.

Up above, an aeroplane streaks through the clear blue-and-white sky, a silent self-contained ship of human beings, drifting briefly through their world. She feels a brief, familiar spasm of anxiety at what a plane can do, and then an older, calmer feeling fills her, envy of the luxury of those on high, capable of dispassionate examination of all those spread before them on this tiny, insignificant patch of earth Here and now: the hardy joggers, the tabloid-reading biker in his heavy red-and-black leathers who glances up sharply, at them both: Dan and Anna, in their dark clothes, sitting a few feet apart; the city coming to life all around them . . .

'I always used to think how much clearer it all seems. When you're up there,' Dan says quietly, following her glance skywards.

'Yes,' she says, taking his hand one final time. 'I expect it does.'

ONE OF US

Melissa Benn is a writer, journalist and campaigner. She has written one previous novel, *Public Lives* (1995), which reviewers praised for its 'acute intelligence' and 'incredible subtlety'. Benn writes regularly for the *Guardian* and other national publications, and her non-fiction includes *Madonna and Child: Towards a New Politics of Motherhood* (1998). She lives in north-west London with her husband and two daughters.